The

Change

Chronicles

The
Change
Chronicles

Paula Friedman

Lillicat Publishers
USA

Lillicat Publishers
402 N Cuyamaca St
El Cajon, California, 92020
USA

Cover art by Victor Habbick, Copyright © 2018 by Lillicat Publishers

This is a work of fiction. With the exception of historical events and personages, all incidents, names, and characters are fictional, despite any resemblances readers may see to actual events or persons. Because of the dynamic nature of the Internet, any web addresses or links contained in this book may have changed since publication and may no longer be valid. The views expressed in these works are solely those of the author and do not necessarily reflect the views of the publisher, and the publisher hereby disclaims any responsibility for them.

First Print Edition: June 2018
Printed and Bound in USA

POD ISBN-13: 978-1-945646-46-1
Ebook ISBN-13: 978-1-945646-48-5
Mobi ISBN-13: 978-1-945646-49-2

Dedicated to the people of the
Port Chicago Vigil
and all others who risk nonviolent action for justice, love, and
peace

CONTENTS

Part I
Eden

1

Gates of Eden

July 1965

It was already late that Bastille Day afternoon when they clambered down the bluff, Ri at her side and the boy and girl rushing ahead, slipping and sliding on the sharp descent between two granite boulders to the beach below. Far over the Pacific, a shaft of sunlight gleamed through the fog.

"You see?" Ri gestured toward the laughing children. "Here there is no fear." Drops of fog glistened on his black hair, and his words, with their slight Spanish accent, encompassed the whole shore—the screeching gulls, the surf, the beach below.

Only I am afraid, Nora thought. "Look at that wave," she said instead. "So beautiful."

But he turned to her, and, amazed at his attention, she laughed. In his own country, people said, he'd fought in a revolution; he had risked dangers she couldn't imagine. Now as he walked down the shallows, she splashed beside him, briefly forgetting the war and the ever-lurking threats of nuclear war, and barely aware, as she splashed, of the waves' spray soaking her black jeans and dark tee shirt. He must be thirty-five, at least; if he *was* attracted, she would have to tell him how much younger she was, barely twenty-two, and how little she'd done. How twisted and unwomanly was the little she could offer a man.

Seashells scraped her toes, slid across with the retreating surf. A wave broke, crashing; another crested in its wake.

But he might not be attracted at all.

The fog was thickening and the air was turning cold. Ri had been so anxious for these children to enjoy today's trip. "Come help me," he'd said. "Their mom's on her own, you see; she works as a clerk, she can't afford a car." His voice had made clear he knew she too was trapped in the city.

Up ahead, the little girl's rhythmic "Build me a castle, building a castle," as she dredged the damp sand turned into a shriek, and Nora saw the boy kick hard and bring the structure down.

"So ends that idyll." With a sigh, Ri spurted off to calm the fight. Again Nora splashed in his wake, following the water's edge, but then dove sideways into a wave. Longing to swim farther out, she instead held back, curving to dive again, arms smoothly arced, thankful for the slim litheness gained in years of modern dance, and hoping Ri would see her. Not, of course, that the grace from dancing had ever prevented her body's failing at crucial moments—a lesson the years with Murph had engraved in her.

Farther down the strand, both kids were splashing forward, pretending to rush into deep water. Ri said something, laughing, so they jumped back out, but of course they would try again. She should run over there, help with them. Except—no, she mustn't intrude. On the drive here from the city, Ri had kept pointing out Jeffry pines, eucalyptus trees, seagulls, and a golden eagle swooping over a bluff, until he'd got the children singing, but afterward he had driven silently. It was a silent sadness she had glimpsed in him once before—back in April, when her old friend Len had introduced them at the Math Department party, saying "You must meet Ri; he's my closest colleague." Since then, the few times she'd run into Ri in Berkeley, he'd seemed lively enough, but—no, something was wrong. She pushed herself forward, stepped from the surf; even if it did "intrude" she'd help him if she could. Foam splashed the backs of her knees.

In a shallow curve, driftwood broke the shore; beyond, she could see, the girl was kneeling on the sand, impatiently stretching a fistful of shells toward Ri.

"C'mon," the girl was saying, "*you* look."

"Who, me?" Ri knelt, too. Smiling, he picked out three shells. "Eileenie, did you know these lines are called 'flutes'? You know how seashells get them?"

"Me. Ask me." The boy stepped forward. "I know."

"Do you, Eddie?" Again Ri smiled; the lines around his dark eyes crinkled. Laughing, both children moved in closer.

Well, so it's all right. Nora felt her own lips smile. And then, drawn into their swell of happiness, she ran forward and crowded in beside them, hands on the kids' narrow shoulders, listening while Ri, still kneeling, spoke of what sort of creatures had lived long ago in shells like these along this strand. And, looking across, above the children's heads, his glance met hers. *Do you see, Nora? We're making them happy.*

Ri got to his feet. "Ed, Eileen, let's go check the tidepools."

Still clutching two shells, the girl jumped up, racing her brother down the beach. Letting them run ahead, Ri turned. "At least"—his words were so quiet Nora barely made them out— "now they'll have this memory."

His face was deep-lined. These children were simply "my friend's niece's kids," he'd said, yet he'd given up a day to bring them here. Clearly they mattered to him. And apparently so did she, from the way his glance had confided in her. She reached out to touch his hand.

Then pulled back—he might misunderstand. And she didn't want to hurt him; he was a *good* person. Too good for her.

He did not know the truth about her, not the things Murph knew. She held herself back, letting Ri walk on alone toward the kids, watching him show them more marvels of the shore pools, seeing the three turn finally and, waving, start back toward her.

Above, on the bluff, the fog already hid the manzanita. "A rough drive back," she said, again wishing she could help him. This whole time, all summer since that moment at the math party when she'd said, "I left philosophy to stop circling the same issues," laughing as if it didn't matter, and Ri had asked, "Because you did, or didn't, still seek truth?" he'd been there for her, supportive yet questioning.

"It will clear up, inland," he said now. His voice was tired, but he smiled and she had to look down. Blindly, she grabbed for Eileenie's hand and then for Ed's, and laughing, began to spin with them, twirling them 'round and 'round and faster and faster until, squealing with glee, feet helicoptering scant inches above the sand, they drew her with them in the giggling dance. Her hair swirled, and they cried, "More, Nora, more! More, more!"

Another moment, and she let them slow to a reluctant stop. *Here*, she thought. *Here is a way to live.*

Several yards to her right, Ri stood leaning tiredly against the bluff. She saw him glance, briefly, at his watch. Through her arms, a longing pulled to touch him, to pat his shoulder and make things be all right.

But the wind had strengthened, and he led the way upslope between the boulders. In the sand beyond grew yellow poppies. Picking one, he raised it aloft; it glowed translucent against the clouds. He turned and placed the yellow flower in her hair.

Nora blushed and ducked her head. She took a step nearer but stopped; he might not want her to.

With his left hand, Ri pointed overhead. Traversing a shaft of sunlight, a line of pelicans flew single file, against the wind, to sea.

2

Troublin' on My Mind

August 1965

To Nora's left, squad car sirens blasted. All around, people milled—must be near a hundred here along the tracks—preparing to confront the troop train. She willed herself forward, frightened. Any moment, the train would come, engine looming down upon them—and, unlike the activists around her, she had not been here, the previous Thursday, readying to step out on this track and halt that first train. Such actions could do no good, she'd told herself then. And if she got arrested, how could she brush her teeth, keep herself clean, be *ready*? Ready for whatever might happen.

But now she understood: such trivia did not matter. Must not matter.

Just as trivia never could have mattered to the people in Selma, the Freedom Riders in Mississippi, the people Ri had marched with in his country's revolution— "our faction," he had called them, lightly touching her shoulder—or to people in Vietnam. No, here, too, trivia must not matter anymore. Today's action had to succeed, must not be stopped. Not by cops, certainly not by fears. The troop train must be halted, those draftees kept from the war—kept from distant Vietnam, where oxen carted crops and people tilled rice paddies in flooded fields beside the huts that were their homes.

People—people like herself, people U.S. bombs could massacre, people these draftees soon might murder. Innocent people, far from here.

In the white August smog, the protestors moved in silhouette before her, carrying handmade picket signs and rushing to gather between the tracks and little wooden houses along the railroad right of way. It was here the train must be stopped—and here that police would attack, arresting whoever tried. She squinted into the smog, trying to glimpse the engine before it could roar in. Oh no, she was not ready, not ready at all. Her legs shook; she needed to get out of here, go home. Fear must not win, though; it wasn't fear-filled, self-protective people like herself, but those who were brave, who forgot themselves and trusted that change was possible, who'd halt this train, maybe end the war.

She tried to laugh, to brazen through, "Yeah, a few bashed heads make fine publicity, and the VDC sure loves publicity." Back in May, the VDC, the Vietnam Day Committee running this demonstration, had taken over her tiny peace group. Her defiance had deterred nobody. "You think your Berkeley Citizens' letters gonna end the war, babe?" VDC leader Rubin had asked. "You gonna write your congressman on perfumed stationery, or what?" His friends had laughed, and after that she'd pulled back into herself, retreating through the summer even as the soldiers, day by day, shipped off to war.

Except, one evening she had gone to drink wine at the Albatross Bar, and Ri had come in and slid onto the wooden bench beside her. "Unhappy doesn't help," he'd said. "It does no good. They'll have their war."

For hours, they had talked, Ri leaning back with his legs stretched forward, chatting as if they'd been friends for years. She had hunched over her drink, hair hiding her eyes. At some point, "You probably think revolution's romantic. It's not," Ri had said, and asked did she think it would matter what the VDC did. Now, trembling at the sirens, listening for the train whistle, she could only remember, of that whole long conversation, Ri saying "So either I publish lots of research so the university looks good, or else I lose my visa and have to go back home."

"But you'd rather be there, wouldn't you?" She'd wanted him to know she understood how much he missed his country, and that she cared.

"I—no." He'd finished his drink, put down the glass. "There's nothing for me there anymore. Sometimes we think there are possibilities, but . . . Come, let me drive you home." He'd extended a hand, and she had stood quickly, not wanting to delay him. Ready or not.

And now—now too she must be ready. No matter what. No matter what she'd done or who she was. Stop the war, end the massacre. Only, her legs wouldn't stop shaking.

With a cry like the shouting of football fans, abruptly the crowd jerked her back into the moment. "Look, look! Watch out!"

And there— "Look, look!"—it loomed: the diesel, eight cars long. Fast and inevitable, more suddenly *here* than she had ever imagined possible. Reflexively, her hands rose up.

"No, stop the troop train! Stop!" Her cry rose with the others'.

And like these others, now she was rushing forward, racing to answer this oncoming urgency. To end the massacre, save the far-off victims of the war, protect these men and women like herself, too vulnerably human as they fled, carrying their dark-eyed children through the panicked nights' bombardments.

Racing forward, her pretty, new suede boots thumping hard. "Stop, stop!" Running with the others, ankles twisting in the loose, sharp gravel of the track. Crying, raising her picket sign. Ready. And yet even now poised to flee.

For how could someone caught in "self" as she was think she'd any right to risk arrest like these brave people? No, but choice was gone; forget all questions. The train plunged toward them through the smog. White steam erupting—stark, unnatural.

As if her body were outside her will, her feet slowed, *would* not keep pace beside the others. She must not risk jail, she wasn't ready; demonstrations could not . . . Slowing, she felt the train roar past.

And in its wake, three dark-clothed men were speeding forward, limned against the hazy sun, rushing the train cars through the steam. The man in the lead leaped, long and feral, grabbed the open half-door of the second coach and, hanging by one hand, flung a stack of leaflets to the stunned draftees inside. A whirl of paper, someone's cheers, a sharp cry as the man jumped backward to the ground. Silence for five seconds.

Then everyone ran on and on, and, trembling, Nora found she was again beside them, breath coming hard and gasping, choking—until, clothes soaked in sweat, lungs heaving, unable to go farther, finally they, one by one, fell back.

As the train pounded past, spewing steam and gravel, in the clattery aftermath she stood, hands on knees, gulping for breath with everybody else, smarting from scrapes along one arm. *All right, I've dared this action, but from what motive? And my legs still tremble, and—no, I don't really know. Only, we have to stop the war, no matter what.*

It wasn't over; the action wasn't over yet. "C'mon girl, this is dangerous," some man was yelling at her, grabbing her and trying to drag her from what had turned into teargas-drenched steam. "Get outta here— more cops moving in." People were still coughing, hacking; "Yeah yeah yeah, teargas," an old man snapped.

She staggered, still choking with the rest, kept moving. Coughing uselessly, she stumbled with a half-dozen others down a sidewalk and between two poplars, across some grass. A block farther on, and down a flight of stairs, she cut through someone's yard onto an empty street. Beyond, through the clearing air, as she fought to fill her lungs, she made out houses—homes. Somebody's grandpa sat out on a porch.

"Get inside," she tried to cry, throat sore. "Please get inside."

"Oh, I'm all right." The man had thick white hair and eyes that shone. "Everything's cool. Go on now, darling, those cops'll be right back."

Probably a veteran of the General Strike. Waving to him, she turned down the street. But no way to know; that strike was a long time gone.

A very long time. Most people living then were now dead. *Time does that.* No, but she didn't want it to. Vietnamese were dying under bombs. People everywhere, in every hospital on any day, died. *But I don't want to die. This—all this will end. No escape.* The fear of death enclosed her, familiar as the old worn rhythms of her heart and mind. Ahead, the street turned unreal, as if part of the living world and she, on some other side, walked through smog still stinging with teargas, past someone whistling a Donovan song.

Suddenly she was exhausted, emptied by adrenaline and fear, and from running as if she were like these others, trying to confront what had become the enemy.

In fact, she felt famished—time to go up to Telegraph and grab some Chinese take-out. Or pizza near the U.C. campus. Drink something to rinse the teargas taste from her mouth. Too hard to think, and her clothes hot and sticky, dusty from spattered gravel and trackside grit. Down the elm-framed street behind her, past the flatlands and Bay, shone the white towers of San Francisco. In her apartment, south across the Oakland line, sunset would soon turn the western windows to gold. Some days, she liked to watch that gilded light, but this evening, once home after modern-dance class, she'd close the blinds tight, let the room ease into darkness, and try to forget the hopeless emptiness.

Oh, c'mon, you can tough it out. Grow up—stay cool. Not to cry, not to snap in anger or sadness. Wasn't this what she supposedly knew? What she told herself when times got tough? Only, it wasn't enough, not just now. She shoved past two mothers with baby strollers into the Eats Shop and slumped into an empty booth, her eyes still tearing from, she told herself, the gas.

Wiping a speck of chili off her lap, Nora reached for another napkin—there had to be extra napkins. "Excuse me," she said, reaching across a short man's shoulder to grab two from the counter. "Thanks." The man smiled back—or at least it looked like a smile until, a moment later, it turned into a snarl, one he seemed unaware of but that made clear he'd not excuse her until he chose to. *No, dammit, I'm too tired for this stuff,* she thought, hunching her shoulders. Why on earth was she even in this place?

Back east, in college, people had not been so unpleasant, or had they? True, the few men there who attracted her—lithe and dark and quicker than she at math—at finding truth, as she'd thought then—were seldom attracted back; "You're not very womanly," the math grad Richard had said, "or you'd just relax with me and listen," and her friend Pete, the only physics major on the soccer team, had explained, "Because you're skinny as a spider, and your words sting." Yet after a while she'd made good friends there, thoughtful in a way rare here in Berkeley.

Now she pulled out a cigarette—*better buy another pack soon*—and lit it. Better she not romanticize those snowy college days. It was there that, after two fumbling years, she'd fallen for Murph, a brilliant older full-scholarship student who, with his tight-muscled body, his understanding smile, and that long jagged scar down half his face, exuded toughness. Or, as Pete had noted, kicking a snowball down the road, "yeah, one tough fellow, Spider, way ahead of all you one-note intellectuals."

"Don't call me 'Spider,'" she'd snapped back, still not afraid to.

He'd kicked another snowball. "At your command, Lenore."

"Call me Nora," she'd said, and made it her name ever since. Well, except on rent checks and stuff, and with her parents. "Nora's pretty, too, Bubbie," her father had said, "but we named you Lenore"; well, someday they'd learn. *My name is Nora.* She took another puff on the cigarette. Out the dusty window, the sunlight glared, white and flat.

She'd been having her period the evening when Murph first took her out, and, as his strong hands spread her thighs, she'd realized, shocked, that he would soon discover she was not a tampon-wearing woman but a virgin who still used a menstrual pad. And a moment later, feeling like she had to pee, and hearing her stomach rumble, she'd understood something new—something no one had ever mentioned: the body's uncontrollable grossness could never be escaped, for this body wasn't separate from herself. In silence, she had pulled away. And Murph had lifted his fingers from her skin and smiled—his quietly paternal smile—and risen to his feet and walked her to her dorm.

But late that spring, he had asked her out again, and, after they'd shared spaghetti dinner in a downtown restaurant and started back uphill toward campus, he had run a finger down the back of her right hand, and their world had turned electric. Clasping each other, unable to let go, they had stumbled into the gray converted house where he had a room and fallen onto his sagging bed.

Where, though they tried and tried, he could not enter her. Later, as she huddled ashamed beside him, whispering "Murph" but unable to say more, he had leaned forward, a first tight sharpness in his voice quickly fading into soft, assuring words, "You too—you too could benefit, I think."

She'd searched in the words for absolution.

"There's a lot, Nora—I'm finding, too—lots that can help in psychotherapy."

"Oh, therapy," she'd said.

"No, it can help you too. So someday you may find your true self, whole and womanly and free. Free of that angry, castrating vagina that would turn men into swine."

She remembered her head had hung down while he clasped her tight. Somewhere beyond the outside wall, a group of students had walked past, laughing with knowing irony. It had come to her with clarity, that moment: she was not of those laughing people's world, and never had been, for her vagina, her sexuality, and thus she herself, was a failure. Even if Murph's body, too, had failed, she had been the cause—closed and tight and not warmly open but, clearly, unconsciously frigid.

Immature. In womanhood as in her pointless attempts to "find truth," land a job, even cook a decent dinner. Her pattern. At Murph's insistence, she had gone to a psychiatrist, and at the ninth, last session, the psychiatrist had told her, "Look for patterns."

Hers were all too obvious, stark and intractable.

Flashing a dirty look across the Eats Shop at the snarling man, who had moved to a seat by the nearest window and kept eyeing her, she lit another cigarette and pushed away her bowl of chili. *Don't even think of coming over to join me.* Her tee shirt stank from teargas and sweat—not that that would stop him. She should get up and walk home, take a bath.

Except—no. People might be regathering by the draft board; she should get there. Except, too late now; they'd be long gone. Once again, she'd missed the action. Just as she'd missed so much in life.

C'mon, don't exaggerate. She had her apartment, low-rent but beautiful with its wide west windows; she had her friends. Lennie, for one—her old shadow, who'd been in love with her since college. But also the street-singer Nadine, though Nadine was more an ex-friend. And Ernie, who was gay and, having "saved you, dear Norie, from that creature," meaning Murph, liked to escort her places—the Tilden Park merry-go-round, North Beach cafes, and once a gay bar where, though she'd felt out of place and whispered "They don't want me here," he'd insisted, "Too bad for them. Time we stop hiding out," and made her stay while they leisurely sipped their drinks.

In fact, everything was much easier now than those first two years in Berkeley, when she'd known—except Len, of course—only Murph. For, despite her body's shameful, childish failure, Murph had followed her out here.

"Hah! Wrong. I don't follow, Lenore. Don't kid yourself. Look, computer science here is tops," he'd said, "and that's where the world's going. You watch. I'm gonna ride that baby." He'd held her tight. "Hey girl, you're the best too. Yeah, you are."

Days later, he'd helped her paint the barnlike apartment she'd found—a cheap place down on the Berkeley flats, though she'd still had to ask her parents to pay the rent. "Sure, I'll show you how," he'd said, fixing the leaking faucet, and then driven her, in his old Volkswagen, around the Berkeley Hills. Soon afterward, they'd hiked, one evening, on Grizzly Peak. Then one night when she'd made him dinner and he'd praised it "though this chicken's overcooked," they'd talked until 3 a.m. and she'd wanted to say "Let's try again"; awkwardly, she had reached an arm around his neck. Turning, he'd clasped her tight. *Happy together now,* she'd kept thinking, embarrassed to be so unsophisticated.

"Excuse me, can I borrow one?" Mr. Snarl looked pointedly down at her table, hand gesturing toward her cigarettes. *Yes? No?* She pushed the pack an inch in his direction. *Okay, just go. Just go.*

But he wasn't leaving, only hovering an intrusive yard away.

Just then, a college couple walked through, leading two large dogs; Snarl spun away. But he still didn't leave, just lingered by a different window. No, Telegraph was not a pleasant street. She'd started hanging out here during that second year she'd lived with Murph.

Murph hadn't believed in marriage. "Our feelings, at least, can be free," he'd said. By then, they'd been together, calling it "marriage" for convenience, close to three years and he'd decided to bring in a colleague, Martin, to help pay the rent. She'd quickly understood— a mature woman wouldn't make objections but would simply adjust to having a third person around and recognize financial reality. But she hadn't—hadn't adapted to "living together" either. Not with Murph, anyhow.

But she hadn't known all this—had only been thinking *Happy together, happy*—the evening Murph had asked "Why so quiet with me, girl? You used to talk philosophy all the time, and smile at me, back in Ithaca, and laugh around your cigarette," and—after she'd made herself tell him the truth, "I'm scared you'll leave me"— he'd knelt, gold-hazel eyes gleaming in the darklit apartment, and grasped her hands, saying "I love you, Nora. I do, girl, marry me," and, reaching into his jeans pocket, pulled out a ring.

The ring had two sapphires and one diamond, and they had laughed, unable to stop, about being bourgeois, and she'd said "Yes." And for the next nine weeks, they had indeed been happy together. Both dark-haired and lithe, each dressed in black tee shirt and jeans, she with her dangling earrings and he in his Mexican poncho, they had wandered the city, humming songs in each other's ears, and playing with stray kittens. She had danced in the firelight for him, and in the rain—and discovered that his strong, taut body danced better than any man's she'd known.

Then, one drawn-out rainy night, lying together on the whitish-gold rug, Murph had told her about his childhood. A childhood not at all like the "middle-class nuclear-family intellectual" childhood she had known, but rather the hungry, angry family strife and crowded rooms of a west Manhattan slum, in imminent danger whenever his father struck at him or his younger brother, Shel, and later the street-fights where he tried to protect his brothers, and the ongoing gang fights with razors and lead-tipped poles and butcher's knives.

"That's how I got this," he'd said. By then, they were snuggled warm under the Indian blanket. He'd run her fingers along the jagged, ugly scar that marred his face.

"Knife?" She'd managed to whisper it, barely touching his cheek.

"That too. They'd already done Shel." The answer had been sharp, and he'd abruptly turned, raising his head, and stared at her quizzically.

"No," she had said. She'd looked away and pressed herself closer against him, longing to hold him even tighter—as if somehow she might have been him, been with him or become him and so helped him save little Shel and shared and taken away Murph's horror and the pain; and she had kissed him, over and over, stroked his hair and leaned across him, her lips to every inch of him, as if he were a hero to be tenderly adored. As if she were a wounded fighter too and had fought to save a brother and thus been disfigured—it had all ripped through her, while she held him, like a sudden sword. "Oh Murph," she had whimpered, "oh no."

For a moment, it was silent in the Eats Shop, the crowd somewhat eased. The sunlight outside was amber now. Nora looked down, lit another cigarette. She could not remember anymore how their argument had begun— it must have been the third or fourth night after they'd lain so close along the rug. She remembered only that she'd retorted sharply, something like "No, you have no idea," after Murph had snapped "Why the fuck wouldn't I know what a woman likes?" From the kitchen, he had turned, eyes glaring, and slammed a steel pot, hard, against the doorpost. "Or maybe you really think I don't know? Because, little girl, I do." He had glanced at her crotch. "I do. Like with you—we both know you enjoyed hearing my story."

Only the one moment. It had taken only the moment—that sentence and the single glance. Her universe had turned upside down.

And this inverted universe had been empty of all but horror. The horror, at first, of knowing what Murph had been through. And then, the next morning, as she'd stared into a sun-glazed shoestore window, the glaring reflected horror that was herself—for what perversion, what sadism, must have caused her to respond with such intensity to Murph's tale? To have, in his words, "enjoyed" it?

Carefully now, she watched Mr. Snarl again move away, heading toward the Eat Shop door. No, that Freudian stuff— "sadist," "castrator," all that—was absurd.

Had to be absurd. Even when she'd been with Murph, she'd known that much. And yet what sort of anger—some twist of desire, some fundamental, ugly immaturity—must a person like Snarl keep inside? Was she, with her body's failure to open and her twisted response with Murph, any less repulsive? A failure, shuffling out the door, gladly gotten rid of. *Unwomanly. Castrator.*

It had required those entire first months with Murph to make her understand, but, standing at that mirroring shoestore window, finally she had, and the full shame had engulfed her. Afterward, through the long spring and summer of that second Berkeley year, she no longer dared go outdoors, or do anything but hide, for any word that resembled "scar" or "attack" or "knife" (and, after a while, most did) could make her blush. And people would see her with Murph and would see what she was; they would *know.*

Just as she knew with this Snarler—*something wrong there, dangerous.* And—oh damn—still there. Still staring, his mouth in a sneer, right hand stirring, stirring his coffee. Better here, though, than to get waylaid going home.

Never could she have thought like this, considering how to protect herself, during those two years she'd lived with Murph—or even those first months after finally leaving him, when she'd walk into the Mediterraneum Café, some rainy Friday evenings, and invite a stranger home, trying to verify her sexual maturity, her normalcy. Two unknown guys, there'd been—no, three.

But not you, sweetie. I wasn't that desperate. Now Snarl stood at a table scarcely fifteen feet away. She turned her back to him. *Get lost.*

She should be damn grateful none of the one-night stands had killed her. There'd been that one guy with a snake tattoo who . . . Carefully, trying to move inconspicuously, she pulled her pack onto her lap. The better to run—no, walk—to safety if she must.

Yet not to let danger block her. This evening, after dance rehearsal she would have the dark walk home. Even Nadine, so ready to sing even outside bars, had acknowledged, "That dark street of yours, with all those bushes—wow, Nora, it freaks me."

Besides, and more important, soon other troop trains must be halted. And someday there'd again be lovers and relationships, though not until she was whole. For now, better the simpler closeness of friendships—with "comrades" like Mark. With Ernie, her gay friend. Or, for that matter, with Ri. Except she barely knew Ri, hadn't seen him in more than a month, since the beach trip. But Len, of course, there was Len—except, he was a disaster area; during the Tonkin Gulf episode, a year back, he'd stumbled into her quiet blue room one evening, taken her hand, and, dropping his copy of *Kafka's Prayer* on the coffee table, begun to cry. To cry.

So, hey look, Mr. Snarl or whoever you are, just don't follow me, don't. 'Cause I gotta get outta here. Body taut, stepping lithely as if to dance—or run—she slipped from the crowded Eats Shop. Glancing around, making sure Snarl wasn't following. Then she took a long, quivering breath.

You got one life, girl. Find its clear music, dance and dance harder. And stop the goddamn war. Even if she was inwardly vile, she could still try to love. Even if life had no meaning, she still must try to end massacre. No matter what. This much, she knew.

"C'mon, Nora, get that back straight! One and-a two, and-a-one and-a two." Marinda was into it again. "C'mon, now—Jenny, Richie—heads high, point those toes, *relevez, relevez encore.* Kick! Kick! Center that balance, Jenny, higher, higher!" A very traditional modern dance teacher, delicate as a drill sergeant, but that was good. Modern dance out here was full of candlelight and "breathe your spirit," but Nora had missed the discipline of Ivy Jake's old Ithaca studio.

Because she needed that discipline, needed her body firm as possible, rehearsed and ready—ready even though it always might again fail her.

"First position!" At Miranda's call, they came alert, four women and two men here tonight, darkness falling outside the plate-glass windows of Berkeley Dance. They'd a performance Sunday at St. John's; Nora and Jenny shared the lead. She felt honored; in the dance, her body always shone. Last night, she'd made herself lift the phone and invite Ri.

"Of course," he had said, with quiet seriousness, "I'll come."

Afterward, they would go for coffee. He'd wear his European leather jacket; they'd sit in the dark coffeeshop and he'd talk about his research or a film; she'd ask how those kids, Eileenie and her brother, were doing. Ri might discuss the struggles against the government "back home" in his country, but only if she brought it up; for him such things were simply events that happened, to be met with grim gentleness, protecting where one could. His eyes would gleam in the low light, the lines by his lips would ease.

"Don't slouch, Nora. Head up, abdomen in!" She needed to stay lithe, be ready. For the performance. For when the trains came through. For Ri, in case he wanted her.

He didn't know about her—not what Murph knew. If ever she were to risk more with Ri than friendship, she would have to tell him.

3

Because

It happened because she was looking for a poem to take him, maybe Roethke's "In a dark time" or some early anonymous ballad, something that could sing but not say too much, and so was crouched by the bookcase beside the door, wearing old torn jeans and a wrinkled sweaty tee shirt, hair straggling, prickly, over her shoulders, when she heard two quiet knocks.

She rose to her knees. Likely the landlord out there— and her rent payment was late, September 8 already. Better make up a story fast, and hope he'd believe it. She looked sloppy, a mess. Never mind; still kneeling, she opened the door.

Feet stood there, a man's feet in brown leather shoes, dark pants above. *Okay, the landlord,* she thought. And then blushed—seeing, as her gaze rose, not the landlord but the familiar light blue workshirt, the lined face—Ri, gazing back at her, eyes round with surprise. He half-smiled and then his expression turned serious, almost tender.

"I'm"—she tried to smile back— "you know, looking for a poem." Laughing weakly, she bent her head to hide the awful blush; it would give her away.

"I'm disturbing you?" His voice went awkward. "Am I? How are you?"

"Me?" *Dumb thing to say.* Her heart pounded. She tried to push the blood from her face, force calm. "Glad. Glad to see you. I've been depressed." *From missing you*—she might as well have announced it.

He stepped past her, walked across to the purple couch. "Well, I've worried about you." Then, seating himself, he asked if she'd heard the news. Down south, in the San Joaquin Valley, the grape pickers had walked off the fields. "The migrant workers," he added. "This morning. This may be big."

"This morning? They're striking?" Trying to think, she shook her head, jumped to her feet. A thin streak of white smoke rose from the ashtray on the bookcase. She stubbed out the still-burning cigarette.

"Do you know how they live, down in those migrant camps? Nora, we see pictures, but imagine living there."

She tried to murmur something sympathetic.

His glance challenged her. "Don't you see? It's the racism. When I took my car in for repairs last week, they heard my accent, suddenly they had no time. But—no, never mind that, listen to me, how are you? And thank you—that dance program was remarkable. I wanted to tell you afterward, but I had to take Anita home, my cousin; she has no English to get back alone."

But if you had stayed, maybe now we—

"Your dance is a gift, you know. Don't get so caught up by the war you let a gift, a gift like that, go."

"No. No, I don't." It came out in gasps. "I won't."

But if he saw her tension, he wasn't letting on. "The VDC's new project," he said, meaning probably the antiwar march in October. "Can they possibly believe that is enough?" But all she heard was the sound of his voice.

If he knew what she was feeling, he would despise her. With that same irritation she felt when someone she didn't want desired her. "They think it's good tactics, a march," she said. "I guess."

"You guess." He laughed, eyes pleased.

She smiled back. Quickly. "Yep."

"Well. Yep, then." He tossed back his hair, the familiar sadness changing to delight.

I do make him happy! The thought flashed, instantaneous. *See, I do! So then, all right. Why not say it?*

Besides, what other choice? With her hands clenched tight, legs twisted so taut, her voice thick and faltering, surely he must realize. And that was always the most repulsive—people trying to hide their longing, defensive and pretending and false. Better to admit—be direct, show courage. Just tell him.

"I want you."

Don't. No, don't.

Too late. Now, no going back. And Ri was reaching out—only not in the way she'd dreamed. His right hand reached out and held her wrist.

Once, years before, Murph's hand had clasped her wrist. But then it had been Murph who'd made the first move.

Now, "I mean, want you," she repeated.

Ri patted her hand. Gently, he squeezed her fingers. Surely he cared. Or— No, what did he mean?

Earlier, back in July when he'd brought her home after the beach, she'd served him coffee and, leaning back on her couch, he'd closed his eyes in childlike trust, as if with her he'd found some sort of peace. She'd wanted to hug him then—simply hug him. Yes, surely he cared for her, as she for him. As if they were not separate people. His eyes, at the beach, had sought hers.

"Nora, it is all right."

She bent toward his voice. His tenderness must surely be real; certainly such warmth was not possible—not toward an importuning lover—unless one loved in return. As if she were certain, she fell against him.

But clumsily. Embarrassed, she hid her face against his chest. She breathed his warmth, made out each long cotton thread of his shirt. Unspeakably tender, his left hand pressed lightly on the crown of her head. "It is all right."

Except that it wasn't. Because this hadn't been a rehearsal. Not some "mistake" that could be taken back. This moment was everything. This was Ri—his warmth beside her, his hand on her hair.

"You see," he said.

My friend, my friend. This had to be real—Ri holding her, Ri here, trusting her. As she trusted him. She would be honest with him always, never demean him by lies. Never let the ugliness arise between them, the twistedness that Murph had seen in her. Ri was too good for that.

Too good for her.

"Nora, you needn't be afraid with me."

The light had faded; they lay on the purple couch. Through the windows, spruce branches swayed in the evening wind. After a while, she felt his hands slide up her arms, caress her breasts, begin to stroke her abdomen and thighs. Warmth spread with each touch.

Ri turned, crouched in the half-light above her, weight on his knees and elbows, hands weaving a sensual net across her skin. Carefully, half-laughing so she also laughed, he slowly pressed forward, began to enter her.

Only, suppose she couldn't open? If her body failed, as it had with Murph? Or if her feelings really were the sick, perverted things she had believed?

No. Keep all this away from Ri. Or— But if he didn't want her?

"Wait. Ri wait."

And, before she could stop time—have not said "wait"—Ri, *sensitive, not like men here,* pulled out. Breathing hard, he rolled onto his side.

Three minutes, four.

Silent, they watched each other. His hands stroked her hair.

"This is ours, Nora," Ri said. "There are no judges."

She had said, "Wait." She had held him out. He had trusted her.

"Look at me," he said. Shadowed, his eyes glowed. "You weren't the only one, these weeks, who was unhappy."

These weeks apart. He too had been unhappy. So it was true—he loved her.

Except—and she despised herself for thinking it—wasn't there again an ambiguity, so unlike him, in those words? An ambiguity now even in his quiet laugh, as if to reassure a child? Yet obviously he did care.

It made no sense.

"Here in your country, everyone has these dreams—why shouldn't we?" Again he was laughing, and this time with a rueful smile as if they shared the parody.

Unless he thought she'd not understood the parody. Or . . . what had he meant? What did he want? No—rather, what did *she* want from him?

But she mustn't get caught up in old issues, not now. She mustn't build new barriers after what she had just done. "What do you mean?" She forced out the words. "Ri, what did you mean, 'people have these dreams'?"

He stretched his legs out on the couch and pulled her close. The lines by his lips were deep grooves. "Listen, better we just be natural. We all have our pasts; we live how we can. But, Nora, let's not talk about these sad things. If I start feeling close to someone"—again, his words sounded like parody— "then I have to run."

Yet clearly he respected her; he did not find her repellent; he was holding her the way a person does who cares.

My friend. My friend.

Ri brushed back her hair. "This is ours," he repeated. "No judgments. But this means you, too—you'll not judge me, Nora."

He understood; he accepted. His smile creased each line of his face. There was only this moment, and it was real; this night was forever. She loved him beyond what she'd ever thought possible.

She reached out her hands to this person who was everything. "Ri, I want to touch you, and touch you again and again."

He caught her hands and, standing, bent to kiss them. "I must leave now," he said, "but I will come back, very soon."

Nora's universe had lasted those six hours. Then the time of outer space began.

For a few minutes after he left, she still felt his touch, breathed the warmth of his skin. Kneeling on the couch, she put off lying down, trying to stave off her separation from him.

In the morning, an American flag flew. It hung, white red and blue, over the front porch. Surely the couple in the apartment downstairs must have raised it for a holiday—some obscure state holiday, no doubt. Only, it felt like a threat. A threat to Ri, from which she must protect him. But why think that? Unless, underneath, she really wanted to . . . *No, no—don't think like that.* She took an old blue burlap curtain from a box in her closet, sewed a circle of white cotton and three narrow strips onto the center to form a peace flag; fumbling with a hammer and three nails, she hung her flag out the kitchen window in the wind. Lighter than the tricolor war flag below, it fluttered, bright in the sunlight. Satisfied, she sighed, then drew a long, warm bath; sometime while she bathed, the scent of Ri on her skin dissolved.

But at some point soon afterward, while using the toilet or washing her hands or brushing her teeth, she understood—she could never be truly ready, never be sure her body would be clean, desirable, and open, in whatever hour Ri might return.

And besides, be honest, that's not the real issue; the real issue is, he doesn't love you. The thought popped up, a sharp reprise. She didn't know if it was true.

And truth was necessary. For, as hours, then days, passed, questions and answers began to rush through her mind, changing with each hour, with each minute, each second. Because, clearly, her awkward confession of love—*grasping at Ri, as men have grabbed me*—and her body's closure, her saying "Wait," weren't unrelated. She needed to understand. For before Ri, there'd been other men she'd loved; and, even before Murph, there'd been twists and closures. A *system,* they formed—some sort of system, a system composed from silly warnings and "insights," from words of men she'd been with and her own mind's voices, from darkly counseling voices, voices she had loved, voices of this time and place But why believe them? Why believe she must protect one she loved from herself?

Again she watched her thoughts march by in worn review.

After the first week, sometimes she would search, cigarettes and ashtray by her side, through her volumes of Plato and Russell and Wittgenstein, seeking some way to separate *truth* from its human formulators, to distinguish *decision* from thoughts that judged. To go to Ri, to see him, laugh with him at some worn-down Wittgenstein joke and be glad together, she needed to find the truth of her feelings—and of his. But for that, and for there to be no judges, she must abandon all systems of judgment and truth—live without systems and be, as Ri had said, natural.

Early one morning, sitting cross-legged on the polished floor, smoking another cigarette, her hair uncombed, the old dance skirt askew, she tried to decide, without logic or words, what to wear, and whether to make Ri a gift—would a beaded pouch be too personal? —and whether to go to him. Shifting position, she wondered if her hair smelled fresh enough, and who was she to "understand" Ri—she, who had thrown herself at him? And why—to challenge him if he did not return? No, what did she really want from him?

After ten days, she wrote him to warn him, "I've guilts and shames I thought long gone, old fears that my body and feelings aren't good. In my dreams, Ri, I sacrifice myself or my beloved to elders, rulers—those 'parent' judges who pronounce the system's warnings and enforce them. Or else, to protect you, I must flee into pathless chaos, for bounds become rules, reason becomes judgment. I am so sorry, Ri. I thought I was free. But this 'I' stays locked in false voices, in systems of thought; there is no 'self' who truly loves. Ri, I did think I loved you."

To write, though, was pointless. If he didn't care, it would annoy him; if he did, she would entrap him further. *Just go to him, be natural.* It would be all right; he had said "There are no judges."

Sure. Sure, she could go see him.

Jumping up, she reached for her Grecian sandals and new scoop-necked tee shirt—he would like these. No, but didn't this mean she would see him to make him desire her? To draw him in, entrap him?

No, it had to be all right.

Across the window, the light shifted; her mind turned over. Concepts changed; the world recomposed.

Of course he would come back. Only wait; she had to trust him. She put the sandals down and slung the new tee shirt across the chair.

His palm moved down her cheek.

In the morning, she'd dressed in jeans and an old tee shirt, leaving the Grecian sandals and wearing her Keds. "I know you need your privacy," she said. He was hugging her. They stood outside his apartment, on a porch overhung with yellow flowers. His right hand slid along her thigh.

"Ri, you don't understand!" He was touching someone who might want to hurt him, who might *enjoy* it. Except no, who had said that? After all, it meant nothing that— "Ri, listen." But she mustn't draw him in. Yet he had to know.

His hand pulled back. "Well, it's all right. We needn't discuss these things. Let's just be happy today."

Three shallow wooden steps led up to the kitchen. Inside, sunlight slanted through an oval window. He poured two cups of red wine. "To you," he offered.

She tried to smile. They stared at each other. She couldn't speak—must not, must not draw him in.

To fill the silence, he spoke of the war, of "your country," of his work in math "describing limits, you understand, for certain Abelian recursive functions," and of the two kids she'd helped him with, that day on the Bolinas beach. They sipped more wine. She saw him glance toward the door.

No, she mustn't bother him. She jumped to her feet.

"Nora." He stepped in front of her. "Tell me what to do. Should I come see you soon?"

Only if you love me. But how could he care so much, unless he loved? *No, because I can't love. Please, you mustn't come too close.*

"I was frightened. I wasn't going to come back." He spoke as if such things still mattered. "Nora, you misunderstood."

Quietly, the wall and ceiling turned upside down. Or rather, inside out—reversed.

But better this way. And he had things to do. People to see. She tried to step around him to the door. "I have to go."

"I don't want you to leave. And if you must, I'm coming with you."

Come, go—whatever he wanted. It didn't matter now.

Entering her cold apartment, he had hugged her again. Here with her, even though too good for her. Even though he had said "You misunderstood." His voice pierced her heart. "Don't you see that I, too—? Nora, listen to me. We are too old for dreams." He was too close, his hand reaching to touch her shoulder—trembling.

"Ri. Please leave."

"Listen—"

No way out.

"You bastard!" She could hear her words scream, "You bastard!" Saw her left arm flapping, slapping at the air. *No, no, that's silly, a child's act.* She slid down to the floor.

Oh no. Oh Ri, you deserve so much better.

But before she could rise, he had stepped to her side. He was leaning above her. "God damn, Nora. Why? God damn." His eyes hard and glaring. Like someone furious.

Only, already, one hand supporting her, he was lifting her to her feet. His lips were set. "Look what you've done." His voice cracked. "Nora, *why?*"

She knew it was too late.

Yet, even as he stepped back, for a moment the corners of his lips rose. Only slightly, but as if to parody his anger. As if to smile with her. Somewhere beyond the window, a church bell rang, the deep bell of the old cathedral two blocks down the street. Even now, she thought, she might smile back, laugh at herself, say "I'm so sorry," and maybe save something. Something inconceivably important.

Except, it *was* too late. Across the cold white room from her, he had walked back to the doorway. For another moment, he stood watching her, like someone who cared. Then, as the bell chimed out again, he turned and was gone.

"Learn your lesson." The words rang in her head with the chiming bell. She sank back on her purple couch. She had understood.

The fears that her feelings were perverted, that she might want to destroy someone she loved—those fears were simply false. And these falsities had led her, in these crucial moments, to act like a maddened child.

As the therapist whom Murph had had her visit had explained, when she'd spoken of Murph's stomping out because she'd screamed, "Anyone would deny you if you act like that." And as every psychology article or book agreed, a person's actions always showed a pattern. Now she understood: hers, too, showed a pattern, her pattern. By not opening her body with Murph, by her earlier spider-sharp retorts, and, with Ri, by saying "Wait!" and, now in this last moment, slapping the air like a "freaked-out" Nadine or a spoiled child—by such acts, over and over, she created a set-up *to keep a man away.* Clearly, this was her pattern.

"Learn." The bells re-echoed. "Learn."

Yes, and what the pattern, the explanation, meant was clear. It meant that Ri, and every other man she'd thought she loved but had held away, could not be whom she really loved. For she did not heed the man but only the *system*—the vagina that stayed closed, the voices warning that her feelings must be wrong. The system—

with all its voices, from her parents' "Watch out or boys won't respect you" or her dorm counselor's "You know what they're after" to the old compelling folksongs of deceptive lovers. The system, in all its voices, which, though she might dread it or laugh at it, were what she always heeded, always seemed compelled to follow. Compelled because the system—or rather those whose voices formed it, this system she lived enclosed in—must be whom she really loved. Must be, to have such power over her: the power to make her "act like that," to make her believe she was twisted and close herself down, the power, thus, to hold men out.

It was as if she were an infant caught in a "grown-ups'" world, heeding its accusations that she was "sick," sadistic, helpless, and all the rest, because she loved those grown-ups. Believing its judgments, too, of fearsome men out there. Yet believing also its lures—its fairy tales—that said that only someone most brilliant, or some suffering hero like Murph, or a man who could understand even somebody like her, a man like Ri, could possibly be right for her, be "someone I really love." So that when she found such a person, her desire must leap forth in too intense a longing—doubts rising with equal intensity until she would push the "loved one" away, remaining the system's child. *Like the girl in the folksong whose mother claims to hold a silver dagger "that says I shall not be your bride," and is believed because she is the one most loved.*

And there was no escape, no awakening from this nightmare dream. Unless— Nora sat up on the couch, surprised in the slanting light of approaching evening. In fact there might be an escape, a way out from fairy tales. And that way was simple—to love not those the system judged "right" for her but, instead, whoever was out there.

Only, knowing this now did no good, unless she could stop thinking she loved Ri. Belief in such "love" was the very trap of fairytales. The one way out was to move onward—throw off the false self with its dreams, rebuild a true self, become whole. She had to reject the infant's universe and climb, as if herself a child, to a new maturity, become someday fully a woman, someone who would never fall back into old dreams and cry "You bastard" or, as if unworthy, implore "I want you."

Time to mature—and in the only way possible, replacing dreams with the natural closeness arising from ordinary needs, replacing the system's judgments of whom to love with openness to everyone around. In this, only this, way she might come finally to love with the encompassing empathy she'd felt in Ri. A hard quest, but, if she accepted it, she might someday love genuinely, fully.

Through the next days, washing the dishes or dusting a windowsill, sometimes she'd think that her belief that Ri cared had been delusion, an adolescent crush. But, moments later, she would remember his hands on her hair, how his eyes had shone when he'd said "I was unhappy, too," and his arms around her through the golden afternoon. *I do not understand.* But none of that mattered now. All that mattered was this necessity—to find new ways, to push aside her fear, her vulnerability.

"Nora, I'm glad you are here." Ri's hair was matted, his eyes heavy with fatigue "I've worried all week; I shouldn't have walked out like that. I was thinking too much of my own despair. But you—*you* were in despair." He gave a rueful smile.

She longed to soothe him, to reach across the table and touch his hand. Except she must not; she did not really love. This longing to comfort him could not be real. She'd only come to him because—no, she didn't know why. "You were ... in despair?" She half-whispered it, must not get close. "I don't understand."

He shook his head; his hands stroked the tabletop. "When there's been so much loss, you see. But listen, what I do know, it's this—if someone is sad, and I can give some happiness, there is pleasure in that. A sensual pleasure."

She tried to smile, to soothe them both. She watched his eyes. *"To give some happiness."* Happiness to the children, at Bolinas beach. Or to—

Whatever he might mean.

He had stood; he pushed back his chair. As he stepped around the table toward her, his hands slowly lifted. His fingers spread to touch her hair.

"Ri, I cannot give." She mustn't lean into those hands. "Not the way you do." She mustn't think those hands beloved. "I cannot love."

He stood still a moment, took a step back. "Yes. You can love."

It would be hard, the path could easily be lost. But someday to love—which meant first to wholly give, to empathize without bounds.

Careful not to stumble, she rose to leave, but his arms went around her, and he pressed her face against his neck. She leaned close, breathing him, accepting the gift, then raised her head to go.

Part II
The Streets

1

Marches and Media

October-December, 1965

Near the U.C. campus, the noise grew louder—the music, the shouting. In front of the Mediterraneum Café, the crowd on Telegraph Avenue became impassable. Down side streets cruised unmarked police cars. Nora could barely light her cigarette, her hands shook so. Now that she was no longer in the Berkeley Citizens group, it was hard to keep track, to find out what was happening or who the leaders were. But fear wasn't slowing her feet anymore; she had moved beyond her paralysis at the troop train demonstration. And as for not knowing the leaders, she understood now: that was only a status issue, arising from the judging self that had closed her in and kept her from reaching out beyond herself. *Whether I spoke well at meetings, how well I danced, how pretty my new suede boots*—that "I" had been a child's ego, its world glassed-off from others'.

Around the campus, people massed, silhouettes too dark to recognize any individuals, street noise too chaotic to make out the speakers. She leaned against a metal railing, sweating in her black flannel shirt and black jeans, feet sore from the new boots—trivial irritations, she reminded herself. Utterly trivial; unlike her, some people here planned a serious action against the war tonight, readying to march the six miles to the Oakland Army Terminal and force a way inside, to risk their freedom to save unknown others' lives. These were people who cared. To be like them, like Ri, she had to break away from ego, reach out instead to help others— to *need* to be one with them in their own need.

Meaning right now she must do much more to end the war. To hesitate in fear, perhaps, but not to slow or stop. *Yes, yes, I'm doing that.* But this night was only a beginning.

In the surreal chiaroscuro from dozens of glaring camera lights and hundreds of flickering handheld candles, the mass of shadows began an uncertain shift. Up ahead on Telegraph Avenue, a sound truck slowly passed, carrying the Vietnam Day Committee leaders and followed by the long marching column, people young and old singing, shouting, carrying signs: END THE WAR, STOP THE BOMBING, SUPPORT OUR TROOPS—BRING THEM HOME. Surging from the campus, people jammed the intersections; they spilled from overcrowded sidewalks to fill the streets. Overflowing the road, this crowd was far larger than any demonstration she'd ever seen. An armbanded monitor bumped into her; he snapped "Watch out there," and she turned, furious. Couldn't he see her good intentions? Wasn't she one with the rest? And then she paused, stock-still, frightened by her anger that rose to judge him. In the darkness, she couldn't even see him well; no one could be clearly recognized; truly, this was the first demonstration she'd been to that was so large as to absorb everyone into one single, surging determination.

Suddenly she understood: that determination, like she herself, must act from love. Squeezing past the nearest, close-packed marchers, she broke into a run, rushing to catch up to the front. The police weren't interfering yet, but they would, they always did, and someone in this crowd might throw a rock, a bottle, whatever else, and police retaliate. She had to reach the front and make sure people acted without violence, without judging people, without divisions into "them" and "us." *Show we care for everyone.*

Only, she'd waited too long.

The march stretched at least a mile ahead. A man raced down the sidewalk. Television cameramen squeezed out from a side street, headed onward. Somebody in a lawn-green poncho was handing out memorial candles for the murdered Vietnamese—and, all across the Avenue, people cupped the flickering candle lights in their hands to warm them. On the sidewalk in front of Cody's Books, a couple stood, seeming dazed— *faculty types,* she thought, and then recognized them as Lennie, his arms dangling awkwardly and his feet slightly out-turned in his usual stance, and his shy blonde wife beside him; they were wheeling their twin toddlers in a stroller, and, approaching, she could hear them telling each other little algebra jokes about Movement factions; "If Protest Group X loses 3 people to Protest Group Y, which loses 4 people plus half an 'undecided' to Protest Group Z," Len quipped, "how many FBI men lost their jobs today?" Smiling, she joined them, standing under a flashing traffic light; they seemed unsure themselves if they were marchers or observers, oblivious—*like half the parents here,* she thought—of all the cops along the march route carrying teargas. Suddenly she wondered if Len had seen Ri recently; surely he must have, working in a neighboring office. But when she had mentioned Ri, a couple of weeks before, "You're making that guy into some kind of god," Len had said, lifting his glasses to rub his eyes. "Maybe so you can worship someone?"

Now Len said, "Out of the street, Nora, you may get hurt," his voice climbing an octave and several decibels. "You're such a fragile thing."

He's still in love with me—it was in his voice. *But it's been years now.* Years since they'd walked the paths of Ithaca and he'd fallen in love. And here, tiny beside the lanky mathematician, his sweet-faced wife stood silent and pale under the flashing light, nervously rolling the stroller back and forth in short strokes, all the while eyeing his profile.

Abruptly, Nora turned away, boots stepping hard. It was embarrassing, this glimpse of the couple's intimacy, the way each held the stroller handle but their hands stayed carefully apart. And their minimal, detached involvement with the march felt pointless, alien, something she was leaving—no, had left—behind. All around, people chatted and laughed, playing Beatles tunes on gleaming guitars, singing old union songs. Couldn't they understand? Didn't they see? At this very second, Vietnamese people were being bombed.

But what to do? Again, she broke into a run, compelled by the need to *do something* to halt those bombs.

Up ahead, everyone was swaying, voices singing "We Shall Overcome." Near the next intersection, she saw a few marchers starting to slow down, already dropping out, but others—late shoppers, mothers leading schoolchildren—were coming in, replacing them with new mass, new energy. Not many blocks ahead, people seemed to be crowding up, surging around in front of the Co-op supermarket, spilling out onto residential streets.

And just beyond that, she saw as she reached the edge of the Oakland border, people were wedged together, covering an intersection and spreading halfway down two blocks, standing on cars, balancing on each other's shoulders, even climbing telephone poles. They had spilled onto the lawns and pavements, filled the parking lot beside the laundromat and a second lot across the avenue. Why? Was something blocking them? The cops, probably, and she could find no way here to get through to the VDC leaders on the sound truck. Under the garishly pink floodlights, many voices were clashing, still shouting "Forward," "On to Oakland," "Out of Vietnam"—only, there was nowhere anyone could go. Nora leaned against an ancient green parked Chevrolet and—hesitating, afraid her boots might scratch its paint—delicately climbed onto the fender.

From this vantage, she could see, nearly a block ahead, helmeted cordons—three long lines—of Oakland police. Legs spread, tapping their clubs in impatient rhythm against their palms, they stretched across the road and sidewalks. Beneath their floodlights, the VDC leaders stood confronting them. Here, anything might happen.

Anything.

Was this how change was born—balancing awkwardly on tiptoe on the fender of a Chevrolet?

She'd slip if she jumped down to run.

But she had no wish to run. She wanted to do what? Rush up to those leaders, the VDC politicos, and implore "We must be human"? Tell armed cops about "the system"?

Yeah, fat chance. She was not among the leaders, and even if she were, who'd listen? And anyhow what was there to do—exhort the people here to charge through the police lines? There were families in these lines, schoolkids, old people, babies. Even if the march got through, they would all be harassed and attacked on the long miles through downtown Oakland to the Army Terminal.

Now, squeezing back into the front ranks of the demonstrators, the VDC leaders were making their way through, calling out "Go right, go right!" Crying "To Berkeley Civic Center! Tonight we'll rally there." Did he mean, instead of marching into Oakland?

Surrounded here by students and a half-dozen older women thrumming a compulsive beat on snare drums, she hopped down from the fender. No, who were these people? She could feel their tension ease as, surprisingly quickly, everyone turned, swinging sideways with the surging march line, song and laughter pealing forth again, and everyone stepped lively, rhythmic, though behind them, loud, some voices kept on chanting "No— go left, go left!" Her legs began trembling so she thought now fear would surely stop her, but it didn't, hadn't, not this night, and even as they headed back toward central Berkeley, someone on the sound truck shouted, challenging the darkness, "Tomorrow we'll be back! Tomorrow, on to Oakland Army Terminal!"

But not tonight, no. Not now. She paused at a street corner, relieved—and suddenly, acutely aware she'd been very frightened. But, really, what self, what bounds, was such fear trying to protect?

"Nora, help me." From the shadows, a sylph-like figure stepped toward her. Golden curls framed the sweet, childlike face. The street-singer Nadine, wearing a dirty orange dress. "I can't stand it. Roger won't leave his wife. He's blaming me."

Surreal again. Yet she had to respond, must not keep judging people. "Blaming you, Nadine?" Probably not wrongly, either, yet there must be some cause, which a caring friend would try to understand, for the singer's compulsive seductions of whomever another woman valued. And the singer's eyes overflowed with concern. "I've been so freaked for you, Nora. I, I've, I keep seeing visions of you—you, alone on an iceberg, cold, grasping a silver knife."

"A silver knife?" *No, this is Nadine's game, this is not me.* "Weird. Like, thanks, Nadine." But why a silver dagger? *Saying,* the song went, *that I'll be no man's bride.* No, only coincidence, the singer's hippie-styled "freak-outs" just one more attempt at control, *childish and ugly as my own ego's traps.* Murmuring understanding and reassurance, saying "It'll be okay, truly it will," she hugged the singer tight and then, thrusting forward, broke away through the dispersing crowd.

A block down the swiftly emptying street, she almost walked directly into Murph.

"No," she said. Jumping back, she stared at the taut, tough-muscled man before her, his upper lip cut by a sloping scar. "No." But it wasn't Murph.

"Fuckin' bitch." The man's eyes darted past her, shifted sideways. The lips moved—not like Murph's.

"Sorry." She'd taken another step back.

But it wasn't this street tough that scared her; it was knowing that Murph could reappear at any time. More warily, she resumed the walk home, but once more the Murph from her past seemed real, as real as that tough. Walking, feet tired, up the tree-lined blocks, she recalled the old scenes. *It wasn't Murph's fault, though.*

She'd thought it her fault, then. From the morning, three years back—*so much time out of my life*—when she'd stood on the Berkeley sidewalk staring into the mirrored store window that seemed to reflect her soul's depravity—the depravity of, in Murph's words, "enjoying my story"—she had loathed herself. For months afterward, she had stayed indoors until night fell, away from people's eyes. Until finally the fact she never went out, her "hiding inside"—as, much later, her gay friend Ernie would call it, saying, "Hah, think I haven't been there?"—had infuriated Murph.

He must have suspected why I hid, she thought now, taking the sharp uphill back to Telegraph Avenue. Or maybe he hadn't, but soon he'd begun staying late at the computer lab and objecting, "Don't you think it's time to grow up?" "Can't you cook a decent meal?" and the rest, condemning whatever in her he'd once loved. When she had tried to "talk things out," to analyze herself and show him that soon she would grow well and love him better, he had acted tired and repeated, "Nora, it's a therapist you want, not me." He'd gone to New Mexico for a month, and, afterward, insisted she "remain over there" on her side of the bed until she "learned," and sometimes he'd stay up talking with friends all night, and would shake off her hands if she touched him. The August of that year, their final year together, he had a new job, programming for Standard Oil, which took up most his time.

"No, you are not trying," he had snapped, one Sunday that last October, when she'd again asked "Let's talk." Knowing he'd be furious if she asked for grocery money, she'd made do, for their dinner, with five eggs— two for Murph, two for Martin, his partner in their department's Navy contract, and one for herself—and the omelette had come out soggy, strangely grey.

"We're supposed to eat this shit?" Martin had pushed away his plate.

"Nora." Murph had pushed his chair back and stood, voice threateningly quiet. "We've talked about this, haven't we? This façade you play of incompetence? You know you can do better when you want to." He'd lifted his and Martin's plates. "But I'll tell you what—if you really can't cook, go get yourself a friggin' job. That way, we could eat out, at least. If nothing else." And of course she'd known what the "nothing else" meant; it meant that what they called her "sex problem" had come back, even though she should, by this point, open easily to him. Only, she couldn't.

Carrying the plates off to the kitchen, Murph had sighed, "Okay, Marty, let's go out to Hot Wings," while she'd stared down at the table and her own cooling egg.

"I'll get work somehow," she'd promised, knowing it wasn't possible. Always, those rare times she'd managed to get a typing test or interview, she'd failed. And when, after Murph had started at Standard Oil, she'd asked he refer her for a clerical slot there, he'd just laughed, "Girl, they do expect basic maturity."

A maturity she'd been sure, by then, she lacked, given her failures not only in work or graduate school, but also sexually—her *abnormal* response, that night on the white-gold rug, and all those times her body had kept Murph out or, more recently, had clung to him "like a nympho," as he'd said. "A mature woman just seduces her man."

Leaving her egg uneaten, after Murph and Martin left she'd gone outside for a walk. The October flowers had been blooming, that evening, all over Berkeley.

But, coming home, she'd realized they were still out of food, so when Murph and Martin returned, she'd asked Murph for the grocery money. With a shrug, he'd pulled five one-dollar bills from his wallet—then, slowly, a sixth. "This enough?"

Nodding, she'd reached for the bills. But instead of handing them to her, he had grasped her hand, pulled her into the living room, and sat her on the rug. There were grass stains on his sandals. "You want the money?"

"Four-fifty." Stupidly, her voice had trembled. "That's plenty."

"Well, of course. Since money grows on trees—"

She'd looked up, seen his paternal smile. "Before the Co-op closes," she'd said.

"Nora, don't you thank me? Don't you even say 'please'?"

"Before the Co-op—"

"Nora." Or was she only imagining it? "Say 'please.'"

Martin had sat down nearby on the plaid armchair, opening the *Chronicle*. His eyes had met Murph's and they'd smiled. Head shaking, Nora had stared into the ashes, seeing the firelight flicker in the barnlike living-room. *No.* She'd leaned to one side, stared at the octagonal window over the mantel, remembering she and Murph once had been close here. *No, I won't.* Raising her head, she'd got to her feet. She'd stepped off the white rug.

Inch by inch, she'd lifted her Guatemalan purse from the coffee table, stepped across to the front door. Slowly she'd opened it. *No.* Walked down the outside stairs.

Only later had she realized that not only her leaving, but also Murph's constant certainty that he was right, had saved her—especially when he'd gone to work, a month after she'd left, for a NATO contractor somewhere in Scotland.

Carrying only the Guatemalan purse, that evening she had walked to the Mediterraneum. She'd sat at a balcony table, rereading an old copy of *Newsweek* that someone must have left—nowhere to go and no money for a room. Because she hadn't even the maturity for a job. *No,* she had thought again, *no,* and tried to hold on, rereading the paragraph a third time, a fourth. Because beneath her feet lay emptiness. *You are worthless, nothing.* No, but it would go on and on, unless she . . .

"U.S. Army rangers bring Vietnamese women," the caption on the photo read, "to safe haven in an enclosed strategic hamlet." She'd practically memorized it. "There, after questioning, they may pick up their accustomed lives, secure from Viet Cong incursion."

"You're not planning to dive into someplace cold and wet, are you?" A hand had gripped her shoulder. "So look, I'm gay, absolutely no danger to you. Come home with me."

"*What?*" She'd jerked away. "Come *what?* Let go of me, you—"

"Miss, I don't like watching folks go under." The short man had perched on the edge of the chair across from her. "My name's Ernie Strydmer. I'm for people."

Three weeks later, Ernie had said, "In honesty, I do get tired of sharing my digs. Even though you're a charming ornament. It's my only extra couch, dear," and after another day of futilely searching for work, "All right," she'd said, "You're right, best I do it now." Because anyhow it wouldn't matter; even a steady job couldn't turn her feelings less vile or make her more mature. Yet she had dreaded taking money again from her parents, like a child dependent on an allowance. While Ernie was out, she'd made the phone call. Tried to gloss over the broken affair— "failed," her parents called it. "We really saw ourselves as married, Dad," she'd said, and "Yes, he loved me. Mom, it was *me,* it wasn't Murph's fault." And, over and over, "I'm fine; I don't need to come home."

The next week, Ernie had driven her, clasping her parents' check and a second-hand suitcase holding a new skirt, tee shirt, jeans, and not much else, to the rooming house she'd found. "I daresay you can do the rest very well," the small man, now her friend, had said. "You can be charming—don't worry so."

But it hadn't been worry; it had been the ongoing horror of realizing she was failed, depraved, insane. In the weeks that followed, the only times she forgot herself were in songwriting sessions with Nadine and a piccolo-playing downstairs neighbor, "exploring our energies," as the singer would put it. For three seasons, they'd presented skits at bars and parks. But then, back in January, Ernie had happened onto a session and, within a month, Nadine had met and seduced his beloved Rich.

"But why?" Nora had asked her.

"Roger's taking me for an ice cream soda," Nadine had answered, smiling—then collapsed in tears, "I'm sorry, I'm sorry." *Warm-hearted, if one can reach her.*

But no, all of that was over. It was just some random tough, Nora calmed herself, who'd appeared here on the street. Not Murph and not her past. She could move on, someday she *would* be whole. She looked out across Telegraph Avenue. It was empty now; everyone had dispersed. *Tomorrow I'll march again. This time, we will go on.*

"Jan, I wasn't so scared as at the train tracks. And it's not that this march was bigger, but yes it was, and in the morning we all marched again, and . . ." No, it was too hard to explain, Nora thought, the Oakland cops charging, and the Hell's Angels roaring in, "And then there was a confrontation and people sat there on the street, nonviolent and brave. *(Not me. But I stayed.)* And they sang." At her square desk, lamp already lit against the November dusk, she tried to describe the march down Telegraph and the next day's clash for her former, now quite staid, college roommate. Sturdy and rational, Jan had become a biochemist in Manhattan—still the warm, attentive listener, the comprehending mind. "Jan, I used to think I loved," she wrote. "And maybe someday I really shall—and be whole, like you." Nora pulled a cigarette from a new pack. The problem was, for words to have meaning required structure—but then that structural system controlled how one analyzed issues, how one experienced phenomena, how one knew the "self" or understood the meanings in Ri's eyes.

Indeed, there was no way to explain these complications in a letter. Pushing back her chair, she slid the page aside. Later, then. The Vietnam Day Committee was holding an open-mic meeting in an hour. There too, of course, people would cocoon themselves in words and systems, a few of the serious leaders— Weinberg and Delacour and Goldberg—were friendly, but everyone would sit around judging what to do; she could get caught up in those arguments, but she mustn't judge. Yet she needed to be present.

As she stepped outside, the mid-November rain was pouring, soaking everything. It held a sense of imminent finality, like the rains during the Cuban missile crisis, when she had fled with four acquaintances upcoast in an ancient car. Now, to her left and above her head as she started up the tree-lined street, a caterpillar crawled along a dripping leaf; somewhere in mud a toddler in a reed-thatched town looked up and saw the falling bombs and could not flee. After the meeting, she would phone her parents; they were simply people, real people, not "archetypes of the culture." *And I can risk this now; I am on my path and I will find new ways of love.*

Only, the path was still easy to lose. Aware of the fragility, she let speeches at the meeting pass without judging them, protecting herself, and later, back in the silent apartment, she again put off phoning her parents. That night, she dreamed of children "after the Bomb," knowing she must save them, but by morning her direction was less clear. The sun lit the table where Ri's hands had trembled so that, turning to her, he had spilled his coffee; blue-and-white tiles gleamed in the kitchen where he'd put his arms around her. The light brought it back—the golden afternoon, the touch of *that person I once thought I loved.*

The next day, she did call her parents; they were expecting her for the holidays, and she would have to disappoint them. Yet at least she could be generous and kind; they'd always loved her. "We should visit soon, though," she offered. "Like maybe sometime this summer? It's warmer then, easier to travel." And by then the new, giving self would be stronger. Sturdy, really—if she continued on her path, reaching out without judgments or bounds.

In the early dusk of New Year's Eve, Nora stepped silently down the gravel drive under Ri's windows and halted beside a sheltering rosebush. Half-hidden, she peered toward his living room window, where a yellow light glowed. By now perhaps she might dare visit.

Only, she saw figures moving, shadowy behind a light blue curtain, and heard voices through the windows, voices that rose—Ri's, and then a youngish woman's and an older man's—in anguished tones. Then there was silence, then murmurings again.

To not risk being seen if any of them looked out, she glided, in a long dance step, almost a leap, across to the grass beside the drive, and backed away.

2

Up the Trail

Spring 1966

Leaving an evening rally, Nora walked the mile south on Telegraph Avenue. Up a quiet leafy street, she saw the white-pillared house, office of the *Berkeley Barb*. Lately her churning thoughts had grown calmer. Now sometimes she could discuss Movement tactics again, as she had this evening, and even again tell jokes without getting caught up in the logic. But she still had to weigh her vulnerability. With exaggerated care, she watched each thought, yet she had to hear people's arguments, even "try on" their judgments provisionally. For, others' views, if merely provisional, at least couldn't drag her back inside the system's fairy tales. Skimming along on such judgments—on "common knowledge" or what the hippies called "ordinary frames of reference"—might even sometimes be to step toward maturity.

Of course, half of what people at the rally had said was just dumb— "When the cops charge, jam a fuckin' stick between their legs," for instance. Even though she'd not yet separated from the voices of the system, still she must find some way to make her "own" decisions in this struggle against the war.

For that struggle never halted. Even though people marched and rallied, the photos in the newspapers showed, each new spring day, worse atrocities and a widening war; each moment made clearer the need to act.

And here, in that pillared house across the road, the *Barb* was one of four U.S. "underground papers" confronting that war. True, the editor, though a leftwing journalist who took some risks, was not known for risking his own well-being. But the paper spoke up for people in Vietnam, for the peasants beneath America's bombs, and carried accounts by protestors on the streets, offered a voice to people who needed protection and to those struggling to protect them. To work on this sort of paper, reporting actual news, would allow her to help real people, give her voice to the real world—*to speak for others, give to their needs not speak the words of a dream. To save others, end this massacre.* Here, or wherever the path led, she must learn the sort of caring she'd glimpsed in Ri.

If I do this, I shall lose myself. Exactly. She tossed her head, crossed the street.

A regular Brenda Starr. Her story, "Radical student picket line confronts scab workers," was the *Barb*'s front-page lead, the paper's biggest scoop in months. For weeks, the editor, Max Scherr, had let her handle only the entertainment page, phoning bars and clubs and turning every "Here's our hottest new group" from Jerry Garcia, each "Really the best band this country's ever heard" from Bill Graham, into "ROCK, Jeff Airplane (see MON), $3," "FOLK, M. Farina, Jabberwock, 8pm, free," "BEN. Lincoln Brigade—P. Ochs, Fish, lightshow (see SAT)," "SPECIAL, Mamas & Papas, dinner, Berk Aud, $6," and the like; the *Barb* used tight style. By now she was sure the paper, with its sleazy graphics, numbed and disinterested reporters, ancient typewriters in the crowded main office, and recurrent sexual innuendo around the dinners that Max's tired wife prepared, was no path to any sort of caring. Yet people needed to read the paper's articles, to learn what truths they could about the war.

So she stayed on after that first scoop, soon getting another and then a story on scholarship blacklists and one on defense-contract funding of a famous U.C. physics lab's entire "basic research." She was learning to talk to city commissioners and restaurant owners, to deans and police captains, being recognized by politicos, acknowledged by local Left leaders, and becoming quick with strangers on the phone.

"How can you call this work 'nothing'?" Sally asked her. "The *Barb*'s a rag, okay, but we're reaching people who'd never look at *Socialist Worker* or *People's World*." Sally had been with the paper from the start, specializing in human interest features and reviews. She was thirty, a divorced mother of four, graceful in the wide blouses and full skirts she wore despite her weight.

"I liked your piece about the guys getting black kids into that daycare," Nora told her during staff dinner one evening. Sally looked her over and patted her arm. *Sure, we're friends.* But now, over coffee at the Mediterraneum, Sally barely glanced up. "Your problem, Nora, is you want caring acts to be done caringly."

"Don't you? I mean, don't we have to get beyond the system's structures?"

"Ah, a theorist. No, caring isn't theory, not to me. See, if there was 'caring' daycare I could afford, I'd still have my kids. But as it is, see, their dad's got a nice new wife who can be home to 'care' for them all day."

Oh, that. Nora just nodded. Sally's world differed from hers—even from her parents', though probably equally immersed in the slow boredom that crushed down feelings and closed off possibilities.

"You think I'm a middle-aged momma," Sally said. "Ending the war's more important, right? And the music, too? Bet you love 'Sounds of Silence.'"

"Well, I do. You know, that song speaks of the inner dance—of what covers the inner dance. Of the unheard voices lost beneath the lies."

"That so?" Sally's grin was cold. "Noise, honey—it's noise that cuts those voices down. The 'noise' of our lives."

Of course, at Sally's age, music must mean differently. Nora watched the hip people, students in jeans or tie-dyed skirts, some black guys, a few aging beatniks, tracing their way through the endless coffee line. Whatever the inner silence, this room was noisy and smoky.

"But, Sally"—because it's not just theory, it's what I need to live— "some people must give of themselves, around here. Those guys you wrote about, don't they care about those kids? Because, what I mean is, we need to give our voices *for others.*"

But while she spoke, she couldn't help noticing how Sally just sat there seeming sure of herself, and how the satin stripes on Sally's full skirt made her hips look even wider.

And now I'm judging her looks? "I mean, for our own sakes, too," she finished. "Mostly for others, though."

"Think so?" Sally laughed. "Hey, you really think so? Like, you know what you know. And I know what I've lived. Let's keep it all going, okay?"

Nora's fourth scoop concerned a bank's denying a pro-abortion group an account because, in the bank manager's words, "They're controversial." She quoted him. Fifteen minutes later, while she was still grinning. Max grinned back. "You swallowed one sweet canary," he congratulated her. And more canaries followed, and by April, she was handling nine stories a week, mostly first-pagers.

But for what, prestige? She mustn't lose the path, must write to help *others.* But, even though Sally thought the paper and its coverage important, it seemed now a wrong turn—the job dulling, the interviews unfelt, the paper's aims unfocused. And the schedule, ten hours a day from Sunday until deadline Wednesday night, left no time to think. There was an ugly quality to that first half of the week, the stories to be covered often trivial ("Dog owners lose rubber bones at party"— "Too many private cars in Berkeley?"), and the other reporters acted bored by everything. Then, after Wednesdays, the emptiness came in, the dangerous nostalgia, falling into memories that pulled her down into thinking she loved Ri.

Yet she had to stay on here, helping those she could by telling their stories ("Young mother to lose apartment because baby cries," "Activists get record bail—come to courthouse Monday!") Besides, through reporting she might yet meet Movement people who truly cared. She'd not found them yet, though—the generous, loving people she needed to be with, to become.

One April morning, seeking them, she interviewed at the American Friends' Service Committee office in San Francisco. She felt strange, dressed in an office skirt again and a white buttoned blouse, her hair rolled high, smiling at the middle-aged man across a wide desk—for a volunteer job helping children. *Just like missionaries,* came the thought, but she assured him she had no better-than-thou attitude and hoped to learn as much from the work as would the kids.

Across the table, he watched her silently. She could hear water bubbling in what must be the office coffee machine; the man's stomach rumbled.

"But, you see, we're looking for someone much simpler." He didn't smile, didn't explain why having more than one reason was a disqualification. "Somebody who simply wishes to help." After a couple more minutes, he escorted her out.

A week later, remembering the kids on the beach, and that Ri had called them "prisoners of the city," she forced herself to go to a City Council meeting, and to put in her name and wait her turn to stand up and argue that there really was need for a bus out to the beaches, "so poor kids, too, can get to the ocean." But no one responded, except one woman, a newer councilor, who came up as the meeting ended, and, taking her by the arm, said "Thank you for your enthusiasm, dear—there's so much to bc donc."

Other times, as the evenings lengthened, she stayed late at rallies and meetings. When she suggested, to the small group An-Tee-War, the possibility of civil disobedience, a bearded man laughed her to silence while the others walked down a hall to the kitchen, discussing whether to order olive or sausage pizza.

Back home, she took a long, soaking bath. As on one or two other recent weekend evenings, she caught herself thinking *It's been months—by now couldn't we be friends?* The beauty she'd felt in Ri made so much around her—the *Barb*'s strident prose, these politicos' egos, rumored squabbles in the VDC—ugly and painful. But she understood, watching the sunset through her wide west windows, she must not succumb to this tempting sorrow over "lost love." Instead, she had to keep on, still seeking people who generously cared, even as she doggedly wrote the news and tried to act to someday change it.

Just go farther up the trail. Hope will come.

That Monday, an attorney she was interviewing about the new Council for Justice, or CFJ, that would "give legal-team support to Movement actions," told her of plans "by very dedicated people" to shut down the UTC napalm plant in Redwood City— "nonviolently, you understand, but it'll be much more than civil disobedience." *People who genuinely care, then?*

"No, of course I can't give you a contact number yet," he added, with a little laugh. "I shouldn't have even mentioned them." *No, you shouldn't have,* she thought, *because, you know, this tastes like a super-canary.* And perhaps these really were the caring people. But days went by—days she spent adjusting her new cat, a pregnant female rescued from the pound, to life in her apartment—and her attempts to reach Movement people who might know people who might have heard of people planning anything in Redwood City still got nowhere. All she could find were more rumors—not the activists.

"So check out those CNVA folks at Port Chicago, if you're so stuck on civil disobedience," Max said, and sighed. "You people, you Lefties, narrow your view too much. This paper has to cover the entire Movement."

So on May Day she hitched a ride to the vigil that the CNVA—Committee for Nonviolent Action—was holding beside the town of Port Chicago at the gates of Concord Naval Weapons Station, the giant base on the Sacramento River where the Navy shipped munitions off to Vietnam. CNVA had billed the action "a time for caring, for opposing murder with our lives," but when she got there, thirty miles east of the Bay, in the dry valley heat the straggly line of sweat-stained, grubby vigilers—eight of them, she counted—seemed ridiculous, their sleeping bags heaped like trash by the roadside, hand-drawn posters barely legible, while they silently stood, as if half asleep, hands lifted and fingers spread in the *V* of the peace sign, smiling at passing weapons-truck drivers.

This is moral witness? Their optimism seemed insane, a joke. *Or am I merely scared to be seen as one of them—and maybe get laughed at?* Really, she thought, scribbling in her little notebook the two good quotes she could get from them, this action needed much more publicity, planning, and even hope, to bring in the crowds and be effective. These demonstrators must have cared, once, though now they seemed only to go through the motions, but it would take people who still had hope and also knew the media, knew how to make events "newsworthy."

These Redwood City protestors, however, might really be both caring and effective—the sort of generously loving people she sought. As the week's news deadline neared, however—only an hour until midnight, Jeff finishing up in the photo-processing closet, the other reporters gone home, and the paper, in Max's usual terms, a disaster—she gave up on finding them, and leaned back on an old white chair at the *Barb*'s kitchen table. *Forget that; just get the scoop instead on the VDC anniversary event.*

But "scoop" or "cvcnt" was far too strong a word. According to the *San Francisco Chronicle,* LBJ was about to bomb Hanoi and Haiphong. The war would enlarge, China would come in . . . and the VDC was calling for a "Movement Picnic."

Right. *Make it a short-short,* she thought. But no, that was being judgmental. *Works so well around the Barb, though.* Shaking her head, she lifted the phone, trying to escape the humor's distancing allure. *Just get the details. Like what, recipes? No, stop that.* She dialed the VDC office.

No answer. "Guess they're not on night watch, Max."

She waited as the editor dug through a mess of papers on his desk in the living room office. He tossed a yellow card through the doorway, and it fell by her feet. Reaching down, she picked it up with two fingers. On it was a pencil-scrawled phone number. "Try this one," Max said. "Dave used to be on Steering Committee. Don't worry, he's up—it's dark outside."

On the eighth ring, a man's voice answered. Sleepily, but turning sharp. "Fuck, babe, I know *nothing* about that picnic. Like, that's how we're gonna end the war—a picnic? *Barb* wants a story, how come you're not covering Redwood City? You know what people down there are doing?"

"You know about Redwood City?"

"Oh." The voice went quiet. "Sure. I've a whole portfolio of stuff. Clippings, photos, everything. You know what those napalm trucks look like? Do you—those silver crates full of bombs?"

She hesitated, not sure why. "I've seen them." A guy from CNVA had pointed them out, during the Port Chicago protest. Max had put the story on page 3. Right on the fold. "Yes, you've got photos?"

"If you're serious. Sure, give me an hour. I'll drive them over there."

"We're on deadline." She stared down at the phone, not sure what made her say it. "Get here in fifteen minutes. If you really want to end the war."

But it was a full hour before Dave slipped into the *Barb* kitchen and, crossing the room noiselessly, dumped a portfolio onto the kitchen table, covering the documents she'd been reading.

"Take some coffee." She nodded toward the pot.

"Yeah, that's what I should drink. Coffee." He was lean-faced, straight blond hair too short, watching her reaction from ice-blue eyes, lips curved in a cheerless grin.

Now she realized who he was, the notorious "VDC Dave," with his history of "adventurist" actions—the cool-headed heavy drinker alleged to have emptied the Berkeley draft board office with a stinkbomb, the

Movement near-legend who'd run a sailboat up to Alameda Naval Air and got the sailors loading ammunition until he'd laughed and they'd had to drag all the boxes back off. Above those elegant cheekbones, his eyes stared back at her, measured her—for what? Blue as a freezing winter sky. In the steamy kitchen, she opened the portfolio and tried to focus on reporting.

Because, whoever Dave was, his account of Redwood City was unfocused and confused, yet the way he moved pulled at her body and his eyes fixed on her like a cougar's on its prey. Still, she tried to piece together some coherence from his press clips. A citizens' rally in Redwood City, a public meeting where three women chained themselves to the UTC napalm factory gates— and a flyer: "Persons whose conscience impels them will walk onto UTC's death plant and make a silent stand" against the war.

More moral witness, then. Nothing more.

And this guy is drunk. An adventurist. Or an agent? Could be an agent—that haircut, tough talk, could be the CIA. She lit a cigarette—her turn now to measure him.

At least the portfolio was a reporter's treasure. Photos of napalm bombs stacked in open fields and pistachio orchards, articles from the *San Jose Mercury-Sun* on the zoning fight against the UTC plant, sketches of loose bombs piled up on docks in the Mexican-American town of Alviso. "In San Jose," Dave added, leaning close behind her and clutching her hand to light his cigarette off hers, "thcy'vc bombs storcd right bcsidc the road. In unfenced lots." Reaching into his scuffed backpack, he pulled out a glass jar. It held a light-colored clear jelly. "Guess what?"

She dared not flinch.

"Oh yeah?" He slouched against the wall. "Babe, if that scares you, what'll you do when we have to fight? You know how much of this we're dropping on those people this year? This week? Do you *care?*"

His judging was relentless. It infuriated her. Only, she forgot everything, with him standing right there. Close to her. Watching.

"The thing is, you have to go now, Dave." She reddened. "I'm sorry, but I can't write this up and make conversation. Not at the same time." He went silent. Then, "Okay. Okay, come to San Jose with me on Saturday. We can take a look around." Blue eyes brightened, fixed on her. "You're not scared?"

She dared not flinch.

3

The Lion

Spring 1966

The tract homes beyond the freeway's screening hedge were middle-class, but wasn't she? Ticky-tacky isolation boxes: *You can't play in our yard.* Keeping people out, just as she had. But she could change—was changing. They could, too, and they must, many more of them, to stop the war. She stared hard out the window, away from David.

She mustn't withdraw. Yet even this morning, waiting for him, she'd had to force herself to concentrate on her young cat, petting it as it nursed its kittens and purred and licked their fur. She'd kept rotating her wrists, stretching each leg separately, pouring tuna cat food into the bowl, lighting another cigarette, trying to stay calm. She'd feared coming with David but, in fact, reporting on the South Bay napalm sites was necessary.

"Look there." He gestured toward an airport, set low between the freeway and bare hills. He kept edging the van off the road as he drove—but it was his presence, not his driving, that frightened her.

"How the hell you gonna do anything, with those nerves?" For the second time this morning, he squeezed her wrist. Not in assurance, but in challenge. "That's the trouble with the Movement. We're all fucked up."

At least he was watching the road again. She closed her eyes; there had been an hour of this. "No, it's the System within us that's fucked up. *We're* not."

"Yeah, we are." He smiled, an American movie little-boy smile. How practiced was that seeming guilelessness? Yet her abdomen quivered, a twinge of desire, even through the dread.

"All the same, Nora, we can act." Again the smile. "Remember, last year, the draft board up by campus closed down for a week? 'Come back some other time, boys, we can't stick around to enlist you'? We didn't get those workers out by moral witness, you know. We had beautiful lettering, elegant print on cream-colored stationery, with that quietly underlined "Warning" and a Bureau of Investigations logo at the top to look official, and we had stamps on the envelope—but not cancelled, so it wasn't mail fraud. But when those nice clean citizens in that nice clean office, deciding who to send to Vietnam, opened up those envelopes and read what just might happen, right there—they started thinking, babe. Wondering, 'Suppose the next one blown to hell is one of us?'"

Something was turning her voice weak, like an admiring but fearful child's. "That's a—a great action, David. Really is. But so isolated. I mean, with marches, people learn." *Why am I begrudging him? Because I can't reach out and act with such daring?*

He glanced at her, the van again swerving. "Damn it, don't any of you understand? Do any of you who saw the VDC leaflets even realize we really napalmed that woman and her child? Do you? Listen to me, Nora—if people want to demonstrate, or Women for Peace wants to boycott Dow, or the whole damn city wants to sit on its ass expounding its collective ego—or exercise its legs with bigger, longer marches—fine. Fine, I'll give them what information I've got, just like I'm giving to you—but that is it. There isn't time for boycotts and debates and marches."

Flowers—lupine, poppies, some sort of white daisies—grew by the roadside, and near the turnoff to San Jose a mockingbird sang on a barbed-wire fence. Just beyond a sparse wood glinted the southern tip of the Bay. He pulled the van into an overgrown lane by an old stonework bridge. "There's Alviso. And we're out of gas."

She watched him drag a gas can from the back of the van. While he filled the tank, she crossed the gravel lane and began picking wildflowers—mostly, the blue lupine—in the warm grass. The bridge formed a high arch over a tiny creek; downslope stood an old wooden church with a tall steeple, small houses clustered around it.

He called, voice softer, asking wasn't it strange to find lupine here or see such clouds before summer. He looked gangly, even boyish, eyes hooded. But those eyes demanded, and those deft long hands and high cheekbones drew her. *Caution, danger ahead. Nora, don't let yourself be used.* The old thoughts.

Then David tilted his head, grinning the movie grin. Glowering back, she tossed the wildflowers to the ground. His grin widened. They climbed back in the van.

It hadn't disturbed him—her flinging away the flowers like that, such a childish gesture! Her heart jumped in her glad surprise. It hadn't bothered him, as it would have Ri. She felt her mouth curve upward, and laughed.

Ahead of them, weekend crowds, probably Alviso's Mexican-American residents, promenaded along the embankment that held back the Bay from the town; across the narrow estuary hundreds of napalm bombs gleamed in open crates.

But several miles farther south, on the edge of San Jose, the crates of bombs were stacked fifteen feet high beside the highway. David parked the van a half-mile down the road, and, ashamed to be frightened, she followed him back to the bomb site, across the broken curbing, and down a potholed drive. It opened onto a sort of entranceway—a break amid the hundreds of slatted, bomb-filled crates that formed a roofless chamber, crisscrossed by narrow aisles stretching high above their heads. No one could see in here from the highway, or even from the nearby side street, but she couldn't escape her fear.

"Come here, come look." Crouched like a cat, David glided toward a far corner. She could make out his hands in the shadows, moving over a crate on the bottom row. Forcing her feet forward, she could see the nose-cone deep inside the crate, uncoupled from its silvery shell, long green-and-red cut wires sticking up like the antennae of a metal insect.

"Want to borrow my knife?"

She ran her fingernails along the insulated wires but could not make herself feel they were lethal; here, the reality seemed pretty, shiny things in boxes. She shook her head.

"A knife's a weapon, that it? So you won't even touch one? Tell me, babe, what do you think those bombs are?"

Of course—of course—but at this moment, her reality was his unending pressure, her own confusion. *Stop telling me what to do.* While she knelt beside the first crate, he was stalking among the rows, crouching over a crate now and then, apparently at random, knife in hand.

A security guard could enter, any moment. Her stomach hurt. If David hadn't brought her here, she'd be back home, fifty miles away and safe. This was crazy. *Dave let's get out.*

"You know, I realize what you do, Nora, informing people, making them aware and all, that's also important." Coming closer and pressing his knife against a nearby crate, he began to remove its yellow stickers. She leaned forward to watch.

"You hear me, babe? I know this is a big jump for you." Somehow, his words released the tension.

She nodded. "It is." A moment later, her own fingers began to peel the first sticky papers from the next crate's slats. "Flammable," the stickers read, "U.S. Armaments— Firebomb-BLU." For an article, a picture, an unlikely but possible injunction. She no longer felt sick. From her patchwork purse, she pulled out the *Barb*'s ancient camera and, hands almost steady, started snapping photos. Caption them well— "Napalm-B—half polystyrene, one-fourth benzine, one-fourth gasoline— the super-stick stuff that water cannot quench." She would have to write it forcefully. She'd be writing to save lives.

Removing those wires might save lives.

"Want my knife, after all?"

But before she could decide, David pulled out his cigarettes, shook one from the pack, and held up a match.

Slowly, she grinned back—a cat's snarl. *Stop trying your daredevil scene on me.*

The flame burned out between his fingers while they stood together between the stacks of bombs and she watched his grinning, high-boned face. No, she wouldn't try to stop him—wasn't about to give him that satisfaction. The flashpoint of napalm was far too high for a match to set off. Knowingly, she too kept grinning.

"Looks official, doesn't it? That's how I do things." A few evenings later, David, wearing a construction hard-hat, leaned against the cab of what he and his "handpicked driving *compañeros*" called their "napalm escort truck." It was, as she'd written for the *Barb,* "a half-ton pick-up with bright red fire extinguishers hanging on each side and, stenciled across the back, a wooden sign, USE EXTREME CAUTION. NAPALM BOMBS AHEAD. Tonight the truck stood in the driveway outside her apartment. He'd first stopped at the *Barb,* he said, but "that fat woman," meaning Sally—*nasty put-down but at least he's not attracted to her*— "told me you'd gone on home." Removing his hard-hat, he held it at waist level, his long, thin hands pressed together. *As if he's courting me*—the thought made her smile inside.

"Those truckers," he said, hat still in his hands as he followed her upstairs to her apartment, "maybe they'll think we're Navy, or maybe UTC or DOW or something. But Mr. and Mrs. Jones driving down the freeway—bet they've been wondering lately what those shiny bombs they've been seeing out there are; now they'll know. And you know what? They get frightened enough, they may start understanding what it's like for the Vietnamese."

But upstairs the bulb in her wooden lamp had gone out and the room was dim. Just inside the doorway, David stood still, as if struck by the tree-sheltered quietude. His voice went hollow, the insouciance gone.

"Nora—Nora, suppose this war meant your own family's lives? Wouldn't you do more, lots more?" He prowled the room, pressing his fingertips against the spines of her books and peering sideways at their titles. He said, "Don't any of you people actually care? I need to know." Balancing on his heels, he squatted down across from where she sat, her legs wrapped tight together, on the purple couch. As though intent on prey, his eyes fixed, half-closed, on hers.

No, no, best not get closer; do not get used. It was the old trap of her cautioning voices and she knew she mustn't listen, but her hands shook. *Could get knocked up. And what if he doesn't care. Men run—remember, men run.*

"You're so fucking nervous, you're worse than I am." His words cut into her thoughts. "Hey, do I scare you? I scare all these people—these student types, Women for Peace, your CNVA pals—but you, you claim you're serious, you say you're ready to take chances, and then—"

It's one in the morning, and you attract me. You too much attract me. But no longer would she confess this. "I . . . I pick up on other people's tension, David."

"Oh—I'm sorry. Then should I go? I'll leave, if you want."

"No." But he was grinning again. "Come here."

Wait. May be an agent. Silly to fear, but at least an excuse to hold him away. And she needed to.

He held out a hand.

Wait. He's dangerous. Use extreme caution.

The hand pressed her fingers. "There's a bottle in my van, babe. Should I go get it?"

Later, after he had pulled her down next to him on the couch and set the wine bottle near them in the half-dark, his voice gliding through yet another activist adventure, it began to sound like a movie soundtrack, a well-used seduction script— "I thought I'd be shot, nobody else had stuck around, the cops kept creeping closer"—on and on, but pulling her in, even so. *And if he uses me, leaves me?*

She stared at his long, lithe form in the dark room, studying him with the same intensity he focused on her.

Trying not to care too much, to be glad he seemed to wish no deep involvement—waiting and waiting until the dangerous yearning, the false fairy-tale love like she'd once believed she felt for Ri, faded. When she was sure it would not return, she pressed herself against David on the couch, placed her hands along his thighs.

He asked no questions. His bony hands moved knowingly—smooth and confident. Her abdomen quivered, surprised with electric feeling.

But the silence went on too long. Much too long. *Only dreams—only dreams again; this isn't working.* She turned away, head shaking, trying not to speak.

"What is it?"

"Nothing, Dave." She mustn't ask. Must not fall into old fears; this time, her body would work. "I don't want to force my body. That's all."

Voice gone soft, he laughed. "No, no, I won't force you." Gliding, almost dance-like, in the moonlight he rolled over on his back and, with another graceful motion, pulled her to him. Her breathing raced and he held her, his own breath speeding. Then, as they moved together, hesitant at first but quickly finding the other's pace, matching each other's motion, heat began to spread out through her groin. When he entered, the movement was sudden, swift—but sure and gentle. His eyes locked hers. Their bodies turned electric.

Yet what she longed to tell him could be only—by now she understood—the words of dreams.

With dawn, Nora woke, sad with uncertainty, circled by the endless thoughts. David hovered by the bed, already dressed in his jeans, looking down at her and buttoning his work-shirt. "Want one, babe?" he asked. He held out his cigarette pack. She shook her head, but he lit one for himself. "Don't get up," he deadpanned, and grinned.

She watched as the door closed behind him. She wanted to make him happy, that was all. She doubted she could.

4

Kittens and COINTELPRO

June 1966

Shortly before dawn, a man called: "Baby, you're in our sights." In the moment after he hung up, an operator came on, "ringing you back with the charges on your call to Tijuana." The next time it happened, about twenty minutes later, Nora tried to dial the police but her line went dead. The night was still hot, but she dared not open a window; branches swayed in the darkness just beyond the panes—branches nearly wide enough for someone to climb—and screening the windows from the street below. There had been three of these calls this week, always a man breathing heavily. "Everyone gets those," the pony-tailed reporter Michael at the *Barb* had said, shaking his head, and the gray-haired columnist Jeff had asked "What are you doing in the Movement if you're scared?" Even Sally had only looked pensive and said, "I'd just try to ignore it."

But who was phoning? And why the mention of Tijuana—the Mexican abortions center? *And why do the* Barb *people just presume this is political—what if they're wrong? What if it's sexual, an attacker?* No reason, after all, that she'd be a political target; she'd done so little. Still, one of her articles ("No demonstrations took place at the unfenced napalm storage sites on the Alviso docks or alongside Highway 101 in San Jose") might be considered classified information, and she had given her name to the Marine MPs at Port Chicago. Mostly, though, what she remembered was David using her phone to call *compañeros* all over the Bay Area. And one day, when people had been discussing provocateurs, over dinner at the *Barb,* Max had turned to her and asked, "You know who I think's an agent? Yes, you do."

But surely that was paranoia? Another form of judging, another way to hold a person away? Yet there were, of course, real agents; as Jeff said, pulling his grey-brown mustache while he chewed a spicy tamale, "Someone's gotta keep an eye on us, make sure we don't start trusting each other." They had all laughed, but she was still afraid. But what actually frightened her wasn't that David might be an agent—she didn't really think he was—but that he might leave her.

That evening, as he again stood with one hand poised on her phone, her suspicions returned. Dragging on the cigarette he'd lit for her, she barely mumbled "Thanks." *Thanks for the light, and let go of my phone*—no, she couldn't say that. But someone had somehow got her number, and, further, agents weren't the only ones who used people, not a bit. What was he doing with her phone, anyhow? He used and tested everyone—even the kittens now. They were racing across the couch to pounce on each other, tripping over their own feet and making "eep-eep" sounds, but he kept picking them up to see which would fight back. Laughing, he put the last kitten down, then began to dial as if she were not there. Making long-distance calls, expensive. And why? "Enough contact with the outer world, David." She clamped down the receiver, hard. "Organizing's great, man, but I can't afford it."

"Hey, what the fuck are you doing? Doing to yourself, I mean. 'Cause, babe, it's like, 'Oh Dave, oh Dave, I can't afford this phone call,' blah-blah, and the next time it's 'Oh Dave, let's give to everybody, let's not judge people," blah. And you, what about *you* in all this—you don't want anything?" He let go the phone and flung himself back on the couch, scattering the kittens. "You never say a thing about yourself." He lit a new cigarette, threw the old one into her stone ashtray. "Look at me. Something happened to you. You broke, somehow." With a strangely delicate motion, he reached over and encircled her wrist.

Use extreme caution. And he would never give in, never let her give in. Someone she could care for. "No. Nothing, Dave. Nothing 'broke.'" These so-called depths of closeness were unreal, fantasies that blocked any paths to mature, encompassing love. And did he even want more closeness?

"Tell me, Nora."

Staring down at the grain of the floor—*just like with Ri*—she choked back the dream-love that could trap them in the system's fairy tale. *Unless I've trapped myself by thinking there's a trap.* No, crucial not to go there. "Don't, Dave."

He'd sat up; he leaned toward her, upper lip curled. "'Don't'? 'Don't'? Babe, I've seen stuff I shouldn't have, yeah, but what I'm sensing, what I need to know, is what is it broke you? You're as broken as me."

A statue I am. But that's all you get to see. Because there's a trap inside, a maze. "Yes." And that was it. If he did understand these depths, he'd go away.

"That's your answer?" He stretched his arms toward the ceiling, scattering cigarette ash. "But I was hoping—hoping if I got you angry enough, you'd say what's wrong." He flashed the boyish grin. "How come I frighten you?"

Don't let him see. "C'mon, David. You push too hard sometimes, that's all."

"Uh-uh. You're scared. You're scared shitless."

"*What?*" She jumped to her feet. Without meaning to, she glared back at him, voice rising. "Don't tell me how I feel, you— You know, you brag, you flash your—"

"Do I?" He kept grinning.

No, don't push another man away. She sat again, head bent to hide the blush.

"C'mon, babe, tell me you don't like it."

But she stopped the sharp reply, shielded them both from the dangerous cuts. As had he, she realized. Nor was he walking out; he wasn't leaving.

And so—she saw it in a moment's vision like the sturdy granite of a mountain cliffside—her anger and closures did *not* always drive a man away. And so possibly, someday, someone . . .. She lay back on the couch. Dave wasn't looking toward her but outside, though, toward the lonely night. Toward the starlit chill—Or whatever those images had been.

She must have slept. Moonlight shone through the wide windows. Damp with sweat, she listened to Dave's breathing. Still half-asleep, she caught his stifled sob.

"David, what is it?"

He shook his head, sat up, and reached for the pack of cigarettes on the table. His slim form moved, graceful, in the pale light. "I don't know, I don't know anything anymore. No one cares enough. You know, all these people claim they're against the war, but they do nothing. Nothing. Only a few of us keep trying. Like me, like *mi compañeros* on the escort truck, but we're not enough. And you? Like, I'm sure you care, but you're so frigging scared." He laughed. "Sure, you're going to 'change'—but change what? Your beautiful 'self'? Fuck it. I don't know why we even stay alive."

Just comfort him. Her hand reached out.

"God damn you!"

But his slap didn't touch her hand. Didn't touch her at all.

He had laughed. Leaped to his feet and stood laughing there in the moonlight, mouth spread wide.

Don't laugh at me, don't! But he wasn't.

"Damn kitten!" He thrust two bleeding fingers into his mouth. "Little critter—he attacked me." She heard the match scrape as he lit a cigarette. "That's your protection, Nora? Huh—that leopard?" In the brief illumination, he stroked the purring kitten's arching back. "Tough little guy."

Moonlight still streamed through the windows, but the stars had gone pale. Close to dawn—she must have slept again, David spent the night beside her. But now he went taut, an animal alert to all the early sounds of morning. "Come here," he said.

She turned. "David, David"—she pressed her abdomen to his, wrapped her arms around his neck, stroked the narrow angles of his cheekbones. His hands moved gently; softly they encircled her, slid lower.

"Cold, cold moon," he whispered. "Let's give what we can to each other."

Too close. Too close. She dared not answer. *Yes, but if he's using me?*

"And you'll never say what's wrong?"

She only shook her head, pressed further toward the safer, sensual silence; her breathing quickened.

"Babe, am I hurting you?"

"No, not hurting." She could feel him start to enter, felt his member large and firm inside her. In silence, wary, she began to move in rhythm with his thrusts, responding to that ease and swiftness—swiftness she was coming to know as David's. And soon she felt the rush of dark intensity, and in those moments it took every vigilance to not say—and under her breath as they came, she whispered— "Yes, I love you."

Only dreams, only dreams. Sleepily, much later, he asked what she had said.

"Nothing, David. Just—oh, I don't know." She shook her head and added something about human openness.

In the morning, since he lingered to read the *Examiner* that he'd picked up somewhere the night before and sat around hand-wrestling the kittens and discussing antiwar tactics, and since they'd briefly been so close, she knew he wouldn't return. But sadness over that would be delusion; she should be glad they'd avoidcd falsc "closcncss."

Leaving, he smiled crookedly from the dusty hallway, eyes heavy and a cigarette sliding, between his fingers, from the pack. He stretched out his free hand, a quick gesture that asked no response. Chin lifted, she returned the smile. "You, too."

5

Suppose a Woman

June 29, 1966

On June 29, the United States bombed Hanoi and Haiphong. Nora had just got home from the gynecologist's, turned on the radio, and pulled a cigarette from the pack when she heard the news. She watched the kittens lunge at a toy helicopter on the rug. It was the "war toy" she'd bought Ri for a Christmas present back in December, hoping they could laugh together, but had found no way to give him. The calico kitten rolled on its back, paws killing this peculiar mouse. And suppose a woman, in some hooch downriver near Hanoi, had gone to a clinic, her period two weeks overdue. Nora turned the dial. "Stay tuned to ABC Broadcast News. We will bring you late-breaking reports as they become available." *I pulled only four wires from those bombs.* Even though she'd wanted to do more. She straightened her tee shirt, lit the cigarette, and stepped outside, closing the door behind her carefully so no kitten could run out, then headed for the *Barb*.

Hours yet before the lab would have her test results. In the *Barb*'s back office, she picked up the phone to call Movement groups, "What do you plan to do? We've just bombed Hanoi and Haiphong." But it was too early; most hadn't heard yet, no one had a statement. Someone on the August 6–9 Committee—what was left of the VDC— said "We'll discuss it at our next meeting, probably," and the Soviet expert Bill Mandel exclaimed "Oh my God" and talked for an hour on probable Soviet responses. Usually good for quotes, the activist Marvin Garson just replied,

"The only meaningful reaction would be to blow up New York harbor, which no one's about to do. So stay cool."

But the phoning gave her direction. *In the crisis, she holds aloft the struggle, marches forward despite the heart's secret pain.* The image helped. And she could call anyone—almost.

At 4:30 p.m., she phoned the gynecologist.

"Yes, yes. Your test came out positive."

"Which means?"

"You're pregnant, dear."

When she had first sensed the new softness in her vagina, she had felt joy, but now there was instead a heart-thumping fear. Sally, who was paying support money for her four children, stroked the green cotton of her handmade skirt and said, "Well, so you better get doctors' names in Tijuana. That's where people go. Unless you're crazy." With a crisp smile, Ernie asked, "Now wasn't that careless?" and Nadine said, "Pregnancy freaks me. I really don't want to know all this." Even Lennie, answering the phone between changing the twins' diapers, said, "Don't you have to decide pretty quick? Stick with kittens; at least, they can be left alone." The messages were clear, as if she had an illness— "You go take care of it." She rolled the toy helicopter back and forth along the shiny floor.

Downstairs, the couple who always put up their American flag on holidays were singing "Ballad of the Green Berets," either celebrating the bombing or getting back at her for pasting war-atrocity photos on their flagpole. When the phone rang, she didn't answer; it was probably the breather. *Don't get scared; don't let them win.* She hurried outside.

The evening was still light, sidewalks crowded with people, the sky hazy with smog. Everything unchanged, as if nothing had happened. If she walked to Ri's place, she might see him, silhouetted in the window, readying to work all night. They would make conversation—about the bombings, the FBI raids, rumors of concentration camps. "We are all in despair," he would say, and then she could answer, "Ri, I have learned." Would he put a hand on hers? *Oh sure.*

Besides, what if that woman was there, the one whose anguished voice she'd heard through his window, back in December, perhaps a woman from his own country who would make his features go soft as they had, once, with her. She knew nothing of his life now. Except he did not need the burden of her problems, her sordid situation. Even her presence—would he find even her presence a burden?

But her feet had already turned, following the way down the gravel drive. They seemed to clunk against the wooden stairs as she stepped to the vine-covered porch.

"Nora." He opened the door, stared out. But then, first glancing behind him, "Wait, stay here a moment," he said, and half-closed the door. She could hear papers being shuffled, and what sounded like something scraping the floor, inside.

Then again he stood before her, smiling in the open doorway. She peered into his eyes, as if to find there the key to what she might dare tell him.

"It's good to see you," he said. She tried not to guess if the words seemed flat. "Sorry, but I had to put some things away. Some things I work on. But come." He gestured to the living-room table. "Come sit down."

Still searching his eyes, she started forward. He was asking, "No, truly, how are you?"

But as they reached the table, he abruptly pressed his hand down on a handwritten sheet, perhaps a letter, and began sliding it and another, typed paper into a large envelope. "Excuse me," he said. He held the pages at an angle, so she couldn't read the text.

"I won't look," she offered, then caught his quick grin.

"Here, I've cleared us a space." He tossed the envelope onto a shelf and then, relaxed, brought out a bottle from the white-painted sideboard and, with a quick sommelier's gesture, offered it for her approval. "A very good *Côtes du Rhone*, mademoiselle." He brought two mugs from a cabinet and started to pour the wine. "For us."

Behind him, on the far wall, hung an expressionist painting, a clear sky over a silver beach, one seagull flying. He followed her glance. "Oh yes, very pretty, but is there time for 'pretty,' anymore?" His gaze lifted, hard.

No, she had interrupted something here; she felt his tension. And truly she had no idea anymore what his life involved. He was busy; she must let him be. She lifted the mug, but her fingers shook. Quickly, she lowered it.

"Nora, it's all right." Ri placed a hand on her arm. "But do you understand—here, it is still possible to believe in nonviolence, in social kindness. But in my country now, sometimes people—sometimes perhaps it is not possible."

And what was in that envelope? Something she should not know of, certainly; no, she should not be here. She started to rise.

"Wait. You've not even finished your drink." His gaze held her. "Listen, listen to me. You don't need to leave. Don't you know I want—?"

"Please, Ri. I—" But she mustn't tell him. "Don't, Ri. Please."

A minute passed in silence. Then his voice went sharper, different. "Remember, I told you once how it was at home. Nothing has changed there. Only, now it is worse. In the cities, it is not so bad; even people here can understand. But out in the countryside—no one here can know what that is like—on the dry farms, people still keep trying to raise crops but they cannot. And they cannot live when the crops dry up. And the water. There are towns now with no water, where there is no hope. First the babies sicken—the babies, then the children. There is nothing."

Ri, I'm pregnant. But this "I" felt less important, here.

Ri had walked out with her onto the porch; they stood in the darkness. The scent of the yellow flowers was strong with spring; she had to get away.

"Nora, you never—"

Because I mustn't. Because I can't really love. Because, because, do you—?

"You never saw that envelope tonight. All right?" He pressed her hand. "You understand. But—seriously, tell me. Tell me. Something is wrong; how can I help?"

No. Even if she hadn't glimpsed now his wider world, no. She couldn't. To tell him meant to explain the whole of everything she'd thought, to explain it all—these months, the system, logic, the world.

And it's not Ri, she reminded herself, walking home, *not Ri I seek, but David, father of my child.* Except, not a child—a fetus. And she mustn't act toward David the way this closed-up social system said to, must not act the "righteous victim" must not judge, demanding he care. He would not care—and, more important, she must follow her path, the path to maturity, especially now.

Yet, since the fetus was his, too, shouldn't the decision be shared with him? Someone as flawed as she in her love, and ignorant about the world, how could she alone make this decision? The decision of a child's whole life.

6

People

July 1966

Red, a friend of David's, who'd been reading Zen, said "Dave's gone up to the mountains to seek his way."

"The mountains? Where?" Nora asked, but Red just mumbled "Sierras" and passed her a joint. "Have a hit. You're always uptight."

When she called the VDC office, a woman said "David? Gee, he hasn't been in since, wow, gosh, God knows how long."

No way to reach him.

For three weeks, the hospital "considered" whether to grant a rare therapeutic abortion. She sat by the phone with a list of Mexican abortionists in Tijuana. She'd finally got a new, unlisted number, but the breather still called, always after midnight. Twice this past week, the line had gone dead afterward when she tried to phone out. Spruce branches—*anyone athletic could climb those*—scraped on the windows in the dark. When she asked people at the *Barb*, they just shrugged, and the old reporter, Jeff, said "What're you doing in the Movement if even that frightens you?" And Sally, leaving after deadline, said, "Well, I think it's something else you're scared of." Then, in mid-July, when Nora opened her door to a quiet man with graying hair from the county health department, he handed her a notice: "The thirteen cats your neighbors reported on your premises comprise a public health hazard. We have thus authorized complainants to dispose of any appearing on their premises." But how could there be such a notice? One cat and four kittens didn't make thirteen, even under Big

Brother. Sally wanted the black kitten, and Len's teaching assistant Jane was adopting Tiger, but this still left the other two. And the cat. No, this notice—plus the breather's phone calls, plus the twenty-one parking tickets for a car she didn't own—these were actual harassment, whatever *Barb* people said. Unless they were a threat of worse, of something that might endanger the fetus too.

No. No, they mustn't!

Nora closed her eyes, trying to make herself laugh it off. *I'm worrying about the fetus—and, at the same time, phoning to Tijuana?* But what if the FBI knew it was David's—or if David was an agent and somehow knew and didn't want her pregnant? Or . . .? This time, she did laugh. *I'm hardly some major activist they'd target. And no one—no one—targets fetuses.* Or did they? But already she'd begun staying inside after dark. Already this harassment—*or whatever it is, a lurker like the Snarler, or worse?* —this self-protective caution—or was it paranoia? —was dragging her back, locking her inside away from the path toward open, generous loving. *Because this struggle is still fragile.* Now she must keep struggling toward new habits, habits of *not* judging, of *not* "deciding" who was dangerous, or desirable, or worthy.

Soon it would be August, and the hospital stayed silent. Lennie took her out for coffee at the crowded Mediterraneum. She tried to explain: even if telling people "No" meant barring them away, she'd had to, lately, "because people keep visiting, now when I need to decide about, you know, the fetus and life and—" Abruptly she reached out a hand, for at "people keep visiting" he had jerked away as if struck. "No, no, Len, I don't mean *you* shouldn't visit! *You,* I'm glad to see." She focused on his eyes; they watched far too tenderly. Still, she had to tell someone. "Murph's back in town, Len. Since last week, and now he wants—all at once, he wants—to live with me again. And I can't stop thinking *No!* and putting him off when he calls. I keep thinking how his damned analyses, and his 'You didn't want to, last night, so don't try to touch me now' and—you know, all that stuff—how it pulled us into hell. I won't! Not again. But in five minutes, Len, it might happen; he could still reel me in. Listen, I need to not judge, I need to care for everyone, but when he's there—" She shuddered. "That must not happen."

"He knew you're pregnant? He came out here knowing you're pregnant?"

"Yeah. I said, 'You have to leave.'"

"Trying to stake his claim on you. You were such a lovely, fresh—oh, maybe sometimes silly in your philosophic whirlpools, but those were genuine issues. But he dragged you down—excuse me, he did—into ridiculous quagmires. Really—you were so vulnerable. I saw, he made you hate yourself. I saw, he treated you like an, an *accoutrement*. Even back in Ithaca, I saw it— and worse, out here. I would have—" Len drew himself up, right hand keeping time with an imaginary baton, like an orchestra conductor, the way he used to. "Let me say it—I am so glad Ri was good for you."

"Ri? Why bring him in?"

"That respect he has."

Oh, but respect wasn't the issue. It was love, the unbounded, *open* love she'd seen in Ri. "I'm not talking about Ri. Let's just—"

"What? Discuss Murph?"

"He's not a bad person."

"You told him to leave? To get lost, right?"

She sipped her coffee. "Well. Yeah, but he hugged me. Too hard—I had to say 'Stop, stop, I'm pregnant!' But he apologized, he was very sweet. So, stupidly, I told him about last year, how I thought I was perverted and frigid, all that stuff. How I saw those were just the system's accusations. Yeah, I told him all that; I told him I had to stop judging, to escape that stuff. I said, 'You used to analyze me way too much.'"

"He kept staring at me. 'You fucking need analysis,' he said." She shivered. "And kept staring, like someone confused."

Len laughed, a hard laugh. But his eyes looked puzzled. "To be really honest, Nora, I'm not sure I get it, either. By 'the system,' just what do you mean?"

"This, right here. All of it. The culture. *This*. Society, the warmongers. All of it. And the people one's cared about."

"Like Murph?"

"All of them. It's in us, in our own thoughts, too. In everybody."

"*Right*. Even when we critique it, huh? Just can't get away. Hey, listen, Nora, one thing I don't do, even for you, is take these social science constructs seriously. Okay?"

So he'd asked but he wouldn't listen; he was avoiding the issue. Just as Murph always had, and still did—like ignoring her tapping fingers, the evening before, while she sat perched on the edge of her couch waiting for him to leave. Right at the end, though, Murph had shrugged in his old dismissive way, "You do know I went with someone when we—you know I have a child, right? Jannie's a bitch, but she's a woman, a real woman, and we made a great kid. And even you, Nora—listen, I can tell you—even you, whatever happens, you're gonna feel love for that child in you. And maybe, maybe you'll even rediscover those feelings people had—well, most of us had—as babies before we even . . ."

"Got born?" She'd not asked it nicely.

"Screw you, Nora. Go see a therapist." Slapping a hand against the doorframe, Murph had walked out of the apartment.

"Finally!" She tried to laugh. "But Len, he may come back. And it's not just him, but all these people who . . . Like Mark, you know? He stopped me in the Co-op, 'How's it coming, your liberation—I mean, abortion.' And Nadine, she's scared, but when she said 'That gives me really bad vibrations,' I could've—! It doesn't matter, though, what anybody said; what matters is how I react. I must not, must not laugh at them. I mustn't judge them." It was her anger that dismayed her; she could barely remember anymore the grace and naturalness with David, the peace with Ri.

Lennie lifted one hand, again as if holding an imaginary baton. "Don't do this to yourself. You're trying to be utterly open, yet keep certain people out—as if anyone could resolve that. It's a contradiction, that's all, only a contradiction. Look, I guess the way out of judgment leads through judgments, but—Nora, you have to go on anyhow."

Just then, a couple in hiking clothes and thick boots jostled past, slamming against her chair. She grabbed for the table edge; Len caught her hand to steady her. He kept on holding it and, pulling away, she caught only his last words, "—wish it were *my* baby."

Oh God. Yet his concern was so real. "Sure," she whispered, "wouldn't you just love one more to have to cart around?"

Yet that night, thinking over the conversation, she realized it would be all right to put up bounds when her needs—and the baby's—were ignored. And she had to. Because, what if Murph came over again? She must not return to that, ever. Both for her sake and for the baby's.

No, better she call it "the fetus." This was not like really being pregnant. No, never mind all that; the point was something else; the point was, maybe it really was possible to set bounds without blocking love. After all, those shouting matches with David had not chased him away.

Except, none of this was certain. Every door she opened, each person she kept out, could wreck the fragile balance—and she had to be whole soon. To decide about the baby. Once, she had thought, almost singing the words, *I'll have us this child, Dave,* but it was never David at the door, or late at night when the phone rang. And no way to know what awaited the baby—a caring world, or only loneliness and a mother frightened not only of herself but of who might lurk outside under the dark trees?

Two evenings later, jammed among the crowd on Telegraph, she casually opened her notepad. Here, briefly she could forget, and simply report the news, jotting figures on the narrow pages and noting "speeches by Savio, Rubin, Camejo, [blond woman—find out which 1] of the San Jose 3." Deadline tomorrow, and the speaker in a black shirt had just said two Vietnamese hamlets were reporting cases of bubonic plague.

Alert, shifting abruptly into journalism mode and grasping the notepad firmly, she pushed forward; that last speaker's statement was important. Only—

She stopped herself at the curb. Any day now, she could be in the hospital for the abortion. No time to track down news. She had to focus, to think things through. Was it giving and generous to bear life, or was it an attempt, like a cheap scenario, to possess David through his child?

All around the intersection, people pushed and chanted. But she had to decide now, become someone *now* who loved generously and maturely enough to determine the baby's life. Delay was mere luxury; there was only this need to soon act.

Dark shadows pressed, shoving her onto the road. There, approaching across the dull pavement under the lampposts, cloaked in a poncho as in some drama of communal glory, David came driving, steering the escort truck down a narrow pathway that opened through the center of the cheering crowd. He must have glimpsed her, but he did not look her way.

No one looked her way. Carefully, she walked home. Twelve blocks to the winding road that led to her apartment. Reaching the intersection, turning to walk up the dark hill from Telegraph. Narrowing her eyes, watching the shadowed spaces under the elms. Watching out for the breather—or Murph, or the Snarling Man, or FBI, or whoever would know her by her shadow and could hurt her and the child. Watching and moving warily, when she needed to love.

7

Simple Life

July 28, 1966

"Nora are you all right?" The man beside her on the purple couch pronounced her name "Noh-ra." His hand shifted on her wrist.

From the phone, a woman's voice was saying, "We have scheduled your therapeutic D and C for 9 a.m., August 4th." Nora jerked her hand free and tightened her hold on the receiver. Hot smoggy sunlight spread gold bars along the wooden floor. *Children love the patterns in wood.*

That morning, Sally had invited her to Stimson Beach, but, leaning across the *Barb*'s long table, she had answered, "No, I really need to work on my decision." Later, afterward, she could go to beaches, flee the ugliness. Something was crushing her, now when she needed to open and reach unboundedly to people—and the *something* was not only the ugly city or Murph's visit or even the silence from David, not the harassing phone calls and fear, but this decision.

And, the night before, her parents had phoned, "Remember you suggested, back in December, that we come visit you sometime this summer? Because, darling," her mother had said, "last weekend, the Millers told us of a lovely hotel in San Francisco, very clean and quiet, right on the wharves. So your father's made us reservations—"

"Ma, it's hot here. Humid and everything."

"Humid—in San Francisco?"

"Yeah. It's almost August." No, if they came, they might realize—and they must not find out. *"Come home, darling, we'll take care of you. Nobody needs to know unless you want.*" She'd be sucked back into the D.C. swamp, like a child.

Yet her parents were only parents. Not some "elder representatives" of the system, but real people, who also stood up to injustice—*like when Daddy told off the White House guy, last year when the administration threatened to cut hours for senior staff.*

"I'm sure, Mom, you'll like it anyhow," she'd added, and then her father had got on their upstairs extension. "It'll be great to see you, Bubbie. You're still our child, after all. We need to make sure you're taking good care of yourself."

Not only of myself. But she only said, "Thanks, Daddy."

Children love the patterns in wood.

"Noh-ra, are you all right?" Now, even as she answered the hospital's call, "Yes, August 4th, right," and lowered the phone, thinking *D and C—what an innocent name for it*, she looked up again at the man beside her. His hand again had grasped her wrist, and he peered at her, insisting. Insisting—but someone she barely knew. Someone barely a friend, and someone not the father of this fetus, not David—why was he even here? This man with the cut-off name *Ted*. This awkward person who, nevertheless, wore an elegant rust-gold scarf and a quizzical smile, and had conned her address out of Max and was sitting here, now, on her purple couch. She frowned. "Let go."

"Sure. But are you all right?" He smiled, but intently, and without the sardonic edge he'd shown at the *Barb*.

When he'd come to the *Barb* two days before, he'd been carrying the CNVA press release announcing a new demonstration out at Port Chicago. *Oh Lord, another Army veteran*, she'd thought, seeing his military jacket. Veterans kept popping up lately, always claiming to be "hundred percent antiwar," half of them probably agents. But this man, with his quick and self-deprecating humor, had seemed sincere; after a few minutes, everyone on staff had gathered to listen.

"That fence out there," he'd recounted, meaning the miles of fencing surrounding the weapons base— "it's full of holes," and, playing to his audience, had tossed his scarf back over one shoulder. He'd spread a score of photos on the littered glass table. "See how that chainlink's all ripped? And those guards off playing softball. Security out there's a joke, it really is." Everyone had laughed and leaned closer, passing the pictures around. But she'd barely paid attention.

Until Ted had mentioned driving the escort truck the night before, with David.

"He's back?" She had turned to him. "Dave is back?"

"Somewhere out there, I imagine." Gray eyes, too casually looking her over.

The next day, she'd been home, packing—Ernie had offered his apartment while he spent a month in Hawaii meeting "genuinely *nice* boys." It was only a temporary sublet, but she had to move, to save the cat and kittens and flee the phone breather. Kneeling on the floor, missing her apartment even as she prepared to leave it, she'd been stuffing dresses into a suitcase.

"I made Max give me your address." Suddenly Ted had been there, leaning against the door frame, looking like a lanky cowboy yet strangely elegant, no longer wearing the rust-silk scarf, but, on his finger, sustaining that stylishness, a ring of chased silver with a small turquoise stone. "Way you sounded over at the *Barb*— last time I heard someone speak like that, next morning he'd shot himself." No sardonic tone, not even a half-smile, entirely serious. "I'm going to help you, if I can, Noh-ra." Ever since, too, he'd pronounced her name that way. "Hey, this life we're all living is hard, but look, we can't give in. I would like to help you. You deserve that."

She didn't know why she'd felt so sure he meant it— still felt sure—but she did. In any case, he'd been sharp, even witty, at the *Barb*, and aware of what the war was doing to people, and obviously he'd known precisely how to check out Port Chicago. A couple *Barb* staffers had said he was the one who "kept the engine going" in CNVA's white Port Chicago Vigil van, and who'd "hyped folks up" for the pre-vigil rally, but he'd also rushed off from the interview, obviously worried, to drive a sick friend to a doctor.

In any case, there he'd been, leaning against the doorframe while she stuffed the last clothes into the old suitcase. She had tolerated his presence, listening absentmindedly.

But finally she'd given in. She had told him only of her simple needs, like moving to the sublet—and, before she could object, he'd started helping pack up her books and dishes, and then climbed to the attic over the kitchen to catch the white kitten and the calico, scooping them into a cat-carrier for "a one-way trip to Jennie's"— his old pacifist who, he said, "keeps saying how she wants another kitty."

But when he'd sat down on the desk chair across from her couch and repeated, "Now tell me what's wrong, Noh-ra," she had snapped, "Not Noh-ra. *Nor*-a, my name is *Nor*-a," and only after the anger passed had spoken more—and then only in abstractions, to avoid using words that led into the maze of self-doubt.

Now, hanging up the phone, she pressed her hands together so he'd not try to touch them. "Of course I'm all right."

He looked down at the few boxes she'd got packed during the night. "You can count on me. Seriously."

"No, I can't ask that sort of promise." She hunched forward, hands together, elbows on knees. "You're very kind, and I thank you. Only, please don't play therapist. I can handle things. Like, I can move myself."

Gracefully, he leaned back. He lit a cigarette. "Sure. I know you can. Look, I don't have your education, I did the Army and then some cheap-shot engineering courses, that's all. These abstractions you brought up yesterday, like needing to 'become the giving mother,' all that—I don't know psychology, I really don't. But"—was he teasing or sincere? She couldn't tell— "I meant what I said. I hope I can help you." His gray eyes, wide set, were like clouds without a hint of blue.

She would have answered, but no words came.

"Never mind." He ground out the cigarette and rose to his feet. "Let's get this over with. Then you can rest. C'mon—your stuff, let's move it."

The whole time he carried her heavy boxes to the van and dragged everything up the stairs at Ernie's, into the jammed little sublet, he spoke only once, seeing her struggle to carry up the diamond-patterned rug. "You don't need that, for God's sake. Between your cat and those straw rugs your friend stuck into this overheated dump, you're courting fleas." He paused for a moment. "Hey, how you doing?"

"Fine. It's fine."

"Is it? Really, you can tell me if something's wrong. It's okay." He pulled a cigarette from his pack. "Although right now I do have to get going. Got a meeting at Ahimsa House—our communal house, so-called. I told you at the *Barb*, right? Anyhow, I promised them I'd be there." He laughed. "You should see it—all these nonviolence advocates ripping each other by the throat. Believe me, I'd rather stick around and help you unpack."

Forcing her back dance-straight and lifting her chin, she sat taller. "I'll walk you downstairs." That way, too, she could breathe fresh air; it was so stuffy here. The cat was rushing around, frantic.

Downstairs, Ted climbed into the van. He clutched the steering wheel. "Better get over there and help them figure how to stop Port Chicago—or something. I'll be back. I *will* help."

She stepped away. "I said, I'm fine. Everything's fine." *Besides, I'm pregnant.* If he would just go away. It was confusing, this kindness.

Upstairs, Ernie's apartment was far too hot. By next month—afterward, when she would have *decided*—she must again find housing. But meanwhile, here there were no thick branches leading up to the windows, no phone number known to police and the breather. Only— no, she was failing; if she'd even begun to love maturely, givingly, she must halt this possessive wish to bear the child of someone who didn't want her.

Except, the fetus's life was its own, its sole life. Surely protecting this life was real.

Unless, of course, she sought the child to replace its father; that was known to happen with unwed mothers. But, even then, wouldn't bearing a child be giving life—giving love?

Unless— No, she needed to speak to someone. To escape her mind's voices. She could call Jan, Jan was also pregnant. But differently. Jan was a *real* mother.

It was up to herself, alone. To decide this.

She lit another cigarette. *I shouldn't smoke. Do what is best for the child. For love, for—*

No, she should abort, since otherwise—

Unless—

Decide.

8

Chasing Dreams

August 1, 1966

STOP PORT CHICAGO!
The poster flashed into her vision. And Ted, holding it and leaping toward her.

"Guy, get outta here," Ted cried out. He was rushing toward her, lunging through the doorway, into the apartment.

Good thing she'd kept the door unlocked, not given in to Murph's "Hey, you don't trust me, girl? You explored this with a therapist?" He was snarling now as, rushing forward, Ted slammed into him. Off-balance and infuriated, Murph half-fell against her as she shoved herself yet further into the corner of Ernie's bed, arms still raised to hold Murph off.

"Fuck you." He spun toward Ted, fists rising.

"Come on, come on, man—man, let's cool it." Ted, lids lowered so his eyes seemed turned to long gray slits, stood gazing at him. "Murph? Just let the woman be, Murph."

"I said, God damn, fuck off."

"Like, what's going down?" Ted's eyes looked mild, almost curious. "What's all this crap about?"

And, as he spoke, Ted had moved up beside her; she felt his left hand squeeze her shoulder. She tried to speak, to thank him, but could only nod, aware she wasn't feeling anything, and shivering as her glance turned, wary, toward the furious man who'd once been "like a husband, really," and now, blocked by Ted, stood at the foot of the littered bed. *I'll tell Ted it's okay, he needn't stay, he's done so much. I'm a grown-up and can*—Yes, she should say that. Murph wouldn't really hit her. She would be all right. Except she shuddered, and her arms were cold, and her legs, and finally she cried, "Just go! You go, Murph," forcing the words and staring from the shivering cold.

Her cat leaped, with a mew, onto the refrigerator and began to lick a paw.

"But why?" Murph's eyes gleamed with tears. He had turned to her, his fists unclenched. "Don't hate me, Nora. I love you."

Once, this man's touch had been everything.

Ted tossed his red-gold scarf across one shoulder and stepped back, away from her and Murph. It was almost as if he'd leave, so they could work things through.

Murph, if you had only . . . After all, it had been her own doing too. "Murph, I know." She mumbled the words. "I was so immature."

"But someday, Nora, someday you'll be a true woman. It takes time, but I'm here and someday, someday when you're—" No longer trembling, Murph's lips held a paternal smile.

She felt her left hand reach out for Ted's and hold it. "Ted," she said.

Murph stared, the smile fading. Then, as she watched, Murph, who had once been everything, turned and walked out through the doorway and away.

"He'll be back." Ted cocked his head to listen as Murph's steps, taut and sharp, descended the stairs and the outer door slammed.

"I think not. Murph understood." Nora paused, for it was hard to say. "I don't really care about him anymore."

For several moments, they waited. Then Nora pulled herself up and went to stand beside Ted. Her body was calming, as if she'd been hunted for days through woods and at last was come to a safe meadow. Ted draped an arm around her shoulders.

"Thank you," she said. "Thank you."

"Yeah, well . . .." He laughed. "You know my friend Jennie's really happy with those kittens. A real love match."

"You do help people, don't you? Everyone."

A few minutes later, when she'd fed the cat and they'd rearranged the posters in Ted's van, she heard him pronounce her name "*Nor*-ah," stressing the syllable, and she laughed back, "Yes, that *is* my name!"

"At first I thought they were just mispronouncing it, over at the *Barb*."

Three hours later—the image of Murph, one furious fist raised, fading—she followed Ted, a sack of STOP PORT CHICAGO! posters slung on his back, through the evening darkness. He had left his long scarf in the truck and thrown an old red bandana around his neck, making her put one on too, "in case there's fumes in that lot. Used to be industrial there." He treaded carefully just ahead of her, finding their way past the jutting blocks of jagged cement and cracked and broken pipe across the glass-strewn lot. Her sandals slipped on broken boards and sudden potholes. For these three hours since leaving the apartment, they'd been doing this—playing this serious child's-game, slapping antiwar signs across Telegraph Avenue storefronts, covering the walls of the Berkeley draft board and even the gates of the Oakland Army Terminal, pasting the posters like a medieval decree: *This war has plague.*

"We'll get hundreds of people out there," Ted said.

"Wait." Hopping across two boards, she stepped lightly forward (*look! I still can dance*) to take a poster. "Here, I'll put this one up." On her right, the windowless side of an old brick warehouse offered an invitingly blank façade, and with dawn it would be strikingly visible from the freeway ramp below.

"Yeah! That'll stand out, Nora. You do a great job."

She gave a smile back. This constant encouragement made her feel like a child—but better than fending off his questions about her life.

Yet—here they were, and he'd been so kind and helped her so—she did need to answer his questions, finally reply to what he'd asked, even if it risked the old pain and was dangerous. Spreading glue beneath the poster so it would cling to the bricks, she looked across to the gentle, lanky man—a man who was safe, distant enough from the sort of person who attracted her that she'd never drag him down into her mazes and that trap of thinking she'd entrap him.

"Ted, listen," she said. "You wanted to know, so—okay. Listen, and please understand me. I used to think, see, that my love was sick—perverted, ugly. But then I realized that thinking this was just to fall for the system's—the social system's—theories. So I asked myself why had I got trapped in those theories at all? *Why*, you know? Because, if someone thinks she's perverted, then she'd better hold off any man she feels she loves—has to, to protect him, right? So why, *why* would I think that way? Unless—here's the thing—unless the system and its structures, or rather unless the people who'd taught me the system, back when I first loved *them,* were—are—whom I still really most love. Still them—them I'm forced to love."

She paused, her right hand smoothing the poster against the cracked, rough wall.

"That's what you fear, Nora? That you may push someone away?" He had taken out his lighter, the silver one she'd noticed that first day at the *Barb*, and, leaning forward, was lighting two cigarettes, the small flame flaring against the darkness. He handed her one. "Or you still fear you'll trap someone? Or 'hurt someone,' is it? Guess I'm not quite following."

She felt his hand—a movement too quick—brush her shoulder. To reassure her, or something else?

"Look, Ted." She threw the words out. "Look, I don't mean, by 'system,' only what people call The System, like the war machine and everything, but all of it. Not just Murph's putdowns, either, but everything—theories, traditions, everything—our parents' warnings, friends' suggestions, what they say a woman should do, the whole society—how it teaches us to see or stuffs its little voices in us. I mean, imagine . . . All right, imagine this: imagine that people are all separate, that we cannot feel another's pain, and someone's swimming out there, in a pristine sea, alone between flesh-colored rocky shores, like in that Antonioni film *Red Desert*, and the white ship approaches, but when one swims to it, it speeds away, and one can see the shores are like a mother's flesh, or like one's own. I mean, it's like, do I seek only a mother's love, my own, my society's love?

"But of course not; of course I seek the lover I feel I love. I mean, those theories are pop-psych nonsense, right? But—okay, here's another pop-psych image—my love cannot *transfer*." She half-laughed but stopped herself, concentrated on holding the next poster firmly in place so it would set. "No, listen, this is dangerous, even to speak of this stuff. It gets too involved; it can trap people. And you're a good person."

Yet of course he would be safe. *It's only when I start thinking I love someone that I rush back to those familiar shores.* She looked down at the ashy soil; broken glass surrounded their feet. "But there's a different love, a mature love, and, understanding this—understanding all of this, really—I'm finally free to want that love. Do you see?"

"Not in the least."

She grinned back, glad for his humor that was so honest—for his presence.

"Hey look, I told you." Lips curled in a rapid smile, he rolled the dozen or so remaining posters between his hands. "I had to help out my family, once I got back to the States. I didn't get onto that college track. So some of this stuff . . ." He touched her sleeve. "It's 'not my field,' okay? But one point you made, one point I do see very clearly. If you're still afraid of this 'system,' Nora—I mean, if you're still afraid you'll trap somebody if you dare to love—then, no matter you keep telling yourself you're free, you're not." His hand moved again to her shoulder. "No, wait; forget that. You are free, of course you are, struggling so hard like you do. You're a brave person." He turned away, skirting a heap of rotting boards. "Look, I don't know what to say."

Lifting her feet high, again as in a dance, she followed.

A rusting fence marked the end of the lot. They climbed over, her sandals catching briefly on the wires. On the other side, a ledge of cracked pavement, clotted with weeds, hung far above the freeway. A roar like a river rose from the cars below. She was thinking to surprise Ted with a couple of *relevées*, see how he'd take *that*—but best not to get too close to the edge. The roaring nearly drowned her words, "Hey, I didn't make up that metaphor about the shores and ship," she shouted. "Really, it's from *Red Desert*."

"Good thing I missed the film, maybe."

She barely made out the words. For a moment, she leaned forward to pull loose a wire that had caught against her jeans, then she straightened again. Ted was asking, with no change of tone, "What do you plan to do about the baby?"

The building on their left was decayed, sagging gray shards covered with twisted wire and John Birch Society signs; she leaned back against it. "How did you know?"

"I guessed. Well, I've been around pregnant women, took people to the clinic sometimes, back in Japan. And how you looked that day, at the *Barb*."

She ran a hand through her tangled hair. He'd done so much for her, but even so. "What difference does it make?" No, that was unkind. "If you really want to know, I've no plan, okay? I thought if I knew what the baby's father wanted, I could decide. But I don't know." She paused. "Truly, if I do have this child, it won't be to possess him. It won't."

"This guy's claiming it will?"

"No, no. Me—I was claiming. Not anymore, though."

Ted peered over the ledge to measure something. "This guy, the father—that's Murph?"

"Of course not! Actually—actually, you know him, the father." She had thought she'd never tell.

"I know him?"

"Yeah. David. From the escort truck."

"Good Lord." Ted spread his hands. "Well, damn good you didn't push him, then. Dave's in bad shape. I spent half last week keeping him from doing something dumb. He's suicidal."

"Suicidal? Most people just figure he's an agent." Quite a witty line, she thought, especially in the circumstances, but Ted's voice turned rough. "Do they? Well, if Dave's an agent, he's one of the best *we've* got."

She hadn't realized, until she felt the tightness in her neck begin to ease, how much that fear had weighed on her. Even after Sally had said, "The guy's agenting his prick, if anything," the suspicion had remained. Suspicion and fear. Fear for herself—and again for the fetus. For what David might do, what the FBI might do, what *someone* might do to this fetus, if she couldn't protect it enough. Protect this baby enough.

"Paranoia's an Establishment weapon," Ted was saying, voice muffled as he leaned far over, still examining the ledge. "It makes us turn against each other." Abruptly, he pointed. "Look there."

Ahead and to their left, maybe five yards away, a scaffolding rose sharply from the concrete, four beams connecting it to the ledge, the two horizontal beams about six feet apart. "Wait here," he said. Carefully, he placed one foot, then the other, along the lower beam. Clutching the upper one with both hands, he began to step across the chasm of the sunken roadway, leaning far out to stretch a long, shiny STOP PORT CHICAGO! banner over the SACRAMENTO I-80 EAST sign.

Nearly slipping, he turned sharply around. Another few seconds, and then, almost slipping again, and breathing roughly, he clambered back.

"Not fun." Ted hopped down to the ledge. "Let's hope it stays up there. I'm not redoing it." Stepping over to her, he lightly took her hand—an easy, friendly gesture. "Tell you what, Nora. If you decide to have that baby, I'll help you through the pregnancy."

Scores of headlights flowed below.

"You'll what? I mean, you don't even know me. I mean, even if I have the baby, I'll be giving it up—for *its* sake—but there's still these next seven months. That's a long time, Ted—a long promise to someone you don't really know." She couldn't stop watching the lights. Hypnotic. "I've told you, I can't hold someone to this sort of promise."

"Me, you can. Whatever you decide. Look, I'm here for you."

The living-bedroom was too crowded; with Ernie's bed, the velvet sofa, tables on the straw mats, there barely was room to walk around. She said, "That's a dream."

"A possible dream. We can have something beautiful."

Not my type, he's not my type. So, not a dream, then—just reality. Reality had been this wandering all evening, like brother and sister, putting up the signs. Reality had been to laugh and joke together about "snipe hunting" out where the Navy partied, over on the Sacramento River out toward Concord. Reality was relearning this friendship level, being comrades and no more. Reality was to give of herself, to offer what even Sally had called the "warmth that is a woman's gift."

"Here." In a half-unpacked box, she found two glasses and her silver wine decanter from those years in college, mementoes of that once-prized sophistication, trucked along to every apartment since, and now finally useful. She set them, with a bottle of Red Mountain, on Ernie's wobbly coffee table. "Pour it in the decanter and we can pretend it's decent wine."

Ted laughed, crowding onto a dusty corner of the couch. Already the apartment had taken on a cat-litter odor, she noticed; the air was sticky and hot.

But it was safe here. "I'd never have made it here without you, Ted. You don't know how grateful—"

"Hey, no need for that. I already told you."

Among the groceries was a box of glazed doughnuts. She offered them on an un-cracked plate, then sat in half-lotus on one of Ernie's floor-mats, watching Ted across the table and trying to shift the conversation to *his* life.

"Well, I always felt different." He bit into a second doughnut. "These are good. I was in high school before things changed, I learned how to play the game, to be 'one of the boys.' I could hold my own there, and besides I was smarter. And damn good at baseball, and I could fix things—cars, televisions, whatever they wanted." His hands fiddled with his glass. "Once I was out there on my own, though, taking dumb jobs and then the Army, I knew something was missing. Lots was missing." His eyes fixed on her—those gray eyes. "There's one way, you know, you really can help me. You asked and yes, there is a way. You studied philosophy; I wanted to. Especially the points where science and math and philosophy meet. Maybe you can suggest stuff to read?"

"Of course." *So long ago, all that.* Surreal, a different life.

"Thank you." Without the sardonic edge, his voice was gruff.

Then it shifted, too abrupt. "*Thanks,* kid!" Suddenly too hearty, loud, almost as if from someone else. During the *Barb* interview, she'd heard such a shift—he'd moved so quickly between sharp humor and that gruff sincerity. But the voice now was different, the tones of "one of the guys," of Army canteens and night secrets. Of someone with jagged edges. A worrisome shift, really, as if even to ask help had embarrassed him. Or as if he was someone who didn't stay in any persona, or maybe anywhere, very long.

But at least he wasn't so sure and simple as he'd seemed; he saw, though differently, just as much as she. Very differently, though—they were very different. She must remember that. And it wasn't likely he'd understood what she meant.

Except, that's like still thinking I'm "superior" so only someone "superior" can possibly be right for me—or that I've such enormous "problems" that only someone even more "superior" can understand me. She tried to force away the thought.

And fortunately, Ted was opening up about his life. "I met people overseas, you know, amazing people. There were farms near the base, and we'd go to dances. One day, this guy's daughter sat beside me—I was helping her dad fix a plough. I fell in love with her. That fast, just like that. And I was teaching some of the kids arithmetic, his and others. It was different there, the possibilities. I felt something new.

"Then I got rotated home. It was really lonely here, after all that. Everything empty again—no point to anything. But I decided to get out and *live*. I was curious about life, straight-out. Which is what I tried to tell Dave, last week—be curious about life, the way children are. Look and don't look away. Nora, there's this dream I have, this dream about . . . I call it the dream of possibility. Because it is possible—to stop the killing, to change people. Or—hell, not even that, but to help people figure who they are." His gray eyes widened. "Because, when people do look, they see the possibilities. They see they care and want to care. You know? Nora, that sort of love you talked about, a new sort of love—it *is* possible, I think. People can care about everyone, just like children do. Children don't look away. Children open up to everybody. I call it a dream, but it's reality. It's a possible dream.

"And in this dream, there's a woman."

She glanced pointedly at the clock. Her hands began to clear crumbs from the table.

"May I sleep here, Nora, on your couch tonight?"

Payback time? "Sorry, I didn't hear you."

"May I sleep on your couch tonight?" His smile flashed, the sardonic smile she recognized as his. "They're squabbling, every minute, there—over at Ahimsa House. Nonviolently, of course. But the rest of the time it's 'Ted, Ted, *you* know how to speak with lawyers,' 'Oh Ted, please fix the plumbing,' 'Ted, would you mind—?' I *do* believe in community, but really, really, I could use some sleep. I haven't slept in a week."

Wine glasses balanced in her hands, she listened. Not payback-time, then. And after all he'd done to help her. Of course. The only mature thing, only decent thing, was to offer him the couch, and a quiet night's rest. He was saying he'd leave early, had to get out leaflets in the morning, to write up another press release for the demonstration.

"Ted, of course. Even if you sleep in all day, you're welcome. Very welcome." Her own warmth surprised her, the generosity in her voice.

"Hey, you know, you're really a good person." His voice held a note that made her turn. "Not everyone would do this." But his eyes had closed. Stretching out along the couch, he was asleep in another second.

For a long time, she stood before the two narrow windows. Ted lay on the couch a few feet away. Something in his words had moved her—his dreams, his longing to help people. But if she cared for him, it would only be in this moment, not in any way that *identified* with him, not in any way she might mistake for love. A safe caring. Lithely, she glided around the coffee table. A half-smile crossed his sleeping lips.

But the baby . . ..

Even those pamphlets in the gynecologists' office stressed that lovemaking wouldn't harm a fetus. Besides, she was going to abort; she had decided. The D and C was already scheduled—only another three days. She stroked Ted's eyebrows. "Come over here onto my bed."

Whatever she had expected, there only the tingling of their skin, the slippery dampness of the sheets. The swift beginning, with smiles and groans but mostly silence. Neither said it was too soon. When he tried to enter her, she jerked back, thinking *No, you see, I still cannot,* and when he didn't speak, she forced herself against his thrust, making herself open. When he came, she moaned and called his name.

Later, Ted started to cry.

In the darkness, she made out the tears along his cheeks. He said, "I wanted to show you something beautiful."

"We don't know each other yet." So few men cried. *He's not my type.*

"I *will* show you. I promise you."

She lifted her head. "Let's just have what there is. No point to chasing dreams."

9

Child

"You'd rather we not have come, Lenore?" Her mother glared, clearly aware of the answer but not wanting to show hurt.

Sorry, Ma. It's just I need to think about this coming abortion. About my new lover—we just got together last night. About whether I can love.

And they could have called first, not just grabbed a cab to come pick her up—no warning this evening, no time to prepare. *Or at least not used my old name.*

La Cucaracha du Sud seemed safe enough, though— too expensive a restaurant to be part of her own life. But here with these two middle-class, middle-aged people, her parents, she felt the trap press down. Her father looked distinguished with his high forehead and professorial manner, but her mother appeared helpless and uncared-for, prematurely wrinkled with a cigarette dangling from her lips. And meanwhile her father kept explaining he'd banged his knee on his suitcase in the hotel but "You know your mother and I won't use a bellhop, Bubbie—no way to treat another human being."

"Pick whatever you want for dinner, Lenore," her mother said. "We're on vacation."

"You need to enjoy yourself a little," her father added. "How come you don't wear your hair up anymore? It looked so nice that way." *You're so pretty a girl. Look out for yourself—be careful, Lenore, don't go where—*

She knew it by heart; it was the trap: *stay in, watch out, don't let them in, be wary whom you would love.*

Then Ted came through the narrow glass doors. Finally. He'd promised to be here, so she could remember who she was. A white "aviator scarf," obviously chosen for her parents' sake, was draped around his neck. He flashed a sidewise smile that made her lips tug in response. She jumped up and ran to him. Her hands shook. "You won't say anything?" she whispered as they hugged.

"I told you, Nora, I'll keep your secret."

She briskly pulled out her chair when they reached the table, before Ted or her father could. "Daddy, Ted knows electronics really well. And cars." Her reflection smiled back from one of La Cucaracha's framed mirrors.

"Sorry to be late." Ted carefully spread his napkin on his lap. "Had to help people set up the stereo, over at the house." His voice changed to its heartiest sound. "Ahimsa House, I mean, Mr. and Mrs. Seikh. That's where I live these days. It's a group of people building community. Or trying to."

"I hear you work in electronics, Ted?" Her father was now also speaking *hearty*. "Must get some interesting projects, out here."

"I've been rewiring a home for troubled kids." Ted paused, voice going deeper. "It's down in Oakland. "The older kids 'help' us, you can imagine. Tracing circuits and all. Mostly I work for peace, though." Pulling them in, she realized, protecting her from feeling trapped with them, but also protecting them from her fear.

"Sounds good," her father said. They all began to study the large, shiny menus.

Later, while Ted and her father spoke together over enchiladas, her mother picked at a quesadilla and said, lowering her voice, "Darling, you're doing all right?"

"Fine, Ma."

"Are you? If something's wrong, dear—"

"Nothing's wrong, Ma. I told you."

Ted had leaned alertly forward across the table. "Mrs. Seikh, Nora said you work in interior design."

"Well, not really design. Colors. I do colors—walls, fabrics."

"Because I was thinking, maybe you could help us with Ahimsa House. We need a space, somewhere people can find quiet." He held out his elegant silver lighter and smiled, as at something wonderful. "You understand." Carefully, he lit her mother's cigarette. "It would be a space, someplace with the right colors and tone, where everyone can find peace together."

Her mother nodded, voice taking on a new precision. "People—some people, that is—claim that green is calming. But I often think of green as prisons. Ted, if you'll sketch out—here, let's use a napkin—what sort of shapes you may want to include . . ."

He was making it all work. Her mother's design could help Ahimsa House, her dad was finding the Oakland project intriguing, her mother's antennae had ceased their probing—and in twenty-six more hours her parents' visit would be safely over.

"They're not young, you realize?" Leading them to his car, Ted whispered the words, though her parents were several yards back. "What we need is kindness to everyone. *Everyone.*"

"You haven't understood."

"They love you, kid. They're 'not the oppressors,' in your own words." He draped an arm around her. "Two more minutes and we'll be driving them into the city. Be gentle." His hearty voice took over again. "What if we go the long way, Mr. and Mrs. Seikh? And go across both bridges? You ever been over the Golden Gate?"

4

Take This Handcuff Off, Please

August 4, 1966

The hospital gleamed fluorescent white; even the waiting room reflected the glare. Ted had offered to come but she had refused; he seemed irrelevant now. She stared into the bright, ugly light. This room, this building, had become, for this moment, her life. It was a symbol, too—of hopeless struggle, of undesired destruction, of abortion of a baby conceived in the struggle against the war.

Only, symbolism was romanticism, fairy tale—offering no answer, just bunk. These were final moments—*keep decision free of panic.* No last-minute grabbing for the fetus or its father. *The decision is made.* She must stick to it.

Just to sing my own song, / so to know, 'fore you— No, no, silly words, silly song. Deal with reality.

"Like, I had to take the bus to my abortion, David."

"Have you ever seen new eyes watch yours?" Hadn't that line been in a song she'd written, back in college? *Don't get dramatic.*

She could have decided differently, after all, could have told her parents—had started to, with that last hug. They'd loosened up so much around Ted, laughing when he danced with her on the wide flat parapet overlooking the Bay. At the airport, when he'd gone over to check the schedule for someone at Ahimsa House, she'd squeezed her parents tight, actually started to say "I have to tell you."

Then, "If something's wrong, darling," her mother had repeated.

"Wrong? No, things are fine, Ma." It wasn't as if she would go back there, ever. Back into the past and away from the path she'd found to wholeness. No. But it wasn't as if she were a starving "unwed mother" either; she had the money they sent each month, the four hundred dollars she'd saved when she'd managed to get work. She had friends, wasn't really alone.

But all this was not the issue. The issue was whether it was *possessive* or was *giving,* to bear the child of a man who'd left her. Was it to bear life—or to cling, clutching the fetus instead of freely giving in encompassing, non-possessive love?

No, no. No time left for this. *I have decided.*

Across the room, two doctors and an immaculately dressed woman in a green-gray suit marched stiffly past a row of patients and their families. Everyone spoke politely, as if pretending this was not a place of pain and death. *Why doesn't the Movement look in here?* Even the flowers in the vases looked artificial, shiny and machine-cut.

Here—this soft steel innards of America. This killing center. Not a place to—

In the small lab, the technician raised the needle for her blood test. He was fast; in no time he had checked the number on her plastic wrist bracelet and was asking "Which finger should I prick?" And during that moment, it had become entirely clear. *The system's disposal machine. And I have come to it, bringing my baby.*

"Wait, wait a moment."

"Which finger would you prefer, Miss Seikh?"

How can I know? I've not decided yet. How does one make such a choice?

"Miss Seikh, you need to—"

They take it out—take it out and then—? Of course your mother's frightened; it's too cold for you, outside.

"This handcuff. Take this handcuff off me, please."

At the front desk, the British nurse glanced up, her voice unsurprised. "You wait—be sure, dear. You want to be sure first. Wait until the crying stops."

No, better not to wait. There would be seven months more, and the baby's future. The baby's whole life. From a phone booth a block away, she called Ted.

"I'll come pick you up," he said.

It was hours later, trying to read in the stuffy apartment, before she saw the failure. *I have chosen to possess, to stay in the fairy-tale trap. This cannot be to help the fetus—the baby. I have not changed.*

And Ted had simply let her off outside, not stayed to understand. He'd had another vigil meeting to get to, had work to do at Ahimsa House, needed to take groceries to the woman who'd taken the kittens, had to— Anyhow, he could hardly help, right now. No one could. She lit a cigarette. Again decide? Maybe ask if the doctors—

The phone rang. She lifted the receiver.

"Oh yeah? Still care enough about the world to pick your phone up?"

"David."

"I've rediscovered television, babe. They're off in the bar watching it, and we climb up into their cab, and we fix things. Me and Embey—no one else cares."

"How did you find this number?" Her heart pounded.

"That's what matters to you?" The bitter tone was new. "Doesn't it matter that people are out there dying? Don't any of you care that we're risking our lives?"

"David." She swallowed. "I'm pregnant."

The silence lasted a full minute. Then, "And so?"

I will not judge, I'll not claim rights. "David, I'm taking care of it. But you should know—I mean, since it's yours. And"—no matter how possessive the words, she forced them out— "I need to know how you feel." If she changed her mind and aborted, would he feel she'd killed his child? And if she didn't, would it burden him—disgust him? She couldn't ask that question, or whether he wanted her to have the baby.

Ted had said, "Dave's suicidal," and what if David said, "Don't. Don't have it"?

But David's voice had gone flat, covering what sounded like a moment's trembling excitement. "Do what you want. I have no feelings either way. I wish I did, but, babe, I can't feel anything anymore."

Any reply *asked* something. Time to become mature. "It's all right. David, it's okay."

11

Wait

August 4-5, 1966

Toward midnight, she heard the ringing. But it was the front doorbell, not the phone. From the outer hallway, she peered through the glass-windowed door at the bottom of the stairs; it could be Murph out there, or the Breather; whoever it was, was in shadow. But she must no longer let fear enclose her. She pressed the buzzer to let him in.

"I've been worrying about you."

Ted. He did care. She spread her arms out.

But an hour later, as he lay naked above her, long body pale in the darkness, she shivered and stared away. The ceiling seemed too close, his breathing too rough. What if the gynecologist's pamphlets were wrong, their reassurances misleading? She had to protect the fetus. *Yet, to give is to open—unafraid, nonjudging. Loving.*

Only, she loved the fetus, too.

Except wasn't that merely animal love, any mammalian mother's response? And Ted's eyes gleamed like long-familiar depths in a dark-gray sky.

But "Let's wait a minute. Ted, let's wait a moment."

He raised himself and carefully sat up. "You're wise, you know. You really are. We shouldn't be hurrying what we have. I can wait for you. It's all right."

Part III
To Love and Comfort

1

Stop Port Chicago

August 7-9, 1966

llBut what do you think of this lead? 'Nearly 500 people left Concord in sizzling heat.' That okay, Nora?" Marty, the younger of the *Barb*'s new reporters, stuck his field notebook in front of her. She was standing, with him and Benjamin, the paper's photographer, among the demonstrators just outside Port Chicago's Waterfront Gate.

"'The long procession wound forward,'" Marty continued, reading his work over her shoulder, "'through hostile countryside five miles to Concord Naval Weapons Base. Motorcycle toughs cruised back and forth, hurling rocks and bottles at the marchers. By 5:30 p.m., the march reached the base and weary demonstrators squeezed into a narrow roped-off area between the road and railroad tracks. Across the way waited 100 cops and armed Marine security guards.'"

"Nice work, Marty. Just maybe cut the repeats, okay?" She was glad to encourage him, but it was urgent she start the interviews. Ted had shown her how to change the big reels on the tape recorder; only, then, before she could hug him, he'd given that sidewise smile and hurried off, a dusty black scarf dangling from one shoulder, to gather equipment for the speakers' platform and help Meriwether and the others prepare for civil disobedience.

"Yeah of course you can handle the tapes," he'd said, impatient. "Just record everything—all of it's important. Hey, it's like news reporting. And, listen, when this red light blinks . . ." Again his hands had led hers through the process. He had smiled encouragement, but impatiently, eyes tensed in the sunset haze. "Nora, people really need to hear this. They need to understand *why*—why folks exactly like themselves are risking so much. Their freedom, their lives. Oh, and look, if I'm arrested, you get the tapes to KPFA, okay?" He'd moved off into the crowd, not stopping to look back.

Now, all around, people broke into a chant. "Stop Port Chicago / Bring the Boys Home." Carrying the recorder, she walked through the crowd, feeling shy but stopping here and there to do an interview. "Those people are *my* people," a Mexican woman said; a retired longshoreman compared the protest to the 1934 general strike in San Francisco; a former engineer from nearby Martinez said he'd quit his job to work against "the damned war profiteers." The young pregnant mother of toddlers, who'd been letting people planning civil disobedience stay over at her house, said she too would stop a truck— "Pregnant or not, yes, I shall." And when a professor's pregnant wife, who'd driven out in a new white Volvo, said "I support my Vietnamese sisters, who also carry life," Nora had to lower her eyes. *Theirs is the courage.*

"Citizens prepared to risk arrest will separate from the main body of demonstrators and, one by one, step out on the highway to nonviolently confront the napalm trucks." The words from the loudspeaker were the same as those on the leaflets she'd helped distribute: "One man, one truck, a thousand lives." *Meaning women too, of course,* she thought—*pregnant women included.*

"Each life is a universe," the professor's wife was saying. "I stand for all mothers."

But this is my child. My child who is utterly dependent on me. Yet what if giving everything to this one life meant not saving others?

Oh, but never mind; today's action cannot stop the war. In fact, it was absurd, what this woman, and all these people here, claimed. Ted, for instance, this morning had insisted, "Yes, we *can* end the war—we can, right here." Really, it seemed as if humor, skepticism, even rationality, had fled, with everyone here arguing that moral witness alone could halt the whole war machine.

Yet of course "common sense," "rationality," were only the system's judgments. *To keep us tame and quiet.* Ted had added, "We can stop this war, kid, if enough people see they do give a damn."

A beautiful belief. But how could he think such a hope possibly true? No, she couldn't ask this, couldn't risk fracturing his belief.

Ahead and to her left, directly in front of Waterfront Gate, there was shouting. Marines, police, and a bunch of motorcyclists were gathered, baiting the demonstrators, obviously trying to provoke a confrontation. Clasping the recorder tightly, she shoved through the crowd, frightened but committed now to tape whatever happened. Benjamin and the Barb's other new reporter—the elegant Gar, said to be a selfless, longtime pacifist—moved forward beside her, jostled by a reporter from a San Francisco daily.

"Catching their last words for posterity?" Benjamin's cynical words, as she lifted the recorder's mic to another demonstrator's lips, held his familiar East Coast ring. "Lots of idealists around today. Not to mention green Marines." As he laughed, she laughed with him, momentarily forgetting danger and doubt.

"But Nora, what about this line—'Most of the hecklers and demonstrators faded as darkness came'? That sound okay?"

She looked up. In the starry countryside night, Marty's silhouette was barely darker than the sky. Wrapped in her poncho, she lay against Ted, who was asleep on the sparse grass. "'Toward midnight, some remaining protestors headed over to the Weapons Station's other entrance, the pastoral Main Gate.'"

"Shh," she hushed, "Just 'Main Gate' will do. And how do people 'fade'? But yes, it's fine, Marty." It was cold on the grass, her fingers numb around Ted's wrist; he did not move—important not to wake him. *Be as kind as you can.* Let him rest while that was possible; napalm trucks could come, any time. All around them, here across the highway from Main Gate, cows grazed in the low flat pasture and along the wide hills. Only, those hills covered bunkers laced with anti-personnel shells and nuclear missiles; somewhere far away a terrified mother clutched a baby, hearing helicopters approach.

How could I have dozed off? Nora woke with a start. Not far off, vigilers huddled under blankets or curled in sleeping bags beside the road. Her eyes blinked, strangely teary. But what she felt, unexpected and mixed with Ted's warmth and a new admiration for these people—*was* this the generous caring, the encompassing love for the many? This longing that each sleeper here be safe and no one be afraid?

"What is it, Nora?" Ted shifted onto one side, groggy. His hand brushed her cheek.

I do care. Ted, I do.

But before she could speak, his hearty tone broke in, "It's all gonna be up to you soon, you know." Yes, up to her: to take the photos and tapes to the media, to run off a second leaflet, to get more people out to the lines. "Kid, you can do it. This time tomorrow, Nora, some of us'll be in jail."

"Don't get arrested." She hadn't meant to say it.

Still his fingers stroked her cheek. "Kid, I know you care. But look, I have to."

From across the dark field, Lee moved toward them, stiff-visaged, grim, the Agit-Prop organizer whom Benjamin called The Valkyrie.

"How you people doin'?" she said and flopped down on the grass. Her face had the lined sadness of a tired farm woman, which someone had said she was; on her hair perched a jaunty cowgirl hat.

"Doin' just fine," Ted answered. "Gettin' ready for the mornin' wipe-out when those trucks pull in."

Lee dipped her head and grinned.

How good to see this. To listen, warm against Ted's chest, watching these people connect, hearing them joke.

Both of them country-raised—good to laugh at her own voice. Out here, the world was more desperate, but maybe more whole.

Benjamin had left the roadway, come to sit beside Lee. It *was* good here, here in this community, here with Ted, who gave so much—who had helped her, who helped everyone. But he'd pushed himself so hard, these past few nights, pushed beyond himself, like all these people, struggling to stop the massacre. Had they always been like this—caring for others, beyond any self or bounds? If she could just become like them . . ..

An hour passed. Everyone's thoughts were on the coming action—arrests, the danger of police violence. In the headlight beams from a parked squad car, Samantha, the frail-looking law office worker, studied *Legal Case Reference and Research.* "Kids from my street go directly to jail," she'd said, speaking precisely into the tape recorder Nora still held; "Friends I grew up with, those are the people they draft for the front lines." Near the road, immediately across from Main Gate, Juliet paced nervously back and forth.

"Jeez, you know that woman gave up a career with the Joffrey," Benjamin whispered. "The Joffrey Ballet— tossed it away so she could go work with refugees." He pulled out a match to light his cigarette. "You people are nuts."

A serious dancer, then, Nora thought—Juliet's whole life must have been ballet.

As if sensing the attention, Juliet spun around. Her gray cape swung back as she came a step toward them. Uncertain, she peered at Nora. "But we have to reach people," she blurted. "To reach past everyone's anguish. You know what I mean."

I? But why are you asking this of me?

The stars had faded when a man drove up from Waterfront Gate, three miles away, saying police there were beating demonstrators. Benjamin grabbed his camera, Samantha closed her book, and they drove off to learn more. Most of the others stood and began brushing grass from their wrinkled clothes. A few hoisted picket signs and trudged to the road edge. Hooded or cloaked, they stood in the predawn wind, profiled against the sky as they readied to confront the napalm trucks.

Over the hills, the morning star rose.

Back in May, a few ragged protestors out by this road had seemed ridiculous in what she'd judged their futility. But now such judgments had to be behind her— and indeed that tiny group had led to *this*. Nothing here was laughable, *nothing*; that easy skepticism was a tool of those who guarded each chainlink fence. *How clear that is, here.*

Under a lamppost, an older man, a union organizer from San Francisco, was making sandwiches from donated bread and salami. Slipping from Ted's side, she walked across the road to help. *To feed my people.*

Soon the light turned pink, and she heard Ted call her, sleepily laughing. She put down the loaf she'd been slicing and started toward him. His eyes met hers. She smiled, then saw his gaze turn, fixing on something beyond her, up the road.

His stance shifted.

Two women, one small and thin, the other tall with dark blonde hair, had stepped away from the picket line and, carrying peace flags, started up the highway toward the low rise near the railroad crossing a hundred feet away. There, the weapons trucks would have to slow before making an oblique turn left onto the base. Between the turnoff, called Overpass Road, and the highway was a dusty triangle of ground, a narrow space where people could legally stand to await the trucks. It commanded a clear view of the route from Concord. A tactical view, Ted had called it, picking the location for the action.

"Guess I better make sure it really works," he said now. Dragging himself out from the blanket, he stood. He stretched and shook his head as if to clear it, then waved to her backhandedly and headed off to stand with the two women.

Never mind, just make more sandwiches. She needed to stay with Ted, but she also must give to them all. She had lifted the loaf, but she lowered it. She took four steps toward the road. *Here is my community.*

Except of course she was not of the community; she was the "support person," who would write an article, would take tapes to the broadcast news, but was not going to step onto the road and be arrested.

But, which acts were most important, which showed courage, all that was only judgment. For her, what was necessary was, rather, to stay on this caring path, this hope that she'd finally glimpsed in these past few hours.

Another four steps and she was trekking uphill to the narrow triangle of ground. Across the highway, lining the road the whole way from the turnoff and adjacent railroad track down to Main Gate, thirteen squad cars waited in the morning haze. Watching them and the Marine security guards, Ted and nine others stood arguing last-minute tactics, planning their civil disobedience. *I have no right to be with them.* No matter; whether or not she'd a right, she was here, committed to recording this action.

When the first truck appeared, the tall woman by the Overpass Road turnoff lifted her peace flag and almost casually stepped in front of it. As if he'd rehearsed, the driver braked, a deputy strode out from a squad car, and the woman was led off, making no resistance, to the car and placed in its rear seat. A second truck approached; the second, much older woman stood before it; the second arrest was made.

Soon a third; then a fourth. As each weapons truck approached, a demonstrator stepped out to halt it. The ritual established itself. Between times, they waited under the hot sun.

On every half hour, a young, crewcut Marine, bullhorn in hand, stepped to a chalk line drawn across the Main Gate drive and read out a warning, "This white line denotes the access and egress points of Concord Naval Weapons Station. Any unauthorized entrant is subject to a fine of not more than $500 and up to six months in jail."

And then, as each new truck approached, another demonstrator stepped toward it, shaky or calm but determined, crying out "Stop" or standing in silence, committed to halt this oncoming vehicle—this machine of war.

Yet only briefly, Nora could not help thinking. *How many lives, if any, this morning are actually being saved?*

Now, though, she accepted what her job required. She taped each confrontation; she taped the squealing brakes, the protestor's message squeezed into a word or two— "Stop the murder," "Stop the massacres," "Choose—choose." Gripping the recorder, her own gaze locked on the oncoming truck, she stood beside the demonstrator on the sunbaked road. Feeling as if, despite all doubts, these acts could really end the war.

But if I get hit, what happens to the child?

The day grew hotter, the dust thicker. Down the road, another truck appeared. It was Juliet's turn, and the tall dancer began to tremble, shaking all over as she adjusted her white tailored blouse and long full skirt.

"Julie, you'll do fine." Ted wrapped an arm around the tall woman's shoulders, hugged her until the trembling ceased. With a grateful smile, she pulled herself taut. As the weapons truck loomed closer, she stepped out on the pavement.

Close at her heels, Nora felt her fear, felt *for* her, felt a longing to help her, felt *through* Ted—though it could not be possible to feel through someone else—felt for Juliet and, the next instant, for all of them. *For this, my whole community.*

The driver swerved; the truck swung hard. Swung sidewise, braking with a sound like fury. Hampered by her long skirt, Juliet barely moved.

But then Nora saw what the dancer was attempting. Leaning slightly backward, Juliet had tautened and then, from a standstill, leaped suddenly upward in a swift, long, twisting *relevé*. Leaping not to escape, but to stay before the truck. And there, standing firm upon the pavement, gaze fixed on the driver's eyes, still-shaking voice sharp and clear, "*Now* do you understand?" the dancer cried. "Now do *you* understand?"

The recorder caught the words. Fast, but so scared her muscles barely worked, Nora shifted her feet, tried hard to stay at Juliet's side. "Good girl, good girl," Ted was calling. Over Juliet's head, the silver bombs loomed; the truck inched forward slightly, then slammed to a final stop.

One by one, the vigilers' hands rose in silent V-signs. Someone began singing "We Shall Overcome."

And it would all be on the tape.

And be broadcast to the world. But would the seriousness come through—into the yellow-lit kitchens, the quiet porches under overhanging flowers, across the six o'clock news? None of this could matter unless someone heard. None of it, until people were moved to act.

When only she and Ted remained, standing in the dust beside the triangle of earth, Nora wrapped the recorder in Ted's scarf, laid it atop a dry clean blanket, and took the Pentax from his hands. She had barely time to squeeze his fingers. Already, in the noon glare, another weapons truck was coming, climbing the mile-long rise from Concord. Once Ted started toward it, the whole responsibility to make the world see and hear would be entirely hers. "Hey, and maybe they'll figure it out now," Ted laughed. "Who knows?" He touched her hair and, as if crossing an ordinary street, stepped onto the highway before the approaching truck, his arms spread wide.

She carried the recorder, the camera, the notes, and names down the parched slope, and stood facing toward the Main Gate. From Concord, napalm trucks, three and four at a time, were passing, bombs stacked high—the beginning, delayed by only a few hours, of a normal Weapons Station day. A Marine again read aloud the warning "This white line denotes the access and egress points . . ." Across the road from her, Ted, Juliet, and a third protestor sat crammed into a white, unmoving squad car. All around, new people were arriving—from Berkeley, San Francisco, the entire Bay Area—to keep up the line. They climbed out from cars and turned to the gate, eyes taking in the armed Marines, the white police car with its prisoners, the bombs piled on the distant wharves. One by one, they began to sing "We Shall Overcome."

She had got it all on the tape—and now the singing too. But these singers were *new people,* people who *did not know,* who had not "been here" and did not understand. They had brought canteens of water, but, while Ted and the others were locked into that baking car, she too would take nothing to drink.

Again the guard repeated the warning; more trucks lumbered past. Slowly the white squad car lurched into gear, pulled out, engine racing, toward Martinez and the county jail. When, finally, a carload of demonstrators left for Berkeley, she went with them, carrying the precious messages from her community. Riding through dry farmland, idly wondering if she had time to stop home to use her bathroom and feed the cat, she understood that she was free, could sleep after taking in the tapes and photos, could return to the vigil, do what she wished— but others were in jail, she had not stopped a truck, and the weapons still rolled, the bombs still fell. There was community, and no end to the trucks. There was her search, and no end to the war.

2

You Really Fight for Your Friends

August 1966

Grime on the stove, layers of dust in the straw carpet—the sublet felt filthy. Constantly the cat scratched at fleas, which must be multiplying endlessly in the heat; the kitchen smelled of cat pee and garbage. She had to clean the place now, before it got worse. After bathing without even waiting for the water to get hot, she pulled on fresh clothes, then hurried back out. No time for housecleaning, with real work to be done.

But on the upstairs landing, someone stopped her. It was like falling into a loop in time. Nadine, the singer, her former friend, vivid in green and yellow, sat on the doormat. Looking "freaked out," in the singer's terms. Nadine must have used a plastic card or something to open the downstairs door.

"My voices," the singer faltered, "they told me that you're caught in something."

"Right." Nora stared carefully across the landing at the old, striped wallpaper. "I am."

"That you need to be freed." Nadine's voice trembled; her eyes blinked back tears.

Extending a hand to touch the soft arm stretched across the hallway to block her way, Nora said, "I have to hurry. I can't stop now, Nadine. People need me."

"Roger's wife is back. Listen, she's taken him back."

"This is—well, more urgent." Thinking *I should be kinder,* she remembered that, long before, she and Nadine had written songs together, the singer composing the music, she the words. She gave Nadine's hand a warm squeeze. But no time now. Lifting her legs high, she hopped over the singer's extended arm and, making her way downstairs, grabbed her mail from the hall table and headed back out.

Out—to hitchhike to San Francisco with the film for the AP. To catch a ride back to the East Bay, carry the tape recordings to KPFA-FM and, there, ignored by the all-male radio staff, stand tapping a foot until finally the motion, and her words "the tapes Ted promised you," reached one man's attention. She felt tired, hungry, had a baby growing inside, *have to lie down,* but it was necessary to keep going—write a quick article, get out more leaflets. Her people needed help, and in Vietnam people were dying.

Ted had said CNVA's Ahimsa House would let her use the mimeo machine for running off leaflets. Leaflets to stop Port Chicago. Leaflets to raise bail, to free the demonstrators. To get Ted out of jail.

Then they could comfort each other. In the *Barb* office, where nobody understood that Port Chicago was not "just another story," she marched over to Benjamin: "Come help with this, man. You know how to work machines." He laughed but, finally, grabbing his camera and saying, "Hey, whatever you say," followed her.

But at the stone-and-brick communal house, a tall white-maned man blocked the doorway. "Of course you can't 'just pop in to run off some leaflets.' How do I know who you are?"

"But Ted said—your coordinator, Meriwether, said—"

"Oh, did they really? And how do I know that? Like, get this straight, you two, *I'm* manager here." The hand poised to slam the door.

Benjamin pointed his camera.

"*Your* people. Leaflets for *your* people." Nora kept repeating it. "Your people are in jail. In jail."

"I told you." The man sounded, she thought, like someone kept from dinner. Too bad—no one was eating now. *Leaflets to free my people, our people who'll stop this war.*

"You two—we've rules here."

She had held back, staying inside the lines, she was thinking, yes that white line of propriety. But Ted, Ted and the others—now, they needed help. "*Rules?*" She almost shouted it. "You know, it's people like you, it's—" Her voice was rising; she saw Benjamin's eyes widen, his grimace as she shouted. But she wouldn't stop. "People like you, man—people like *you*! You, with your locks and rules and power games and—" *No, watch out, he could call the cops. Be quiet, shut up.* "Like you—who make these wars." *Just stop.* "Don't close that door. You—it's *your* people's, *our* people's vigil will stop Port Chicago, will save those lives, will—only you, you won't let us, you—"

Mistake to have shouted.

Except, the white-haired guy was not there anymore. He had backed into the hallway, and the door was open. And he was walking away, out toward the giant cedar silhouetted against the salmon-and-green horizon. "Not too long," he called back over his shoulder, voice nonchalant.

They found the mimeo in the basement, down a long brick staircase. The steps were slippery, the ceiling so low it was hard to stand upright. Only a forty-watt bulb shone above the rusting machine.

Benjamin shook his head. But not about the mimeograph. "Jesus, woman, you even had *me* scared." There was a swagger to his voice; that morning he had climbed across two weapons trucks, chasing photos for the AP. He grinned, carrying stencil blanks and reams of paper to the workbench. "*And* you got us in here. You ain't one bit helpless, girl."

She grinned back but felt nothing, only a longing fear. *Are my people, out there, all right?*

"Yep." Benjamin began turning knobs, coddling the ink drum to a slow start. "You sure can fight for your friends." The drum began an unsteady turn. "Or should I say, *for that man?*"

Her victory was empty, though. After a dozen cycles, the drum made a groaning noise and snapped. Twice,

Benjamin restarted it before it gave out. No matter what he attempted, no matter how she tried to help, nothing made it move. Finally, they just stood crouched under the low ceiling and glared at the stalled machine. No way now—no leaflets would appear, no flyers would pop forth to help raise bail and bring more people to the vigil. Again she had not done enough, just like the whole time she had stood apart on the line, never stepping forward like the others to halt the war. And who, this ordinary Tuesday busy night, would even hear those broadcast tapes? At the Council for Justice, people would be phoning for bail, frail Samantha arguing with the sheriff's department, Barry the legal assistant racing through supporter lists; and out on the line more people would stand before the trucks. There was so much to do, and nothing had changed, not one step come closer to peace.

She should go home—feed the cat and clean the sink and wash her hair and . . .

But, half an hour later, when she and Benjamin stopped at the Council for Justice office with the forty-four smudged leaflets they had managed to run off, Ted stood at the top of the stairs. He looked exhausted and triumphant. She started up the steps toward him, but her clothes were dirty, she had done nothing, it was he, not she, who had stood before the trucks—and here so many people could see them, people like him who also had spent time in jail and just been freed. People with courage.

But these are judgments. Don't get caught in them.

And Ted was turning to someone beside him, a young Council for Justice attorney wearing a grey suit and tie, and was laughing in that hearty voice, saying, "Yeah, sure, you think they'd even take us back into their jail? No chance!" Not looking her way, Ted followed the attorney and several other demonstrators toward the back room, where their first defendants' meeting had begun.

"And I'll be there/ to love and comfort you . . ." In the white van, the radio kept playing the song. Over and over, during the forty minutes' drive—apparently, the month's big hit. Ted drove; the meeting had ended late;

he was taut, anxious to return to the vigil. With Benjamin and eight others, she'd squeezed into the back of the van, sitting on the metal floor as they bumped along through the night. A newcomer rode in the passenger seat, and Ted kept encouraging him, "Man, those Marines couldn't block a football pass, that's why they joined up," then forcing the balky gearshift lever, "Guess I better check this thing tomorrow." The hearty voice again—he was committed now, exhausted but still caring and struggling against the war, again caught up in the vigil.

These people respond to him so! Truly I do care for him, too—but I can't stay out there all the time, like them. Not just the bladder, not only the tiredness. It flashed through her mind again, *Maybe I still could change my mind and abort.* But it seemed a silly thought.

Climbing out with Benjamin at Waterfront Gate— together they could interview more demonstrators tonight and write up the in-depth story of the protest— she saw Ted's gaze shift toward her, and his expression change; his lips half-opened as if questioning—she was sure—why she was leaving him. Surprised, she halted. She could clamber back in, reach over the back of his seat, for that moment hold him.

Only, the people here—these committed, brave people—were watching. And again, immediate actions called—the interviews with protestors to give people hope, the writing to bring more people out to end the war, taking her own next steps upon the fragile path of learning to give to all; everything must be done. Ted surely knew this; he had to know she cared for him—and wasn't their longing private, self-centered, compared to this struggle to end the war? Tonight they must wait, she and Ted—but soon.

Meeting his eyes, she waved goodbye.

Exhaustion kept her in Berkeley, the next few nights—exhaustion and the thought of having failed Ted when she'd climbed from the van. She scrubbed the apartment, though this did not stop the fleas and she had to—her cat was frantic. Laundry had piled up, too, and garbage—everywhere fleas could breed. If she couldn't stop them soon, she'd need to use flea-spray—and that, some people said, was dangerous to the fetus. So she must—just stick around for a little while more and get the place seriously clean. Besides, she could shower here, shampoo her hair, wear fresh clothes—life was different here—here in this apartment in this city far from trespass lines, this place with running water and no constant fear of someone's—of Ted's—arrest, without the thought at every moment *Step out on the road now and give your all; risk freedom and your life, your child's; stop this war.* It had become far away, that roadside world, a reality difficult to recall.

Then it was Tuesday again. Ted knocked at the door. "We need another hundred people."

A week had slipped past her, a week when she might have changed her mind about the fetus but hadn't, had not even thought about phoning the hospital—or about anything but Port Chicago, and already the pressure on her bladder had become familiar, the extra weight a habit; it was already a new weekend, a humid Friday evening. Ted smelled of the oily dust of the Port Chicago roadside; it covered his skin and clothes.

"A hundred serious, committed people, not the drifters we've been getting," he was saying. "Scores of drifters, they keep hanging out with us. But we need people out there who are serious—who'll pick up their signs and stand by that road, people who *will* stop the trucks. Then we can block those shipments, Nora, and shut down the frigging base."

She had meant to wash the kitchen again tonight, to read a new novel she'd just bought. And Ted sounded nearly fanatical, the way he had ten days ago, when the vigil first started, like the humorless passive-ists she and Benjamin laughed about at the *Barb*.

"You know this vigil can't stop the war," she said. "Ted, you know very well. It can't even stop the trucks."

He stood silently by the narrow window, lips compressed.

No—no, he was too vulnerable. "I mean, I mean, how do I know? Yes, you keep on, Ted. Do keep on." Her words surprised her. "I—if you want, I'll stop a truck."

"No! No, you're in no shape for what happens in jail."

Except, if she didn't reach out, and try, and give—! But there was no way to explain. It wasn't only about becoming whole, anymore. She'd started having nightmares all the time, as if she were Vietnamese, a Vietnamese mother with a baby, a little child. She was failing these people far away; she must help save them.

Unless this *must* was not truly caring either, but simply others' judgments—the vigilers' judgments— trapping her in *their* commitment, her own caring not yet real enough yet.

Ted had flopped down on the bed, eyes closed. She took a step forward and sat next to him, then stretched her body alongside his. As she turned to him, he turned on his side and opened his eyes. In silence. Ernie's old mattress not even creaking beneath them, they reached forward, with tired awkwardness, to drag off each other's clothes. Soaked in sweat, smelling the cat sand and garbage in the kitchen, wordlessly they began to make love, bodies struggling to move together.

I'm so sorry, Ted, I want you, but I . . . No, this was no time to explain all that, the what-had-been's and the welling-up of old fears whenever she thought she loved. He was exhausted, and she wanted to comfort him, to bring him into her. She wanted to, wanted to, and even if her body wouldn't open, still she—

"You're right, Nora." Suddenly he was saying the strangest words. "We do need to slow down. Yeah, we do. And you know why?" His left hand stroked her stomach, and he gave a quiet laugh. "Not just your pregnancy— though, hey, you're starting to swell. But there's another reason, Nora. We've got something real going, you and I." He opened a pack of cigarettes and pulled one out. "Out there at the vigil, some folks—you know, it goes on and on forever, and I'm not sure they even know, some of them, who they're with anymore. But you and I—"

"But, Ted, don't you mind?" *When sometimes I can't open?* Only, she couldn't say it.

"We need to take our time. We've something real."

Lying back, she took a puff on the cigarette, and they shared it. After a time, she watched him put out the stub on her old stone ashtray. His left hand began to stroke her thighs. Her breasts felt swollen, longing. With an index finger, she traced his lips.

In the morning, Ted said, "I better get back out there and make sure the Sleeping Bag War doesn't erupt again. It's—don't even ask."

Perhaps an hour later, after he'd left for Port Chicago, the day began to heat up, and the apartment's fleas again started multiplying; at times they felt like a punishment, at others a bad joke. She had got all the dishes washed, but not yet done the laundry. This was her real life. By evening, the community was again far away, that world unreal.

But soon, in a day or two at most, Ted would come back; he would say, "Yes, we can end this war. Yes, it is possible." This time, she would agree, "It *is*—it *is*," and he would answer, "Come out there with me, Nora. This time, *you* stop a truck." Because it was necessary—for her own sake, but also, though it did sound silly, because he and that community, and possibly she, together might stop the war. *Might*—and that uncertainty too, all the uncertainties, formed a wearying wall.

It was noon on Monday when they learned at the *Barb* that police at Port Chicago no longer made arrests. Instead, the Navy sped the napalm trucks through the gates, rifle-bearing Marines running beside them, knocking any protestors off the road. This meant less chance of arrest and jail if one tried to stop a truck—but far more risk of injury Yet Ted was out there, and the others. And those Vietnamese mothers, the ones in her dreams and the real ones huddling under bombs, had no safety for their fetuses—their babies. *No safety at all, unless we care. No protection, until we do more here.*

3

We Shall Overcome

August 16-17, 1966

She was bent over her worktable in the *Barb*'s back office, scratching a flea bite and writing a feature on the new Diggers' "free community," when Ted rushed in.

"The key. The key to your apartment, kid." He spoke in a rush. An old silver-gray scarf hung across his left shoulder. "I need to work there, get this leaflet out *now*."

She could feel their distance—the distance between here and *out there*. "I'll meet you back home," she said, handing him the key. "Soon as this story's done. You go ahead. I'll make us tuna sandwiches."

"Yeah, but hey, gotta hurry." Briefly, he hugged her. "Look, not to neglect you, but I have to get back out there, soon as this is done. Skip the sandwiches, people are in terror. Bunch of Nazi thugs been driving back and forth all day, right by the line. They're 'Like, got one big blast tonight for y'all.' Loudmouth punks—but guns in their pickups. We need folks out there fast, lots of folks."

She watched him leave. Tonight, then—tonight she had to get there, be with him and the community.

Yet courage and caring were not these people's alone; stopping the weapons trucks was not the only way to end the war. Her job tonight was already determined—to cover the rally supporting the activists subpoenaed by the House Un-American Activities Committee. All Berkeley, it was said, would be there.

Under the green STOP HUAC banner, hundreds of people squeezed through the two sets of double doors into the crowded auditorium. She pushed toward the front, repeating "Press—make way—press," which usually worked, but here only at the last minute could she find a seat, far at the end of a row. Just ahead, people from the vigil had gathered—Samantha, Lee, the teacher Peg, the labor organizer Rich, several people she didn't know. *Those who've been out there. I'm a reporter.* Then she saw Ted. He was still wearing the ragged silvery scarf. Caught between two vigilers anxiously addressing him, he only nodded and smiled to her.

Onstage, a blond athletic man, one of the peace candidates in this year's elections, had taken the mic. "Now we've seen that HUAC and McCarthy could not prevent the Civil Rights Movement," he was saying, "and, by the way, its offspring: the Free Speech Movement and the Students for a Democratic Society and Women for Peace and the Vietnam Day Committee—and everyone else who's organized against this war. We have watched the Dow boycott grow, have we not, despite the naysayers? We are finding hope in San Francisco's Diggers." Taking a quick sip of water, he smiled toward the network television cameras. "So, my friends, tonight the time has come. Tonight we—you and I—we too shall take a stand. Tonight we shall drive to the guarded gates of Port Chicago. Port Chicago, where"—he shifted so the cameras caught his profile— "we see already a microcosm of what America will soon become, unless we win this struggle—an America where by day sheriff's deputies rule the roads, and by night Marines and Nazi thugs know no authority. And so tonight—now, my friends—we shall go out to the vigil line, and *stop* this madness and *end* this war. Just as these brave folks"—lifting both hands, he gestured toward the row of vigilers— "have been doing, night after night after night.

"We *shall* go join them—there, on those dangerous roads—and put *our* bodies, too, on the line."

The chanting erupted, "Stop Port Chicago—stop the war now!" Chairs were scraped back; people leapt to their feet. Gathering belongings, bumping inadvertently against each other, people began pushing toward the exits; they crowded through the doorways, flowed across the grass, piled out to the street. Already, the first few vans and cars were starting up, engines grinding, and moving out, forming a long, fragmented caravan to drive the thirty miles of crowded freeway east to Port Chicago in the night.

Swept forward with the rest, she glimpsed, far ahead, the ABC television crew tossing gear into their van and pulling out in the bumper-to-bumper line. "Maybe tomorrow," someone beside her laughed, "we'll see ourselves on the evening news."

It looked like the landscape of the art-house film *Red Desert*—desolation, stagnant swamps, the three looming towers of the oil refinery, tilted slightly toward the top. Caked with rust, the towers glowed with bulbs strung like Christmas lights on every side, reached high into the darkness. Creeping along, the old car finally gained the north end of the refinery, and the driver paused. After a moment, he turned the wheel to head upriver.

"This the direction, babe?" he asked—new to the vigil, lost since this car had got separated from those ahead.

"Man, watch the road," someone on the back seat shouted. "Last thing we need's a cop to . . ." His words trailed into soft puffs as a joint was passed around. Already, the car was turning again, curving smoothly onto Waterfront Road. They passed a swamp, skirted the river's edge.

"Have a hit, babe?"

She shook her head. They skirted another swamp, what might be railroad yards. The chainlink fences of Port Chicago rose, tall and shadowy, to their right.

But there was no safe place to park by Waterfront Gate. Following the road, they turned with the long curve of the hills, beyond a meadow where a sleepy cow grazed and then on, another three miles, toward Main Gate. About two hundred yards beyond it, other cars were arriving—more new people come to swell the line. The driver pulled into a tiny parking space.

Nora stepped from the overheated car as soon as it stopped, and she slipped away, squeezing past the newcomers. There were scores of newcomers—milling around and eating sandwiches and sipping coffees; she saw few walking forward, though, to join the still-sparse line across from Main Gate. None of these new people looked ready to stop a truck.

Yet the crowd, and especially the ABC-television presence, meant that finally they might get real publicity. To bring more people—to end the war.

"Nora—hey, kid." Ted came rushing toward her, arms out, tears of joy in his eyes. "You're here!" She saw him, saw the tears, and then saw nothing but his eyes. A moment later, though, as if from outside, she seemed to watch the two of them cling together, bodies forming an arch, a vision as if sculpted out of time.

Leaning against the wood rail-fence, she clutched him tighter as they embraced, the fierceness of it surprising—yet reassuring. They sat together in the long grass, leaning back against the wooden fence.

"Yeah, Nora, yeah." Draping the silvery scarf around their heads for privacy, Ted pressed closer, his face against hers. She breathed the salty odor of his sweat. Surely they had gone far beyond comradely warmth or laughing comfort. As they held hands, she knew there was nothing, for now, she should say. She looked up at the stars after a while, repeating, what, long ago she'd done many times, picking out Arcturus, Deneb, Vega, and then turned her eyes toward what was, here, again her own community.

None of the Nazi pickups had returned, but rumors had spread that several Nazi toughs were hidden among the hecklers, out in full force. Worn down, the veteran vigilers clumped together in tight groups; a few hung out beside the water containers or the smelly port-a-potty, leaving the newcomers to wander around alone, risking the marked and unmarked trespass lines—lines everywhere, by Main Gate, by Overpass Road, beside the train tracks, and in places along the fence. An argument had broken out around the food table, another between two hippies, and "Ted, come help!" a voice near the highway called out. Across the road, too, Marine guards stood around baiting Rickie, the vigil's only black, who was arguing loudly; one of the vigil's rumors was that Rickie carried a gun.

"Oh fuck, let them all go at it! Thought we could bring out some serious people tonight. Listen, kid, I don't even care anymore what they do."

The words startled her. "You *what?*"

"Hey, I've got to get some rest. Hold me, love."

I know. I understand. Ted, I do—I do. Rest on me, rest.

But at that moment, other words rose inside her, cold words, coming from that reservoir of judging voices, speaking before she could stop them. "Now, Ted, you listen. If you're really committed to the vigil, you can't just suddenly not act."

No, wait! She thrust both hands across her lips. *I didn't mean that. I meant, I meant to say . . . I love you, too.* "Ted, wait."

But he was on his feet. He hadn't heard.

He gives so much, he goes beyond the rest of us. Only, she hadn't said that, either. She watched him move off, loping easily up the grass-patched slope, heading toward the triangle of ground by the Overpass Road turnoff. He was not looking back.

A minute later, she could see him standing with the vigil in-group—Lee, Samantha, a few others—pointing out tactics to two young men who were readying to halt a truck. He would stay up there. *With his clique*—she silenced the thought; it was ugly, judgmental, wrong. And, besides, it was she who had just said those words to him, *You can't not act.*

However, self-reproach had no importance here; besides, there was no time; this demonstration required her, too. She walked toward the food table, where the newcomers clustered; at least she could help them find their way. Across the road, armed Marines stalked back and forth, thirty-some neo-Nazis gathering beside them.

"Tell people!" A man's bony hand grabbed her shoulder. "Look, you see those new people going up there?" The man, an old pacifist with cracked-rim glasses, jerked his head toward the little triangle of ground at Overpass Road. "They're giving support to those guys committing c.d."

"So?" She nodded vaguely. His thumb kept pressing her arm. "Don't poke, please."

"You've been here, Nora; you know the situation. Tell those people the rules: if someone gets attacked, they're not to try to protect the person—it'll only make things worse."

Again she nodded. But pulled away, annoyed, and hurried, forgetting him as she reached the top of the slope, stunned by the presence, here, of these committed activists, and by the tension in those armed Marines. She wasn't brave enough—it wasn't just being frightened for the child—she wasn't brave or self-forgetful enough to be standing here. She wasn't among these who planned to stop a weapons truck, who had stood vigil here every night, outnumbered by police and hecklers and Marines. The brave ones, these—these few especially, waiting on this triangle of ground—Lee, hands twisting her cowboy hat, fragile Samantha grim but laughing while she argued tactics, the older woman who said little but sat quietly on a three-legged stool and ate a plum. Nearer, Benjamin seemed idle, almost careless, but his "Joining the suicide team tonight, Nora?" was hollow and humorless, and his eyes stared toward the road.

It was past midnight. Ted and Lee whispered together, and Samantha, closing her book, strode over to join them. Nora walked restlessly among the silhouetted protestors, made a cardboard press card, lit a cigarette from her nearly empty pack. Down the road, some of the new people were starting for home, walking sleepily along the dusty pavement to their cars, but none of the neo-Nazi hecklers were leaving.

Here at the top of the slope, Marines lounged against the chainlink fence not far from the closest police cars.

The television crew, looking bored, lounged on the tailgate of their van and chain-smoked cigarettes. In the pasture, crickets chirred. A police radio sputtered.

Someone said, "Look."

Far away from Concord shone the five yellow lights of a truck.

"There's another." Lee was pointing, cowboy hat held bunched against her side. Behind the first five lights came five more. Across the road, police rushed to take up positions; the television crew removed their cameras' lens caps and readjusted lights. Tall as houses, the trucks drew nearer, rumbling up the slope.

Too fast.

They were coming too fast.

The first truck swerved, lurching in toward the gate, the heavy momentum of its bombs behind it. Bracing to a stop, the two young demonstrators who'd been racing toward it faltered and fell back. Bomb-crates swaying, the truck lurched forward, speeding through the gate. Across the road, a dozen hecklers laughed.

Out from the blackness, the second truck loomed. Its five lights gleamed.

Again, too fast.

Someone, in the television lights, was running toward it.

The person—for a moment, she could see him—was Ted, his tall form leaning forward, arms bent as if to shield himself. She did not like the way he held his arms. This person, he was going—whoever he was, she could not see—to be killed.

And there's nothing I can do to stop this. I'd confuse his timing; I'd distract him. Her eyes turned away into darkness—the flat white road. *And if I move, the hecklers—and the people and the baby could be hurt.* The road's particular whiteness. *If this is even happening—*

Gears ground; the truck braked hard.

She half-glimpsed Marines, in the white light, rush forward, attack the person. Blocking her vision, the high-packed truck lurched past. Whoever this person, they were dragging him along the pavement in the camera lights, hitting him with nightsticks, knocking him to the ground. Her feet would not move.

Not I who's stopped a truck. I, who'd only make things worse. A movie, unreal.

Samantha had run out onto the road. She was throwing herself across the demonstrator, one hand upraised toward the Marines. A Marine sergeant shouted something, raised his club. Seconds later, he lowered it to his side, snapped a command; the Marines began pulling away.

In the camera lights, people were helping the demonstrator back, covered with gravel and bruises. There was a wide-eyed focus to each person's face. The demonstrator leaned on Samantha. Nora could see now; it was Ted.

As people's hands rose in *V* signs and the vigil lines began to sing, she stepped back, away from the television cameras, away from Ted. "We shall overcome someday," people sang.

Now I shall never overcome. If I couldn't do this, I have already died.

Barry, the legal assistant, came forward out of the darkness by the roadside fence. He was carrying witness forms and asked had she seen what happened.

"I couldn't identify the Marines."

"But you did see what took place? You saw it was Ted?"

She watched him write her name on his yellow pad. "Yes," she said. "I did." Nearer the fence, Ted was laughing off the attack and trying to set up new tactics. Hands spread, he was arguing with Samantha, who was insisting on stopping the next truck; Samantha's clipped "Okay, we share the risks, then," met his gruff "Tonight's my turn."

"Nora." Benjamin had come up beside her, voice tight. "Can't you seduce him or something? So he doesn't kill himself?"

"No, a woman does not do that." But that wasn't what she meant, but she couldn't explain. "If he wants to—"

"Jeez, you people *are* nuts." Benjamin's words parodied their cynicism, calm as if nothing had happened. Only, his hands gripped his camera too hard.

Beyond Ted and Samantha, the road stretched off. She could hear them still debating. She was carrying a child; her actions didn't come, like these people's, from a generous caring, and, any moment, more trucks might arrive; Ted might again . . .

"Listen to me." She leaned toward him and Samantha. "Listen. I will stop the next one."

Neither replied. Even the vigilant Lee made no answer. As if nobody heard. *Nobody knows.*

"C'mon." Benjamin was at her side. "Let's get out of here before the slaughter."

It didn't matter what she did. She hadn't gone out on the road, and now it was too late. She nodded and headed downhill with Benjamin toward the main group. Two dozen or so of the newcomers still milled around, there, hanging out by the food table. While Benjamin wandered among them, asking about a ride back into Berkeley, she waited, smelling the stale sandwiches and staring at crusts of a blueberry pie. Then she looked up. Benjamin was returning, gesturing thumbs-up. Beyond him stretched the dark gray road toward Concord.

She saw it coming. Saw the five yellow lights.

"Let's get going." Benjamin was grinning. "Like, I found us a car."

"Truck. Truck, Benjamin, truck."

His hands jerked, flung open the camera, reached to change rolls of film. Moving too quick to follow, but her gaze fixed on them.

"Nora, run. *Run.* Throw your arms around him, or something."

But her sandals caught as she raced onto the gravel, slipped on the narrow strip beside a ditch. The napalm truck—*no, I must halt it!*—roared on past.

Far up the slope, from the triangle of ground, three demonstrators—Ted, with Samantha and Lee on either side—were racing out to meet it. Marines were leaping forward—*like a movie, like a movie*—shoving the two women, flinging them aside. And for an instant, like a repetitive loop, the high-packed truck blocked her view. Then it had passed, and again Ted lay on the ground, surrounded by a cordon of Marines.

But this time her feet, as in a dance, could move. She ran across the road.

On every side, Marines barred the way. Joined by two other demonstrators, she faced the cordon. There had to be some way around—but there was none. Marines formed too deep a wall. A sheriff lounged against a fencepost, gazing up at the stars. She heard Ted scream.

Plunging against the Marine line, scratching at their shoulders, she scrambled to get through. A baby-faced Marine grabbed at her poncho, caught it, and began to push her backward with one hand; his other hand lunged out and grasped Lee's hair. Shoving them backward, he was pushing them toward one of the long white trespass lines.

"Aren't you human? Aren't you human?" Shouting, she tried to dodge away. Her foot slipped on the rutted ground. Her sandal strap broke, and she stumbled against Lee. Struggling not to fall, they tilted off-balance—and suddenly the Marine let go. Nora shook off her shoes and—*dance now, dance*—ignoring the gravelly pavement, raced, barefoot, back toward Ted.

Out of the darkness, a silhouette lunged, blocking her way. She shifted, dodged around it. But more guards were ranged before her; another moved in from behind. And two Marines were laughing—one was black and one was white—and then there was a space. She ran to Ted.

Kneeling, she leaned across him; she touched his shoulder, saying "We are here." Her arms were spread, her back arched between him and the Marines.

The baby's shielded, deep inside. He is, he is.

Ted said, "I'm all right."

"Don't try to move. Just rest." Only, if the Marines closed tighter, wouldn't staying here provoke more danger?

But other demonstrators had come up; she could glimpse Lee, and a guy named Jim, and two or three others, all crowding around. The Marines began to pull back. Nora straightened and looked around.

And saw it move in, from Overpass Gate—just a little truck really, just the security guard pick-up. Only, coming directly at them.

This has got to be a joke. But everyone was jumping out of the little truck's way. She bent over Ted, thinking to move him to safety—except she wasn't strong enough. It could hurt him if she tried. And certainly, really, the driver would stop. Stepping forward, she stood between Ted and the oncoming little truck.

Twelve inches, six—the headlights of the truck.

Her feet took root.

"What did you intend to do, kick in the headlights?" Benjamin walked beside her as they all made their way down the slope.

She couldn't answer. *It would have had to hit me first. Somehow I would have protected Ted.*

Lee, on her left, broke silence. "You did well."

No. No, if she had stopped anything, it was only the tiny truck, a child's-size truck.

Half an hour later, Nora watched as the television crew, under the white camera light, interviewed Ted. He sat against the pasture fence, injured leg stretched under a plaid blanket. "Only wrenched my knee, I think," he was saying, "bunch of fuckers, pulling a person around," and he laughed. And, a moment later, was speaking again of hope, "People need to see we do care—that they also care. If a thousand people come out here, if even a hundred see it's possible, we can close this base and we can end this war."

Everyone hovered, lingering at a too-respectful distance, as if suddenly Ted were sacred. Not far away, Lee sat cross-legged, holding the remnants of his silvery scarf. Benjamin chewed cracker after cracker, chatting between-times with the television crew, like someone who dared not stop to rest. Exhausted vigilers had drifted to the road-edge or lay under blankets or sleeping bags. *Caught, as I am, in a private struggle.* She walked a bit apart, near the lone lamppost across from Main Gate. Whenever she passed Ted, he was engaged with other people. Twice, she heard someone—Samantha, then another woman, maybe Julie—say they'd drive him to a doctor, but he laughed this off. *Ted, you should*—but she dared not approach him now.

Not caring if a car ran her down, she lay back under a pink blanket, at the very edge of the road. She could look up and hate—see the trucks again roll by, the bombs' silver gleam, the Marines lined, like vultures on a spit, along the opposite fence. To turn them and roast them, to slice them off with a sword at their knees, to press a loaded gun to their foreheads, to— The violent images spoke a terrifying failure.

Slowly, over the mountains, the morning star rose; light tinged the sky.

"Decide—do you want to ride into the city with me?" Benjamin's words woke her. Dawn could bring some safety here, but for how long? And when would the Vietnamese be safe? She had not stopped a truck, and now she truly would have to ask Ted's permission first, or it would be as if she followed him, as if she sought to possess a lover's heroism—to be too close, to become one with him.

"C'mon, decide. I have to make the AP with these photos, fast. Gotta scoop the competition, you know—competitive capitalism and all."

She dared not go speak with Ted. "Benjamin, let's leave."

The road was empty. Benjamin packed his film, started the sputtering engine of the borrowed car. "Hope we can reach the City before I conk out."

Through the window, she glimpsed Ted, over by Samantha and Lee and the rest. "I should go back." *To Ted, to stop a truck, to vindication.*

"Should I let you off, then?"

Or simply to stand pregnant and self-centered in the dust and sun of Port Chicago? And if the Base could not be closed—if to stop a truck were indeed become possessiveness, *too* close—or if the war could only bring new loss and no hope . . .

In the passenger seat, Nora covered her eyes. "No, let's leave." But was Ted all right?

"Then let's get going, before somebody tries again."

Frame after frame of blackness—there was nothing on the film. Benjamin in his torn shirt, she holding broken sandals, they stood barefoot in the AP office watching the rolls drop to the floor. The editor was genial, "Guess you got too tense." He and Benjamin grinned.

But the film was blank. As if it had not happened. Did anyone even know?

"Benjamin"—early in the afternoon she left the note by his sleeping form on the couch in her apartment— "I can't sleep. Going over to the *Barb.*" Headlights of trucks, the headlights of hundreds of weapons trucks, trucks high as a house, trucks looming *too fast*—moved forward whenever she closed her eyes.

4

Separations– "All You Women"

August–September, 1966

IITwo hundred people moved out from Tuesday's anti-HUAC meeting and made the long drive to Port Chicago." She leaned her head on the typewriter, then jerked herself awake. "By 2 a.m. most had left. Apparently, they'd found no excitement."

"Write about the meeting. Stop taking sides." Max was peering over her shoulder. "You political types get too emotionally involved."

This was a different world, these rooms at the *Barb*—this whole city—where the confrontation last night at Port Chicago was no more than one event. "I can't write this today." She had to think—no, no, write it up.

An hour later, Benjamin was standing by her desk. "Want to see yourself on television? Time for the evening news."

" . . . And here we see a demonstrator behind a cordon of Marines. He had tried to halt a napalm truck, which was not stopping—apparently a common practice out at Port Chicago. Marine guards dragged him from its path, hitting him with nightsticks."

On-screen, a female form glided forward, suddenly and briefly visible, wearing—*yes, it's my poncho, must be me*—and leaned across the demonstrator.

People's hands lifted high in V-signs. The camera panned across the line of singing demonstrators.

"Our cameraman was knocked down by Marine guards, and valuable photographic equipment destroyed. We have requested a full investigation."

In a final tight shot, the camera pulled back from the cordon of Marines and past the demonstrators' line.

"Like a corny movie, Benjamin. And all mixed up." After the broadcast, they walked the four blocks from the *Barb* to Si's Charbroiler; they sat hunched over black coffees and too-dry hamburgers. "Embarrassing."

His dark eyebrows lifted. "Why on earth should you be embarrassed?"

She dared not risk getting trapped in the maze of explanations. *Scenario of the all-daring hero and his girlfriend.* "But, Benjamin—on nationwide TV." She squeezed her eyes shut and shook her head.

After she took out the garbage, she cleaned the cat-box and scrubbed the kitchen floor. Too tired to sleep, she lay down anyhow, trying not to see the oncoming headlights of the trucks.

And then it was completely dark outside. The buzzing sound was the doorbell. Throwing on her coat, she ran into the hall and leaned on the buzzer at the top of the stairs, unlocking the outer door below.

Even as Ted pushed the door open, she rushed down to meet him; she flung her arms around his neck. "Don't ever, ever, ever do that again. I thought you might die. I thought—"

He was grinning, holding her. "You really are some woman, you know. Out at the vigil today, all those women—well, like you, like what you just did, but you— see, you're *you*." He laughed, but it was a hearty, one-of-the-boys laugh. Startled, she realized the tone comforted her; it said she'd reacted normally. "People there kept offering me new scarves," he said. "Too bad it's so hot out." She helped him up the stairs, and in the studio set out wine and cheese, sat beside him and stroked his uninjured leg.

"God," he said. "I am so glad you're all right. I was worried."

"About me? But you—!" Of a sudden, desperate, she reached again to hold him. But, inside, she was pulling back, unable to stop herself. In these few hours since she'd left him, there on that frightening roadside, terror from the night had brought back those old doubts—especially that fear that her love sought some heroic "romance," the very sort of scenario those mixed-up television shots had portrayed. Did she really want such a thing, even at the cost of him being hurt—want to possess and be one with "a hero"?

Adoration was dragging her back into this, setting off these self-accusations, these mazes of shame. Instead, she had to put forget this, put "self" aside, simply hold him, hold him. And act—*stop a damned truck.* Except, first she'd have to tell him . . . everything. So he'd know who she was, her past, her thoughts on those vigil nights. But this was hardly the time for that.

In the stifling hot apartment, she poured more wine. She curled beside him and held him against her. At the clinic, he was saying, the doctor had X-rayed his leg, announced "Got yourself a bad sprain," and wrapped the leg in bandages. "Of course, they're way too heavy, but he gave me two aspirins." Laughing, loosely holding her wrist, he wrapped his other arm around her. Eyes smiling, pleased with her. She dipped her head, surprised. After a few minutes, he put down his glass and lay back on the bed, watching her.

Yes, it would be all right. She didn't have to explain anything. She wasn't romantically adoring him. Tonight would simply be what it was. "You know"—she threw out the words in a monotone, as if stating the obvious— "I must go back and stop a weapons truck."

"You *what*?" He sat up. "No. Good lord, no. Definitely not—no trucks."

She must have misheard. But he repeated it. "Why should you? There's nothing happening out there now. Last night, we nearly killed ourselves, right? But, for all the publicity, you know how many new people came out today? Two. And one left after, I don't know, half an hour. And nobody, the whole day, blocked any trucks." He spun the wineglass. "If a hundred of us—fifty of us— go out there ready to do whatever it takes, we can shut it down. But we're not a hundred, we're not fifty, not even fifteen who'll act. No, there's no point anymore."

Too late, then. Now to act, to stop a truck, would be only moral witness. At worst a futile gesture only for her own sake.

"You fought hard for me out there, Nora. I saw you."

"No, no. Only to get through those Marines."

"'Only'? I saw you. You were fighting, fighting hard."

"I was out there." That, at least, was true. Again, they went silent. The cat, who'd been sleeping on the kitchen counter, jumped through the doorway and onto the bookcase, avoiding the straw rug, and hopped to a window ledge, scratching at fleas.

"Your kitty's not very happy here."

"You saved its life. I mean, you got us here."

"You know, people out there today, they wouldn't do anything. And they wouldn't even let me *near* the road. Not that I objected much."

She realized she was stroking his wrists with a new shyness, terrified because this felt like adoration for him "I wouldn't stop you. Or maybe I would; I was so afraid—you might have got killed.

"Every day, Vietnamese are—"

"I know. But, listen to me. I wasn't trying to possess you, Ted. I wasn't. Please understand."

Putting down his drink, he stared at her as if stunned. "To possess me? Good Lord, no, you don't seem at all possessive. I don't understand. Hey, Nora, look. These fears you have, sometimes they're not clear to me. You need to *tell* me. Try."

She stroked his left palm. "If I do, it opens the mazes. I can't." She tried to look into his eyes, but he looked away.

She lay down beside him, silent. She played with his fingers; his lips moved over her eyelids. But when he slid one hand along her skin to stroke her abdomen, and heat spread through her, she clenched, fearing what its intensity might mean. She stroked him, too, but hesitantly, careful not to hurt the scrapes and bruises along his legs, but then only held him. She mustn't love too much—if it even *was* love; she was feeling a strange pride, pride in him and in herself, aware of what he'd done, and she wanted this tenderness and caring to go on and on, wanted everything between them to go on, and that the ugly bruises and scrapes and burdensome, heavy bandages be gone. If there could be some peaceful time, here and on the line! A time to just be together, and him healed, strong, loving, with her—wanted him *now*. Yearning, she pressed closer.

Or had she been wrong, these months, the old fears been true?

But why think this way now? Because I didn't act on time?

Ted whispered something. His hand moved up her thigh.

She started. *Wait.* But she wouldn't say that, not this time. Even if her body wasn't ready, or—she wrapped her legs around his. "Love," she said.

Then, arms taut and fierce, he was clutching her. She reached, grabbed for him, his shoulders, his thighs. A poignant sharpness raced through her, and she did not halt herself, rising as their breathing turned to hard, quick gasps.

But if I—

For an instant, Ted was grinning. "Hey, we can slow down, if you want. But I'd rather"—his fingers touched her nipples so she cried aloud— "show you how beautiful love can be."

But as her hips lifted in welcome to his deepening thrusts and he nuzzled her neck in electric yearning while they both laughed, the questions *What if I can't open, be a woman for him?* and *Isn't this adoration wrong, perverse?* hung like veils, screening her feelings off.

No way to say anything. They cuddled close, yet even this serenity hid something true. When he squeezed her hand again, she responded only briefly. Yes, they'd found at least some closeness, and she must not risk prolonging it if they'd stay outside the false scenarios of dreams.

Later, half asleep, he turned to her, "I'm all right, you know. We'll bring them all home safe."

Near-record temperatures, days later, in the valley, fleas and smog in Berkeley, sleepless feverish heat on the vigil line. Light from the rising full moon shone on the hills and road. She sat on the ragged blanket with Ted, away from the others—Barry, Lee, Samantha, and two guys she'd not met before. One was a veteran pacifist called Richard the Tiger-Hearted, and the other, young with a short new beard, had been among the hecklers but tonight had come over and was helping Richard tune his guitar.

It was her first time back here since that night, over a week ago. She felt overwhelmed around these people, ashamed because, pregnant, she'd had to walk, twice this hour, to the "potty van" and pee, and abashed because these were people who had been here, day after day, as she had not. Yet now she was annoyed by their humorless discussion, their discordant guitar strings—!

Yet none of this was why she'd said "Let's go sit by ourselves." A hundred feet up the road, shimmering in the moonlight like something miraculous and dangerous, lurked that triangle, that dirt-and-gravel place of heroism. There—where he had been heroic and she . . . *though finally I did step forth, enough to be, perhaps, a bit heroic too.* There, where she'd felt . . . what? She could not remember, caught in fear.

Enough. Just be like these others, be simply here. Here, simply loving. Here, braving the trucks, braving fear.

"Ted, let's go. Ted, it's after midnight."

He stood, smiled at the guys tuning the guitar, and waved to Lee and Samantha. "Come on, kid, I'll take you home."

There were two worlds. The first was the vigil and Ted. The second was the unquiet home where heat and fleas never let up, nor her constant questioning. It sometimes seemed what could bring the worlds together was simple—a clarity, a space of silent calm away from the angry haze. Then these worlds could merge and the loving community be reopened for her; her love and this child would grow whole among these people. One night, a week after they'd sat beneath the moonlight of the Port Chicago roadside, Ted suggested they rent a house "with some of the others—we'll build a real community."

"Oh yes," she answered—and couldn't stop smiling. It was a rare city night of clear stars; they kept feeling giddy, joyous; something new seemed burgeoning. But when Ted, crying out, came inside her, she forced herself to hold back, calming her longing, until she felt sure the baby would be safe—and her feelings not too intense.

Afterward, Ted seemed near tears. In the morning, he kissed her and left for the vigil—where that triangle of earth would shimmer in the starlight with memories she mustn't approach; the roadside there had become a place she dared not go.

"Come out, I'll come get you," Ted said, the next time he called. She agreed—and then, realizing she could not be sure and her feelings might be perverse—she phoned him back, "I have to cover a rally tonight." Another evening—already a week had passed—Ted said a van was "bringing more people out to fill the line, they'll pick you up, kid," and, this time without even thinking, sure that her fear would close her in, "No," she answered, "I have to be here today and tomorrow." Then four days passed, then five, and when he phoned, it was to say he was busy struggling to hold the vigil together but, "soon as I can get a free day here, I'll come visit." Yes, he said, he'd been to town to pick up posters, "but I had to rush them back out there. Everyone was waiting."

One hot evening—again, five days later—she called from a phone booth in the Co-op Groceries parking lot, three blocks from her apartment. No word from Ted, and she realized he must be too caught up with Vigil House, that shabby farmhouse near Port Chicago where the vigilers were staying between nights on the line. After she'd asked, three times, "But is Ted there?" the young man who'd answered said he'd check. A grumpy voice, distant. Through the glass wall of the booth, she could see people walking past in the usual way, carrying groceries, chatting with friends.

"Hey, Ted isn't back, babe. Like, he drove Samantha and some folks—Lee, of course, and Rich, Jan, April, those folks—up to the mountains, get some R and R. Why?"

It was ten days later when Ted arrived. Nora went quiet: *I mustn't demand, but why didn't you take me, too? I'm trapped in town—you know that. Yet you haven't even called.* The thoughts filled her mind, tried to leap out, but they were petty—a childish voice; the real issue was she'd missed him. Besides, he had wanted her with him out there; it was she who'd held back. Now she'd have to say why she had—would have to say everything.

"Nora, tell me." Again he was asking, "What is it? What's wrong?" and saying again how glad he was, here with her. But not why he hadn't called. And he didn't keep watching her, not at all.

In the morning, over their instant coffee—she'd been too tired to go for groceries the day before—he said, but no longer laughing as if testing an idea, "The vigil's collapsing. It's coming apart."

"You don't mean that?"

"Yeah, but I do. Most the folks there these days are just grubbing a place to stay."

They stared—at each other, at the table, at the cat hopping from the window ledge to dodge the fleas. Saying "Hey, kitty," Ted stretched, reaching for his pack and the old rust-color scarf. "Guess I better get going, Nora. Kick some folks off the couch at Vigil House, see if anyone'll lift up a picket sign and walk the line. But"—for the first time this visit, his smile felt real— "we will stop this war. We'll change things. It *is* possible." She reached out a hand. His words had no sense of hope, though, and what was he speaking of besides the war?

"Yes," she said, and lowered her hand. Yet during the night, laughing on Ernie's squeaking bed, everything had seemed new and near, and she'd tried not to say "Wait."

5

The Other Side of Midnight

September-October, 1966

She lay on the purple bedspread. *Too difficult,* she was thinking, yet in fact finding a place without Ted's help had not been hard. The couch and her purple spread filled half the main room of the tiny cottage, but it really was a cottage and somehow—miraculously, she kept thinking—she'd found and rented it. It was quiet, affordable, an escape from the overheated sublet, somewhere where she and the cat—and the fetus—could be safe. Difficult? Maybe, but she'd done it.

Still, something was missing; there was some other way she needed Ted. *You promised to help me. You said you'd come back soon. I need you.*

Even though she'd managed just fine. She'd been walking to the Co-op to check the "for rent" notices but seen the sign across the street and crossed to look; she'd seen that the landlady was black and thought *Oh no, she'll never rent to me,* but tried; she'd expected the rent would be too high, but it was not; and she could bring the cat. *You were right, Ted—I can do more than I thought. Yes, help's not what I need from you—or not anymore.* Pregnant and alone, she'd found this home for herself—and for the baby.

Yet the longing for Ted remained. Clearly, shelter, food, safety—simple needs—were hardly the only needs. The vigil and baby and much else beautiful could live safely within her, but the sense of betrayal—and the doubts about her feelings—could destroy, even now, any chance of wholeness. And this fear too, its mental mazes, was dangerous.

Absorbed in thought, she almost missed the knock.

But the door wasn't locked Dumb to have forgot that, this late at night.

Ted stood there in the doorway. Could the Vigil House people have given him her address? It was two weeks since she'd phoned and left it with them.

"Now you come walking in"—not at all what she'd meant to say— "after letting me worry this whole time? Like I'm your whore, or something?"

"Nora. Nora, no."" Gray eyes sorrowful, he stepped forward. He reached to hold her. "No. No, I'm sorry. Truly."

Lips tight to not start sobbing, she stood stiffly, letting his arms enfold her.

"May I?" He gestured toward her pack of cigarettes on the stone ashtray. Lighting one, he sat on the far end of the couch. His glance took in the room. "Wow! Hey, this is a fine place. You talk like you're so helpless, but this is wonderful here. Look what you found yourself! I knew you could do it."

"Yep." She couldn't but smile in response. She, too, liked this cottage; she liked it very much. She laughed.

Then it surged through her—the *community*, the house he'd spoken of where they would all live together and care for one another—she and Ted and the vigil people and— *A place where the baby could be born, where everyone would love.* She burst into tears. "If your promises meant anything—!" Only no, this hadn't been the issue. No, certainly not. "You might at least have helped me move!" she heard herself cry. But that was not it, either. This was all wrong.

It was I who first held back, saying "Wait" whenever we'd start to make love, I who'd say "Not yet" when he'd ask I come with him back to the vigil.

And he didn't know she saw now past her own attacks and demands, and at this very moment was seeing past *this* anger. He couldn't know she saw more in him than he knew, or that she was more than those clingy words. Dumb, angry words that spoke the system's lines—words powered by a dumb anger that could not even say *I'd slap your face.*

Yet none of this was it. *Just hold me. I'd love you close.*

"I *would* have helped," he said. "I was worn out, out there, people needing so much. None of us were getting any sleep, the cops going nuts and smashing people, everyone on each other's case . . ."

"I see. I understand. It's all right."

"Yeah." He must have said something else, though, something she'd missed hearing, because all at once he was speaking of other things—dangerous things. "Not just the vigil," he was saying. "I've had it with Vigil House, with all of them. But that isn't it." He lit another cigarette.

She thought, *I knew this would come.*

"There's something else, Nora. I need to be alone. I've realized, the past few days, I need to get by myself and think about things. About what I'm doing. About everything."

"'Everything' meaning . . . like us?" She couldn't prevent it—something sharp and bitter came rushing out. "Now *you're* pulling that." She *did* have needs—real needs, simple or not. "You, too?"

"No." The embers of his cigarette sparked. "No. Listen, I promise you. I will be here for you." The gray eyes held hers, as if to soothe her pain. "I do care."

She could hear the seriousness. It dissolved her doubts. It made the anger and bitterness go away. He was here. At least in some ways. "But I, too, Ted. I care."

Just as you've cared, all along. Just as, out there, you've needed me. She laughed and cried out loud suddenly, not sure why, "Ted, come." Her voice deepened, "Come to me." He'd left the cottage door open, but at her tone he thrust it shut. She sank down on her knees on the round rug; running a hand through her hair. She leaned back against his legs.

"Hey, Nora, I do need you. You know that."

"Yes. Ted, I—" *I do need you.*

He too had knelt, and he turned her toward him. She reached to touch his face. Carefully, quickly, he rolled to one side and pulled her close. For many minutes, they lay still on the rug, gazing at each other, hands tightly clasped.

If I could tell you everything—

But this was no longer enough. Breathing harder, he sat up. He began to take their clothes off, tossing her tee shirt and jeans onto the floor, and then her nylon underpants, and dragging off his own dusty jeans and shirt. He pulled her over to the couch and briefly stood there. Then, "Hey, kid," he gasped, and, leaning forward, lowered himself upon her. She felt his slightly sweaty body, lean, taut, rough like the life they lived, hard against her own.

"Ted," she said, and his hands moved, fondling her breasts and abdomen, and, as she pressed herself against them, sliding to her groin. Hesitant, yet ready, she let her hands explore his body, too.

An hour—at least an hour—must have passed, she thought. Sheathed in an electric clarity, they moved together, shivering in this rediscovery of each other. Caught like with him in the new intensity, she watched his gray eyes yearning like her own. Around them, the dark cottage seemed to glow as if illuminated. "I need you, love," Ted cried, "I need you."

She was afraid again, but—it must have been from the truth in his words and the way, hearing their yearning, she desperately yearned for him—but, unable longer to hold back, her own truth cried "I need you, too. I do love you."

Hours later, Nora woke. Through the windows, three stars shone in the black sky. Her neck felt stiff, weighted by Ted's outflung arm. She slid forward, trying to free herself and sit up. His eyes opened. He cleared his throat.

"Hey, woman."

She snuggled toward him.

"We sure do have something real," he said, and laughed. "Guess that's pretty obvious."

Were those the stars in Orion?

"But, Nora"—he had cleared his throat again—"there's something you'd better know."

Then was it over, so soon?

"We have so much, we really do." He paused. "But look, it gets lonely sometimes out on the line. You know?" She heard his breathing change. "Okay. Hey, look, I slept with someone out there. Out at Vigil House."

Was that all? The relief was so sudden, she laughed.

"Nora?" In the dark, he was peering at her, expression so puzzled she laughed again. Suddenly he did, too. "Thank you. Nora, thank you for that."

She shook her head, giggling. "I mean it. Well, obviously."

"I didn't—wow, I didn't know you'd take it this way. You're a generous person, you know? And you're right to laugh. Because it's nothing. Nothing serious, like with us."

Obviously, again. Because, when two people love, why fear "rivals," as the system's clichés insisted? Sometimes people simply slept with people; it just happened—and was nothing. *It's me he loves.*

"Not like with us," he repeated. "Anyhow, she knows it's over. But I thought you've a right to know."

And she—? That woman too has rights.

But she laughed again. She felt a loosening from the system's bonds, a fearlessness, lifting her over the system's maze to see, if not a way out, at least that an *outside* existed.

In the morning, walking into the little kitchen, she found Ted sobbing at the sink. "You're such a good person," he said, "so good a person. I'm afraid I'll hurt you."

"You won't. You won't." *Men flee when they feel guilty.* "I'm fine."

But she wouldn't go back out to the vigil—and would try not to think of the community there, or of stopping weapons trucks, or of waiting again unsure of Ted's return. What she needed was to trust in his return—to trust him, trust his love. Besides, she could no longer force herself to the confrontations out there, confrontations with Marines but, even more, with her own fears and doubts. And she dared not risk the child in her body so much anymore.

There was work to be done here, besides—with the war still worsening. Her child and *all* children needed protecting.

In any case, forcing herself to the vigil from fear of "other women" would be absurd. If one loved caringly, reciprocally, nobody could "take one's man away."

"You think not?" It was the end of the *Barb*'s workweek. Sally and she had carried their tacos from the *Barb* kitchen out to the back yard. At the far end of the dandelion-filled lawn, Max's wife was playing with her daughters in a sandbox.

"See that?" Sally said. "That could be you, a year from now. I've been there." Her blond hair fell around her mouth. She bit into the taco. "Isn't it always what we go for? This lady out at your vigil, she's going for it too, be sure."

"But to love means not trying to possess. Mature love, I mean. If he loves me, then—"

Sally shook her head, bits of cheese and lettuce falling to her lap. "Uh-huh, have your ideals, sister. But what I advise—you be like a gardener. Tend that love."

"You mean, go back out there? Sally, I'm no help to him there—or to anyone, out on the line." Except that he needed her.

Sally lowered the taco to the paper towel on her lap. "You've missed my point. D'you ever read *Ladies' Home Journal*? Like, 'Coddle your man.' For real. Not necessarily out there, no, but, for God's sake, Nora, give him a break. Like, there he is, out on that vigil line week after week, trying not to get busted, sleeping on some dusty floor, and meanwhile trying to keep up everyone's ideals, including his own, and maybe it's just getting too much, too damn much, you know? But then finally it's Sunday night and, all worn out, he comes to you—and he's ready to be loved." Sally paused. "To be *loved*. And he gets to hear your self-analyses? Your complaints that he's not there enough?

"You know, some guys grab what they can, all that—but I don't think this one's like that. I think he cares for you. Would it really hurt you—would it really hurt, Nora, to fix him something other than macaroni and tuna for dinner? To shut up about *you* and let him talk about who *he* is. At whatever length he wants. And—well, you know very well—pregnant or not, you *do it*. You follow me? Your man needs comfort."

I know. Now might be too late.

In the yard, the girls were making a castle, not with sand but by piling blue and yellow blocks together.

"Mrs. LBJ to Attend S.F. Opera Opening September 20." The headline was on the front page of the *Berkeley Gazette*. She ran to the back-office phone.

"*Berkeley Barb* calling," she said. "What do you people have planned when Ladybird Johnson comes to the S.F. Opera opening? On the twentieth, yeah. Tickets are eighteen dollars. I checked, yeah. Fifteen for the balcony."

From the SDS office, a young man replied, "We do not just react"; the UCV, formerly VDC, had "other plans"; the AFSC—the Quakers— "will not go disrupting others' events." When she phoned San Francisco Agit-Prop, an old sounding woman answered, "yes—just write 'Yes.' Never mind how—we'll be there." Lowering the receiver, she joined Max and his friend Ed, one of the Young Socialist organizers, to plan tactics, moving back into the comradeliness of struggle, with its necessary judgments, a simpler task than being that vigil-self of caring and community.

But if, here, her work was limited, still the caring and community remained, out there. On September 20, she feared, these two worlds of hers might collide.

White lines and trespass signs, sirens and police—
the curious crowd outside the Opera House held more
wealthy than poor people, as many LBJ backers as
radical protestors; the police dared not attack. This was
neither Port Chicago nor Vietnam; this was civilized,
peace-ville; here many lines could be safely crossed.
Besides, whatever the risk of arrest, it was she who'd
catalyzed this demonstration, simply by making those
phone calls asking groups' leaders "What have you
planned?" So now it was up to her to discover where
Ladybird Johnson would arrive—whether through the
grand courtyard entrance, or up the front staircase, or
through the distant back door around the far corner of
the block.

Within the courtyard, hundreds of spectators
jammed together. Demonstrators, signs hidden under
jackets as they passed through the gates, slipped in from
the picket line across the street. Carrying three roses
given her by a little neighborhood girl, maybe eight or
nine, who'd seemed awed by her visible pregnancy and
pink Mexican dress, Nora entered the gates, stepping
with pointed firmness, as if to say "Here we are free," on
each white line.

Television crews and newspaper journalists had
crowded in with the rest. Squeezing her way closer to the
main door, she switched to an ultra-feminine stride, a
timidly mincing gait. She made her voice high,
breathless, sidled up next to the *Chronicle*'s silk-jacketed
society reporter.

"Ma'am, excuse me, please? The President's wife is
coming this way?"

The reporter had the majestic upper-class profile of
an elegant raptor. "That's correct."

"Soon, Ma'am? I'm supposed to babysit."

The hawk-eyes turned toward the ceremonial
archway. "Around 8:30, dear. That's what they told us.
Excuse me, please."

Unless the cops shift plans. Careful to keep mincing,
Nora forced a way back through the crowd, then out the

gate, rushed along the bright façade, hurried toward the white-lit avenue along the building's other side.

Running closer to the rear entrance, she could see Agit-Prop already there—and Benjamin, camera at the ready while he laughed with the troupe. Flinging out her information in a few staccato words, she didn't stop to talk more, or even look around, but, saying "Yeah—hey—hi," rushed away, hurrying back toward the main mass of picketers with her news.

Muffled in a red scarf, a picket captain, Mark's friend Erin, stood talking with two women. "Which is it—8:15 or 8:30?" he called out, "Oh, never mind—either's too soon," and began rushing demonstrators into a tighter circle. Then, "Okay, into the courtyard we go," he called, sending them jogging toward the gate. Two hundred strong, they crossed the busy avenue, stopping traffic and pressing on, into the crowded courtyard. She could see them, dark in the half-lit courtyard, lifting signs high— "Johnson Murderer," "Out of Vietnam!" "Bring the Boys Home Now;" mounted police came pressing forward on their trotting mounts, clubs uplifted, determined to force people back.

She followed the pickets forward, focused only on this moment. Ahead, bulbs flashed; the famous diva Joan Sutherland ascended the stairs. The *Chronicle* reporter, never raising her hawk-eyes from her writing pad, took notes. Thrusting through the crowd, a cop on a tall curvetting horse advanced up the drive, club raised.

"Hey, hey, Mrs. L B J—" But where was Ladybird? It must bc 8:15. *If I've messed this up . . .*

"—how many kids didja kill today?"

People pressed tight—too tight, too tight to move. And actually the handsome, snorting horse was bearing down directly on her, plunging from the darkness, prancing forward too fast.

By now, the time must be 8:30.

A beautiful horse, dark bay with a silvery blaze.

"Hey, hey—"

Bye, horsie. She slipped backward, shoved between two onlookers in fragile silk suits, and spun around, back toward the gate. The watch on the nearest wrist read 8:32.

No way now to get enough demonstrators to the other entrances ahead of Ladybird. No—better try. "C'mon," she shouted, gesturing to one group, five or six guys all standing together. "Don't cluster up like that. Come on!" But no one heard. At the sidewalk, she started to run.

"Nora." A hand grabbed her wrist. "Nora. Stop." Looking awkwardly formal in a suit jacket and cords, Lennie stood blocking her way. His free hand rested on his little wife's shoulder. Slowly his eyes focused on Nora's abdomen.

The far entrance again—I have to get back there. Now!

"You didn't abort?"

Yes, yes, I'm pregnant, I'm pregnant. Okay? "I have to go. Len, I do."

But at least his presence, his being here demonstrating tonight, meant they were reaching the liberals. Lennie demonstrating was totally out of character; it meant people were changing. It meant—

No matter; get to the other entrance. Len, let go my wrist.

"Jessica, meet Nora. My old college friend."

The blond woman smiled—*so sweetly though you know he's still half in love with me.* Voice soft, the sound almost lost, Jessica leaned closer. "If there's anything we can do, anything, please don't you hesitate to ask. We must get back to our daughters now, but please don't forget."

"Thank you." *Hurry, have to block Mrs. LBJ*—and that was far from the hardest confrontation. Because maybe—surely—Ted had arrived. He would be here somewhere; somehow, she would have to force her own barriers aside, find a way to tell him, finally.

She pulled away and broke into an awkward run.

Only, everything was over.

Because, even if Ted was around, somewhere here on this corner where the wooden stage rested, under a single spotlight, beside the building's backdoor entrance and people milled confusedly in the dark, it would not be possible—too rushed, too many words—to say it all. To say that she, who had not risked danger night after night, felt proud love when she recalled his heroism, yet still feared her love might be shameful or unreal. And so on and on then she would go, talking of "the trap," of judging, of a thousand words to say that she must ask, first, for his permission and be—no, not forgiven but, perhaps, understood—before she could rejoin him at the vigil and be with him there, caring, saving lives. Impossible to say all this, certainly not here amid this crowd and her own tumult—not possible here even to say she understood now and she *would* give more. Besides, she had to somehow get people back here, sneak them in toward this half-hidden back door to block Ladybird.

No, that too was no longer possible.

Peering into the spotlit corner, she recognized what must have happened. Only Agit-Prop—and Benjamin and a few vigil people, with the dozen or so pickets who'd heeded her shout and raced this way, had been there when the Secret Service, changing course, had brought Ladybird in through this back entrance.

But that *Chronicle* reporter had been sure—sincere, trying to help a naive young woman. *If I just hadn't told the picket captain to move people to the courtyard.*

In front of her, the Agit-Prop troupe were laughing in triumph. In no great hurry, they were taking down the stage, while, across the wide street, two people in the Port Chicago van kept revving the engine, shouting it was time for Ted to come drive them back to the vigil, their voices distinct and hearty. On the single step beside the stage, Benjamin was happily lowering flashbulbs and film into his leather case, wearing the big smile that meant he'd scored a scoop.

Except, when he saw her, the smile turned strange. Glancing up, then peering toward the bare wooden stage, she suddenly made out Ted, his eyes beaming with laughter, the rust-gold scarf draped elegantly around his neck. He was lifting an armload of costumes across one arm, and his other arm was wrapped tight around Lee's shoulders, his hips and hers lightly touching as they smiled into each other's eyes. On the street, the van engine roared again. Sandwich wrappings crinkled and skittered underfoot.

"You—you and Lee!" Nora heard her own voice screech, tight with tears. *Screeching like that goddamn raptor reporter's.* "You and Lee? 'Oh Nora, I understand now'—sure. What about goddamn human caring?" With the half-running, half-waddling stride she'd been using all evening, she rushed to the wooden stage. Clambering up, she raced across. Lee and Benjamin stepped back; Ted stood still, just gazing at her. Hard, decisively, she drew her right hand back, slapped him hard.

Too late. And now it really was too late.

Except—except, as she hopped back off the stage, "What is it?" he cried out, and, turning, she saw him reach, stretching forward, toward her. "Nora, it's not what you think. And there is—damn it, there's something else going on with you. What? Love, tell me. This is not only about—" *All right, all right. But I can't.* For a moment, she stood, wanting to soothe him. To undo her anger, undo her constant hesitations of those first weeks, make the slap go away—undo everything gone wrong.

Ted had knelt down and bent forward at the edge of the stage, leaning toward her, and she reached to stroke his hair. "Tell you? I can't tell you."

"I know, Nora. I do understand. And I know you're not bothered about Lee. But truly, she and I, we're just friends. Just friends." Only, then he was saying other things, things that made no sense. "You're such a good person, Nora, be proud, you can do so much, you care so much. But somehow, however it was, somewhere you lost your confidence. And you need confidence."

She was shaking her head, her whole body trembling. Trembling with anger, shaking at the trite, *trite* line. "'Confidence.'" She laughed the word.

"No, Nora. Love, I need you."

But the whole gap was crashing open, a hole in the starless night sky. She spun away.

"Come back, love—come with me tonight. To the vigil."

Any gap can be leaped; it really can.

She raised her eyes, wishing she could make this possible. "Not yet. Ted. Soon."

"Well, don't be worrying about not halting Ladybird. You made her pay attention." Sally stuck a gold-white card, "ACE ACTIVIST!" on Nora's desk. "You made that whole gilded city pay attention. And I wouldn't worry about the little Valkyrie; she's a convenience for him."

Nora shook her head; she went back to typing her copy. At least she'd instigated a solid demonstration and could write it up. Five hundred people on five days' notice. That was her lead, as if there'd really been a victory and not a farce. She forced out another page, then wrote about the flowers.

She had carried the flowers that a little girl had given her. Except one flower, which she'd put in her hair—there had been no chance to hand any to Ladybird. Or to Ted, for that matter. She'd protected the child in her womb from the crush, but the flowers had got smashed in the crowd's initial charge into the courtyard.

"The pickets chanted," she finished the story. "The Agit-Prop sang. Ladybird could hear the protest even from inside. She bore no living flower."

In the fog of the bluff above Agate Beach, near those rocks sometimes called the Gates of Eden, Ri had reached across and placed a yellow flower in my hair.

"I need you," Ted had said. *I love you, too,* she would reply.

"Your information was correct." In the evening, over cheeseburgers at Si's, Benjamin kept grinning. "See, they changed plans, that's all. I happened to be standing right by a squad car—just happens, you know—and happening to hear the radio calls, and they were saying, 'Guys, we got a whole mess of pickets in there, better bring the old lady in through the back.'" He took another bite. "I don't get it, Nora. You did great. And with Ted, too—you were cool. Is it absolutely required to pick yourself to bits?"

6

The Leaving

October 1966

Not yet one o'clock, and already the day was smoggy with Indian summer heat. She stood, chain-smoking, in the cottage doorway.

Since the Opera House, Ted had visited only once. "I need you, Nora. Maybe we *can* work things out, after all"—the words had seemed rote, but surely only from her self-doubts, or from fearing Lee. But he'd also said, "I don't want to hurt you," almost as if in warning.

No, she needed to escape this—these constant thoughts, this sense of helplessness and betrayal, of shame and worthlessness. There was something or someplace she needed to find, for her own life and the baby's.

But soon Ted would be here. The night before, she'd phoned Vigil House and he'd answered, "I'm coming into town tomorrow—what if I pick you up? Maybe we can finally get to the beach." *Sometime after lunch,* he had said; it was silly to expect him this soon. She lit another cigarette.

At 3 o'clock, she opened a second pack.

After another two hours, the sun nearing the horizon, her anger bubbled over. *As if this stupid despair would tear into everyone who's helped create it, tear in and force me to give up, and . . .* The thought had no ending. *Ted, we could be somewhere by the water, in white snow, in a place of beauty; we can still love.*

Or were there no solutions? For a woman like her—pregnant, frightened, knowing that any fear or loss might thrust away what she'd learned with Ri—could be any resolution? Or would there be instead nobody who truly cared, no giving persons, but only the functionaries and the murder-trucks and green Marines, forcing anger to overwhelm hope?

Don't overdramatize. She stubbed out the cigarette. Yes, stop this childish melodrama. Problems never came only from others. Locking the cottage door behind her, she started to walk. The streets were baking, even in October.

As the first cool of evening fell, she started down the gravel driveway, climbed the steps to the back porch. What few flowers remained hung, dry and brown and crinkled, from the vines overhead. She knocked—a moment later, heard the turning knob.

And was sorry to have disturbed him. Ri moved like someone who'd not slept, and his gaze looked preoccupied, almost anguished. *But can I help at all?*

He said, "Come in." He stretched out a hand. Not near enough to touch—but that was good, she thought.

He had pulled out the old velvet chair beside his table. "Here, come sit here, Nora. It is good to see you."

She felt immersed in the peace around him, the *way* he cared. And he understood her as Ted did not. But if she gave in to the peace, let go the urgency . . . But this was not the problem; the problem was she'd come uninvited. "I cannot stay long," she said. "How are you?"

I cannot go on. No, don't say that. It would be absurd—another childish drama, *not-me.* She had come unasked, and she mustn't ask help from him. What she wanted was not that. Better to be quick, direct. "I am pregnant, you see. It doesn't show yet, but, see, I don't dare do anything. And I need to find something—I don't know what. You know? But I need to. It's silly.

"I am scared."

"Of course you are." He sat down on the chair across from her. "Anyone who's pregnant. Tell me how to help."

Leave him alone.

On the table, two letters and a document lay open next to a tiny leather box. Something was wrong, she could see the anguish in his eyes, and she didn't know what it was or how to help. How distant his life was from her now.

"Tell me," he repeated. "I'll do anything."

She squared her shoulders. "It's strange. Have you been out to Port Chicago?"

"No. I should have, but I've had to work."

Only, she'd meant something else, deeper. "Because I saw a glimpse there—a glimpse of a way to be. I saw it before, once. Remember when you took those kids to the beach, how you were with them and how happy it made them? Out at Port Chicago, I've seen it, what people give. I've seen such wonders. But when things have been so ugly here . . . Ri, I mustn't lose that glimpse. To care the way people there care, the way you do. I *will* not lose this—I *will* not lose what I've found."

He half-stood, leaning toward her. "Don't you know, here people are always saying 'Change yourself,' as if what's wrong must be in us? Nora, you *do* love. You won't lose this." Gently, he squeezed her shoulder. "So. Let me pour us some wine. We can rest quietly awhile."

Later, descending the steps, she realized the air was clearer; the evening star shone. They had spoken of the war, spoken of a researcher's fight against the draft, of a former friend "shot in our second revolution." She had nodded, tried not to cry, and patted Ri's hands.

"If you need anything, I'm—" he had said, walking with her down the driveway.

The peace had been there, each minute. Ri *would* have helped if she'd asked. Maybe this was all she'd needed to find.

But, the next morning, news came to the *Barb* office of a baby left in a deserted daycare, an old man dwelling in a downtown trash lot, another village "saved" by bombs; she thought really no one had actually done a thing for anyone—or not enough. *And Ted? I guess he forgot. Used me, with his usual promises and vanishings. Banking on me to not make any hassle.*

No, was that really it? She mustn't get sucked back into such judging. Yet Sally's comment was too reassuring, "The man's way overextended, but he cares. He wants you." Maybe—she could test it. *Be* mature; phone Ted not to ask anything of him but instead to say "I will come out there again. I'll stand with you."

So, that evening when she called from the Co-op parking lot and heard his voice, she let her own go husky. "It'd be so good to see you, love. It's been so long."

His deepened in response. "Tomorrow, then? We do need this—we both do. I'll be there."

Nora sipped from a glass of water. Waiting for Ted, she had flea-sprayed the cottage a second time, standing outside the door afterward to protect the fetus. The cat clung to her footsteps, mewing. She set out a fresh bowl of water, saying "Kitty, good kitty." She would have to spray the fleas again soon; people lately were saying bug sprays could harm fetuses, but they didn't really know.

Overhead, the sun glowed, a too-hot ball.

And if my anger, too, has flared, "banked-up," extreme—or if there's been no change in me, if even our community has hardened, and I bring this child into a world that can't be loving, where people betray each other—! The sunlight merged with the question in the glowing haze, the violence of ordinary denial spilling into old nightmares of The Bomb. Across the narrow walkway beside the cottage, the wooden fence ran toward the street. *And if that sun becomes a monstrous ball of fury, flaming above and rolling down to smash them all—them all, dammit! —Ted and Lee and Daniel, David and Murph and Sally and the lady with the plum beside the road, and yes, even Ri, all of them and their betrayals—you whom I trusted, you people I've loved!*

No. It wasn't true. Those were lies. She clasped the glass of water. She didn't really want to kill anyone, not at all—only to break something, though she didn't know what, some barrier. Leaving the door open to dissipate the bug spray, she sat, exhausted, on the couch.

She was asleep when Ted arrived. He half-stumbled on the doorstep; she saw dark circles of weariness ringing his eyes. His hair hung lank, he wore no scarf, and his clothes were stained and wrinkled.

Briefly, he embraced her. Briefly, seating himself on the couch beside her, he smiled. But nothing was the way she had expected. Reaching into his jeans pocket, he pulled out a cigarette. He carefully lit it. The time had come, he said; he didn't meet her eyes. "I've finally understood, Nora. It took me too long a time to realize, but I have. And I don't want to pretend with you. You are too good a person."

"'Don't want to pretend' *what?* You've realized *what?*" Only of course she knew. And knew—even as she struggled to light a cigarette, her hands shaking—that she needed, immediately and more than anything, *a way to fight.* To fight what was coming, what was clear from his downcast eyes. *A way to fight back, to not be defined away, as I was by Dave and Murph. To define—equally to define—our reality.*

"You've been right, Nora; you have. This isn't working."

I don't want to be right—not about this.

"I really thought we had something." He let the ash fall to the ashtray. On his right hand, he still wore the white-silver ring—*like a flash of hope.* The thought made her grin, but he didn't look up. "But out there now, it all goes on and on, and I'm worn out; we all are. And—okay, I haven't said anything to you, but there've been days I— well, just hung out in my room and worried about you. So what I've been thinking is this. Are you the person I want to spend my life with? Am I, for you? Because, if not, we better seriously—I mean seriously—think do we want to go on with this."

But why is he saying this stuff—Ted, who's cared for people he doesn't even know, who reaches out beyond what's possible, who doesn't give in? "Why are you throwing away how we care for each other? You're putting bounds—like, who should we worry over, what is their role, for exactly how long?" She forced a laugh. "You're joking?"

He shook his head. "I thought we had something going, kid. I know we did. But I was wrong—it couldn't last."

"But *why?*" No point to these words.

He kept speaking and she barely heard. At some point, he said "What you need—I've thought about this— is confidence. I know what that sounds like, but think about it."

"Sure. For how long?" She couldn't resist the line, though everything was hurting. Only, she should have said something else, something to show him "confidence" was just a word, a way to toss her off, and his decision mistaken—because he kept repeating that he'd been wrong, that 'what went wrong' had been his fault, and, again, that he feared he would only hurt her, "I understand it now, Nora. I told you, once, I had a dream of something beautiful. I still believe it's true—we *do* care about everyone." He pulled a cigarette from the dwindling pack but put it down unlit. "But you and I, we're not in that dream together. We're not together, out there. You know that too."

But we can be. We can, now. Only, to say this, she would first have to tell him—

His hand made a stroking motion beside her face—a lilting, loving, tender motion. "We've talked about so much, you and I, and you feel so much for people, and, believe it or not, I really care about you. And I'll try to help you through your pregnancy, I promise you. But, if you thought there was more"—again he glanced toward the doorway— "you must have misunderstood."

Her throat hurt from smoking; her hair hung in tangles down her back. But she straightened. "Misunderstood *what?* The English language?"

No! No, *this* was the moment to struggle to define truth, to not let it be defined away; she must stay calm, cut sharp and clear. Fight back, but directly. She had to, and quickly. "You listen. Listen, Ted—and don't give me garbage. Misunderstood you *how?* Like, somebody told me that once, last year, somebody who had reason to, but *you*? No, I don't think so."

Because, whatever had happened with Ri, Ted had loved her—*and that does give me grounds to stand on. It does.* Even if "rights" did little good. "You people, you people"—only, her voice was starting to get shrill, she could hear it take a wrong turn, veer off from the true, hard struggle, and she mustn't get splintered this way, reduced to a babbling child. "You people!" But she couldn't stop. "You people! You people don't really care, you destroy whoever's different"—on and on. A child's voice.

He was looking down, twisting his hands. She realized he'd taken her words seriously.

"I don't believe that's true, Nora." He took her hand. "Some of us care."

"Then why—?"

"I know you care for me. I wasn't sure, for a while there, but now I am. But—"

"'But' what? What? Or 'who,' maybe? Maybe 'Lee'?" She looked into his eyes. Eyes that for a moment gleamed with humor.

"Good lord. Lee's a friend. You know how it is, out at the house there. We're just friends."

She peered again into his eyes, gray eyes that did not see what she saw. *Remember, you were going to show me something beautiful? We still need to find it.*

Because, though it seemed too late, still there was something—he was right—that she needed that could fight, that did not have to ask permission or offer explanation but could confront, and keep confronting, *as if with a right to,* what she must. She had to find this "something"; it greatly mattered.

And no, it is not "confidence." With a harsh laugh, she turned to say so, but there was a sharp meow. The cat had come over to them, tail lifted high. But when Ted, saying "Hey, kitty," reached over to pet it, it scurried from the room. They heard it in the kitchen, lapping water.

"People are expecting the van out there," Ted said.

"'But' what, Ted? You didn't finish. You said, 'I know you care for me, *but*.' 'But' what?" The tears weren't helping.

But he, too, looked close to crying—crying *with* her, she supposed. "It's not just you or me," he said. "All of us, we're getting used up. Not only from the war. I don't know how we help each other, anymore, I really don't. I thought I could, for you—well, be what I'm not, or not look down the road, I guess." He hugged her hard. "I wanted to show you so much."

Once, seeing him hug Juliet on a heat-hazed road, she had shared in the caring community. Now she didn't know, wiping away tears, if they were hers or his. Once, there'd been connection; they'd all felt together, natural as children, caring for everyone.

"We do want to help people," he was repeating. "You do—I've seen you. You're scared and you're pregnant, but you keep coming out to fight. So—why, Nora?"

She lifted her head, hearing his real question. "I've not been out there for you much, have I?"

"As much as you could. I know that. You're a caring person, a good person. And I"—he shook his head— "am not."

"That!" She'd been sitting by him forever, she thought, but she jumped up. "*That!* Ted, of all things, *that* is just not true."

She wasn't sure how long they'd sat there. "Well, that van needs a new distributor cap," he said, rising to his feet. "And I said I'd get it back out there by dinner time." He put out his cigarette. "Nora, I know you think discussing stuff traps people, but I don't. I believe it *can* get through."

"Get through?"

"Through our barriers. There've been so many barriers between us, but, you know, we crossed quite a few."

To respond truly, to say "I'm still here for you," she *would* have to say everything, define a path for them both. Still, she had to try. "We both care."

He was pulling the van key from his pocket. "Yeah. We've been out there together. And you've fought so hard." He stared down at the key. "I really did need you." *And when you did*—but it was she saying this, not he— *too often I wasn't there.*

This time he hadn't said "Maybe things *can* work between us" or "I'll show you something beautiful." But there was this other form of caring love, and, if he couldn't be everything he'd promised, still he kept reaching out.

And no, I didn't misunderstand, not in the least. She walked him out into the sunlight; they clasped each other's hands. *But never mind—and no way anymore.* As they hugged, she whispered "You'll be all right," just as he said "You will get through."

Closing the front door, Nora stepped inside. She could have urged, "We still love. Let's keep trying," she knew. But again, saying the words required the *something*, whatever it was, she'd not yet found. Besides, this time it really was too late.

Part IV
Time of Changes

1

Aquatic Park

Late October, 1966

She needed to tell Ted, but the words had to be ones that could get through. She kept starting over—really should just stay home and think it through. But she was running out of paper; heading up Telegraph Ave to meet Lennie for lunch, she stopped at the dime store and bought a small notebook.

"Ever since you phoned," Lennie began, speaking around the roast-beef-on-marbled-rye special, "Jessica's been saying 'Get that woman outside. She needs to forget that jerk and take care of herself and her child.'" He wiped his mouth with one of the café's huge paper napkins. "Funny about marriage, Jess and I are like one person now, it's weird. But here's my puzzle. See, I can understand you with Ri, of course, but, Nora, I met Ted out there, you know, and—I mean, you can argue rings around him."

"Wrong. Besides, you're being elitist. Mistakenly." She swallowed a bite of her sandwich. The food was too heavy here, not good for the fetus. "So you've been out there, then—to Port Chicago?" Usually, liberals like him just gave donations.

"I was curious."

Because it affected her? She raised her eyebrows.

"Far more than curious. It's what I told Jess—my work's important, I won't stop doing math, but something's got to be done about this, too. Marching gets nowhere, and there's no congressman I've written to can give a reason we're in the war. No sane reason." With one hand, he conducted a nervous tune. "But you think writing those guys is entirely dumb, right? They don't hear, they won't act, and so on?"

"Well, yeah." She shrugged, relieved he was talking politics. "Isn't that obvious?" Talking with Len was distracting, at least, but she watched him as through glass, anxious to leave.

And on the way home, walking through Faculty Glade, where oaks shaded a creek beneath a high stone bridge, she stopped, attracted by the silence, and lay down on the grass. Since Ted had left her—barely a week, it felt longer—she would wake each day intending to phone him out at Vigil House but not knowing what to say. She would decide instead to "get practical"—phone doctors and adoption agencies—but then start crying. Sometimes it seemed she'd always been waiting—for Ted, for David, Ri, someone—through months and years. And meanwhile there were the heat and fleas, fear and, too often, anger. And now this other, growing fear of what might happen, fear of labor and delivery. *Child, I want something better than this for your legacy.*

Watching the sun low in the west, she remembered the hazy hot ball, the fury ball. *Then let it roll, that sphere! I'll roll it, murderous and huge. I'll write the FBI, inform Ri's boss, snatch David's gun. I'll roll up every article the* Barb's *afraid to print, the words I can't tell Ted—finally, finally say the unsaid—pack them in one mega-orb of light and sound—*

And let it roll—a plague upon their houses. Smash!

See, "Smash"? She couldn't help smiling. The grass here was soft and cool and, after all, a metaphor was only that—feelings, even "banked-up" bursting feelings, just didn't explode. Besides, what she wanted to destroy was only *what came between*—between Ted and herself, between a Vietnamese peasant woman and the slightest safety, between the people who were attacked and those who would rescue them, between the "prisoners of the city" and the rock-strewn beach. If she could only break through these bars between the people who longed, if she—she and Ted together, she and a whole community—could as the folksong had it, tear down the walls.

She remembered the white light in the fog, that first afternoon at the beach, when she ran to Ri through a cresting wave. Swift through that crest, the water no bar. "The bars between," the walls between—words she watched glisten while she lay on the grass. Words that glistened like the shining feathers of a jay bird on the nearest cedar. Glistening as each person glistened in their many facets—no, their different "selves," their *personas*, each bounded by its warped-glass globe of ways to see, to understand, to act. Child-selves, workday selves, *giving* selves—each a globe bounded by refracted thoughts, by echoing words proclaiming "no" "no entry,"—by, that is, its own verbal green Marines, its mental barricade. Glittering selves, these were—forms, chimeras—but they veiled hopes, bounded what was called possible. Shiny, shiny, crystal globes, yes, glinting like these narrow sun-shafts striking between the clustered trees around the glade, sparkling on cresting waves . . . *Wait, I'm thinking in my sleep. Yet how this light can soothe.*

Even without him. See, there a woman moves, glides from the trees, dances through the leafy circle with her little boy, stands by the creek and holds his hand. I must—oh, wake up! Wake up, it's late, it's getting cold.

On the way home, she thought what she should write in the little notebook. She needed to tell Ted why their love was still possible, but if she could not say it fully, he might not understand. "Yes, each of us waits in such a crystal globe. The problem is to know that breaking the globes will not break what is warm and beautiful inside—to see that there is strength and love in the other, not confuse the fragile, veiling crystal with a person's self." Surely he would comprehend; she only needed to show him these words. Carrying the notebook, she walked to the kitchen for a cup of water. The water glistened, light swirling behind the porcelain's translucency. To *break through* required, then, not fearing to break the globes, not withdrawing, not being crushed by another's limits or one's own—required standing up, instead, to whoever said "It is too late," "You're wrong," "You must have misunderstood." She watched the water bead along the cup. "Even if that person's you, Ted."

But over and over, the same problem. To stand firm, to break through, she must first be whole, trust the strength and love in the other—*or else be nothing, silent in my cold-space globe.*

Two days later, she took the F bus to San Francisco, and a cable car to the wharves. White, clear light surrounded everything, the ocean breeze sharp with salt. On the shore in Aquatic Park, eight old men and women hunched in a circle around a bonfire, like yet another group maintaining a vigil. The oldest man, with thick white hair, invited her to share their days-old bread, extending the loaf in one hand. She started to shake her head, hearing the cycling inner warnings, "dirty," "dangerous," but stepped up to the man and tore a small piece from the loaf, eating as she sat with them and watched them pass a gallon of red wine around. When she rose to leave, the white-maned man said, "My dear, your pregnancy is beautiful." She smiled at him, blushing.

The waves were shallow here, the Bay's green water flashed with gold in the sunset. Where the low waves swelled near the sand, she walked barefoot, swinging her sandals vaguely to their rhythm. Seagulls glided past, circling and circling; a pelican flew above and peered down, head to one side. *You see, Ted, I could get here, I can find some beauty, on my own.*

Before heading home, she began skimming the book she'd brought, *The Hero with a Thousand Faces,* that so many hippies were reading; "Who bars the trail becomes, when you ask the right question," she read, "the guide who points you to the grail."

But of course they're not real persons, only conjured shadows from the past, who bar my path. And what she needed to confront now were not shadows, not theories, or even Ted's denial or the war, but her life, her whole life—and decisions yet to come. Like, decisions about the child. Only, to confront these decisions, she had to discover that same "something" that she needed for confronting others' definitions so she might define her world and so might . . . No, the thoughts had no end. As if not even a crystal globe but a hard, encircling mental wall, indeed like a line of Marines or *like, even, our own lines holding me back with warnings "You'll endanger someone!"*

Like the "No!" of all the world.

And yet she'd sat with these people here, shared their bread. She looked around; they had left. The beach was emptying, stars already shining in the water.

Riding home, she opened the notebook again. Important to keep the letter simple, avoid having to "say everything first" or trying to convince him—of *what*? Surely it wasn't to him she wrote, anymore. And surely, that "something" she needed, something that could break through the encircling barriers of "self"—shames, guilts, refusals, and those same barriers in others—wasn't just "confidence," but something deeper, much deeper—a *core*. Without it, she hadn't the force to break through—not through all the inner and outer barriers in Ted or herself or those whom the song called "masters of war."

The notebook filled, and the weather stayed unseasonably hot. Neither with an end in view.

But whatever the core, one thing she knew. All those barriers or walls or obscuring crystal globes, or whatever she might call them, came from shames—old bodily shames and later shames about her feelings, like when she'd believed, running across the road in the television lights toward Ted that night, that *she'd be seen as some sadistic castrator trying to possess him.*

And so a few days later she picked up a new book, *On Shame and the Search for Identity,* in the Co-op's book nook and eagerly scanned its pages. It spoke of two sorts of guilt, "a socially constructed and constricting" guilt versus "a natural remorse that warns us of needs we have overlooked," but mostly it spoke of shame—"usually a learned response. Behind any shame, and especially when we are *most* ashamed, may hide what, if we look further, is most natural, even beautiful."

Reading, she reached for a cigarette; her elbow skimmed her abdomen.

She put the cigarette down. She would wait five minutes—no, ten—before taking another. She read on.

It was two weeks since Ted had left.

Behind each shame may hide what is most natural and beautiful.

2

Clarity

End of October, 1966

Too easy. There must be a mistake.

It was the very end of October, and the week before, despairing of Ted's love, she had written a mock epic, *a wee musical for you folks out there, Ted,* she'd laughed, *so take that!*

> 'Way on the road out of Concord town
> Holding up signs as the war trucks bore down,
> Folks ceased to breathe as their hero stepped forth,
> —for the trucks would not stop, nor hope e'er be thought,
> And the cry "No!" resounded—yet forward he leaped
> With a love full and deep as had not yet been reached—

But no. She'd realized even as she wrote, this was not an action to be mocked. Not at all.

And meanwhile, in the countryside around Khe Sanh, half-grown children were being rounded up for interrogation and men and buffalo died among the rice stalks. On the vigil line, new signs read "Napalm = Auschwitz," and four truck drivers were rumored to be "reconsidering their jobs."

One evening she realized she felt happy, and the next day she woke at dawn, laughing. Because there it was. The "something" she must find was not in a book, did not come in a wise friend's or some ancient guide's voice, would not take more long months of learning, but, *like a cartoon lightbulb going off,* suddenly was obvious—*there* in a moment's clarity. There all along, but seen now at a clearer angle, like a painting obscured for years by critics' "renovations" until, in this moment of realization, all those "improvements" painted by society dissolved, and she could see with clarity the brightness that had always been there. The yearning love, the longing to protect, those feelings that men whom she'd loved had called "castrating," "angry," *perverse* "enjoyment," or desire for mere clichéd dreams—defining her away and leaving her in shame and crashing her world—these feelings *were* the grail. Were the core. She knew now. The core was *herself*, these feelings, this love. This self, bound by no rules, defined by no voices of others, determined by no others. This self, this depth not only in her, but in everyone—this need, this yearning, this love.

And, once seen, all this was obvious. The grail, the answer. Self-doubts shredded, crumbled like leaves in a forest windstorm, dissolved like obscuring mist that falls away. But if she'd not gone to Aquatic Park, not read the particular chapter of Lynd's book on shame and guilt, would she have found her way? Or if she hadn't invited Lennie over, trying to be kind to him?

"We're keeping an eye on you while you're pregnant" Len had said, first thing on arriving, that afternoon. "That's what we've decided, like it or not."

"It's kind, Len," she'd made herself say, hoping she could avoid getting irritated with him. "I'll have to go out and make a phone call in about an hour, by the way."

"So get a phone, here. Better you be able to call out, even if you do get harassments. Jess says 'She doesn't get it. Pregnancy's not all that safe.'" He was waving his hands around like desperate to hug her.

A big mistake to have told him about the harassing calls "That's not the issue. I'll have to go out in an hour. As I said. But we can talk until then."

He was staring at her bare feet. "While you spare me an hour from your serious thinking? You know, I went through that stuff once. Lying around theorizing the real world."

With me, you mean? She pulled out a cigarette.

"With Jessica. When she said to wait, I thought I wasn't yet a man." Then he looked flustered.

She gave him a wan smile; they'd known each other for so long. "Len, you want some apple juice?"

Later, as they were finishing the juice and her cat slept on Lennie's lap, she said, "There's something these people at the vigil know that—that, if I understood, I wouldn't have to give in, either. Not to those Marines, not to cops." She paused. "Not to guys, either."

Len laughed out loud; the cat stretched in its sleep.

But Len's eyes were going tender. This whole discussion wasn't fair to him, wasn't fair to Jessica; he should leave, and she should tell him to. Instead, she took a deep breath. "What I mean is, if I had this— whatever it is—I too could define a self, I too could 'never give in.'"

He was wiping his glasses. "Isn't this a bit reductionist? 'If I had this key, then I'd have it'?"

How safely phrased, and how beside the point, just like back in college. She stepped over and lifted the cat from his lap. "This kitty's not very happy. Since we moved, she acts sick."

"Take her to a vet." He put the glasses back on. "That's what I mean. Check out your cat, Nora. Go buy a maternity dress. Instead of this seeking-the-key stuff."

"But there *is* some key. I'm getting close, you see."

"Close to what?" He drained the last drops in his juice cup. "Some internal essence that others have and you mysteriously don't?" His gaze still softened the harsh words. She handed the cat back again; it purred ecstatically. Soon she really should make a phone call, and she ought to go to the Co op; fresh juice and protein were important now; perhaps, too, she *would* phone Ted from the parking lot. Was he all right—was he safe? She said, "It's a question of knowing something in oneself—of *recognition.* Clearing out old veils and finding something—something we all have, maybe. I don't know, Len—some worth in us so it doesn't matter if we lose everything."

He was stroking the purring cat very slowly, his other hand conducting, fingers vibrating too fast to see. He raised an eyebrow, perhaps unconsciously.

She stepped into the kitchen, filled two glasses with water, and brought him one.

"I'm not being cynical, Nora."

"Yeah, just being rigorous." She gave a short, rueful laugh. "Me, too."

"But look at what you're proposing, dear. Our *veritable* natures? Our deepest, innermost needs, some core of lovable inner *essence* waiting for discovery?" Trying for sarcasm, his voice trembled. "There's nothing like seeking human nature. But it's a long way from deducing a proof, you know. I'd feel better if you'd look for a gynecologist."

She set her glass on the window ledge. There was no safe way to show Len she heard his care and honored the gift in his love, but she needed to; he needed her to.

And then, a moment later, she recognized—understood—his gift to her. Because that *was* the issue, exactly what he had just said. Wasn't it precisely what she'd been thinking—that there was a core that she needed to find—and that this core was her deepest feelings, those feelings choked by guilt and hidden by shame. But those feelings—wouldn't they be the ones always there during her loneliness when she'd waited for Ted's return, here in the silent cottage—those yearnings to be back with him and the community and holding him again? Those yearnings deeper than any fear or anger or helplessness she'd felt—just the longing to be back there, simply loving him, loving them all. Maybe, then, this longing, holding firm when other feelings vanished, was her deepest self—this deepest feeling, her "core"?

She thought it likely was. And yes, some "lovable inner essence," if Len wished to call it that.

She knew she was smiling. It was as if she had sensed, like some caring leader of a people, or a mother holding her own child—love, beneath all despair and anger, whole and reaching—love, with its tears that were simply the need to give love. To give love, yes—for this innermost, longing love was not at all distinct from—was the very same as—the outer circle of giving love that she had sought so long to reach. "Mother and child," she said aloud—meaning the one who asked love and the "giver" were not distinct but were one.

"What?" Len looked over at her strangely. Yet every bit of this came from what he had said, thinking it a joke, a silly concept of "essence."

If in fact any of this was true. Because—wasn't it too obvious; how could it be so simple? Or else it was.

You're right on this much, Len—it's nothing like solving a proof.

And then she was looking at her couch. There, right there on the purple spread, was the place where Ted had said "I need you," and she had yearned, yearned so much, toward him. This was what love was—needing his need, he needing hers . . ., the longing sexual, emotional, overwhelming, enclosing them, feelings merged, inseparable.

See, this is what I meant, Len—Ted—people. Love mirrors love; love that would give, and love crying its need to give love, are the same.

And the clear reflecting pool of memory, when she'd been alone here longing so deeply for Ted and for the others, had so purely reflected, then, her gladness when someday she would again be on the line with them, each caring for the others. *Like a mountain pond reflecting the blue-pink sunrise sky, so these needs reflect each other,* she thought, *the needs to receive and to give love reflect, each the same, in infinite mirroring.* And, if this was true . . .

"Nora, you all right?" Len had taken a long step toward her. Too close, but he took a sudden step back. There was a *meow!*

"Sorry, cat." He jerked his foot away.

"You're not scratched?"

"We're both fine." He wiggled his fingers at the crouching cat.

"You see, it's the very same," she whispered—meaning reaching and caring, and taking the cat up in her arms— "and in everyone. Love is."

But Len flung her an I-gotcha look. "Then I guess it's in you too, isn't it?"

Yes, of course. That was the point. "Len, yes, you're right."

He swallowed. For a moment, he was silent. Slowly, as she watched him, his hands, which he'd extended, lowered. "Dear," he said. For a moment he went quiet again, "Dear, if that man is your choice—though it beats me why—go after him. 'Don't theorize, galvanize!' Or something."

Before the thread is lost. Before she forgot that the fearful maze was only permeable veils, or that Ted might, this time, be really gone.

Len was fumbling in his pockets; he pulled out a bottle of pills. "Here, for you. Folic acid. Jessica says in Europe pregnant mothers swear by the stuff." He added something like ". . . and, loving the baby inside you, the way it already loves its mommy."

"C'mon, Len." She forced a sigh. "This baby will have a *real* mom to love."

But the words *baby* and *inside you* rang like carillons.

As soon as Len had left, though, she realized he'd been pointing out the *emptiness* of ideas like "human essence." And indeed, she thought, couldn't the idea of some loving "core" come from desperation, a grasping for a life raft? She picked up the cat from the purple bedspread. The cat purred sporadically; she stroked its fur. "You'll feel better tomorrow, kitty, or else we go to the vet."

Yet the raft found in desperation is real and will not sink. In the morning, she woke with the thought, really an image of people climbing, helped by others' hands, from the sea. These years, she had been frightened and ashamed to show *what*—love? *Oh well, sometimes the obvious can be true, even though needed.* She stood outside the door in the sunlight. *Rest now. You have always been whole.*

"I think I'm going nuts," she told the cat. It looked up, rubbed against her legs. Leaning over, awkward as she shifted weight, she petted it. Loudly, steadily, the cat purred. Dandelions grew amid the sparse grass at her feet. *The glow of pregnancy.* But this hope was more than physiological response. This was the light on the waves of the Bay, the people of the vigil line, Ted warm beside her on the couch, the weeks and months before. *The learning.* She had shattered the glass.

But an hour later, readying to go out and phone Ted, again certainty fell apart. If she was whole, how could she not be with Ted? Was it simply that love's depths did not always "win"? But that would mean there could again be mistakes, be so much loss. *Yet, even then, love will remain.* She started toward the Co-op, but no longer to phone Ted. She could love, that was the important thing, whether or not he loved her.

In the parking lot, across from the year-old grape strikers' table, she ran into Rickie, the black guy who'd been at Port Chicago those first weeks. "You should be taking things easy, sister," he said when he saw her pregnancy, and insisted she let him carry her groceries home for her. For two hours afterward, they sat talking at her yellow kitchen table. She made them sandwiches and explained she'd be giving up the baby.

"You *what?*" His kindly tone abruptly vanished. "What're you saying, Nora? 'Give the child up for adoption'? What the fuck? You can't do that. That's your baby, girl! You just can't."

And you suggest what, instead? Her lips twisted. "You are so right, Rickie—*my* baby." She had stood. "So what the fuck, yourself. Listen, *my* baby has a right, *my* baby has every right, to the very best home I can find him. And you're asking I deny him that? That I deny my baby a good home? To live in poverty, to have only one parent? *That's* what you're saying. How dare you?"

Suddenly his smile broke out. "Hey—hey, I see. Yeah, you'll be all right, girl; you'll do your all, for sure." He laughed though his eyes stayed puzzled. "Mixed-up, you are, but you'll be a good mother, girl—fierce and really trying. Kid's gonna be okay." He carried his cup to the sink. "'Cause you really love that kid."

That night, she wrote late in her notebooks and washed clothes. By bedtime, the new awareness, though fragile, was something she knew, and had known through the whole day. *My depths are love; my love is whole. My child is real; I want my child to grow up whole.*

The next day, she made herself discuss her fears with Sally, though it was hard. But Sally was someone who knew what it was to care about men and yet stay herself, and how to fight for her children.

"Listen carefully," Nora said. "I mean, be honest. Promise? And—Sally, please don't judge me." *All right, just say it.* Taking a deep breath, she told Sally how she'd felt, the awe arising amid the ordinary tiredness and warmth, while she'd touched and held and made love with Ted, the evening in her apartment after he'd risked his life at Port Chicago. She said, "I keep thinking I must've wanted something weird, something sadistic." There was not much air in Sally's tiny duplex in the stucco house jammed-in beside a bank, but Sally had made the place "home" to raise her kids there.

Waiting for the reply, Nora broke into sweat—at best she could expect the sort of easy reassurance people gave each other, at worst a horrified abrupt agreement with her old self-loathing. But Sally looked at her thoughtfully; after several seconds. "How were you touching him?" Sally asked. "Did you want to hurt him?"

Nora turned away, embarrassed, afraid she'd blush, as she had years before when people asked how she could go with someone so scarred-up as Murph.

"Nora?" Sally asked. Then Nora remembered, even in her body, that night with Ted. "No—no, I wanted to heal him; I wanted to make the cuts and scabs go away." Speaking the words, she heard the truth. "I wanted him to hold me. I wanted him. I wanted him healed. And, Sally, to be with him. For us to be happy, so much."

Sally smiled, as if she'd said something entirely natural.

Then, abruptly, running a hand across a stack of waiting press releases, Sally laughed. "*Of course.* Well, of course. You know, Nora, you better learn to start laughing when people start pushing those sorts of accusations at you. Didn't anyone ever tell you that? Like, I don't know, maybe you've been too frightened over the baby or someone, but—like, we're all good women dealing with hard times. And it *is* hard. Yeah, I know."

But that evening, while she cut up lettuce for a salad, she found herself wondering again why she still found that night at the vigil so meaningful. Was her sexual drive sadistic, after all, or entrapped in romantic plots where her beloved must stand forth in heroic glory? For an instant, she stood trapped.

But no. No, for I remember. I remember. Still she stood without moving, one hand holding a pot of cold water. *I touched Ted, shy and afraid and in awe, wanting him holding me, wanting us making love together, strong and close and entwined. Together, simply together—no matter the heavy bandages, no matter the damn fleas—just us.*

Ted, you were going to show me what was beautiful!
She began to cry. He had done exactly that.

Her abdomen swaying under her new wide tent dress, she awkwardly bent to pet the cat. Something in the posture made her remember Benjamin leaning across the Ahimsa House mimeo machine, saying, "Wow, you'll really fight for that man!" Fight *for* him. *For* someone. As she would now, and for the child. For life, for love.

She had seen Juliet outside the Mediterraneum soon after Labor Day, a few weeks after the vigil had begun. They had spoken of the vigil, of Juliet's struggles to get through to the hecklers, of what she herself had done that night. "Juliet, you're right," she'd agreed. "I mean, none of us is going to forget what happened out there, and the—the heroism, you know? But oh my God, I'd rather just *be* somewhere with Ted, alone with him." Somewhere where waves crashed on the sand, where—

oh, it didn't matter the place. Juliet had said "I used to feel like that with Ron"—Juliet's first boyfriend, a dancer himself who nevertheless had left her one day with no word— "I'm happy for you both."

Now Nora set the pot back on the stove. Her mind couldn't stop reviewing its evidence, whirling as her thoughts had whirled, the year before. But this time, she had known community. This time, Ted had been there, had said "I need you." She set the table, mixed the hamburger with bread crumbs and some sage.

Then she peered out the window into the twilight. The fifth month. *When better to recognize that one loves life? Especially when one has witnessed the love for the one and the many.* Inside, the child was growing and moving—her child, this real child. Would it like the new parents she would find for it? They would have to be people who touched others, who were not afraid. They would have to love the child, take care of it. *What if it has a compulsion to run in front of trucks!* Trucks could be dangerous. *Every time you cross the street, look both ways.*

Oh no, she really was trying to protect this baby. She'd better start smoking less, even quit. She put out the cigarette. *I'll cut down.*

Out the window, the first stars shone as the fading light cleared. She remembered how Ted had visited and said "I need you—I need you," how his own need had overwhelmed her, how for a brief time their passion had been deeper than anything.

Yes, my love is deep and whole. This is more than a start. Once, out on the line, when Ted had hugged the frightened Juliet, she too had cared for Juliet; they had all shared a love, spreading among them in the huddled dawn beneath the morning star. She too—each of them— loved, was whole.

Oh, but love, love, love—spinning from first position, she whirled to the imagined song. *And you don't even have to like the Beatles.*

Much later, she moved through the dark cottage. She had decided to drink water, rather than smoke, after midnight.

So much could have been possible, had she understood before.

Pulling her poncho over her shoulders, she grabbed her notebook and sat by the table. Everything she'd not told Ted, she must. Really, it came down to "You were heroic that night, and I was, finally, a bit brave, too. It's good the world saw, even people who laughed at our raggedy lines; they had to see, and maybe be changed. You reached out—maybe we all can, knowing we're whole—through every barricade. Through each veil of self, each oppression. You fought to save the many, caring about everyone; and you're right that our love can pierce even our own bars. You're right; if people see that they love and will risk everything, and that love remains no matter what, then we're unstoppable and no one can prevent peace. I'm still afraid, but I love you, and I'm not asking, anymore—I'm coming with you, you and the others, out there."

But after she put the page in the envelope with the Vigil House address, she realized she would have to polish it really well. It had to say, clearly and only, *I have come through my barriers. Come back—if you want.* "I love and need you," she wrote. But so what? Too late indeed—he had long left her.

She listened to the rain. An hour later, still wrapped in the poncho, she walked out to the sidewalk.

The whole night's thoughts seemed abstract now, important, yet fragile in the ordinary Berkeley morning. Over the dripping roofs, clouds were clearing. From down the street, a pale figure moved, coming nearer in the light—a dark-haired young woman wearing a worn-out white raincoat. The woman was coming from the Ebennigh drugstore, pushing a baby in a scratched-up stroller. The bushes around the drugstore glistened with dew. The air smelled damp. Here was real life, and right there was a baby—*a baby like mine will be, to care for, to love, to protect.* Here was the world; together, world and theory formed reality.

Bumping just slightly on the sidewalk, the stroller rolled nearer. Not wanting to stare but not looking away, she stood rooted, watching. The baby, a boy with shiny eyes and curly hair, glimpsed her and made a chirpy, burbling sound. Reaching from his seat, his blue cap falling to his lap, he stretched out his arms, lips spreading wider as he beamed—*toward a stranger.* Eyes wide and joyous, unafraid. This was no abstraction. *Love is our first need, first depth.*

3

Going On

End of October, 1966

So, it was done.

The autumn storms had begun. She fed herself—and the baby—and the cat. When necessary, she went to the Co-op or the *Barb*. Staff were annoyed by her shorter reporting hours, but her body was tired so often, slow and heavy. Besides, finding truth was most important, and there kept being new explorations and corollaries to the answer she had found.

The answer—which had been there all along. *I have longed not to trap but to give, not to hurt but to nurture, not to flee but to support.* Others' definitions had barred ("You must have misunderstood"), others' eyes could block ("I'd look so silly, so possessive"), but yearning was stronger, the love reflected and multiplied by every heart.

Love with which I'll protect this child, too, and—

For some days, it rained, the air grown cool with November. In San Francisco, the Diggers' held what they called a Death of Hippie march. People on the vigil line shivered under tarps, together confronting the war and the cold.

After the evening news, she sat on at the table, the thoughts unending; so much that she'd thought unreal or wrong, so much hidden under talk of other needs, had simply been love. "It's the whole system that has turned us against our feelings," she could say, citing "I don't need anyone," "Those people don't feel for life as we do," "That guy's using you, he's gotta be an agent," all that stuff, and all the men who claimed to have no needs, the culture calling love mere "dreams," "romance," and those who called others' ways to love "weird," "immature," "perverse,"—as if any form of love couldn't also stand for any other form of love or love itself. *Oh wow, I sound like a Dylan song,* she thought, *or Plato,* and laughed; still, that system, this culture, had nearly destroyed her. But now she would confront it, not give in to anyone's false views, no matter how insistent; instead, she would define herself and her world.

"And fighting back has many forms." She grabbed her pen and, pressing almost fiercely, nearly snapped the point. "But the real fight is *being there.* Being there, as you were there. For we are this need to love; love defines us all." She bent forward, gasping at the pressure the move caused in her abdomen. "Out on that road in the white lights, love drew me through to you—but it was weeks *later* our longing grew deepest. Love can come from any act, heroic or ordinary.*"*

And, really, it wasn't Ted she was writing to. Certainly it wasn't he who needed to hear this. Did anyone, anymore? Reading of the Diggers' free-food actions and listening to the songs on the radio and news of yet another huge demonstration, it was clear that more and more people were starting to understand, to challenge the war and society, awakening. The hope was frightening. Yet even if fear pushed her back, love would draw her out again—it would, and she need not "make no mistakes." To make a mistake was to live.

Right. So she'd better risk phoning doctors and adoption agencies. "You're avoiding dealing with it," someone had said, Len maybe. What Sally had said was "Trust yourself. You take care of the baby, and the baby takes care of you. How it works."

And with the cat, too—the cat seemed well again, but from here on, if it acted sick, she'd get it, somehow, to the vet. Now, however, it was sleeping on the bookcase, basking in the warmth from the heater. Nora filled its bowl with fresh food, calling "kitty, kitty" and watched the bright eyes open.

On Wednesday at the *Barb* came word that, out at the vigil, Ted and another man had convinced a driver to climb from his rig and quit. Another four workers who'd been thinking about quitting did, too, during the next few days. She went home; it was evening. Cooking dinner, she was thinking *we are, each of us, love,* and again that this could make people undefeatable. *Aware of our worth, how can we be stopped from coming back and coming back until we end the war? From going beyond what we think possible?*

Outside, the sky was black, tinged pink, under a steady drizzle. It was quiet. *Yes, we shall keep going. Even when forced back, forced inward, we still love—our depths are the reflecting pool of longing, thrusting us outward once more. On the vigil line, forced back by Marines, we huddled, finding our warmth in each other, then stepped forth again. Fearful in the cottage, I reached past my own barriers to Ted. And by the Opera House, even after I struck him, he didn't leave me. On the line, though first I hesitated, I did fight through, the second time.*

We can get through.

So many people knew this, finally—people creating changes. Everywhere, in cities here, cities across the world—in people's homes, on crowded streets— everywhere, struggle was spreading. For years, no one had marched, but now they were millions. Too many loads of weapons had rolled, until a few—*we in each land, while the world watched*—rcachcd out to save life.

"Yes, this care for many, not separable from love for one, is our deepest need," she wrote, no longer to Ted. "It has always been there. Will always be there."

Will be there even when my mind must cycle, reassuring again and again against my fears. Will be there even when I'm all alone. Will be there, even if the one I most love—this thought, she realized, had crept in before—*is with somebody else.*

Dropping the pen, she reached toward the phone. She wouldn't have to actually speak to anybody yet, not decide anything, just leave a message, "I am pregnant and I want to talk to you about"—what was the term they used, she'd read it somewhere? — "'relinquishing.' Relinquishing a baby." That was it. She sat back, not lifting the receiver.

Not yet.

The rain on the roof came harder now; it made a rough, elusive tune. What had seemed a silly song in the early vigil days now seemed to point a path.

> *"For I'll be there"—beside the road,*
> *—to fight for the one and the many,*
> *—to long for, protect, and heal,*
> *—to reach past every boundary,*
> *—to seek, from deepest need, the deepest need, love*
> *reaching through.*

To hold this child, protect, hold whole this world.
"Reach out—"
She would be there.

Part V
Somebody to Love

1

Songs

November 1966

Rain puddled the sidewalks by the Mediterraneum, beat on the cottage roof. Now when she would pick up one of her notebooks, it was mostly to write lyrics—rhymed, unrhymed, couplets, doggerel, whatever flowed with hope. It seemed forever since she'd filled any pages with writings meant for Ted. And what she wrote were—no, not diary entries, though she'd kept a diary back in high school—but more and more a form of celebration, shifting away from *herself* and turning outward to the world.

And more and more, they were lyrics—not love songs, not narrations like the libretto she'd developed once with Nadine, but a wakening into melody that might reach people in the world and change it. For change at last seemed possible, if not yet inevitable.

Meanwhile, on the blue ledge beside the table, the radio playcd the news—three features this past hour concerning LBJ's "presidential stop" tonight at the San Francisco Conference Center.

So all right, show him, too—everyone can care. The attempt might not work; someone might get hurt; but she'd try, at least, and no longer hold back. *And even if the cops attack, or the FBI, or—no matter what harassments—now I know I'll protect the child.*

She pulled the silver-and-white tent dress from her closet, the dress with braiding like the Mexican dress she'd worn for the Opera House demonstration, and laid it out on the purple spread. New lyrics ran though her mind.

> *So if police attack and if the guns resound,*
> *Yet, for this child and for the whole world 'round,*
> *I'll stand my ground, I'll stand my ground.*

She grinned, hurrying to bathe.

> *And if we have to stand ten thousand days,*
> *While people mock our hope and shout "too late,"*
> *(Hell, even if we're locked inside and cannot bathe!)*
> *We know our worth, we know our love,*
> *We'll overcome, we'll overcome (oh yes) today!*

But what in fact could she do, jump in front of the president's limousine? Yes, in fact—now she knew she could. Indeed, she would get through, right there, right out there on the pavement, step right up to that murderous warmonger, and—well, she'd have to find the right words. But no, she need only do her best, didn't have to be perfect, not for a roadside challenge—not for confronting any man, whether a president, or Ted, or anyone else. She soaped her armpits, her thighs, her rounded belly. Really, when had she last tried to reach Ted? No matter, and surely it could make no difference whether he, or anyone else, was there for her. She would not run, and she would not collapse beneath old shames or doubts, for, even should she lose everything, she was whole.

And, since she would not stop herself, she might indeed get through. Tonight, no reason to assume that LBJ could not be reached. Everyone could love, after all; everyone needed to—everyone.

She toweled off and, careful not to lose her balance, pulled the dress over her head. When that limousine, flanked by the Secret Service, slowed on Van Ness Avenue, she would run out, still gracefully perhaps, floating as in the television footage of the vigil night, unnoticed until she stood before the president, her arms upraised, to cry "You *do* care, you do. Stop this killing."

Quickly, though, very quickly; she'd have to move as in a fearless dance to protect those children, all those children—and especially this child inside her.

Her suede boots lay under the chair. The poncho hung beside it, unbuttoned so she could slip it off instantly if grabbed. Ready, no matter what.

But so was the LBJ administration. Riding into the City, between her Berkeley Citizens comrade Mark and an Independent Socialists organizer from New York, she fiddled with the dashboard radio, and they heard the news. "The White House has just announced that President Johnson's appearance in San Francisco tonight is cancelled. It is not clear if rumors of violent protests—"

"Oh, for heaven's sake. But do you see?" The organizer's voice rose with excitement. "We've won—we've won! Johnson may be president in name, but he can't go anywhere."

His bombs could, though. If this was a "win," it was too small a win. And next time, would she dare to leap in front of that car? And would she have, really, this time?

For days, Nora sketched, with poster paints on large sheets of paper, the images she called "metaphors of the soul." In her old metaphor, people's selves were like the geologic layers of Earth on a high school diagram, childhood innermost with growth layered outward toward the level of maturity and caring. But her new metaphor came from the one night of the vigil—the metaphor of breaking through every boundary, reaching out past the inner lines of shame, the lined-up early fears, the cautionary words of comrades, guilts from when she'd not reached forth, and the bristling cordons of the green Marines of war. In this new metaphor, deepest, yearning love reached up and out beyond those static encircling layers to the heights where caring, giving, protective love shone bright, ever reflected—gleaming through each thinning guilt or shame—in the mirroring pool of that very same tender, deepest, yearning love—each mirroring the other, the pastels and the brilliance, the giving and the yearning, reaching for the other, and the same.

Spreading out a new sheet of paper, she sketched the colors of this second metaphor—reds and golds for struggle, orange and yellow for anger and humor, purple and black for the eyes of others and the undone, and the underlying pool of pastel pinks and blues of tender love—longings reaching inward, outward, cracking through every darkness.

She laughed aloud, "Oh man, a real mandala of the soul!" and lifted more paint onto the brush. Whatever their connection might become, she thought, Ted had shown her something beautiful.

"Even so, his bars made me put up my own." She shuddered—what a self-justifying cop-out *that* was.

"Easy to love people who are lovable, as you folks on the line might say," Lennie replied. He had begun coming over regularly.

She was determined not to pick up a cigarette. "That's the hard part, see—to protect me and the child, yet stay open. And no, I'm not saying love means letting down every defense to everybody—not at all."

He kept pulling books from her bookshelves, then pushing them in again. "'Protect' is accurate, you know. You already love that child, so why not . . .? I mean, isn't it time you start deciding?" His gaze was luminous with concern. Clearly there were many ways to care. "Isn't it? Nora? Answer me."

"Will they bomb again?" She needed to change the subject. "Will they keep bombing Hanoi?"

Len said nothing. Then suddenly he turned. Outside the window, rain poured down on her storm-soaked yard. "That war!" he said. He slammed a book to the floor. "That goddamn, *goddamn* war. Don't get me started, Nora, don't get me started. Nothing works; they won't halt. I see those kids, they're being killed, and damn it, they are just like mine. My cute little twins—you put one down for a nap and the other wakes up to take her place; there are kids, little toddlers, just like them, just like my little girls, in those *hooches. Hooches,* we say. I tell you, I'm getting to where I might . . . No, I don't know. I just know . . . This war could make someone do *anything*."

The rain beat on and on.

That night, she dreamed a moving shape—a living shape that danced and leaped, no globe but a doughnut, playful. *The ball can bounce, and the ball can bounce,* the shape said, *in and out like a doughnut, bounce-bouncy the same.* She woke up laughing. *I've been dreaming the baby's dream.*

Only, there was nobody to tell. She'd stopped going to the *Barb*. Occasionally, the singer Nadine, or Gregor from CNVA, dropped by—and, twice, Mark, chuckling things like "How can we make a revolution bloom without some bloomin' workers?" Sally too, came sometimes, bringing fruit or cheese and greetings from the staff, and now bursting out "You're kidding, girl, you're kidding!" when Nora showed her the mandala of the soul. "So whose soul might that be, I wonder? Hey, pink *and* blue." Sally laughed. "Yeah, no point closing off your options."

But, except for Sally, people didn't seem concerned about her pregnancy, and after a few minutes, she'd ask each one to leave. Few returned. And it was fine, being alone; she had seen she *could* care for most of her needs and protect the baby within; knowing her worth would give her the confidence for these coming weeks.

Only, she wanted somebody to know—the baby had danced! In the morning, she phoned to tell Ted, even though she was not at all sure anymore how much he still meant to her. December rain struck on the Co-op's glass booth.

"Oh dear, oh dear." There was a hesitance in the speaker's reply. He was stoned, of course, mellow, one of the old hangers-on at Vigil House, and had a slight accent she couldn't place. "Ted—no, he is not here."

"Do you know when he'll be there?" She was tired of asking.

"No. No, I think he is not out of jail yet."

Her cigarette grazed her fingertips.

The speaker seemed to wake up. "But you'd not heard? This Contra Costa County has a new rule, an ordinance just for us. Sleeping on the roadside, this is made now a misdemeanor. Last week, Ted fell asleep on the line—he was too tired. He will not be out for some while."

Tears surprised her. Crouched over, she hurried home, barely avoiding bumping into passersby. *For Ted, for me, for the child, the world.* No mere metaphor this time, the bars she had to break.

But when she tried to borrow a car to drive to the jail, Nadine said, "You've neglected me and suddenly you want my wheels?" Mark laughed through his beard, "You can't drive shit," and Benjamin's door swung open to an empty room, packing paper strewn across his abandoned desktop. Sally apologized, "Like, for that guy, I'd be pleased to, of course. But I can't risk it, honey. I utterly *have* to have this car to pick up the kids. You know what happens to my visiting privileges—they call it privileges— if I ever miss?" Evening had come by the time Nora stood, dripping with rain, in Len's doorway and heard him, too, refuse, while Jessica listened as if hypnotized.

"That guy hasn't even bothered," Len began, but stopped, seeing her miserable and soaked. "Just come in, you're wet through." Jessica rose from the table and, a twin under one arm, approached with her other hand out. "Come have dinner with us. You need to eat more, from here on."

Nora made herself step into the warm room, the comfort of it—a big family living-dining room with a fireplace, baby clothes and a blue ball and rattles all over the sofa. *No, no,* she shook her head. But soon she was seated at their table, the pink-sweatered twin on her right and Len to her left, strips of sautéed chicken and green beans and mushrooms on her plate.

An hour later, she stood, still damp, and feeling too tired to move, and said, "I really have to go." Now they couldn't object.

Len put out a hand to stop her. She tried to brush past, but "What are you thinking?" he said. "Stop.

There's no bus out there. They won't let you in if you get there, anyhow." He stood between her and the door.

"Get away." She would *not,* any longer, be stopped by anyone "Move."

"The guy'll be out in a day or two, probably. *He'll* do just fine." Len was peeling her hands from his arms each time she tried to push him aside. "What's he there for, anyhow—stopping traffic?"

"For getting worn out." She glared at him. "Have you ever been so tired that you—?" But Len wouldn't understand, just one more liberal blocking the path with pseudo-rationality and his wife's good food. "For falling asleep on the vigil line by the highway, okay? That's why. Breaking their new law."

"Their new law?" Abruptly, Lennie's voice darkened. "A law against sleeping—that's what you're saying? A new law?" He glanced toward Jessica, then back. "Specifically to stop a protest? I've understood you, correct? Nora?"

She nodded. If she first tried shifting to the right, as if toward the picture window, she might catch him off guard, squeeze between his left side and the bookcase, rush out and find somebody's car, climb in and—

"Don't even think of it. I move faster." He had lifted both hands to block her. But his expression was different now—very un-Lennie-like and grim. "So—you heard that, Jess? A law to keep the war going. A law they know can't possibly be legal. That's what it comes to."

Glancing quickly toward Jessica, where she sat at the table, like a spectator watching them, he said, voice quiet but dark with impatience, "Jess, love, Jess, will you be okay with the kids this evening? I'll do tomorrow night—I promise. *And* the bottles. I'll do the bottles both nights."

"Oh. You'll 'do the bottles.' Thanks." Only Jessica's mouth smiled with the words, her eyes so pained that Nora almost refused when Len said, "I'll just run upstairs, then, and get my keys. Nora, I'm driving you out there."

2

Eating for Two

December 1, 1966

"Yeah, right, and this is the Grand Mount Diablo Hotel?" The prison guard, young, skinny, and dripping rain, shoved his face through the open car window to snarl across Len, meeting Nora's stare. "Yeah, I said it's some first-class hotel here, right, lady?" He pointed toward the long building. "Right, Miss *Seikh*? Seikh, is it? Or whatever-your-name, Miss *Seikh seeks* kindly to speak with Mr. Theodore Whosit, correct? I got that right?"

Nora shrank into the seat. But she must get through—see this through. Yet make no missteps—must protect the child. But not get put down like this, either—not by these guards, in front of Lennie.

"So may I point out, Miss Seikh"—the guard's voice dropped, and Lennie gripped her left shoulder, *Stay cool*— "this is not some fuckin' hotel, this is not some fuckin' college, this is a fuckin' cor*rec*tional facility. And you spoiled hippie rich kids better fuckin'-fuckin' figure that out." The narrow face turned toward an older guard, who was approaching from a pale-lit doorway. Beyond, over the silhouetted prison wall, loomed Mount Diablo. "You fuckers ever look around like *real* people do, you might know what a jail's about. A jail"—he tossed his head— "a jail's about jailing folks."

"C'mon, Gene, stop screwing around." For a moment, the older guard looked bored; then his eyes narrowed. "But actually. Okay, actually, let's take a look." Extremely slowly, he began to walk around the car. Scrutinizing it, checking for evidence, for an excuse.

"You, sir." He stepped to the driver's-side window. "You. Yes." Leaning forward, he stuck his head inside, pointedly glancing across at Nora and looking her up and down. Then, turning back to Len, "Sir. You, sir, let's see your driver's license."

"Clearly," Len whispered to her, "we forget getting in tonight." She saw his arm shake as he pulled out his wallet and handed over his license.

"Um-*hm*." Again slowly, the guard scanned the print. "Brown hair, brown eyes—take off them glasses, *sir*—Caucasian, is that so?" He shone his flashlight over Len's features. "Okay, and now let's"—the big hand reached in, the glove scraping the edge of Len's nose, to turn off the ignition key. "I can take that key, sir. Now, if you will allow me, let's see your car registration, thank you. And insurance—you got your insurance? And actually—hey, Gene?"

The younger man came alert. He shifted so his hand rested exactly three inches above his holster. "Ray?"

"Here." The older guard, Ray, jerked open the driver-side door, body blocking his flashlight's beam. "Right. Okay—here, sir, here, madam, come on out. Let's have you stand out of the car for a moment. One at a time, folks."

Nora let go her door handle. But "He means you, babe," the younger cop said. He gestured with one skeletally thin hand. Struggling, she made her numb fingers open the door.

"Now. Sister, you just lift those hands high." Ray's voice kept turning to a drawl. "I said, high. And drop the purse, if you would be so kind. Okay—okay, sister, that's good, that's good. Hold it! Just like that."

She couldn't make her eyes lift up to see what the cop Ray was doing, but she heard his voice, close behind her back, and then, again slowly, as he stepped back and moved away. "Okay," he was saying, "Okay there, and now you, sir. Sir, you ready to oblige me? I bet you're one of those folks just can't abide a man in uniform, but I certainly hope you'll be making an exception tonight—*I* would, if I was you. So now that's *just* right, actually. *Very* good, sir, and now get out this door. Get out—that's the way. And hands up, please. *Hands up.*" There was a cracking sound. "*Up.*"

Afraid to turn her head, she still saw Ray take two steps backward. He was eyeing Len as if trying not to laugh. "Well, okay. *Okay,* professor." The drawl turned abruptly sharp. "Gene, frisk this character. And try not to break his glasses doing it. Try real hard."

She made herself not turn around. Her knees shook—because she might, at least in her mind, sneer at these cops, but Len had been taken by surprise—and, under this so-called inspection, he was growing angrier than she had ever seen him, ready to strike the thin young cop, who smiled as if daring him, and whose hands—the realization flashed on her—were moving around over Len's balls.

"Stay cool, Len," she called aloud. To protect him. It was she, after all, had got him to drive out here, and now . . .

The big guard whistled in mock awe, a strange sound in the deserted night. "'Stay cool,' is it? Very appropriate. Tough chick, aren't you? Maybe you're packin'? Yeah, actually, we better check."

Love is our depth, our core. No shame, no fear.

"Ray." Gene was giving Len a few last pats. "We got rounds to finish tonight."

The big cop didn't answer. He leaned over to shove the key back in the ignition, then flipped the turn-signal lever. "That light working? Gene, go check for me. We get done here when we're done."

Gene stepped away and, imitating the older cop's slow stride, approached the front of the car.

"That one's working."

"You sure?"

"Yep. Working."

"Yeah? And the other?"

"Both okay, Ray."

"Check the rear." The young cop's feet crunched on the gravel. She waited, stock-still, by the passenger door.

She could see Lennie, staring out past the dark barren yard to the black wall beyond. It rose like a medieval rampart, thick and ugly in the night. Behind that wall, somewhere in the jail, guarded by people like Ray and Gene, Ted was trapped. Ted and how many others? And how many, over the years?

The cops stood together, Gene with a hand on the gun in his unsnapped holster, Ray hunched over a walkie-talkie, checking for warrants, or pretending to. If nothing else happened—if the cops let them go—then she could jerk away, could take the thirty or fifty steps up to that wall, singing clear the freedom songs from deep within, let every person locked inside those blocks for hopeless months hear, know, and hope again. No—a fantasy, a dream. Yet if only she could let them know. *There is a chance for you, someone is here, someone who cares, who would break through and free you.*

"Get outta here. You never heard of visiting days?" The cop Gene chuckled. "And, uh, by the way, Miss Seikh, no conjugal visits here. In case you were wondering. No fuckin' conjugal visits"

"Nora, into the car." Mechanically, she followed Len's words, stepped in. No way past those thick walls.

Len was starting up the engine, then turning the car back toward the gate. Ted wouldn't even know that she had come. Not that it mattered here.

On the freeway, nearing Berkeley, she heard a sound like a half-choked chant. Len was sobbing. His shoulders jerked, and his right hand moved in little jabs, beating sharp time like a maddened conductor.

"Len?"

He shook his head, bore down hard on each word. "I better get home to Jessica, and fast. Soon as I let you off."

I brought him into this. But when she opened the car door in front of her cottage, what he said was "Dear, thank you. I am sorry we couldn't do more, but thank you. I wouldn't want to have missed that." He laughed— the high, squeaky laugh she couldn't stand. "'Cause I guess we spoiled hippie rich kids better fuckin'-fuckin'-fuckin' look around and see, huh? Maybe the fuckin' hell so."

Inside, she changed out of her damp clothes and took the piece of chicken and an orange from the refrigerator. It didn't make sense; she'd eaten already, with Len and Jessica. She opened a loaf of bread. When Ted got out, that's what she could do, fix him an elegant dinner, steak with a sauce and sliced almonds, oven-roasted vegetables—maybe a torte, whatever that was. She looked down at the heaped plate.

"Now what am I doing? I'm eating for two." Stroking her abdomen, she laughed aloud. "No, for *three*—him, too."

3

Taking Care

Winter 1966-1967

But she had not got through the jail guards to Ted, had not stopped the president, not done enough against the war. She listened to the inner songs and thought of what people were saying—at the Mediterraneum, in the streets, on the news—about "being whole" and trusting feelings, the phrases so much like her own recognition of the love in everyone. And yet this was hardly enough, not with the war going on despite everything, and not when she well knew, for herself and for the fetus too, she should be out in the world now, finding a doctor, exercising every day, and "making some plans so you don't end up racing to the ER when the baby comes popping out," as Sally put it. "At least get yourself a phone. Things can happen fast. Really, really fast."

Except, people said pregnancy was natural, not to worry; the books said simply eat lots of vegetables and fish and nuts, which she did, and the fetus bumped and swam around her womb and seemed happy enough. "You need to call your parents, get help with that child," Len had lectured, the only time they'd spoken since the trip out to the jail, but she knew better. Her changes, her new awareness of the depths of love, felt too fragile to risk. Her parents would hover, would see the pregnancy as one more sign she needed help; they would want her "home." No, definitely not; she would keep on taking their checks, she would phone them sometimes, but she would not tell them of the baby. Somehow she would finance a hospital delivery . . . but how wasn't obvious. Opening the phone book in the Co-op booth, she skimmed through the damp, half-torn pages for the number of Sally's obstetrician. Then closed the heavy volume, and instead dialed Vigil House. Yet, what could she say? *Ted, I broke through; I did try to reach you out there.* This was not news; it was always true. *But know it, Ted.* Even if he no longer loved her.

"Hey, there!" It was Ram-Rod on the phone. *Ram-Rod, the Vigil House crazy*, as Ted had called him, and as the black guy Rickie also had, warning "I mean it, sister, don't let that pig near you." But it was Ram-Rod she now must ask, "Is Ted back yet?"

"Hey? 'Back' from where?" Loud music blared, somewhere behind him. "Like, Gingy, anyone here know if Ted's back? Yeah, it's his ex–old lady again." Ram-Rod was tapping out a rhythm on the receiver.

"Hi." The new voice was a woman's. "Like, I'm Gingy. Ted's gone to the City. Yeah, some kind of screw-up. They must of messed his head around in jail, you know. I think he's—Rammy, Ted's staying at Becky's, right?"

She could trust herself. "Where's that?" She could make them tell her.

"Like, *Becky's*." Ram-Rod was back on the line. "See, Ted needs to rest, and Becky's the place for that. Soft bed, warm food, and," he laughed, "R and R's what Ted needs now. Man, don't we all!"

In the *Barb*'s back office, Sally leaned across her desk. "Gross. I wouldn't take them seriously. But I'll tell you something, maybe time to let that man go. Deal with your pregnancy—focus. Ted'll never be that baby's daddy; nobody's gonna be that baby's daddy. You know that, right? It's up to you, every bit of it. My obstetrician—he's very good, he's excellent, Nora. It's way time you move on this." They could hear Max shouting in the front office. "Let's skip," Sally said, lowering her voice. "Hop over to Si's for cheeseburgers. And I got something interesting for us."

Si's Charbroiler was nearly empty. They carried their burgers to a cleared table by a wide front window.

"You seen these yet?" Sally opened a black-and-sepia-covered magazine. It was the Christmas issue of *Ramparts*, the Catholic leftwing journal. On the cover, and on page after page inside, there were photographs. War photographs from Vietnam. Standing and circling the table, Nora leaned over Sally's shoulder, making herself look. The cover image was in black and white, but the other photos were all in color, starkly, glaringly real. Some were square, some rectangular, and each showed some of the wounded, amputated, napalmed, maimed, and mutilated children of Vietnam. That was the article's title, "Children of Vietnam."

"You think our leaders see these, or care?" Sally stood and stepped back, silhouetted against the windowpane as she held up the magazine. "You *really* ready to 'show people,' Nora? You serious? 'Cause I am. I truly am. It'll go down good, too—with you wearing that hip maternity outfit, if I may call it that. You want to be effective? Here's your chance. We'd better take it."

Nora looked down at her gray-purple granny dress; it hung loose and formless over her widened abdomen. Her hand reached forward and clasped Sally's, so both clutched the magazine. "Yes—ready. Let's do it."

Four days later, in a pouring mid-December San Francisco storm, they and several older activists from Women for Peace entered the Federal Building. They wore high-heels and stockings despite the weather, no boots or jeans, no ethnic jewelry, and carried borrowed designer-brand purses over their tailored coats. Casually climbing the wide staircase, they moved forward, two to each festively hung office. Nora, her borrowed black-and-white-checked coat open to show her pregnancy, would take the director's anteroom. All chatted as if with excitement at the coming holidays. Once inside an office, they laughed with the receptionist, asked the way to the ladies' room, casually took off their coats—and unfolded their posters, each a greatly enlarged color reproduction from the *Ramparts* spread. They held the images steady.

The receptionists smiled at first, showing the polite interest demanded by their jobs; then the smiles froze as their eyes widened in horror, and each receptionist would press an intercom or step to a door at the right of her desk, to call her boss out from his office. The boss, a federal official, would regard the well-made-up, well-dressed women holding up the images of ghastly injuries and death, and hurry down a corridor to consult with his own boss further up the chain. Meanwhile, as the women stepped back out into the corridor, other staffers began to congregate around them, some laughing or accusatory but a few saying very quietly "I'm with you" or "Thank you." In this confrontation, Nora and the others stood silently, bearing witness.

For another fifteen minutes, the building stayed quiet. There were only brief, broken-off conversations in the hallways, consultations among dark-suited men on the stairs. Then the first armed police poked gas-masked faces through the wide front doorways.

"Stop the killing! Stop killing babies!" Nora broke into the chant. With all the others, she began, after a moment, to press back against the police lines, row after row—who kept coming up the stairs, then dragging them down the long, carpeted hall. The cops kept pushing her, her and the little woman Dorothy and an elderly black lawyer. "Stop the killing!" she was crying, struggling not to fall as, more and more roughly, more cops began shoving them on the marble stairs and then, half slipping, onward toward the outer doors. No, she should sit right here on the marble floor, make them arrest her—*knowing our worth, we need not stop ourselves.* But what would happen to the baby? And she had to protect the baby. Yes—and now she could, and—

"So how 'bout you watch out for your own kid, lady?" The short sergeant half-lifted her onto her feet. Then, moving almost gently, he half-pulled, half-dragged her through the doorway and, again quite gently, pushed her out onto the sidewalk.

The sky was already clearing, the wintry sunlight bringing the tang of ocean air, and some of the women linked hands, holding the photos high. "Stop, stop the killing," they kept chanting. She could feel the sadness, the horror, for those children. But the chants, the confrontation, the women's excited hope, all felt to her like reiterations of a struggle somehow gone stale.

A struggle she would continue, though. Especially now, with the cops closing around them. She hadn't expected this, not really—jail, with her baby in her womb.

Suddenly she heard, "They're leaving!" Nora followed Sally's gaze. Yes—yes, that was true; the cops were pulling back; they were turning and marching away in formation, going east, some few climbing the steps back into the Federal Building. "Wow!" someone said, "Wow! Oh wow, we're free," and everyone started laughing.

"Let's not stop!" cried the woman named Ellie. "Let's take these down Market Street, confront the shoppers." People were cheering, and Nora lifted the photo she carried—a bandaged baby with terrified eyes—and started forward, the others beside her, for the two-mile march through downtown. They would take the F bus—no, spread themselves through four or five F buses full of commuters, back across the Bay.

Christmas had passed, and New Year's. She had sent her parents a handmade holiday card and neck scarves, one blue and one green velour, along with a note, "Things are fine here," so they'd not get concerned. She had listened, wrapped in her poncho to hide the pregnancy, to her landlady's lonely tales whenever the woman's truck-driver husband was away. For Nadine, who clapped and said, "Nora, it's trippy!" laughing through real tears, she'd bought a plush white wolf with a silver bow. And she'd pasted a flyer from the Federal Building Women's Action on the cottage wall, glad her child would be born here and not in Vietnam. Mornings came earlier again; there was less rain.

"May I come in?"

She felt grubby in her slept-in granny dress, but it didn't matter, all such body shames, all fears and contingencies, did not matter; one's depths were love. She opened the door.

Ted spread his hands awkwardly. "I know," he said "I promised, and then I . . ."

She reached out and held those hands.

"Nora, you're looking well." He kept smiling. "I knew you could do it."

No thanks to you. But the thought skittered off unsaid—*it's false, and besides it's so good seeing him.* She was blushing with happiness. "Ted, I'm so huge. I waddle now."

He pulled her into his arms. She stroked his face, ran her fingers down his neck, his chest. "You're all right, from the jail? They told me—"

"I'm fine, kid. It's good to see you. It really, really is."

For an hour they held each other, alternately kissing and speaking, discussing people they knew, the vigil, the war. But soon—now, finally—she could tell him. Why they still loved, what beauty they yet might find. She made herself begin, "Ted, I do love you." Wondering if it was still true.

"Hey, kid." He squeezed her hand.

She stroked his fingers. He had come back.

"I know you care," he said. He peered into her eyes. "I've realized that."

She looked down.

"We both cared, kid." He cleared his throat. She knew what came next. "But I've got to tell you something."

Well, yes. And again she needed to find the right words—if she still wanted him.

"We could have had something." His voice suddenly seemed older; he had only shaken his head, with a short shrug, when she'd mentioned the antiwar vets' plan to run a peace ship upriver to Port Chicago. He cleared his throat a second time. "No, I'm with somebody else now. And this time, it's serious. Becky's a good woman, Nora— you'll like her. She got terribly upset when she heard about you being pregnant and alone, and my not staying with you. She gave me a hard time on that."

No matter. It was done. Except, he had to know, "I did try. Ted. I did try. When you were in jail, I did get there."

"You went all the way out there?"

"But I couldn't get in."

Shutting his eyes, he pressed her close. "I didn't know this." He swallowed. After a moment, he said, "No one could get in. And, even if you had, you couldn't have seen me. They had me in solitary. Jail was hard, this time. Listen, you're a tough person, you know? You really are, living here all alone like this."

"But that's *independence*—that's too easy, Ted. What I need is closeness. Interdependence." *And you, your love, to give you love. You—or someone.*

But he was hugging her again, hurriedly, saying he needed to get going, needed to be home soon, "Becky believes in having dinner on time. I want you to meet her. She's eager to know you."

Of course. And yes, it was done; it was over. It was enough that she was whole, love reaching out. Reaching out.

She felt as if she'd wakened, the flakes of moldy fear falling away, just as, in these weeks of winter, people wiped dry the flooded paintings and ravaged books of Florence, Italy. Experts there were drying out the damaged volumes page by page, salvaging the artworks' pigments. "Page by page," she thought, "as hope by hope. No, one cannot rush it." Whatever sense it made, seeing Ted again was letting her begin to act.

And after all, she knew from reporting how to track down information. She made five or ten calls quickly, found the best-regarded adoption agency, and learned of a new "war on poverty" clinic for the baby's birth. She took a bus to the doctor, met with social workers—lied, for the baby's sake, about "the father," offering them an appealing tale of two intellectually and socially superior, star-crossed graduate students. She insisted on her ideal adoptive family—full of love, touch, and caring—and did not let herself doubt the worker's promise to "honor your wishes as far as we possibly can." She dared not doubt.

In one dream, a giant mother taught her to weave a black-bug fence so nobody could come in; in another, a lost mother comforted her on a science-fiction battlefield; in the third, a gray grandmother stalked her through a castle's maze of corridors, became her mother and, when she fought back, was herself. A voice boomed, "Only a man who dares the maze can free you," but then it too changed, become a quiet voice saying, "The mother always lives in terror for her child." She woke with her abdomen throbbing, as if—! No, but it was too soon.

Cherry trees blossomed. In the hills, the hippies held a festival and called it a Be-In. The press covered this event far more than any antiwar demonstrations. A highly regarded lawyer gave her an appointment in his paneled Oakland office to discuss "private adoption options"; after five minutes, during which his eyes twice narrowed—once when she said "no military families and no cops" and once when she said "We all can love"—he handed her a chocolate croissant and said, "You know too little about the father." Casually, he shoved a file of three potential couples back on a high recessed shelf. "And you seem ill. Is something wrong? Can I call someone for you?" She did not say she felt dizzy but quickly left.

Outside, she hesitated. She did not want to ask Ted's help; they were no longer together. Besides, it was silly to fear another bus ride; none had hurt the pregnancy so far. *And Ted will never be the baby's daddy—I know that.*

But also knew she mustn't risk the baby's health. She picked up the phone.

"Of course I'll come for you, kid. I'll *make* the time."

Her anger built up, waiting for him, but it vanished once he arrived and fear fled. He was sporting an off-white scarf and smiling. Thinking to give, in return, she asked, "Can I help the vigil?"

"If it doesn't tire you, sure." He hugged her. "This may sound trivial, but it's major. If you could work up a text for our defense fund? And we need a new press release—no, a couple of releases—and PSAs."

That evening, working on the second release, she felt the first contractions.

4

Birth

February 1967

Becky— "Ted's little girlfriend," in Lee's phrase—opened the door. Her features were still an adolescent's, soft mouth smiling and rounded chin uplifted above the neckline of a flowered dress, her curly hair pushed into braids, but her eyes seemed older, serious. She led the way past overstuffed chairs to a door off the living room. "Good, Nora—we were scared you wouldn't come. I'll get you a sandwich, some orange juice." She began pulling food from a large blue refrigerator. Or do you want to lie down? Our bed is up those stairs." *Thoughtful. A sweet child. That "Rammy" shouldn't call her names.* Ted had come over, three days before, and said "Becky's insisting, kid, you've got to come stay with us as soon as you think you're in labor. We'll drive you over there"—meaning the hospital— "when it's time." So very kind. Yet she wished the idea had been his, not Becky's.

He was outside in the driveway, working on an old two door Dodge. "I'm here if you need me," he called. "Beck, where'd I put that plug wrench? Damn, I'd lose my head if it weren't attached— Oh wait, there's the bugger." His voice trailed off as he leaned over the engine.

A half hour later, Samantha arrived—then, wearing a Mexican poncho, Lee. Lying on the wide bed in the wallpapered bedroom, Nora looked across at them, these three women seated around her—Becky on the rocking chair, Samantha cross-legged on the floor, Lee on the straight chair, her eyes constantly scanning them all— the women of the tribe, gathered about the labor bed.

And even rivalries can't make us each other's enemies. Everyone together once more—Nora felt her smile spread—the Port Chicago vigilers, caring, now as then. No, it didn't matter that the bed was Becky's and Ted's.

Four hours later, a hospital attendant rolled her on a wheelchair into a labor room with tiled tan walls. "There's a fifteen-year-old mom in the next room, and she's not crying," the nurse who took her blood pressure said. "You knew the consequences when you did it." Not safe to laugh at that line, though, not here; all at once, Nora realized how dependent she was now on these people. And when the doctor arrived, he spread her legs apart, checking dilation.

But not brusquely. He patted her shoulder in fatherly reassurance. "I can't let you leave—not this far along. Just lie back and rest. It'll be a good long while yet." For the moment, she felt safe. He was a gentle, light-colored black man, with a kind voice, freckles, and careful hands.

But the hospital's visiting policy was strict. RELATIVES ONLY signs hung in all the corridors. Only after the shift changed and a new nurse, calm and old and easygoing, took charge for the night could Nora get permission for "a friend—yes, only one—to visit, since your folks can't be here. But keep the visit short."

And then Ted was at her side, patting her just as the doctor had, and saying, voice hearty, "How ya doin'?" Seating himself on the visitor's chair, he took her hand, a reassurance as solid and genuine, she thought, as his and Becky's domesticity. She stroked the rust-gold scarf, the one she'd always loved. "Dear Ted—" Certainly this was the time, or past the time, if she was ever going to tell him everything. To say that love was in everyone, and he had shown her something beautiful. In the labor room's half-light, she stared into his accepting gray eyes.

"Ted—" She didn't finish. Too late indeed, and he must already know. She squeezed his hand.

"Hey." He smiled. "We're here for you. Lee's out in the waiting room—so's Samantha. Becky's waiting at home.

Don't worry. If you need us, we're here. We'll fight for you." Leaning forward, he kissed her forehead. He held her hand in silence.

They must have stayed this way for twenty minutes, she lying quiet under the light hospital blanket, he occasionally murmuring "You okay?" or "You're doing fine." No need to speak more. Then Ted's eyes began to close. A moment later, "Sorry!" he said, jerking awake. "Guess I better go pick up a coffee, out in the cafeteria— stay up with you."

"No, Ted, no need." Seriously, wasn't it enough that he cared? Time to let him go, let go the past, let go anger and fear—time to only give, to have this child. "Ted, it's all right." Again she squeezed his hand. "It's good. Go home now, sleep. You and the others, get some rest. You've all been brave."

"You're the one being brave," he said and smoothed the blanket up around her shoulders. Carefully, he stood; then he rubbed his eyes. "Yeah, if I don't get moving, I'll keel over. I *will* get back if I can, kid."

By 2 a.m., when the contractions started coming hard and clearly Ted would not be back that night, Nora felt an instant's fury, a terrible loss. But no, he was tired, and what right had she, anyhow—? No, really, what need—?

No, never mind all that. She must not tense, now must just "go with the contractions." The book *Eastern Health* had a line—she'd paid too little attention to this stuff until tonight— "Clear your mind and trust in what will be." And a *New Mother's Guide* on the nightstand noted, "Contractions are what help the baby to be born."

May the baby be born. She must have cried out. The labor pains had got much stronger.

"It's going to be all right, honey." The calm, gray-haired nurse loomed in the doorway. "Let me finish up this paperwork, and I'll come right back and check you."

After twenty minutes, with the nurse not yet returned, Nora thought to call her, feeling the new pain. It was far stronger, and different. It tore through her body in two waves, dragging her muscles to their limit and stretching them yet further, forcing them completely taut. Every piece of them, every part of her, was pulling toward a single goal.

"Hang on, hang on." The nurse's voice was calming, but her hands pried Nora's legs apart inexorably, their clamp like steel. "Don't be afraid, honey, everything is fine." The voice went silent, gasped, and laughed, then deepened. "Dear, you are all the way open! Let me page the doctor. You're going to have a baby."

In the delivery room, someone said, "Okay, bit of laughing gas and oxygen—breathe deep." She breathed and watched the lights; she was sure someone had said "Oh, wow—oh, oh." Between pains, she tried to joke, "just like getting too high." The doctor smiled back.

But then another pain hit, this one with not two waves but suddenly one—a pain like the Greek kings' armies taking Troy—and the baby's head came pressing down inside.

"Push—push! Don't stop!"

She breathed out, pushed—and screamed.

Life—love—love. The baby came plunging out, head first, into the world.

His. "It's a boy." They were speaking of this baby. Saying "A boy." Saying "Healthy." Saying "long and lean." This baby, *flying forth into his world.*

Under the laughing gas while they sewed up the episiotomy, she drifted out from the brilliant lacerating fountains, up among bright diamond stars. She didn't want to leave green Earth, but she had no choice, and she floated now in farthest space. A moment came—or had come, but when? —of completeness then, utter love and happiness.

Only, *had* it happened? Had that moment happened? Because "now" the moment had already passed—and time itself was turning backward, each moment twisting backward, each instant of her life—and it was from this reversal came the ghastly pain. Nor could there be escape, for if she tried to leap off the backward-spinning globe—of time, of Earth—it was impossible, for the very attempt *had not been* made.

"Hold on, we're nearly done! You're practically stitched up."

But were these voices real? *Cling to them. May they be real.*

"Is my baby born yet?" Somehow she'd managed— hadn't she? —to cry the words.

"Oh yes—a beautiful boy." A young nurse stepped near, bringing him back to her, wrapped in a blanket. His features were delicate, his fingers long. She reached to hold him, but the nurse grasped her wrist, turned her hospital bracelet to compare it with his anklet. He stopped crying and began to root in the blanket, suckling. Again, Nora stretched her hands to him, but, as if not noticing, the nurse carried him off to the nursery.

Nora's baby weighed nearly five pounds. She was not nursing him, not going to raise him. But his features were hers, his forehead his father's; his fingers stretched with curiosity. His dark blue eyes, though people said babies didn't really see, watched hers as if he knew she was his mother.

When Ted came to visit, he stood by her bedside, grinning, while she held the baby; he gave her a kiss and showed her how to make tiny silken god's-eyes. But she couldn't quite be sure she still loved Ted—though how could this make sense, if her love could reach through every barrier? How?

Anyhow, Ted was with Becky now.

Looking back down, her gaze caught on the baby's and he smiled, again as if he knew her for his mother. The tenderness swelled through her, deep as—no no, this was too deep. *For the deepest love must first be whole, between a man and a woman. A baby needs two parents. And how could I, alone, raise such a wondrous child? No matter what has changed in these past months.*

And at least if the police, tracking radicals, went after her or David, they could never discover the baby.

Adopted, his birth records sealed, he would be safe. That first afternoon, she'd held him and tried to offer him her breast, but the nurses had given her a shot so she had no milk; when he cried, she didn't know what to do. She'd called for a nurse, helpless. *There's no way, alone. It would ruin his life.* She wanted to hold him even when she couldn't. *My feelings too tender— Yes, tender and whole--yes, they are good— But if I—*

A child must have two parents.

You love him.

I love him too much. And, very soon, this baby would have his new home, a whole, real family. Her love could give him this. Wonderful parents.

Each action and question was for this—to give him love and life. *The decision is made. He will have wonderful parents. They will reach out, opening their lives and love to him.*

The three days Nora stayed in the hospital, she kept crying, and the nurses grew snappish—until, emptying the bag of embroidery threads that Ted had brought her onto her hospital bed, she showed them how to make tiny god's-eyes. On the third day, Samantha came to pick her up. "You'll stay with me a couple weeks. We've all decided; you cannot refuse." A nurse entered, and Samantha left. The nurse said it was time to sign "this form—use your legal name, Lenore. It's a preliminary form, is all, letting the Children's Home Society take Baby into care."

Ten days later, Nora rode the bus from Samantha's apartment to the agency's office. The social worker had agreed she could hold the baby, but he was already much bigger, and different; she didn't know how to hold him. Soon, a "baby worker" came and asked "You ready?" and lifted him from her arms.

Ten minutes later, in a small reception room, she sat across from the two social workers who would witness her signing. Again there was a legal form— "Yes, your given name, Lenore"—this time, the relinquishment.

"It's always such a difficult experience," the gray-haired worker sighed.

Oh, come on! You're being too serious. She wanted to point this out. *See, I'm not crying.* Instead, she skimmed the document and, hurrying as if finishing a news article, briskly signed. *When he's ten, I'll come find out how he's doing. By then, it'll be safe, it won't disturb anything; he'll be old enough to be fully his real parents' child.* The idea shot through her mind; she let it go. *They will love him.*

5

Somebody to Love

February-March, 1967

"Don't you need somebody to love?" Important to clear her thoughts, important to look ahead—there were many out there to hold and care for. There must be.

Songs from the radio rumbled the old vigil van—Jefferson Airplane, Buffalo Springfield, Donovan—barely louder than the ancient clattering springs. Here, as in the dream when she was pregnant, her baby was born and the vigil people hovered near. But the reality was different.

Samantha and her lover Russ cuddled in the back seat. Up front, Becky stroked Ted's neck while he drove. On the rumble seat by the sliding door, Nora sat watching the rolling gray-green hillsides. Their destination was no longer the vigil but a day on the beach, and yesterday she'd signed away the baby, determined his whole life. The van bumped down the Point Reyes road, past eucalyptus and wild roses. The ocean breeze slid in. No yellow flowers this early in the year. They parked high above the beach.

"You okay?" Ted said. "You sure?"

She smiled, turned to help Becky lift the picnic basket—green-checked like Becky's kitchen curtains—from the van. Ted took it and, walking ahead down the slippery path, carried it to where they found, against a broken, long-abandoned fishing boat, some sheltering shade.

Later, standing on the damp strand, Nora watched the pelicans fly, gliding in over the long horizon of cliffs that met the incoming waves. Sorrow, anger, everything mixed with an urge as if to bless these people—Russ and Samantha in the lee of a dune, Ted and Becky racing down the sand, hands linked. Since the baby's birth, she'd felt she could not stop crying, but this afternoon she had no tears. As if no loss. As if no beach. *As if I don't exist. As if—no, but where is he?*

But, as if it hadn't happened.

Barefoot, she climbed onto a boulder wet with splashing waves. She had wanted the beach—*and here I am.* Ted was happy, Samantha was, the others too. And it was growing clearer that the war could be ended, perhaps the Bomb prevented, maybe all war be ended; better days might come.

You have borne your child. Nora, your child is born. He is healthy, alive.

A hundred yards away, beyond the breakers, two seagulls rode the waves. *So many blessings.*

She knew. *Now he's his new parents' child.*

The moon rose as they drove back to town. They watched it climb above the East Bay hills. In Berkeley, they turned onto the narrow streets of the flats, and Ted and Becky let her and the others off outside Samantha's apartment. Changing into a long skirt and angel-sleeve dress, Samantha hurried off with Russ to the opening of a Miwok art exhibit, laughing with Russ as they struggled to start his old Dodge. In D.C., it must already be late, but, alone in Samantha's dining room, Nora dialed her parents' number.

"We were beginning to seriously worry, Bubbie. Three weeks—no, it's been almost four—you haven't called."

"Daddy, I'm sorry."

"Something could have happened to you." Her father's sigh trembled; she felt his fear. "How would we know?"

"I was out camping, is all—with friends. There's no phone in the woods." Her words still kept trying to come out sarcastic; better to apologize.

"Four weeks camping? Darling, don't you think your father and I know—"

I'm no child anymore, Ma. No need to say so. She looked across the table at a light beige paint spot on the wall. "Please, I'm all right. Don't worry."

"But, Bubbie"—now her father's voice sounded happy, gladdened just from hearing hers— "that's what parents are for. You'll understand someday."

Already 2 a.m., and she was weaving silken god's-eyes with embroidery thread, the way Ted had shown her, when she heard Samantha and Russ come in. A few minutes later, sitting lightly on the rocking-chair across the room, Samantha took out her guitar and began to sing, in her throaty mezzo-soprano,

She walks by night in a long black veil,
Visits my grave when the cold winds howl,
Nobody knows, and nobody sees,
Nobody knows but me.

Nora put down the god's-eyes. "That song," she said, "it reminds me of that night." They both knew which night she meant. "No one knows. No one saw all that happened. Even the photos—when Benjamin took them to the AP, they didn't come out."

"I wish we could show everyone what happened, everything that happened out there. People need to know how change comes about."

"Yes. At least *we* saw. I saw what you did, saw what Ted did. All of you, Samantha—giving so far beyond the possible."

"No, we hardly—"

"I saw." There had once been a time—she remembered the Brecht play, *Caucasian Chalk Circle,* with the servant woman giving up everything to save the baby abandoned by the queen. Now, with Samantha strumming "We Shall Overcome" on the old guitar, she could almost remember—there'd been a time once, long ago, when she had known her own parents to be beautiful, brave, generous people. Maybe they were, and she'd lost that vision.

Samantha changed key, began to play a Joan Baez song. "I think sometimes we've been gifted, Nora, to have seen what we've seen."

Reach out. As if the loved one loves. As if whoever's there is loved. As if the loved one is there.

Outside, the street was empty. *His real parents love him; he loves them.* Longing and generous, open people. *I love my child.*

Love the love in everyone.

Grief was the other half of need, loss the other half of love.

Yiskadol v'yiskadol.

Somewhere the child lives, and he loves.

Part VI
The Other Half

1

Someone I Once Knew

March 1967

I'm living "as if." Weaving the little god's-eyes—pastel pink or pale blue, a row of purple, silver, gold, the bright-colored outer rows—she would remind herself, *Yes, someone to love is out there, if you live as if it's so.* Quiet filled the cottage, except when she'd listen to the songs on her radio, the same songs she'd heard at Samantha's in those first days just after the baby's birth. "Ruby Tuesday," "Strawberry Fields Forever," so many. And again "Somebody to Love." The first spring days passed.

As if she believed in her inner worth, *as if* she was needed by someone near she loved, *as if* she would never again let fears or lingering judgments—barriers lined like a mere string of Marines—keep her from caring or acting from care. *As if* only the outside world could ever stop her, for she'd not again stop herself. She checked and rechecked these feelings, re-reviewed her actions, tested the old thoughts and new, winding the thread around and toward each god's-eyes rim.

After all, didn't ceasing—if she had—to love Ted mean she had stopped at a barricade—had given in and so she, too, now was blocking love? *But one has to, sometimes, make decisions; even amoebas make "judgments,"* she'd laugh. *Even amoebas can learn.* Her love was within her and waiting, no matter what, and someday *would* draw her forth again, reaching out toward someone, breaking barriers, reaching through; there was time. For the moment, she would rest, let body and sadness heal; one needn't *always* reach, not always thrust a way through.

Yeah, sure, "And when in doubt, reach out!" How easy to parody her own ideas, make little jingles, laugh "'My love may bring the dream into fruition, make real what was conceived'—hey, good pun there!" Her lips smiled. *Yes, fine.*

No, but this is serious. She lowered the god's-eye, not yet finished. *There must still be time.*

Except, time for what? But the rest of the thought escaped her—something dangerous, but whatever it was must wait. Carefully she picked out a second embroidery thread, this one bright gold-yellow, and two more toothpicks, tied the new thread to the end of a grayish pastel, and began to weave another god's-eye.

Through the early spring rains and the new green leaves, the dogwood opening in the neighbor's fenced yard, Nora sat in the cottage weaving the god's-eyes like protective booties or new mandalas of the soul. It was as if, she felt, her mind spun a sort of peace, and when evening came, she'd make herself eat a meal. The songs on the radio spoke too clearly, "When there's someone you love trapped on the inside," "I'd just be faking it," "I won't be there besi-i-ide you." This was all right, though—*simply my body missing its baby.*

When Jan sent a card, "We have a girl!" she replied with a present of three silk god's-eyes, each wrapped in gold paper and a glistening bow.

2

On the Inside

April 1967

Finally, she'd had a phone installed, but at first nobody called. After four weeks, for the first time, it rang. The sound was raspy.

"Lenore? Lenore Seikh?" The voice, which made her throat go dry, was Millie's—stout Millie, her "primary" worker from the Children's Home Society. She must have told them they should contact her if —

"No, nothing's wrong, dear. Only good news. I'm happy to tell you, we have placed your baby."

"*Now?*" Her muscles clenched. It had been three months. "But I thought you placed him weeks ago, months ago. 'As soon as he puts some more weight on,' you said. 'As soon as—'" But now it wouldn't help him if she complained. "I thought he already had *parents.*"

"He was born so small, dear."

"You said—" No, she had relinquished this too, her right to argue for him.

"Dear, your baby has a wonderful home. That's what's important. His parents are still young, in their early thirties. They touch a lot, just like you asked for— every interview, they hold hands. They love him so."

And wasn't this the whole world? *They love him. Their baby.* The phone felt too heavy to hold. She could think of nothing more to say. "Thank you."

Besides, there was so much mail to read, so much she must do today. Envelopes to open, bills to pay. She had to read the *Chronicle,* catch the news. Later, it would be time to make dinner, clean up, get to bed.

But the next morning, when the phone rang again, the caller hung up before she could grab it. An hour later, she heard the voice outside her door, the familiar voice, shouting her name. She took a deep breath and turned the knob.

David stood slouched against the fence beside the walkway. Lighting a cigarette. "Yeah, babe, the *Barb* folks said you're still around. Come out, we need to talk."

Little late for that, David. Even though her womb throbbed and her breathing speeded up. Twenty minutes later, parked in a deserted lot above the freeway, not far from the Richmond hills, they smoked their cigarettes and stared out the windshield of his old green van. Nearly a year ago, when she'd got pregnant with his child.

He poked her hand, grinning. "How'd you like our latest targets?"

The power stations, did he mean—that explosion the *Chronicle* had headlined? Or the fake-bomb scare at the "glass bank" downtown? Or something else? She hoped not. She peered back at his ice-blue eyes. Seeing him at the door, she'd been frightened for a moment, but that was gone, both the fear and the old sense, around him, of not being brave enough. "Well, David, yeah, you're certainly showing people how to struggle."

Stung, he looked down. Feeling immensely distant from him, she said, more gently, "See, I'm more into pacifist actions, these days."

Through the windshield, the road and Bay and a pastel row of houses stretched away into the smog. He drank from a flask he'd pulled from the glove compartment. A seagull circled the littered beach below.

She watched the lone bird. "David, our baby is a boy. He was born small but healthy and active. He's been adopted. They love him. He *has* parents. He's fine." She saw David start to smile and a momentary softening around his eyes. Then he lifted the flask again, glanced at her across the rim, and began discussing the next planned action.

So this is how you care for people? Out beyond the beach, two fishing boats were crossing paths, gold waves floating in their wakes.

3

In Struggle

April-December, 1967

On April 15, 1967, two hundred thousand people marched against the war through the streets of San Francisco. Everyone sang— "C'mon people now" and "lighter shade of pale," "I'd just be faking it," and "Next stop is Viet Nam"; the entire length of Market Street overflowed with people and their music. Moving with the others through the Fillmore and the Panhandle toward the park, she saw blacks and hippies and bourgeois-looking families cheering from the rooftops or standing on sun-drenched lawns, offering food or a drink or a freshly rolled joint. Everywhere flew peace flags; everywhere shone god's-eyes. Even during the soporific rally with the usual speakers saying the too obvious, people danced, arms intertwined, and peace signs graced each corner of the huge grassy field. Traffic over the bridges stalled in what the news called a "peace traffic jam," and the radio announced a quarter-million marching in New York against the war; millions more were rallying, that day, around the world. Maybe it was turning, she thought; maybe they *could* stop the death machine.

But there was not only love, among the marchers. Stopping to catch her breath at a street corner in the Haight—she must be out of shape, she realized, still recovering from the pregnancy—she saw Ernie; while they stood talking, four hippies in patchwork jeans surrounded a small old woman coming from a liquor store and began to heckle her. "Wow, peace and love," Ernie snapped, and she crossed with him to wrap their arms around the woman's bony shoulders and lead her through the hecklers to her bus stop. At the rally, monitors were stopping people, shooing "hippies and folks who don't belong there" away from the elevated speakers' platform. "Hey, Nora, give us a hand here," a monitor from Berkeley Citizens called, tossing her an amber-colored armband. "To block the 'unimportant people' off?" she laughed and, wrapping it above her elbow, led two teenage girls in tie-dyed bell-bottoms through a monitor-line, giving them her water bottle.

Near the stadium entrance, Ted was standing by one of the first-aid vans. She ran to him, glad for the warmth in his gaze so earnest and unchanged. Samantha sat nearby, the two of them aiding anyone who needed help climbing the van's steep steps. But when she offered to spell them, Samantha said, "Oh, today we have too many volunteers!" *How wonderful,* Nora started to think, trying hard to be glad for this human outpouring, but feeling empty and unneeded; "Don't be like the System," she said, "Samantha, don't turn away people who want to give."

No—what a childish, defensive statement that had been. Quickly, she pulled back. And, eyes intently on the gold balloons, balloons that bobbed a hundred feet above the giant crowd, she hopped aside to let them treat a fainting marcher. But why, she thought, had she got so defensive, felt so hurt, as if left out?

Only momentarily, though; these were her people— Ted, Samantha, all the vigilers—and they and what they were had become part of her. She loved them, she was whole even if sometimes she slipped back into that sense of hurt or down into that emptiness. *And, damn, I am glad*—for the vigilers, the crowd and the too-numerous volunteers, sunlight on gold balloons, the music all around. It was good, their joy, the warm spring light they shared, good to dance together, good to accept—and to not *always* have to struggle and reach out, yet always to stay open and to seek.

But as spring wore on, it became less clear where to carry the struggle forward, where to actually seek. Antiwar activists, too often beaten and jailed and discounted, were turning tough-minded, hard-edged, no longer connecting in a caring community for peace but, instead, rushing to force the war's end through a "war at home." It was rumored another escalation loomed in Vietnam, that Johnson had set June 28 to invade North Vietnam; although some thought the story a trial balloon, there also were rumors of arbitrary arrests and draconian jail sentences—and of plans to reopen the World War II "relocation" camps. With the bombings ever heavier on North Vietnam and LBJ said to be readying a martial law decree, more and more people began to urge confronting the war "by all means necessary." Some spoke of resistance, others of revolution; few urged nonviolence anymore, and no one mentioned moral witness. When the battleship *Enterprise* docked, on leave from Vietnam, only a handful, mostly older women from Women for Peace, joined Nora at the gates of the Alameda Air Station to leaflet the returning sailors.

"You folks are gonna get yourselves killed down there," the *Barb* staff warned them. And, standing in the chilly morning with the five other demonstrators on the empty road beside the dock, sharing with them a warm baguette from the new People's Bakery, and hoping the food would aid their resolve, Nora shivered, dreading the tense wait for the sailors' approach and expected confrontation.

But when the gates to the gangplanks opened, and the newly arrived sailors streamed down, shouting and running and then turning directly toward the picket line, their young bright faces were grinning, and they cried out their agreement with the protest and the "Peace now! Bring the boys home!" signs. Nodding, smiling, they skimmed the leaflets, some flashed V-signs, and a few asked "How, though—*how* do I get out?" The Women for Peace acted delirious with delight, and Nora fashioned a smile across her lips like a doll; in her thoughts, she exulted like the others in the sailors' response and what it could mean for the world, but she couldn't fully feel the women's exuberant joy.

A few minutes later, when a Marine guard threatened one protestor, "Get back across that street or I haul you in," and she moved forward to interfere, boots stiff on the pavement as once she had crossed the Port Chicago highway, again she felt as if she was only living a repetition, barely feeling the present.

One afternoon in the thick heat of July, she reclined on a slightly sweaty cushion in a Haight Street apartment, breathing stale incense and watching, through the dark sweet-smelling smoke, the eight men and women who lounged along the mattresses that covered the entire floor. In the center of the room, someone threw the I Ching. The dark-bearded man pouring the wine spoke of auras and life energies. One of the men, a former activist, beside her rolled a joint.

"Don't be so uptight, girl. Feel the love." His hand trembled. "Get into the moment. Stop letting expectations rule you. Be free." On a pillow, a woman in tie-dyed shorts lay sleeping.

"Hey, even amoebas learn." Nora placed her glass precisely on a single exposed spot of floorboard and stood up. Barefoot, she balanced on the mattress edge, one foot lifted, toes in *pointe* position. "Man, this isn't love, this isn't anything." Stepping lightly around the stoned-out people on the mattresses, she located her boots in the hall and slipped off through the open door, holding the white wood railing as she ran down the steep outside stairs, thinking she should get back soon into dance again. Standing at the bus stop, she watched young hippies pass, thinking *We mustn't let the Movement fritter into parody.*

Two days later, a hundred miles upcoast, she visited with Nadine and two of the singer's "freak" friends in a rural commune near Mendocino. The commune was called North Unity. Marana, a gentle woman who lived in a tiny cabin beneath the pines, taught her to milk the goats. Nadine's guitarist friend Whiskers took a hit and snapped "Don't bring up Vietnam—no death trips here." In the barn, what the black-bearded leader thrust before her was a gun, a heavy-gauge rifle "to hold off the city people when it all comes down." Eighty feet above the ocean, firs and redwoods cradled thick ferns in salt mist, lost amid white fog, but the commune children's clothes were old and thin and their eyes seemed dulled. Standing with their mothers in the filtered moonlight, Nora wondered if these women, too, had gone numb.

Even in mid-October, the Bay Area stayed hot. Hitchhiking down Telegraph to Oakland in the predawn darkness with two of the organizers, she hurried toward the ghetto park that would be their staging point for Stop the Draft Week. As first light broke, she strapped a walkie-talkie under her poncho and moved out with the thousands marching on the Induction Center. Everyone expected to be stopped—to be attacked, as an unpermitted march always was, by cops. This time, however, they would resist, fight from street to street in "affinity groups," communicate through walkie-talkies. Like every other communications point person, she understood that this role made her likely to be the first attacked; as one Veteran for Peace activist had warned, on field patrols, the first person targeted was "the guy with the communications gear."

And meanwhile, as was pointed out in the final strategy session, no longer could people "go limp," acquiescing to state power. Instead they must resist, not by violence but never cooperating, either, "refusing to collude with fuzz in the pay of the warmongers." Today the protest would force the draft center, this pipeline to the war, to cease processing ghetto youth into murderers and cannon fodder.

Carefully, in the strategy sessions and scouting missions, they had rehearsed the plans, the routes, the walkie-talkie codes, and what to wear for protection, how to take evasive action. But it wasn't working—not the way they'd planned. They rushed the streets in the small affinity groups, helmeted, moving fast in their sturdy clothes, with picket signs strong enough for shields, and ready to fight; only, there was no opposition. In the early light, they moved on unopposed, the whole two downtown miles to the Oakland Induction Center.

There, they waited. A few still wore helmets or hard hats, but most people had removed them. Nearly everybody stood blocking the street in front of the Induction Center, between the brick and concrete buildings all around. Packed together, they filled the whole intersection; no busloads of draftees could possibly get past them. Yet, packed in like this, there was no way, Nora began to realize, for anyone to move quickly. They had countered the System's previous tactics, but what ambush lay ahead?

Across the intersection, rows of police stood stiff in riot gear and leather. Hundreds more cops, it was rumored, were gathered in a nearby two-story garage. In front of the Induction Center doors, one demonstrator, then three more, and then another thirty, sat down to block the entrance; buses full of draftees could be seen approaching.

Nora heard a cry, and then there were screams. Police—row after row of police—surged forward, swinging clubs right and left, and firing some sort of weapon, pen-sized cylinders shooting some kind of teargas. Ricky, shoving his way to her, was shouting "No, sister—hey! Hey, Nora, they tested that stuff on us, out at the Port, it's real bad news," and pulling her back from the front line. "Mace," the stuff was called, and cops weren't bothering with arrests but, all around, clubbing and macing everyone. Not only people here on the street or kids sitting-in, but everyone—demonstrators, reporters, passers-by—whomever they could catch.

Had it been an hour? Out here in the park where they'd finally retreated, she worked with the people at the improvised tent with the sign "medics' station," helping the injured. Everyone was sick and nauseated, either from Mace or from the flood of guilt and empathy. "Don't rub your eyes, don't rub your eyes," a nurse kept saying, grabbing the hands of a panicked teargassed boy. Nora tried to calm a woman whose arm had been fractured. Down the few paved paths, volunteer ambulance-cars kept arriving, then taking off again; some brought protestors who'd been injured while striving to block the intersections; other cars rushed off bearing the worst hurt to hospitals. From the podium, speakers intoned, on and on, "We're gonna be back, we won't be stopped, shut down the draft, this war must stop."

Police were leaving them alone here. A few people already were starting home. Somebody had passed around paper cups of water, and two older guys were handing out flowers. Not far from her, another car turned off the street into the park and came rolling down the walkway toward the medics' tent. Seeing Nora's "monitor" armband, the driver leaned out toward her from the window. It was Sally, and Nora started to wave, but Sally just called "Girl!" and shouted "Hey, I got a woman on the back seat here, unconscious, bleeding from a head wound. This is urgent." People pushed themselves backward, clearing the way. Nora grabbed one of the messengers, sent him into the tent for a doctor, and stepped to the side to let the car pass.

"Hey, you—move, damn it! Get outta the way!" The voice was Sally's. Confused by the cry, Nora stiffened. Across a patch of dried-out grass, the car had jerked to a halt, with Sally leaning out again, her hair askew. In Sally's free hand gleamed a water bottle, raised like a projectile, and she was shouting at a stocky giant of a man who stood blocking the path. Walkie-talkie still hanging over one shoulder, Nora started toward them. About six feet away, at the very center of the pavement, the big man hulked—fortyish, round-headed, muscle-bound like a picture-book redneck, a Mister Clean, a human tree. His arms were crossed. In Sally's car, the injured woman moaned, and, through the back window, Nora could see her thrash around. There was blood on the seat cushions and really, Nora thought, she looked no older than, maybe, sixteen or seventeen. A child.

The big man rocked from foot to foot.

Really, really, he's big.

"Say"—Nora stepped onto the gravelly pavement toward him— "say. Say, man, somebody's hurt there. There's someone hurt in that car." She was reaching her hands forward slowly while she spoke—softly, careful only to entreat—but readying to try to push him backward if she must. "That gal in there, she needs a hospital. She's hurt."

The big man didn't move—only that slow rocking back and forth, side to side. "Say—say, listen. If you saw someone injured in the street, you'd help, now wouldn't you? You wouldn't ask their politics? Of course not, you care about people—" On and on talking, "Do unto others, of course, of course you would, and—" Asking, asking; she must keep reaching.

Only, the injured girl's moans were changing, almost gasps. This was taking too long.

She couldn't hear what the hulking man shouted—two, three words only; he raised a fist.

Then he stepped backward.

As the ambulance-car squeezed past, Sally's free hand lifting in a V-sign, Nora let her own outstretched arms go numb and lower, fingers cramping. Her eyes watched the man, in case he changed his mind. *Well, good, I did this.* And in a way, it had been like breaking through the green Marine lines. This too was good.

Yet, since Port Chicago and her baby's birth—*and relinquishment,* Nora thought, hating the term—it was all repetition of what had been real. Those months were gone and nothing felt, any longer, new.

The next day, trapped against the concrete wall of an office building, cops moving in with clubs, she glanced down and, even though her legs shook and she automatically thought *I am afraid, I am afraid,* again she felt nothing. A dozen demonstrators rounded the corner, forcing the cops to break ranks so that she and those beside her might break free, but she only knew quiet gladness, *Yes, I'm safe, I'm free, I can go home whenever I wish.*

But an hour later, with thousands more people taking the Oakland streets, and news coming in on the radios of a quarter-million people marching on the Pentagon, she realized that this moment was a *victory* and this that she was feeling was the sense of victory— the brightly colored happiness of breaking past the barricades. *Ri,* she thought, of a sudden, *Ri, you should've been here.*

Strange to think of him after so long. *You would have loved this.*

She peered across the crowded intersection. Other demonstrators stood, as she did, scanning the streets and leaning against the concrete planter-boxes they had rolled, during the past hour, onto the street for barricades. From the far corner, Mark was approaching, holding out to her a chocolate doughnut. "Here, for you, babe. Saw how you backed that redneck down. Damned impressive."

She smiled politely.

"C'mon, seriously. That was nice work, girl. Give us a real smile!" He grasped her shoulder through the poncho—her old, beloved poncho, the one she'd worn at Port Chicago.

"Hey, cool it." She would define her own reality; she had learned that, learned it with David, with Ted. She shook Mark free. "Like, what's happening, all this, it's great, okay? But don't you tell me what to feel. What's going on, everybody's changes—hey, right on! But, for me, there's also been loss, you know? Guys I cared for, people who left. And I gave—you *know* this—I gave up my baby. So don't you go telling me—"

"Okay, okay. Hey, comrade, yeah. But what I'm just saying, enjoy this while we can. 'Cause it's not over, not by a longshot, Nora—and it's sure not headed forward. 'Cause, you know what?" He grinned. "We forgot to organize the workers." Cupping his hands to form a megaphone, he called out to the crowd, "Hey folks, just now we caught, just a couple minutes ago, an Oakland cop bulletin—you hearing me? —and it says Governor Reagan's just called out the National Guard."

That very next weekend, Lennie surprised her, arguing they needed to try even stronger tactics, "serious resistance, not playing 'Come and catch me' games with the cops, or going limp like lambs." She put away the sponge, slowly and deliberately—she'd been cleaning the kitchen floor—and stepped carefully to the stove to heat coffee.

"I'm not so sure about that." She placed two cups on the yellow table.

"I am." Lennie pulled a pen from his shirt pocket. "No one's hurting in this country, not all that much. Not like the people we're bombing. Yes, yes, people here get crushed by poverty, they get locked in prisons like we saw, but they're not being napalmed or cluster-bombed. And meanwhile look at us, dear—just look at us, right here, safe and sound." He poked the pen against the tabletop. "So yes, I am sure. Completely sure. And so's Jessica, for that matter. Sure that I'm wrong."

She didn't answer. When she had run into him and Jessica at the Peace Poetry candlelight reading on Labor Day, they had barely been speaking to each other.

Len pushed her pile of notebooks to a corner of the table. "You've stopped writing in these, haven't you?"

"Months ago. Been busy."

"Busy not feeling? Living 'as if'? Telling yourself what to emote."

"I don't 'emote.' Nobody 'emotes.' Anyhow, why do you—?" All at once, the conversation exhausted her. "Look, Len, I'm not denying my feelings, really. Like hope, like— See, I'm not 'faking it'; I'm *creating* the possible. I mean, if we act as if we can change things, maybe we will." *I mean, listen to the songs on the radio.* "'Cause we do need to hope. To end the war, to see we're whole. To reach out. Then our love will—"

But it wasn't just Len; everything seemed so hard a struggle, since those last hours of Stop the Draft Week, everybody celebrating that too-momentary victory.

"And if you don't live 'as if'?" Len was saying. "What if you don't? Nora, you do know what's missing?"

"Oh please. Don't start that again." Running his damn theories over her mind. "You mean, do I know *my baby* is missing? Right?" It felt like being smothered by a blanket, struggling to get out. "You don't know what I've *found.*"

He rolled the pen, studying its barrel, gently conducting with his other hand. "I've been extremely afraid to bring this up, understand. It's not my business, but, seriously, think about your baby. Because once you dump—actually *dump,* not just tell yourself you've dumped—your old friend Daniel's Freudianisms, and your Murph's tough-boy esoterica , and God knows what other former lovers' b. s., you're going to see—to *accept*— that you're not at fault. And that neither are your parents, or your—well, any of us. And something else, Nora—you're going to see that baby is your family. And, most important, you're his." He glanced up, so she had to meet his eyes. "And you don't even know exactly how much time is left."

"'How much'? For what?" His shirt looked ridiculous, scotch plaid. If he would leave, she could go take a nap.

"How many months California law allows for getting back an infant."

"For *what*?" She jerked at the meditation beads around her neck; they swung from side to side. "I thought you loved children? You think my baby's some package I should just go pick up? He has parents, remember? He has real parents." She remembered the huge eyes watching her. But newborns couldn't know who was their mother. "Babies love anyone who gives them warmth and milk and—and everything. Anyone, if there's love."

Outside the cottage, November rain pounded on the walkway, on the roof. She put away the *Learn to Sculpt* book, the block of white clay, and a tray of practice figurines she'd worked on that afternoon, before Len came over, and picked up the phone to dial the familiar number in Washington. She caught her mother sobbing; they didn't speak long, but she was glad that, by the end, she got her mother to laugh a little. Across the cottage floor, the new kitten, a black-and-white male who kept ambushing the older cat, and whom she'd named Che, sat on the round rug mewing, as if pleading to her, "Make the storm stop, Momma."

Again, for the hundredth time since those hours of victory on the Oakland streets, there came down on her, her old fear of death. *Today, or fifty years from today, sometime I shall die.* A song had been saying it, too, on the radio, "a moment's sunlight, fading on the grass." *Everything will end, and I.*

Well, this was hardly breaking news—*even too ancient for a* Barb *story.* But through the rest of the month and into December she went in and out of it, that awareness of the *other* side of love and life. Making it both meaningless and yet more necessary to struggle against the war.

And, like everyone, she'd begun to think the struggle might actually be won someday, the war be ended a new way of life possible. Even in their lifetimes, possibly, though did that matter? *But never mind the philosophy—* there was too much to do. In her poncho and boots, she hurried down the wet streets to another rally, pasted up more posters on the downtown phone poles and storefronts, registered voters into the new Peace and Freedom Party. But she felt empty and reminded herself what she'd said to Mark at Stop the Draft Week, "They left and they left—don't tell me what to feel."

And now I can reach out, she thought again, one evening the week before New Year's, *but no one is there; I cannot find him.* Bending low, she worked through the deserted courthouse corridor, side by side with Sally, managing between them to stuff flyers into every one of the commissioners' and staffpersons' mailboxes:

BRING THE BOYS HOME NOW. FUND HOUSING NOT BOMBS. WHAT IF YOUR FAMILY COULDN'T AFFORD A DOCTOR?

However individual and local this action might be, it could still lead to peace, to safety and caring for more people. They could all come together, each tiny action and all the growing demonstrations. They would.

4

All the Roads

Winter 1967-1968

Kids were banging drums down every street, on every hill. People rang castanets and blew whistles from their windows; children stood in doorways and tossed confetti high—or as high as they could. *Revolution, stars above, songs and joy and freedom! Peace and freedom, happy, happy New Year!*

At midnight in the East Bay hills, the Peace and Freedom Party celebrated getting onto the California ballot. No one actually believed that electoral politics could lead to revolution, but "You *know* the Estates General never even considered the monarchy would fall," as Mark laughed aloud, and, from a corner, one of the precinct leaders said "Think 1917." Gathered in a wealthy supporter's redwood home, they were eating huge pieces of roast turkey and drinking scotch and whiskey and cranberry-gin punch from the gold-rimmed glasses on the oversized serving table, everyone warm with laughter, while four couples danced, in the adjoining room, a sort of schottische to "Yellow Submarine."

Yeah right—right on. With a dozen other veteran activists, Nora sat under the picture windows at one end of the living room, the flatland far below, *our sorrows out at Bay, the old world far away.* Change would be coming—obvious, now. Tired from the rush to register "just a few more voters" in the closing pre-midnight hours, they relaxed and sang the freedom hymns, the "Marseillaise" and "Freiheit!" and the "Internationale," "Oh Freedom," and "We Shall Overcome," and twenty-eight more—someone counted them—antiwar songs. Liquor flowed, and people laughed.

"This is the day before the revolution. We'll remember this night for the rest of our lives." It was every perfect New Year, every childhood dream of Christmas, become real. *We are here. The world waits. Loving. Peace and freedom.*

I am here—

"1968! 1968! Happy New Year!"

—and also other-where.

Nora looked out the kitchen window of her cottage toward the blossoming cherry tree across the neighbor's fence. *It's been one year. No—even longer. A year-and-a-half since the changes, two-and-a-half since the beginning, the golden afternoon I lay beside Ri.*

One year since my baby was born.

It was a February day, one of those days when she felt empty. Life had been whole for a time; now Ted was only a friend, the vigil a memory, but the antiwar movement was firm though far from her, and the child . . . She missed him, of course, but somewhere he grew, strong and loving, with his real parents. And her changes were real—*I am whole and can love.* With Sally and a friend who could read astrology charts, she had been throwing the *I Ching.* Over and over, she would get The Well, "My waters are full. I only long that someone come and drink." She had laughed aloud at the possible meanings, but at Sally's question, had answered "Oh it's accurate enough."

She rubbed her fingertips along the purple bedspread. *I am building above a chasm.*

There was one person who might still be reached.

"And all the roads have led me back"—the words ran in her head, lyrics a litany as she approached— *"to this gravel drive, past barriers stronger than the gates of Port Chicago, in this light that filters through the first new leaves and yellow flowers onto these wooden steps."*

In the near silence, she knocked softly on the oval-windowed kitchen door. She listened for the half-remembered voice.

A moment later, someone turned the knob slowly, and the door opened.

Lamplight streamed out. Half shadowed, Ri stood there, wearing old jeans and a faded shirt, a notepad in one hand. His eyes moved, intent on her; his hands came forward with an old respect.

"Nora."

She thought, *He sounds happy to see me.*

"It has been so long. Come in."

"I needed to"—she stepped forward and leaned against a handy bookcase, trying futilely not to tremble or babble, wishing she could smile— "to believe in my worth, you know."

"I am glad you're here."

It was he. Here in front of her, his voice speaking. His dark eyes, his intelligent features, his proud stance. Glad she had come.

"I wanted to see you," she said. She looked down. And then began to laugh, "Oh my God, oh my God, I'm shaking. Ri, it's like facing a police line."

"I don't know"—now he grinned back— "which is harder, sometimes. Come sit down. Have you eaten?"

5

The Other Half

1968

"Once, early this spring, maybe in March"—she was writing another letter to Jan, amazed she and her former college roommate had stayed such good friends— "I started to tell Ri about what happened, I mean Port Chicago and the road and, you know, Ted needing me those months, and about my changes. But to explain—to *explain!* to say love is no dream, love can reach and be reached to—Jan, it sounds like, way too much like, 'So therefore love me.'"

Besides, whatever had really happened on that long-ago September afternoon, the hard part now was to simply accept her gladness—to stop thinking that, since she was whole and needn't stop herself, she *must* therefore keep reaching closer. Reaching to him as she longed to.

At other times, though, she could barely even focus on Ri, for revolution seemed so necessary and so imminent. And when she did focus on her love, it was hard to accept that she might do so—that to pull back at moments from "the Struggle" was all right, and to understand in her heart that the deepest love did not require loving *every* person, joining *every* protest, living *unceasingly* in hope.

Of course, Nora thought, glancing out the cottage window toward the yard next door, the struggle too could obsess one, but this was true of any change. "A period for battening down consciousness against the swell of contradiction, preferably on a day of calm seas," one of the Independent Socialists had lectured at a Peace and

Freedom Party meeting, "is requisite so we may probe all implications." Jimmy, across from her, had only raised an eyebrow.

But one real implication of the world's recent changes was, for her, obvious. The year before, "I alone cannot raise so wonderful a child" had made complete sense; this spring, with communes and open houses everywhere, raising her baby alone could clearly have been possible.

I hope his parents love him. She intoned the words each night, like prayers. *That he is growing and well. May he be healthy and whole, loving and loved.*

She rarely spoke of her child. Len was convinced that now her love for Ri was "a displacement, and you know that," but Len was wrong, his view a reductionism, as if she could only feel for the baby. There'd been *many* losses—and many gains; so much had been found.

One evening, a month after her first visit, she paused on Ri's porch, not sure he'd really meant his invitation, and suddenly he came hurrying across the porch. She felt his warmth as his arms went around her. Then he stepped back, hands lingering on her shoulders.

"It's still so hard," she said, "to know how to act with you."

"I am glad you're here, Nora."

With a jerky nod, she stepped closer. They stood under the overhanging vines. After a minute, he asked some question, then another, but she missed half the words, too caught in being with him—until she heard he was saying something about politics, about "revolutionary hope, as people say." She understood; she had to try to sound alert.

"I do know," she said, "what seems impossible can sometimes become real."

"That's very good." With a fingernail, he picked at the wood of the porch rail. The leaves on the vines hung pale and new. "We know so much, then, of possibilities?"

She dipped her head. Listening to him now was like being with him here both now and three years before. Through the kitchen doorway, his table was stacked, now as then, with papers, the bookcase still crammed full.

"Come in," he repeated. She followed him inside. Pushing up his sleeves, he cleared two spaces on the table and poured two glasses of wine. She turned the narrow stem of hers between her fingers.

But his phone rang, and he stepped abruptly into the next room to answer.

"Sorry."

When he returned, he sat across from her and again apologized. "That call was necessary, though. The work continues, you see; people are very serious. Even your people need help if they've tried to—" He didn't finish, but she remembered him saying, once, "Sometimes people have to leave your country quickly." Now he ran a fingertip along the rim of his glass. "Listen." His voice took on a harsh tone. "You do know I went home for a time? It's grown worse there. It's like years ago, just before our war. People have no jobs, no food; there is nothing. Except, everywhere there are shiny American cars, and the movies show shiny American homes, and people ask themselves 'Why don't we have these things?' They'll follow whoever promises hope. They are very angry, very frightened. Things are 'brittle' there. And your country makes us loans; it's buying itself new friends, you see? And the new friends have asked your government"—he stiffened— "to send 'special' troops. Like Green Berets. Your country always works this way."

"Did you— " For a moment, her hand shook; she put the glass down. "Did you ever talk of this with Len? Mendel, I mean."

"Mendel? Why?"

"I don't know. I thought . . . He's been so upset about Vietnam, these months. Everyone is, but for a moment I thought, maybe, if he'd also heard this . . . He's *so* angry about the war, you see."

"I'm not surprised. Mendel is very fragile." Ri took a sip of wine. "No, we've not talked about this. We don't speak much, anymore. But let's not discuss Mendel today. You wanted to know about my country. It is simple—the poverty is everywhere. People have no choices. Sometimes a father or a mother leaves their child behind; they have to look for work, you see. Listen, Nora, I was coming from a meeting, one night, a very wet night, and I found this little girl. She was maybe three years old, in the rain on the road, alone. Her mother had no choice. What will that child's life be?"

"Unless, maybe—"

"'Unless'? Unless she is a 'lucky' child? And tomorrow a sweet American lady takes her home, and she gets a nice swimming pool and princess dresses? And cookies."

There is nothing wrong with cookies.

"No, I'm sorry, Nora. I didn't mean—"

It would be all right. "I am very sure my son has a good home."

"Yes, those agencies are careful. I'm sure he has. There are great parents out there—you know that."

After a minute, Ri lifted a Spanish magazine from the table. "Nora, look. Look at this. Listen: 'Out along South Lading Pike, some farmers dwelled.'" Translating as he went, he read aloud, "'And there we stopped for water. The wife—for they each had wives—had llamas and a yearling horse,'" and soon he reeled out a third-cousin's long account of a countryside drive, the story of a pony seeking clover in a half-dry pasture, and a lengthy tram ride. He asked, "Have you read Frantz Fanon?" His hands moved in the curving gestures she remembered, gestures now become old friends. At moments, smiles crossed his face, eclipsed the familiar sadness. Her eyes fixed on him, drinking in the remembered dark hair, his dark, dark eyes. Eyes that called her like a baby's, like her son's.

I know we don't actually feel what another feels, Ri. Even so . . . She was caught up in gladness to see him, to be near him. *This is enough. Being with you here, remembering you here.*

That night at home, she felt her body yield to the remembered longing. She wasn't prepared; her hands turned electric as if touching Ri, and she dreamed cathedrals, stained-glass windows drenched in color, windows gliding through the centuries down shafts of light—falling toward Ri and at peace, never there yet ever nearing, without urgency.

Only, didn't the deepest love come in the bodies' union, only *later* reaching outward to this peace? Didn't *not* reaching toward a deeper closeness imply she doubted, still, her own love's worth, and that she thus could still lose truths and self-acceptance that allowed her to be with him? Didn't this mean . . .?

A wrong mental turn, she thought, entering a maze of self-doubt, a maze it took days to return from. But then she did, because *of course*—the realization came abruptly—the deepest yearning was still there, even if she didn't follow it, and whether or not she trusted in her worth. Indeed, her love would always be there, drawing her back when she was lost, calling her to herself, to her truth. *And to my—*

But the thought escaped her, an image only, soft and reaching. *Even if lost, we'll return.* For now, there was this peace.

Yet those few days' mental turmoil showed her how much Ri meant to her. For a time, all the political actions around her seemed mere fragments, shards in silhouette on a landscape she must traverse between the crisp, bright, longed-for moments with Ri.

Or perhaps the events themselves were fragmenting. After King was shot in Memphis and the Oakland police killed a young Black Panther, Bobby Hutton, a memorial demonstration moved through the Oakland ghetto, and she marched in it with the others, black and white, raising gloved fists. Everybody chanted "Free Huey, Free Huey, Free Huey," elbows pumping, circling the Alameda County courthouse, and crying "Freedom, freedom!" but then they went home. During the second Stop the Draft Week, she climbed a pedestal between Lake Merritt and a freeway ramp, poncho waving, and then a bearded television reporter asked, "Please do that again for the camera." At a "New Women, Our World" rally on the

Berkeley campus, Sally and eight other speakers demanded a focus on women and families, but the seniors group and Black Panther activists never came. Every week, she went to Peace and Freedom Party rallies or Independent Socialists events, and for months there were daily actions, but none of it hung together. Often the groups conflicted, and it would seem pointless, unresolved, torn in pieces.

And so at demonstrations she began to focus on staying free, so she might go to Ri. Which meant not only avoiding arrest, and balancing street actions with visits to him, but also balancing her outward reaching with inner questions—meant nurturing her trust in her love and in love's assurance she might reach out again. Reach out to—

Nora tossed her hair, warm in the sunlight of a bright afternoon on Telegraph, playing with a pink balloon while a sweet-voiced guitarist sang.

Watch through the summer
Drink of the dew,
World, how I love thee,
While our summer of '68 comes roarin' through!

"We're on the updraft, but a cold wind's rising," the old Independent Socialist looked grim. "Long decline a-coming." He sprinkled water from his paper cup onto the straggly daisies growing at the base of a STOP sign. "Even if by fits and starts. Look for it."

She only smiled. Every day one heard such commentary, casual sureties and questions that everyone was now finding important. So much of it concerned the choice between nonviolence and armed revolution. A man called Captain had brought two revolvers to a meeting "so you politicos'll learn what to do when they come for you," and she'd carefully turned the cylinders, practice-loading bullets. Really, it was like learning to start a car. *But police are human—and the angers and the barriers are in us, too.* However, if she'd said this, Captain would have crowed, "What happens when those nice fellow humans mow you down?" or "What of the millions we've killed in Vietnam?" and all the rest. She couldn't entirely disagree—and that was a problem since Captain and most everyone were sure of their own answers.

And the rallies on Telegraph were growing more militant— "like they think they can replay the Paris *Mai* without knowing its politics," as Mark laughed, next day, at the Mediterraneum. "Apolitical hippies—they know something's wrong but no idea what. And they'd rather not find out."

"Not everyone's a Marxist," she answered, reeling in her pink balloon and letting it rise again. Lately, most rallies had no politics, and when she'd focus in on street actions, they seemed directionless, without the clarity or care or caring and hope there'd once been.

"No idealists on Telegraph, for sure." Mark stubbed out a cigarette. "Things are getting hard. And people doing hard time, too." He reached over toward her balloon. "And for what? May I borrow this? The whole scene's—"

Fragmented. Not only in her view, then. In others', too.

Yet fragments could come together, and at least the protests *were* against the System, however vaguely. So she worked to raise bail and find Movement lawyers for people who got arrested, and drafted press releases, and wrote short, easily sing-able lyrics for the rallies. Every afternoon, during the sweltering summer weeks, she volunteered in the Advocates for Peace office—where, though the lawyers spoke like radicals, most had no interest in change beyond civil rights and peace. One day there, while she was logging her phone calls and getting ready to go home, the blond attorney, Rick, who functioned as boss though no one called him that, sat down quietly on the edge of her desk. He scratched his scalp but still said nothing; she saw his right hand shift, two inches from her left. *Rick, I'm not judging you, but nothing draws me toward you, okay?* Would she have to say it? She wished he would just move away.

What he was doing, though, was saying "You've been working really hard here lately."

"Well, we have to free people." She forced her urgency. "We need to hope for what's possible, not let people get crushed. Jail is war." A lame finish. Lawyers had a glib way to argue these things. She waited for his rejoinder.

"Sure, sure." He laughed. "But actually, what I was thinking is this: we should be paying you for your time. New Left wages, I'm afraid. But who knows? If you're lucky, they may cover your rent."

She didn't dare believe it. "I'm doing this *for people.*"

"Of course. We all are. But, in my experience, people tend to need a minimum of 'gets' to keep giving. As it were." He shoved his hands into his pockets, then pulled one out and again scratched his scalp. "The fact is, we need you here—by the time you're done with someone on that phone, he's reaching deep to donate."

She bent her head, unable to hide her smile of gratitude, even pride. "Thank you."

"We're hardly being generous." Putting his glasses back on, Rick stood and stretched. "I don't care what hours—couple afternoons, couple evenings a week, long as they're regular. Say twenty hours? At forty a week."

Forty was enough. She could give her parents this gift, at least—pay her own rent, her own food.

Rick stared at her, still stretching. "You're beaming."

It did seem surprisingly important.

For a while. But in less than a month, this too grew rote, the office a place of scheduled work, with the same friendly superficial feelings there'd been at the *Barb*. Of course this work was important—and the other actions, too. On the streets, it was comradely to march, to free arrested comrades; always it was crucial to build songs to call out involvement, words to bring out the press, so that the struggle would not falter and the war could someday be ended, the changes become the whole world's.

Yet, half the time now, she hung back, still protecting her freedom to go to Ri. Foregoing the many so she might reach the one.

On three of these summer after-work nights, a few minutes after getting home, she opened her cottage door to a knocking, and Ri was there. "Come out with me, Nora. Don't you want to see the new Bergman film?" or, laughing, "Come, let's go hear these nice people on campus explain how the Trotskyists will surely win," and, while she quickly changed clothes, he would wait, looking through the bookshelves and petting her old Mama-Cat and stroking little Newcat's back. Twice again, the caring in his eyes drew her in so deeply that, caught in the inner mazes when she didn't dare reach closer, she lost her path. But these times, when she returned to it—after only a few hours, often—she could see him. He was there.

"I *am* glad you're friends again." Across her kitchen table, Len spoke slowly, obviously to stress his earnestness. "But basically—I mean, basically, he doesn't love you." It was near midnight, one of her rare "free" nights anymore. She'd gone with Sally to a meeting on police brutality, instead of getting dinner; she felt desperate to sleep. But Len's words wakened her entirely.

"Did Ri *say*—did he *say* he doesn't? Len?"

The two of them worked in the same building, after all; they couldn't always be immersed in math. Or cvcn in department gossip. Easily, they could have found a moment to discuss her.

But Len looked lost. He cleared his throat. "No, of course not. Sorry. It's just obvious."

Her yellow table needed dusting. *No, listen, Len, every time I think Ri doesn't love me—and that's often—I remember how he watched me, that September afternoon, and how he said it, "I also missed you." It was how he spoke, how he held me.*

"You're wrong. You're wrong." He had to be wrong— or how could that afternoon have happened? That afternoon three years before, with the gold September light on her purple couch, and Ri's eyes, before she'd said "Wait" and begun to block off love. No—before one or other of them had blocked off love.

But now she knew her own worth, she'd never block love again. Even if someone she loved didn't love her, or if she wasn't sure, or if her fear somehow *did* block love, still her love was real—had always been real. Yearning, deep within, and someday . . .

"Nora?" Len had taken off his glasses to rub his eyes.

Everyone loved, everyone. "I'm okay." She poured a coffee for herself. *Don't start, please, just don't. No, and not about your marriage, either.* He and Jessica were separating; he'd said so almost lightly, but he looked haggard, eyes red-rimmed. "I'm just tired."

"From a council meeting?" He put the glasses on again. Behind the thick lenses, his eyes had a glitter she'd only seen that one night outside the jail. "Nora, why do you go to these things? They're sandbox games. Forget that—we have to get serious. I mean, seriously, skip this nonsense; stop getting backed up in your head—what you ought to say, how nonviolent we should be, all that. School's over; skip learning lessons." He placed his hands on the table and leaned forward. "Try skipping Ri, too. *No* more dreaming—that's it. There are people *dying*. Let's go for the solution. For the *win*. It's time. They're playing hardball; so must we."

Now *Len* was arguing against nonviolence? "That jail. That jail." She shook her head. "Those guys—or something out there—really hit you hard, right?" Or the break-up, maybe; they'd been married eight years.

But he was laughing, "'Something.' Yeah. Insightful of you, dear. 'Something.' The underbelly of the monster, that 'something.' You do know—those guards, they'd kill people in an instant. Right? They'd kill for fun."

Serious, then. Len was quite serious. Better stay awake and listen—better not nod off in her chair, even though she wanted to. She lit a cigarette. Okay, hear him out.

"They won't stop themselves." Len didn't wave his arms; he wasn't conducting with one hand. His voice sounded firm—acerbic, even. "It's up to us. We have to."

Slowly she exhaled. Important to answer; Len was so new to this. But instead, she yawned.

"Sorry. Better let you get to sleep." Len stood and thrust his arms into the sleeves of his old jacket. In his normal voice, he said, "Jess is taking the kids, did I tell you? But at least I can be sure they are safe, I can be sure they're not being bombed. In Vietnam, they'd be dying under bullets and bombs whatever she did or I did. Everywhere needs to be safe for kids. That's obvious."

The love in everyone and seeking ways to bring forth the love—that's also obvious.

"No matter how. Nora, no matter how."

The solution, too, must be caring. But she was too weary to find words. Len might not hear them, at this point, anyhow.

Overhead, helicopters roared. During these August nights, with so many people rioting on Telegraph, suddenly the city had a curfew. Sometimes she defied it, walking crosstown to Ri's apartment. They would talk, and she would laugh, and then they might sit quietly, or joke until the other laughed too, and they would laugh themselves to tears. They could discuss anything, really—or nearly anything, she thought; they never spoke of the one afternoon. And it had been weeks since she'd been thinking constantly about her changes, or why to try or not try to be closer to him. He was there, and that was enough; this *was* her happiness.

Only now, an hour after dinner, Ri spread the *New York Times* out on his table— "Russian Troops Enter Prague." The headline and its subheads made it clear; the Soviet Union was retaking it's too-independent satellite. As in Mexico City and in Chicago, the men with guns were clamping down, starting to reassert control over their world.

But she could not react, not yet. She could not take her eyes from Ri, his eyes so brilliant in the darkness.

"What?" he said. His gaze held that softness he'd shown her three years before.

"Nothing."

On the *Time*'s front page, a center photo showed young Czech resisters, most in jeans and jackets, on the streets of Prague, backs pressed against the treads of Russian tanks. Ri gestured toward the image. "Do you know what a tank looks like, from in front?" He lowered his hand. "Now watch, you watch, we'll see all the Big Guys get in line—each one the first to clap and cheer, we can be sure. Listen, what must a person be like, do you think, to invade a country, calculating a certain number will die?"

Those Czech people had risked their lives. Ri's eyes met hers, and the implications of his words suddenly terrified her. But why such fright? He was here, and she, and they were safe. She was whole, and he, and somewhere her baby, and everyone could love, the world would change. But if so, and if she trusted this, why this dismay?

"You know what will happen there next, Nora?"

Without thinking, she reached over and patted his hands. She nodded; now she knew what was wrong. "What will happen here," she said.

When she left—they'd been speaking for three hours—he came out with her onto the porch.

"I'll be glad to leave this country." His hands pulled a yellowed leaf from the overhanging vines. "Only a few more months." He looked away.

Her eyes teared. *Don't ever leave, Ri. You're my friend, my good friend.*

The glow in the evening sky was fading. His hand pressed on her forehead, a tender, sudden comfort. Surprised, she felt her womb throb.

Starting down the stairs, she looked back, seeing the shadows define his lined face, the softness around his eyes. "I'm happy for you," she said into the darkness, and meant it. Aware, too, that the hurt inside had only begun and didn't feel real yet. She turned away up the gravel drive, hand lifted in a little wave of goodbye.

There was a new hardness to the street people these weeks, and, desperate for Ri's eyes, she hurried down the crowded avenue, half-seeing the beaded people jostling in the night, and struggling to feel they too had tears they didn't show and might even seek what was beautiful but lost.

And now truly there was no longer time. Early November, the second evening after the elections, he taped a note on her door while she was out, *Sorry I missed you.* She couldn't decide whether he had meant she should call him. But really there was no time left for doubts and worries. She should have just walked over to his place; what if he were leaving early? Or if he needed her. And what if he stopped by again tonight, while she was stuck here, no privacy for a personal phone call, in the Advocates for Justice office?

"See, it isn't hard, just dial these numbers." She pointed to the list of potential donors, on the desktop beside the phone. "They all say they want to end the war." Jane, the doctoral candidate who was Len's assistant and sometime babysitter, had claimed she wanted to help fundraise, but she seemed afraid to start.

"All right—look, you'll be good at this, Jane, I know. Let's go over it again. You get the person on the phone; you ask have they heard about the protests. Second sentence, 'Twenty demonstrators went to jail last night on trumped-up charges of resisting arrest.'"

"'Trumped-up'? They *did* resist." The girl's long hair fell around her heart-shaped face. The gold-lashed eyes glinted, defiant. "You think that's bad, resisting?"

"No." Frustrated or not, Nora decided, she would not give in on this point. "What I think is we need to move people to donate, any way we can. And we're not the ones being violent."

"I'll say 'arrested on charges' but not 'arrested on *trumped-up* charges.' If you don't mind."

The defiance was way overdone. No one followed scripts exactly, anyhow. Nora wanted to walk out, but sometimes caring for people meant not reacting. And it wasn't her politics that bothered Jane, anyway; it was the fact that Nora had given up a baby.

Jane had been helping with the twins, the night of Len and Jessica's outdoor Sukkoth celebration, weeks before—their last, curiously Jewish, social event before Len moved out for their "trial separation"—when, late in the evening, Jane had pulled her away from the other guests.

"I'm almost afraid to tell you," Jane had said, "how much the girls loved your presents. Didn't you notice?"

The gifts had been guesswork, a silky purple stuffed giraffe for Tanya and a pink plush puppy for Sarah.

"You really know children," Jane had added.

A few minutes later, while they still labored at making conversation, Len had come around the corner. "Janie, Nora's the woman I wanted you to meet!" He'd been rubbing his glasses, not looking at them. "You should talk with Janie, Nora. She's adopted."

Now, standing by the office phone, the younger woman flushed. "Why didn't you tell me you're a natural mother?" Jane's hair matched the gold of the picture frame behind the Senior Counsel chair. "Len had to. Not that he used that expression. But you—why didn't *you* tell me? I mean all of you, you"—her voice rose higher—"you're all so duplicitous. That's it, just duplicitous. But don't go counting, anymore, you, on secrecy. That's over. Like, I am going to find my real mom, and no law—no 'this family not that family' stuff—is going to ever stop me."

"I'm not disagreeing." Nora's voice choked up, matching Jane's, and surprised by her own urgency. "They force it, you know, they forced it on us—their way, or not at all. I never wanted secrecy."

But Jane made a sound like a snort. She turned back to the phones.

It was getting far too late for making calls tonight. But Jane was sitting there, a hand on the receiver—as if still too scared to ask donations, or maybe too stubborn to get up and leave. And challenging every suggestion.

Like, I'm not your mother, girl. Nora pulled her poncho on.

"You're leaving already? Just 'cause I won't agree to lie?"

"Because I'm sleepy. I've worked all afternoon."

"In jail, they're not sleeping. And Vietnamese don't get—"

Okay, okay. It must be after nine, rain pouring from the gutters in the darkness. Zipping up her boots, Nora opened the door and started down the staircase. "It'll go better tomorrow, Jane." *Like, Ri, you should see me handling this practical world.*

But by the end of the twelve-block walk home, she was too wet to think. She slammed open the door and rushed inside to huddle by the wall heater, peeling off her dripping gloves. They would get ruined, lying too close to the heat, though. She bent down for them, thinking how little impact her or Jane's or anybody's actions would have, thinking it was all too late. Phoning for bail did nothing; people, kept getting killed; the war rammed on and on. To protest—had that ever stopped anything?

No, of course it wasn't just Jane that upset her. Jane or the war. *Don't hold back. Reach out.* Somewhere her baby was cuddling—*he has a mother, remember.* And somewhere, somewhere, there'd be others to love; she was reaching out again in the world; there would be people who loved, whom she'd love.

Stepping closer to the heater, she glanced over at the frayed "mandala" of the inner-outer self, the Port Chicago poster, the banner BRING THE TROOPS HOME NOW, a photo someone took at Stop the Draft Week of her wearing her poncho and waving a blue-and-white peace flag. She hadn't eaten supper yet; she could fix a salad, some cold chicken, or maybe cheese. In the kitchen, she set out a plate and knife and fork and opened the refrigerator.

"Nora!" The voice came from the yard, just outside the back door; it had an urgent sound. She reached for the doorknob, but stopped. The voice sounded familiar, but fences hid the garden completely from the street and it was pitch dark out. Pushing aside the curtain over the door's little window, she could make out only a silhouette—a man's.

"Nora, hey, it's me. Len."

Of course—his voice. But, she realized on opening the door, not very like the Lennie she'd known.

His face was chalk-white; his chin and cheeks were a stubbly mess. There were mud stains all over his jeans, and he was soaked with rainwater, his flannel shirt a sponge. As if he'd been standing outside for days.

"Len, you'll freeze—get over here." He moved like someone sleepwalking. She dragged him toward the heater, quickly turning to relock the kitchen door. Prowlers, of course there could be prowlers, but something else, which she didn't understand, made her suddenly wary. Made her feel inexplicably vulnerable.

Shivering, he stood by the heater, the nervousness of his hands, twisting together like fraying ropes, painful to watch.

"Can't live without Jessica, eh?" She hoped the humor would ease him.

But he raised his head. His eyes looked flat. "Nothing so nice."

The cider was hot. If Len would drink a second cup, he'd warm up soon, while his shirt dried. She offered him a blanket to dry himself, but he waved it off.

"Go on," she finished. They were whispering. When he'd started telling her, she'd lifted a hand, signaling *Stop*, and said "Let's talk more about Jessica," then written, with a black ballpoint pen, on a sheet of typing paper, IN CASE THERE ARE BUGS. WRITE STUFF HERE. But it hadn't worked; he kept forgetting, his voice rising in pitch as he tried to tell her. "You know," he implored "You know I don't hurt people."

"Of course." She'd realized by then that he didn't mean Jessica. And he didn't mean simply emotional hurt.

"Remember Professor Dunne? Remember when he said, 'I thought physics would help the world, but I ended up on the Manhattan Project, so I switched to math'? Like that, Nora. Like that, but reversed. Well, not quite." All the while, his hand had waved frantically in its conductor dance.

"Hush," she'd repeated, ignoring his protests and draping the blanket over his still-wet shirt while he tried to dry off in front of the heater. "Come sit at the table, once you're dry enough; get something warm in you, at least." Again, she had pushed the pen and paper to him and urged that he write things. But he couldn't, so she'd said "Well, whisper in my ear, then," barely worrying how he might react to that proximity. "C'mon"—she had shoved him down— "take a chair here, next to mine."

He had complied and leaned close to tell her.

Now, as she said, "Go on," he gulped a mouthful of cider, swallowed, and began to whisper. His hair curled around his face. His left hand shot out, gesturing nervously.

"Math," he said. "Math is not my only field—you know that. I'm *good* at physics. And chemistry. Even as a kid, I did the, the most fascinating experiments, even using ordinary ingredients. And so"—his voice rose higher— "so that was what I used."

"Hush now."

"We *have* to stop what's happening. It's massacre after massacre. If these thugs in power see how deep, how really serious, our opposition is, they'll stop. They have to. But nothing else is stopping them—not moral witness, not resistance, nothing. Well, and so, so that's what I thought. Wouldn't you agree?"

"We need to reach out, even to warmongers." Her answer was starkly automatic. Len hadn't got into this shape just by talking politics.

"We have to save lives, Nora. Give Vietnamese people *their* chance to 'reach out.'" He wasn't asking. "And I thought—you know, I thought others, if I show them how, they'll see to get serious. And nothing is working—nothing else. So, I read up. I know how to research." He started to laugh, then forced his voice down. "I talked with someone—not that 'Captain,' he's bound to be an agent, but someone out of town. Someone I've known since schooldays. And, you know, I am exceedingly good with making experiments."

Her knees were knocking together, she'd had no idea they could shake so fast. That morning, an explosion had injured a watchman—a civilian—at the Navy's Contra Costa Storage Site. Not far from Port Chicago, not far at all. Only far enough to be less well guarded. The news bulletin had said "investigators are seeking the perpetrator or perpetrators" and spoken of "suspected sabotage."

Silly, though, to think of Len in that connection—Len crawling under a fence or twisting wires or planting something explosive, his glasses probably sliding off.

He was moving his lips close to her ear, so close she felt his breath. It was too intimate—uncomfortable. But she kept still.

"I didn't think the thing would blow so soon. Not for at least another hour. I thought it might, you know, knock out some bomb casings. Not to hurt anybody. But to just let them know we could."

Let them know? But the watchman's leg was broken or worse. Possibly much worse. "Len, Len."

"I walked through the gate, right into this big space. It's just off the road, six metal sheds and a two-story warehouse. I went into one shed, and what I did there, I put down my box of bottles, right under a plastic canopy behind a van. I just worked, careful not to drop anything, until it was set. Then packed up my box and lit the fuse, and I walked out. I was still amazed I'd got in, astounded I hadn't been stopped. I wasn't thinking clearly, Nora, not about what could happen. Not about if someone came along, if a worker there happened by to pick up his work clothes—there were bunches of clothes hanging on hooks on the walls. I wasn't thinking, except,

Blow up their armaments, show people it's possible, how we can disrupt the war right here at home. Make clear they cannot keep this horror going; we won't let them; war's not what we want."

She nodded, pointed at the paper on the table: BUT THE WATCHMAN? She printed the words slowly, giving him time to comprehend: he must not answer aloud. A finger to her lips, she handed him the paper. And said, not whispering, "But you know we need to *reach* people, not give up on anyone."

OH YEAH? His pen seemed to write by itself; his eyes stared forward at the wall. TOO MANY IDEALS CAN MAKE US COLLABORATORS. ONLY, IF I'D KNOWN

The pen dropped onto the table. He grabbed it up. HELL, IT DOESN'T MATTER ANYMORE. Grasping the pen tightly, he stared at the paper, started to lay the pen down again, then slowly printed, JESS TOLD ME. WHEN I TRIED TO STOP HOME. SHE SAW ME COMING, MET ME IN THE NEIGHBOR'S YARD. HIS BIG HEDGE. JESS SAID THEY'D JUST BEEN TO THE HOUSE, TRIED TO QUESTION HER.

"Somebody knows a secret." But she wrote, PLANTING BOMBS WON'T SAVE PEOPLE.

"I realized that."

WAS THERE A SURVEILLANCE CAMERA?

DON'T KNOW. MUST HAVE BEEN, he wrote.

But she could hear his panicked breathing now. The breathing of a person who had harmed someone. Who had wounded someone innocent, wounded them badly. And she was *helping* him, though he'd done that. No— she stood up. No—she had to move around, get away. She walked to the stove instead, concentrating on the cider, on heating and pouring more cider. More cider. This war was killing too many people, killing millions of people. The watchman was only one person; sometimes one had to— No. No, that was not it. "Why—?"

No, *no* time for this stuff. "Here. Even so, Len, here, even so. Give me your cup. I'm not sure how to help, but, yeah, I will."

Then it hit her. Of course—Ri would be leaving soon, but not yet, thank God. And it was so clear in her memory, those words he'd said. Only the once, only casually, "Sometimes I helped when someone had to leave the country very fast," and those tales about the *action group* back home, and his offer one night, over a mug of wine, "If it gets really bad in this country, so you need to get out . . ." Yes, all of that. Of course. So many people claimed to be "underground" or "revolutionary," but this was *Ri*. And he was safe to ask, very safe, and Len was his friend.

"Are you still cold? Here, use two." She pulled the second blanket from her bed and put it over Len's shoulders. "You stay put here, all right? Until I come back." But how long could he dare stay? Jessica could've made even the slightest slip of the tongue or got frightened for the twins and said too much, or somebody might have seen Len come to her own door—and, for that matter, they'd start tracking down his friends. No, soon this cottage would become no safer for him than his own home. *Nor for me, if he's found here.*

But she didn't feel frightened. She felt calm, rational; she would work out a plan. "Stay put," she repeated. Len was hunched up, his left hand lightly conducting some melody. "If you keep being cold, Len, get under all the covers." Her voice dropped to a whisper. "And don't touch that phone. Don't open the door. And do not speak first, when you hear me come back—wait to be sure. Okay?"

He managed a nod. He said, "Didn't think anybody would come in." She nodded. She shredded the paper they had written on. Going to the sink, she mixed the shreds with water and old salad bits, and stuffed the mess, with last night's gravy, into a bag to take out to the garbage later. "They collect in the morning," she said. Len kept conducting, but he was trembling. She must go to Ri now—no question. Must hurry.

"Nora," Len whispered. His face seemed even whiter, his eyes huge. "She wouldn't let me stay. She said, 'Consider the twins.'"

"Anyway, it's hardly safe for you there," she whispered back, knowing whispering made no difference. "Or here either, probably. That's why I have to hurry. See you in a bit." She wanted to squeeze his hand reassuringly, but no, he'd surely misinterpret the gesture. Shoving her feet into her boots, she flung on the poncho and hurried out, turning the lock behind her.

The driveway was so wet her boots splashed loudly wherever she stepped. But she wasn't trying to come quietly tonight.

Ri stood silhouetted in the yellow light from the doorway.

"Are you all right?" he said.

Dripping wet despite the poncho, she paused on the top step, cold and shivering as Lennie had been. "Listen, I need help." It was more than two years since she had said those same words, the night she'd run here, pregnant; she could feel the hands moving out to draw her inside. "Come in, it is all right"—those words too had not changed.

A minute later, they were seated on the velvety couch. From the kitchen, he had brought two mugs and a bottle of French wine. "And so?"

"Ri, you told me something, once." She was afraid to ask, but afraid in a new, different way. She had sensed this world in him, but it was one she didn't know. Another world without coordinates—though one where he seemed at home. "You told me, years ago, you . . ."

"Go ahead." He put a gentle hand around her wrist.

As he had, long ago. And it was good to be here again, here with him, at pcacc. The wine glowed red as he poured it. "Ri." If—

They had to hurry. *Len. Help Len.* Hoarsely, "You remember Mendel?"

"Yes?" Ri's hand released her wrist.

"His office is next to yours?"

"Yes, of course. And so?"

"He's become quite radical." She still felt the imprints of Ri's fingers on her wrist.

He took a sip of wine. "What's Mendel up to?" He smiled; it made all the little lines around his mouth crinkle. "No, wait." His hand was grasping hers again, too tightly. "Don't answer that. You're very pale."

"It's—I don't know if you remember." Now she was whispering. "Once, you said, 'If someone needs help, if people need to—'" *To escape this country,* but obviously she couldn't say it aloud. She pressed her face against the velvet of the couch, which must have once been bright blue. The threads were half worn off. But why notice that?

"As far as I know," Ri was saying, "I keep this apartment clean. But let's go out. We can take a little walk. It's such a pretty night, don't you think?"

Under the elm at the corner of his block, they stood, backs to the rain. She told him, "And then, Len said, he kept thinking 'We need to show them what we'll do if they don't stop the massacres.'"

"On the news tonight, they said the watchman—that one of his knees is crushed, you see." Ri kept his voice barely audible.

"No one else got hurt."

"I'm sure the watchman will be glad." He kicked the wet ground. "And to know he'll probably live. Look, Mendel did what he had to do. We would not have, perhaps."

"He's an innocent."

"It's done." Ri sighed. "So. Now we will go on."

Once, in rain like this, they'd stood together, but she couldn't remember where, or what that had been about. Tonight it was to protect a friend who'd crippled someone who—no, Len too was an innocent, except—no, again no time for that; they had to—

"Nora, is he even sure they suspect him? It is very soon. The news named no suspect."

"Jessica told him. When he tried to stop home—I mean, at his old home."

"He went *home?*" Ri put a hand under her elbow. "Oh God. All right, so let us walk back slowly, a nice couple strolling in the rain. We shall go by stages." She wanted those dark eyes to turn, those lips to say "Let's really be a couple in the rain." But certainly not, not now while Len—in fact, they must hurry, *hurry.*

Ri was saying, "I shall phone you, probably soon after you get home, as soon as I can reach . . . someone, a very trustworthy person. Then you will take Mendel outside. Just walk with him to the street. You be there with him, you walk like we are now, like lovers. I will tell you the color and shape of the car. You don't know car makes? No, of course not. All right, afterward, they will meet another car, and it will take him farther. And then maybe another."

"If there are cops—?" The thought made her stomach shudder. "When we go outside?"

Ri halted; for a moment, he held her still. "If anything happens, you didn't know. You understand? Your friend was visiting, friends sometimes visit, sometimes late. But you'll see, it will be all right. Probably he will get out of this country very safely."

Probably. And already Ri was endangered too. And he'd not said a word to question her endangering him. And wouldn't, no matter what happened.

Ri. Oh yes, go through the fear to him—*go toward.* She could turn—right here, right now, the trees all around. But no, of course not. They had to hurry, *protect our friend.*

"In my country"—Ri's voice had turned grim— "we've had so much of this. And you—you can get home all right? While I shall go speak to this person, or possibly two."

After the first blocks, the rain slowed to a drizzle. Crossing streets was less like wading a stream, and she could look ahead, but the streetlights seemed too bright, the shadows less enfolding. And one or two people, here and there, were out now, stepping from a doorway or running to a car, even—as she rounded the corner onto the brightly lit Ashby Avenue, nearing her cottage—an old man came walking by under an umbrella, carrying groceries. Any of these persons might pass again, in a few minutes or whenever it would be, while she was bringing Len out. And these people Ri knew—always he was working, doing math; could he also know these people so well? But if he didn't, what if—? No, but he must; he wouldn't endanger her. Or Len.

Her heart clenched—like a big fist, as people said. It was as if iron clamps squeezed it, trying to make it jump like a trapped fox. A sadness, less frightened than grey and dull, came on her, as if her feet could never take another step. It *was* Ri she needed, and safety. Any moment, from Telegraph three blocks away, or from the driveway by the nursing home across the road, or swift and siren-less around the high-fenced corner, squad cars could swoop in, lights flashing. *"Halt—hands up. Up, up."* And *harboring* was not like three steps over a trespass line, not like pushing forward between Marines.

Except it is. She lifted one foot from the curb and stepped out on the street, the boot splashing onto the asphalt. Her friend needed her. The tree across the way, the spruce beside the grey stone house, seemed higher as she neared it. Passing the next yard, she cut through dripping tangles to her landlady's front lawn. The shadows were dark and still along the walkway to the cottage, so she felt a moment's hope. But a single beam, one shot, still could shatter everything. Or the cops could have come already, be standing inside, and it be too late.

In the shadow's edge, she paused, breathing the moist night air. Even if cops *were* there, even if she went to jail for years and never saw Ri or her child again—*still I am whole, still I love. I can do this.*

She moved down the path to her door. There was silence in the darkness. *Len, we are going to send you to safety.* Pulling out her keys, she leaned forward, shivering again in the cold drizzle, to open the lock.

6

This Strange Defeat

November 1968

"You felt bad just now, back at your place," Ri said.

They were drinking coffee, crammed on their chairs between the tiny table and the railing, on the balcony of the crowded Mediterraneum. "It bothered you not to be serving me a fancy dinner? But, you see, it was simple and fine. You cook very well."

"Thank you." She smiled but then blushed, and to cover, said something about change, switching quickly to politics. "If people *can* realize, then perhaps"—but she felt the force in her voice slide away— "then maybe we will change things. And we must, we must change how people see themselves, if—"

Dinner noises rose around them—cups clattering, people chatting, crescendos of sound.

"Oh yes, let's make the world change." Ri laughed. "But listen to me, Nora, you've seen what happens. When someone tries without sufficient politic, with no preparation—you saw what happened to Mendel. And it would be very nice, of course, if we can get through to everybody, get through and change things. But look around us—here, look right here. Here's an 'everybody,' these people, and they're all over your country, and not only your country. Do you think they care about everybody—anyone but their own? Just look at those faces, Nora—how smooth they are. You understand why? It's because they *will* not show what they feel. Because they know better—because they know not to let anyone see. Because they're out to win. To exploit and to *win.*"

He leaned forward, not laughing now. Not laughing at all. His eyes glittered, sharp and black.

Like a raptor's, she thought. She stared back, mesmerized.

"Because they *will* exploit," Ri repeated, "as they have exploited our countries for five hundred years. Like birds of prey." Again he laughed, but coldly. "Back home, I used to think of that. I would be working, caught up in some theorem, and suddenly I'd start thinking, how can I, too, become a bird of prey?"

She couldn't pull away. Somehow the fact of being together tonight, here at this table in this mobbed café, had come to this—these strange words and intensity. They'd been speaking earlier of literature—he'd given her a copy of *Andorra*—and then, walking from his car, they'd been discussing Len. Ri had said, "I should get another message soon. So far, he's safe over there," and she'd told him of Jessica's hurried visit, Jessica's warning "the FBI keeps on my case, I've hired an attorney. You should, too." But maybe that was what had set Ri off—because when she'd said "If Jess is right, it may be safer for you to not see me," Ri had answered, very quietly, "I make my decisions. They don't."

Now, across the table, his expression remained grim. "If I could teach my people to be birds of prey, Nora—"

She started to speak, but he shook his head. "Wait. Don't you see? Then my people could get back at them."

She was shaking her head. Vehemently. Ri laughed again. "This upsets you, Nora? How nice you are. But see how nice we both are, you and I. Here, I talk, but of course I'm very tame. And besides, there's my work—of course there's too much, it is endless, but then, you see, I like doing math." He turned to her. They were walking down the stairs and his face was wreathed in smiles. He was taking her hand, patting it quietly.

Then they were standing in the doorway of the Med, readying to rush into the rain. "I think maybe we *have* had good years," Ri was saying. His voice turned serious again. "No, don't you think so? You know, these changes you speak of—you're right to believe in them, and to be freer now with your feelings—see, you're blushing. But, remember this, too"—he draped her poncho around her shoulders and then pulled up the hood of his jacket— "let's not forget, those guys are fighting back. You saw what happened in Chicago and in Prague. They've found they can win, and they'll want lots more. They won't be backing off easily. Here, take my hand."

She did, and they splashed across the near-deserted avenue, running for his car.

"But did you understand?" Driving down the dark streets toward her cottage, he kept glancing over at her, and repeated the warning. "These changes are very nice, very hopeful, but this revolution people talk of here, don't believe all they say. It will use you up."

"I know, Ri." And yes, he was being kind, he understood, and yet . . . "It isn't just the politics; it's our feelings, too, Ri. I've no choice; I *have* to keep fighting. Because it's only since my changes that I can even accept that I *can* care, even when—"

"Well." After a minute, "You're a wise person," he said. "And I have no answers. But for me, you see, I've no illusions anymore. I live from day to day."

"Here?" Her voice came out husky. "Here, you mean? But this will change, if you go home?"

"Why should it?" He was driving very slowly. His hands turned the wheel. "One can go back to a place, but not in time."

She glanced at his face, glad for the darkness so he wouldn't see her tears.

The car rounded the last corner, and he stepped on the brake, halting by the walkway to her cottage. She held out one hand and laughed a little. The engine kept running, a thrumming against the rain. "It's silly, you know, but I still get afraid if I—well, if I touch—" She watched her fingers, flat together, press against his shoulder. "I don't know what to do."

"There's nothing you can do."

The rain beat on the windshield. It ran in streaks like blurred time down the glass. "I'm glad for tonight, Ri. Ri, look how hard the rain falls."

He reached up and squeezed her hand. "You see, it *is* better to just be natural."

"Yes."

He shut off the engine. "Come, let's go inside."

In the kitchen, it was warm. They had nearly finished the spiced cider. He leaned back against the bookcase, by the yellow-painted wall.

"There's this way you know people, you accept people," she said, "I still don't understand. It's a way you know yourself, or—I don't know what it is."

"Perhaps it's that I know my limits."

"No, not limits, Ri."

"Oh, but they are limits. You think I accept so much? No." His next words, she wasn't sure she caught. "I'm dead inside."

Five minutes, maybe more, had passed. She'd asked, "What do you mean?" but he hadn't replied. The cider rested, still unfinished, in the white mugs. She still sat here at her wooden table, the light from the shaded lamp dark gold. Ri still leaned against the bookcase, eyes watching her, hands pressing on the tabletop.

"When people here talk about changing," he said, "what does that mean? These changes you speak of— they're important, of course, and sometimes, when we go after something, it makes us very happy. But this stuff people tell themselves here—if I can just get this car, this house, this girl, then everything will change—no. There are things, we cannot change."

She forced a smile. "That "*cannot*" can be illusion, too."

"Oh, that's such sophistry. Nora, you understand better. Sometimes it is far better, far better, we simply live day by day."

But she wasn't hearing the words. Because he was speaking of something else, of emptiness, and she understood—*this* was what it was he'd meant when he would speak of "my country," of possibilities that "also die;" it was what pulled him back to that other place in time.

She said, "What do you mean?"

"Nothing. Nothing real. But those hopes, you see, the ones we believe when we are young, when they are our world." He paused, still gazing in her direction but looking instead into a different place or time. "When we are young," he repeated. "We were, this girl and I. Someone I once loved."

Nora raised a hand. *You don't need to tell me this.* Only, she had asked.

"We did everything together, Nora. We had our plans, the way young people do. It was our first love. We were very intense. Very silly." He smiled. "We were still so innocent— she was quite strictly raised. Oh, we argued, we hugged, we kissed when we could. We laughed with friends and hiked in the countryside; we went to rallies together, the same as people here. But understand, this was a very liberal moment in our country. And, after a year or so, the country had another coup. It was very bloody."

And had happened, though no one had wanted it.

"They had, of course, many tanks from your country. And many guns. Of course we lost. But that's not it. Because, in your country, if a woman goes to rallies, if she marches in a demonstration, it is completely normal. But, at home, this was something new. If a woman did such a thing, she was looked on as dirty—no, not dirty, but as *shameful, unheard of.* And so, after the coup, when the guards would come for a woman, everyone knew what would happen. And there was no way—we were kept in separate corridors, separate cells—no way any of us could stop it." He stepped back from the bookcase, running his hands along the upper shelf. "Sometimes they would give the woman a way out—no 'hard games,' nothing rough, if she will sign this little paper. Implicating herself, and sometimes others.

"There was a day we were let out, most of us. At first, we expected to be shot. But then the fighting moved to another province; the tanks went away. A few among us—and those who had been implicated—were sent to the prison camps."

He turned, as if again seeing her. "Tell me, what do you think we could have done? If they had not hurt only the women, or if later we could have spoken of it—but of course we couldn't. Because if she had been very brave and they had wronged her . . . But to think of that was itself to wrong her. And what could I have asked? 'So did you sacrifice some comrades?' Whatever had happened, you see, we'd been too helpless, we were too ashamed, to speak of it. Soon, we couldn't speak at all.

"We were so young. Nora, at that age, how can one understand such things?"

No, she should rush to him, cry *Ri! I don't want this to have happened.* Only, it had happened, and what she longed to heal was in the past. His past, and that girl's.

"When these things happen to us," he was saying now, "we try to understand. We tell ourselves, 'It must be something wrong in me.' And that's the worst part, thinking what is wrong comes from inside. Since then, I keep the wound open."

Abruptly, the bookcase—something on the bookcase—caught his gaze. "Nora, you made these?" He reached a hand toward her white clay sculptures ranged along the lowest bookcase shelf. Carefully, he lifted the nearest sculpture—two tiny conjoined figures, slim like dancers, the larger bent over the smaller like a mother enfolding her child. "You do know, this is beautiful." He looked up and smiled at her. "I was so worried for you, that night."

"You helped me then. So very much." The night when she'd gone to him, pregnant, seen he *would* help if he could. "Can't you still be with her, Ri—your friend?"

"No. No, we are become different people. Ah, no, don't cry." He placed the sculpture quickly on the shelf and reached a hand to her; his fingers curled around her face. She pressed her cheek against their touch.

There was no sound, only the dripping of rain on the cottage roof. Then the hand slid away.

"Since then, there have been beautiful things," Ri said.

"It's like the flowers, isn't it?" *After you left*—only, she couldn't say that—*when I thought I couldn't love.* "I'd come home and the flowers on the bushes were so clear and bright. As if nothing else existed."

"No, no—"

"Ri, *listen.* Because the next year, the next year—!" She spread her fingers wide. "I've told you of my changes. And I lived again, more than before! It *is* possible."

"That's you." Again he lifted one of the white sculptures, but he put it back. "That isn't me. You have courage, you know; you keep going forward this way. But, for me, no. No, we remember those possibilities of what might have been, but"—his eyes held hers— "those possibilities also die."

It was clear, as if he'd said the words aloud, *You do understand what I am telling you?*

His hands went still. "When people come close to me—listen—what they want is very good. But what happens then—it's never people's fault. But, understand, for me it's too late."

"Ri. I care about you."

"I know. And I never meant to walk off on you then. I'm not leaving you now."

"Except—" Except, soon he would leave for good.

"Not in the way you fear. Your country, but not you. I don't 'lose' people I care about."

There was an old expression, "May God bless your road"; raising one hand, she whispered the words and placed her fingers against his forehead. Yearning but accepting. Nothing more, for now, needed to be saved.

At that time, one of the Peace and Freedom Party's "Dick Gregory for President" dollars hung by her front door, and, as Ri left, she handed it to him, laughing, "Must be a revolution—we even print currency." Then her voice broke, broke on her words of hope, broke on his despair, and in quiet caring—and this strange defeat which was like a victory.

Epilogue

In Our Hearts, the Dream

1969

November 19, 1969. Under the glow from the lightning-bolt lamp, my little Newcat is sleeping, front paws up. The Work-Prop waits, safe beneath its cover, just inside my front door, for Greg and the others to come tomorrow to drag it down the walkway to the truck.

Tonight, the songs from the radio are all nostalgia trippers— "Those were the days, my friend," "Just call me angel of the morning, baby." Okay—I shove the Work-Prop a final four inches toward the door. Trying to shake off the songs' nostalgia—and this other sadness, too, for sometimes it seems, in the outer world especially, that a crest has passed, the trail turning downward from a hard-climbed height. It's a sense of loss different from missing Ri or yearning for my baby. And it's a false sense; there's no need to think our revolution has peaked too soon, leaving this emptiness.

I peer at the Work-Prop. Tonight, I'll just put the final touches on it, cleaning the filters of the press and filling the "bomb bag" with new word-shot. Then Greg and Joanie came across the meeting room and whispered, "You're the one, we've all decided, who'll be riding the Prop. Because you can."

After Port Chicago and my changes, I was whole—and in the birthing. After I gave up my son, for a while I could barely feel. Remember, I remind myself, how the depths of caring save so much.

***

From the start, just after the final People's Park rally on Memorial Day, Nora had found this "Work-Prop" concept exciting. The energy came from the people—only nine people so far, including her, but they were from all over, San Francisco but also New York, Atlanta, Santiago, and in this desperation that was 1969 were ready to use street theater, civil disobedience, nonviolent sabotage, *whatever it may take*— "if nonviolent," most said—to stop the war.

Now, coming in from the meeting, she put down her "practice-prop," just a small-scale plywood model that looked like a shallow shadow box braced by two diagonal struts. If one peered at the model cylinder "desk" set onto the center crosspiece, one could easily imagine the full-scale cylindrical press from which the Work-Prop's rider, high above a shocked audience of "richies" in the rarefied chamber below, would hand-crank silvery "bullets," each a lightweight balsam-wood or curled-up paper message calling for peace. The rider would be loosely strapped into the frame—this, they'd extensively discussed—using ankle and wrist cuffs attached to the corners where the side planks met the long diagonals. The cross-piece desk, painted all in psychedelic red-and-white and dayglow yellow stars—with big blue, dayglow pink, and silver peace signs—would hold both the printer-cylinder and its "bullets," and there'd be, hooked to each edge, a sack for a water bottle and, as defense against teargas, a damp facecloth. Either the desk would rest on a lectern stand— if Greg, their busy New York activist, could scrounge one and attach it to the bottom "footpiece" where the rider was to stand—or else it would be set, well-balanced, on the crosspiece. *Wow, this may be one rocky trip.*

Things would get damn rocky anyhow, of course, just trying to rush the Work-Prop into the auditorium, even if they all rushed it in together.

Right now, though, she was wasted just from carrying this little mock-up the two blocks from Jeanne's garage to her door. Nora took a tired breath. She stepped out of her boots and, standing by the heater, peeled off her socks.

New volunteers kept joining the Advocates for Justice lately. Everywhere around the Bay Area, new optimism had, for a time, swelled—especially after May's long climax, the surge and retreat that had been People's

Park: the wakening joy in the People's garden; the attack by cops shotgunning protestors and hip-appearing passersby, then killing an onlooker, blinding an artist, teargassing children; the larger and larger marches, each met with more arrests, until Memorial Day's finale, triumphant and huge though inconclusive, the people marching between the ranked machine guns of the National Guard and dancing onward in bright sunlight. Since then, everybody seemed involved in what the papers called "the counterculture." Newsreel filmmakers, poetry readings, street art, the *Open Cell* literary magazine she had created, "open to the rising voices of our free communities," Ernie's Queens' Royal Dance group, even Sally's Free Women group that sought new ways to self-definition and, each Friday, put out a manifesto and stood in black-booted vigil at another corporation that hired no women professionals. There were the people, too, whom young Jane knew, the ones who'd met in Tilden Park back in August to discuss "finding our real mothers *now*" and whose hopes—she couldn't quite explain it, they made her cry—felt so *interesting.*

And everywhere the new communes, the gleaming clothes, and the Renaissance Faire, everywhere more "People's music." A cultural booming of change and awareness—though she wondered where the funding came from.

But also, the Movement was splintering, many people said, or was being crushed against the government's unresponsive marble monolith.

No matter what, many still hoped; many yet cared. She did.

And she still missed Ri. Not only Ri.

Even now, though it has been months, missing him comes suddenly, so physical, a sudden blow. Everywhere I walk, my eyes keep seeking him, just as four years ago. I miss his eyes, his voice, the way he moves. It is as if one loved the mountains more than anything and could never

*climb there again. "I'll write to you," Ri promised. "I make
my friends for life."*

*At night, I have dreams of something lost, somebody I
cannot name. This is how I miss the* other, *the one I do not
see even in dreams—the little one who may be crying and
who cannot find me.*

*And then sometimes the sorrow is, rather, remorse.
Remorse because I didn't reach further to heal Ri's
sadness that evening, instead of clinging to my longing—
yet also remorse because I silenced the longing and didn't
move toward him though that would have made no sense.
Remorse because I looked through the doorway of the
nursery and saw the bassinet, the soft warm blanket, and
my baby, on the day I left the hospital, and I didn't
change my mind; I didn't keep, to nurture and raise, my
child.*

*I remind myself again, our worth is also in this
yearning or this sorrow.*

Once, Ri had held her, accepting everything, and
said "I will come back, there are no judges." Now, she
could reach out with love, or wait—but could she yet
simply *accept,* with something like his courage and
respect for each life?

"Our times together, these years, dear Nora . . ."
Reading his letters helped. Six months since he'd left.
She felt more at peace; he was gone but she wouldn't
forget. Each day, she went to work or to the *Open Cell*
collective or rode into San Francisco for the protests.
Each month, she met with Marta, the lawyer
recommended by the Advocates for Justice, and each
time replied to Marta: no, the FBI had visited only the
once and she'd said no more than Marta had okayed; no,
she never spoke about The Matter—or of Len at all, not
to anyone, and yes, she seriously understood that both
the cottage and her phone were certainly bugged, and no
she never left or carried papers that she wouldn't want
the FBI to read, and never threw significant *anything* into
the trash. And yes, she recognized that Jessica, having
rushed at her last month, shouting "Bitch, you caused

it—bitch, he wanted you to *see* him, not use him," must never be taken, under any circumstances, into confidence.

And finally, yes, she understood she must keep out of jail if possible. At one rally, however, she was cited for blocking traffic, at another was dragged toward a waiting patrol van. And she kept going back. She had to—though she couldn't explain this to Marta. Had to, because, even now, though the whole world protested, the war did not end. It only grew more horrific, U.S. soldiers massacring the people in My Lai, ravaging always more villages.

Yet she was sure that most soldiers could, under the right conditions, be as capable of human caring as the sailors who had gratefully taken leaflets at the Oakland docks. It was clear where people's denial of human connection could lead, but, even so and though it would take time, someday everyone could be reached.

Tomorrow, we shall be a hundred thousand marching, another huge November demonstration, the minimal numbers needed to hold back repression and the worsening war. "Come morning, the morning star rises— we shall overcome." We have to. It is all right to give up, at moments, for even after a backward step, love will bring us through—yet better always to struggle forward for the world.

"There's so much rain, this fall." She looked up from writing to Jan, so loyal a friend, and stared out the storm-lashed window. Jan's child was two-and-a-half already—the same age as her own.

In his letter two weeks earlier, Ri had written of a grim cold country, livestock huddled together under winter storms, and of "the way everything suffered, in that ridiculous land," and she had known she was now in his past.

For months, obsessively I would think "No, but if I had truly trusted in my love—known that, whether I reached out or held back, I still was whole—could this have changed things? If, that evening last November, I had crossed what was the hardest road, reached toward Ri beyond all propriety or even sanity, yet faced directly his despair—would it have mattered?"

I would think this, and again, right now, I think this. Only, I know. I know the answer.

The answer is No.

No. No, it would not have mattered. It would have made no difference. For Ri would still be far away, and, even if he were here—this I must acknowledge, and acknowledge in my heart, since it is what I feared to recognize for far too long—yes, he might yearn for someone, but he would not yearn for me.

I accept this, or try to.

Just as I accept—no, I don't, I don't—there is no real possibility I'll ever find my child.

Nora ran her hand along the string of god's-eyes. Jan and her husband taught in a major university these days and were planning a trip to France with their little girl. Picking up the silvery pen, Nora wrote her letter, but she knew that of course it wouldn't be to Jan.

And not to Ri. Rather, it was to the world, to whoever might see its words and use them, just as she'd written those lyrics of hope, two years before.

"For each of these years must now be a path that leads away from war and violence to compassion and love. The dark is real; we love, yet sometimes we must leave what we have loved, or fail to see our way, and some things truly cannot be. Yet, other times, the very fears we've fought or blamed for loss are—like my hesitance to dare intrude upon Ri's sorrow, that rainy November night—only the fear love brings."

These words might have no effect, yet people needed to know. "There are the many and the one; there is the deepest need. We need to *feel with* every struggle, if we can, as if it is our own. Ending the war is not enough unless we let ourselves be empathetic with the yearnings of all peoples, others' fights and others' hopes. It is a feeling for *many* people that fills those who'd build a revolution; this too is a form of love."

A form of love I learned, those nights of Port Chicago and the months just after, when everything—love for Ted and love for my baby and love for everyone—grew strong. Love that I've not forgot and won't forget, any more than I shall cease to love Ri or my growing child.

Enough. Nora draped the blue scarf around her neck. It was nearly time to leave for the planning meeting. There would be Leninist cadres on the march, new Trotskyist groups, more FBI plants shouting "Gotta stick epoxy on the pig's front doors," Weather People arguing armed struggle, and thousands of newcomers who must be guided through the hordes of cops and unanticipated dangers—all the tense logistics of a major demonstration.

Already last week, there had been ten thousand marching, filling the streets of San Francisco. Becky had been there with her women's group, and Nadine and Mark, both wearing green and purple, holding hands inside the drumming-circle. Ernie, too, out on bail after the cops' raid on Queens Care, and saying, "Nora dear, of course we had to run the risk—so our younger brothers can take pride someday in who they are," and smiling sadly below his bruised-up nose. Even her landlady, standing with two other women and a big sign saying "Sisters for Peace" though her husband drove long-distance rigs and, fixing her fuse box onc day, had nodded toward the Port Chicago poster on her wall and said, "Sure, sister, I'm as moral as the next guy, but when we came up here from Georgia, the Navy's who hired black men."

And, way beyond the signs, out past the far edge of the crowd, Captain had been standing, talking with two guys in wrap-around glasses. Then, moving slowly toward the first row, calling for the mic, a gray-haired woman in a wheelchair had half-stood and begun speaking about love for people of all ages, all abilities. Wrapped in a long dark poncho, Ted had cheered the woman; then he too had spoken from the platform, Samantha and the serious mutual-aid anarchists and "forest savers" from their communal house beside him.

Across the world, too, millions had joined in this protest, even though some thought they could have no effect and many doubted change was possible—especially here, where so few people went hungry or without a home. "Indeed"—Nora pressed hard on the pen— "we too shall find ourselves someday beside those hungry others if we cannot bring more people soon to recognize they care."

Yes, true, but *enough*—the meeting!

She glanced at her watch, a present from her parents. Lately she had committed herself to being kinder, phoning them often, trying to listen more. "Good of you, Nora," Sally had laughed, stopping by on a lunch break to pick up agendas. "Motherhood really does make us more understanding, doesn't it?" Nora had offered mulled wine, adding cinnamon and ginger. "Are you sure it's only Ri you're missing?" Sally had asked then, no longer laughing.

Of course, the loss was of the child. Of course. And yes, she had cried when the counselor, that day she'd finally dared phone the agency again, had said, "No further information, dear. He's with his parents. He'll be fine. You need to move on with your life." Naturally her body still sometimes woke her, crying for him. Yet rationally she knew he was there somewhere, safe, and those parents loved him.

Of course—for everyone could love; there would always be love.

But truly she must hurry. She pushed the pen forward swiftly, confidently, tossing back the blue scarf so it wouldn't cover the pad. "We have each known isolation, loved and tried to veil our love or thought we had to give our loves away. But it is through this awareness, these connections with the wounded, the poor, all those forced to give in, that we *can* end oppression—even the dark false consciousness 'I cannot love until I am no longer me; what's wrong is wrong inside.' We need to nourish the deep connectedness we feel, or else"—she pressed hard on the silvery pen—"there may come worse loss yet, darkness throttling generations, should connection falter, having peaked too soon, or come too rarely or too late."

Standing, she kicked back the chair and stared down at the words. Indeed, far darker loss could come. It was only last week's marches, according to KPFA, that had stopped Nixon from using "nukes" in Vietnam. And even if that report were wrong, *too late* could still . . .

Yes, all right—I will.

Yes, she'd agree to it, now; she would be the one to ride the Work-Prop once they marched into the Federal Building and forced a way inside the auditorium. Yes— no going back.

And, truly, it was good how swiftly Greg and Ron had got agreement from Ron's union comrades so that they could stash the Prop, in four big covered pieces, in the maintenance storeroom behind the stage. There, with luck, she, Gregor, and Ron could fit the thing together fast and drag it out and—if they could fight through swiftly, keeping the great advantage of surprise—fling the ropes and hoist her high and yes, *yes,* she would ride it. For she could.

Only, Gregor must lead their charge into the building, he or quick Jeannette, and then into the auditorium; she knew too well she might still hesitate, feet trembling in an instant's terror, before rushing those guarded doors. In crisis—confronting weapons trucks out on the road, or watching Ri's hand reach toward her face but pull away—she still might halt, paralyzed despite love's trust, much as her heart, tugged by reality, had stood outside the nursery door, and her hand had hovered hesitant, that November night with Ri, in love's respect.

Four years ago, in rain like this, I ran to Ri. He held me and his arms stayed tight, I did not have to move away.

But it was already late—no time to think or write more, no time to brush her hair, just thrust on boots and race to the final meeting. She must make clear, this time: they'd have to find a way to break past the police lines by a quicker route.

***

She had been standing, or rather dangling, here attached, for what seemed endless hours, hanging exhausted over the clamorous auditorium. Many had left, but still scores of faces gaped up at her, the Work-Prop's frame hiding all but her hair, her eyes, and her right leg, which had earlier been slashed by a crack in the plywood prop so that, now, sticky drops of blood dripped down. No matter—the blood might lead people to understand. The thought made her grin.

Grin, but not laugh—her balance was too precarious, the wooden prop dangling at this unfortunate angle so that, at any move she made to give the Prop a gentle but eye-catching sway, it twisted into these too-tight circles, spinning her while she struggled to shift and re-brace her arms and legs, the binding straps digging into her wrists and her ankles and threatening, each time the frame slipped farther or bumped the frescoed wall, to give way around her ankles and allow her feet to slide down off the bottom plank.

The Work-Prop was in fact a rectangle of such wood planks, its curving desk set on the cross-bar halfway up adorned with bright gold peace signs and holding the hand-cranked cylindrical press that shot its paper message-bullets past the long diagonal struts connecting the Prop's four corners. Standing strapped-on, feet to the bottom plank, she could, using both legs and one hand, still manage to force the cracked and tilted prop half-steady while her other hand cranked the small stiff press.

Below her, the bigwigs who'd remained stared up, like short prey animals, from the echoing velvet-seated chamber where gleaming gold-and-copper ornamental railings matched the onstage podium on which a leader of these corporate directors stood, his gavel banging as if to command her down by sheer force of outraged decorum, his face tilted up beneath the midpoint of her arc. All those dots down there kept scurrying around— bodiless between their slanted heads and tiny dark-brown shoes—so distant that at first she'd panicked in sheer vertigo and feared that she might vomit; but then, remembering she could trust her worth, no matter what body or mind or world might do, she had steadied herself, even though the tipping universe swayed back and forth each time she moved a muscle, beneath its painted sky.

She reached again, carefully, with the hand not on the press, trying to hone a wider swoop that would not twist around but, instead, draw new attention to the motion and the paper bullet-pellets painstakingly aimed downward to reach these people's minds and hearts. But the movement swung the frame too hard, and, with a quick, sharp lurch, it did spin, slipping as another knot gave, so she fell against the cross-bar desk, her left foot slipping from its strap and dangling, her full weight hanging from her wrists as, for the second time, she felt the Prop begin to crack, and thought *I cannot, cannot,* while years of dance kept each muscle taut and fighting to hold her balanced through this half-upended space.

And wasn't balance itself a crucial issue? Balance of her mind that held fast to knowledge of her love, in ever-changing equilibrium with reaching forth to give new love and caring. Balance of love itself over fear—

The wood frame shuddered. She strained her muscles harder, pulled her left foot higher—*cannot—yes, you can*—until it rested on the lower bar and she could force her body upright. Or as upright as the dangling prop allowed. *It still may give way, can still crash*—the thought came clear—but it didn't matter. *Does not matter, for you love. Now follow where love leads.*

But there came no further crack; the spinning slowed until the Prop swayed only slightly, and she breathed—slowly, carefully—deeply in the triumph of it, and gave a quick sob, and the air of the high-ceiling chamber caressed her forehead in a happy, cooling rush.

The Work-Prop was holding—was holding!

The Work-Prop, which was *her* way, a maneuver unknown to those below and thus more able to reach them, the Prop's cylindrical printer still rolling, churning out those pretty blue-green-yellow psychedelic paper "agit-popper" mental bullets—words, cartoons, quick shapely images to cut through all their barriers—a form of love, she thought, incised with truth and laughter to reach the heart.

Many must surely be laughing *at* her, of course; heads still bobbed and leaned together and guffawed— and soon, today or tonight, she would be dragged down and taken to jail, thirsty, exhausted, wet with her own sweat, legs damp with pee—but all of this mattered little. A few people here would understand; more would see. She was reaching new people, powerful people, was making the news, her Work-Prop helping surge another tide toward peace. No matter what.

She would not stop. She was whole. She could persist, she felt, forever.

God's-eyes glowed upon the edges of her vision, the far walls hanging far into the shadows—purple and silver and green, yellow and azure and red, bright primary colors beside the white, the pink, pale blue. The colors of life, colors of her love, colors for her baby. For everyone.

***

The mattresses on the prison bunks were thin, stiff like the plywood of the Work-Prop. She had tried adding a layer of newspapers, using those she was allowed, even the paper with an article praising her "daring trapeze through a reality we have yet to recognize," but the guards had removed them: "against regulations." Very little was not against regulations here. And the meannesses, the pecking order, refusals of medicines to people who fell sick—all were made to be unendurable. Short-time, though, just two more weeks now. Ted had been right, squeezing her shoulder and saying—that brief moment her trial ended and before the bailiff took her— "I know you can do it, kid." But it was harder than she could have thought. Still, she had done it, would do what she must while the war—the war and the thousand other forms of murder—went on.

Last night, I woke up from a dream. In it, the world was saved and people moved hand in hand, loving and at peace. We stood in a glade in a snow-sparkling woods; I had run to Ri and he was with me. It was simple, "Don't cry, it is all right." But if we spoke, we spoke without words.

A diamond in a raindamp granite block. I woke and cried.

Except I still slept; the guards had left, the caged yellow bulbs were dimmed, the concrete walls gone away. And in this dream, toward morning in the dark wooden homes on the silent streets, men and women slept soundly, our first struggles over and the longer fight for revolution or a good life, in one sense or other, begun. In the November rain, I walked and I danced and I danced, breathing the clearing air.

And then I understood—I cannot find Ri, Ri is not here.

I understood—my child will grow up far from me.

Then the grief I could not feel before, came down. I understood what I have barely begun to acknowledge, what Ri once said, "Our possibilities also die."

Yet I cannot believe I shall not see Ri. I cannot believe I may never again see my son. Except for this longing, I'm empty inside.

Still, in emptiness there yet lives hope. Every march comes from necessity, and it is necessary, each time, that we give and risk. And, understanding, I shall struggle on through laughter, fear, and green Marines, shall care and care again and reach to other loves. For, though I'll not deny the grief, the changes still hold true—love is the depth in each of us and, trusting this, we may love openly, reach through all barriers and years, change lives. Ours is a possible world.

Look past these bars, the narrowed view, all that would silence us; remember.

The lyrics of hope are not mere dogma; there can be moments of the rainbow and the seekers, a lifetime of the struggle and the dream. For Ri, and for my child, and out across a hundred vigil lines, the morning star is rising; our love is for the many and the one. Despair and loss—the dark without night, the light without day—are only half of life; hope—hope, and somewhere—*is the other half of love.*

Acknowledgments

Many persons are necessary to a book's creation. The utterly superb editorial suggestions and encouragement of Andrew Gurcak have been of critical importance for *The Change Chronicles*. Earlier, a wonderful, extensive critique by Barbara Sjoholm was of enormous value. Lillicat Publishers and editor Carrol Fix's outstanding dedication and courage in taking a chance on this and on other emerging authors' works has been especially crucial.

Over the years, too, many writing colleagues have provided crucial, invaluable support and criticism: Norman Davies, Jennifer McDowell, Milton Loventhal, and others of the *Open Cell* magazine collective; "Robert and Marti's writers group" in mid-1990s Oakland, California; Barbara Mullen, Cleo Jones, and the late Avis Worthington of the Albany, California, book authors' group in 2000-2003; and colleagues at the Flight of the Mind Women's Writing Workshops in 1999 and 2000.

A 1990s interview by Wesley Hogan, director of Duke University's Center for Documentary Studies; Kali Tal's publication of my peace movement essay "You Asked 'What Was Happening Then?'" in *Viet Nam Generation,* vol. 6; and that essay's recognition with a Pushcart nomination and as a New Millenium Writing Awards finalist opened the thematic and historical material of *The Change Chronicles* to daylight, freeing it for fictional exploration.

Finally, the brilliant, unforgettable writing, teaching, and encouragement of W. D. Snodgrass, Ursula K. Le Guin, and William Wiegand played enormous roles in my literary development.

About the Author

Paula Friedman's first novel, *The Rescuer's Path*, was called "exciting, physically vivid, and romantic" by Ursula K. Le Guin, "humane and wise" by Cheryl Strayed, "lyrically written" by *Small Press Review*; the Flannery O'Connor Award winning novelist Carole Glickfeld said, "I could not put this novel down—I loved it." Friedman's short fiction and poems have received Pushcart nominations and won awards and honors from New Millenium Writing, OSPA, Indigo Press, the Science Fiction Microstories Contest, and Soapstone and Centrum Residencies. Her works have appeared in *New Flash Fiction Review, Viet Nam Generation, Earth's Daughters, Jewish Women's Literary Annual, Work, Verso, The Future Is Short*, and over 50 other journals and anthologies.

Also by
Paula Friedman

The Rescuer's Path

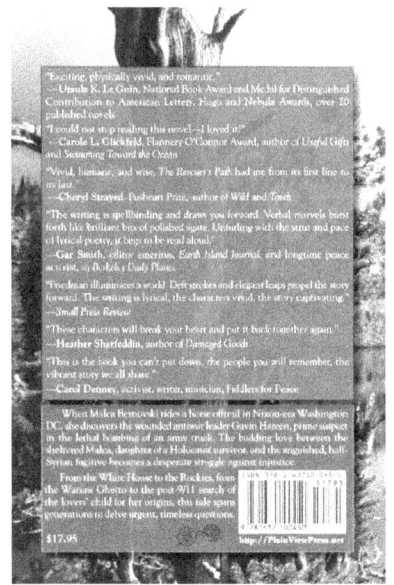

www.ingramcontent.com/pod-product-compliance
Lightning Source LLC
Chambersburg PA
CBHW071100250626
47159CB00002B/529